M000106744

DISCARDED

Other Books by Nick Gaitano

Special Victims

MR. X

NICK GAITANO

A novel by the author of *Special Victims*

SIMON & SCHUSTER

New York London Toronto Sydney Tokyo Singapore

SIMON & SCHUSTER
Rockefeller Center
1230 Avenue of the Americas
New York, New York 10020

SIMON & SCHUSTER and colophon are registered trademarks
of Simon & Schuster Inc.

Designed by Irving Perkins Associates

Manufactured in the United States of America

1   3   5   7   9   10   8   6   4   2

Library of Congress Cataloging-in-Publication Data

Gaitano, Nick.
Mr. X/Nick Gaitano
p.   cm.
I. Title. II. Title: Mr. X.
PS3557.A3586M7   1995
813'.54—dc20
94–37315
CIP

ISBN 0-671-50010-4

For Theresa

ACKNOWLEDGMENTS

These are some of the women whose expensive cooperation made this book possible: Mistress Thunder, Lady Elke, and Submissive Susan ($3.95 per minute); Melanie, Andrea, Tea, Sasha, and Gabriella ($2.95–$3.50 per minute).

Any mistakes pertaining to phone sex are *their* fault, not mine.

On the other hand, very special thanks are due to Lisa of Lisa's Creations, who spent more than an hour during her peak calling period gabbing over the phone with me, then told me to keep my money, as it was her pleasure to help me out.

To the women who hung up on me, accused me of being a cop, or who thought I was just handing them an original line in order to get my kicks: I *told* you I was writing a book!

N.G.

CAPTAIN MERLIN ROYAL was a large, athletic black man, known throughout the Homicide Department for his bluntness and his lack of diplomacy. So Jake Phillips wasn't sure how to deal with this, the way the man was all of a sudden beating around the bush with him.

Royal was an intelligent man, one who didn't try to cover his intelligence up the way a lot of smart cops Jake had known went out of their way to do. They thought that acting stupid, saying ain't and hunh and motherfucker a lot, talking loud and being brutal gave them greater street credibility. It was not a trap that Jake had ever let himself fall into, though sometimes the temptation was strong. Nor had Captain Royal; Royal was smart and he knew it, and he wasn't the type of man to care much about what someone else might think of him.

So why was he acting so strangely this afternoon? On a Sunday, his day off, coming in all dressed up after church and calling Jake into his office, then taking his time getting around to any real discussion, not telling Jake what he wanted. It wasn't like Royal to sneak up on a topic.

The man was self-conscious, Jake could tell, and was surprised by it. And Jake, being barely off Homicide probation, having just completed his first full year in the Death Squad, didn't believe that he'd had time to establish the sort of relationship with the man where he would feel comfortable about asking him what was wrong. As a matter of fact, he couldn't imagine the day ever dawning when he *would* feel comfortable asking the captain that sort of question. He could only hope that whatever it was the captain was concerned about, he wasn't concerned about *him*.

Not that he'd have much reason to be; Jake was good, one of the best in the squad, and he knew it. It had taken a lot of hard work to wrap up the Collector case last year—seeing as nearly everyone involved in the case was dead—yet Jake had done it, had backtracked the madman who'd killed Lieutenant Tony Tulio in the case that had caused the elite Special Victims Bureau to be disbanded. Special Victims had been Tulio's baby, and Tulio, at the end, had lost it. And so, as it always was in the Chicago Police Department, a lot of good cops had suffered, lost their positions, over what didn't amount to much more than the bosses doing what they were best at: covering their own asses. The head man was nuts? So be it. The bureaucratic way to deal with that was to disband the entire unit.

Not that Tulio had come off as any sort of lunatic in the eyes of the general public. By the time Jake had finished with the investigation, Tulio had become a civic hero, his death a true Chicago tragedy. Tulio had not only been a role model for Jake, but his hero, for as long as Jake Phillips could remember. Jake's father, a legendary Chicago police patrolman, had taught Tulio the ropes when Tony had been a young copper himself. After Tulio's death, Jake had used his intelligence and credibility to put everything together and tie it up with a neat pink ribbon that not even the Internal Affairs Division could unravel. He'd come up with answers to the death of not only Tulio, but also that of an ex-boxer named Lenny—a mob legbreaker who'd worked for the guy part-time—and that of a man who'd been sentenced to death by the Collector for committing the heinous crime of simply working as a doorman in the killer's building. The Collector had also nearly killed a young lawyer named Marian Hannerty, whose slickness and clever thinking had ensured that the Collector would never see the inside of any prison or, worse, a state insane asylum.

Marian's part in the deal was just between the two of them, though, and would stay that way until the day Jake died. Her true role in the Collector case had never found its way into the official report, nor would it ever come to light, not by Jake, ever.

Some things in life were just so good you had to keep them to yourself.

Jake thought about that case now, while the captain hemmed and hawed and talked about things that didn't take Jake's concentration away.

Thought about Paul Harris, the Collector.

Who thought that human organs were works of art. What a case that had been. The man picked his victims via computer, through the organ donor network and the Illinois Department of Motor Vehicles.

And twice during that case, while Tulio had been hunting the man, Jake had sat right here in this office, in front of Captain Royal, the big muscular boss lighting one Pall Mall after another, smoking them while he'd explained to Jake what happened to young cops who complained to their superiors about the other cops in the squad.

Chain-smoking back then the same way he was doing now, the man taking his time, tapping another one out on his desk, shit. The room was already filled with dense gray smoke. There were droplets of brown nicotine on the filthy windows behind the captain's head. Jake could close his eyes and imagine that he'd gone back in time a year; it was nearly that to the day. The circumstances were a lot alike, too: the oppressive heat, the fear he was feeling. But back then Jake had hated the man he'd been forced to work with and wanted nothing more than to get off the Death Squad and back to Tactical . . .

"You're assigned to that detail tonight?" The captain spoke the words so softly that Jake almost missed them, lost in thought. He told the captain he was, surprised that he'd even asked. The captain himself had given the order almost two weeks ago, telling the few special Homicide coppers who'd been chosen for tonight's assignment to rent tuxes and save their receipts for department reimbursement. He'd said he'd been ordered to pick his three best men, and Jake had been proud to be included with the other two, long-term veterans who'd earned their stripes. He'd felt too that he'd deserved the honor, and to hell with the petty jealousies of the guys who hadn't been picked.

"You've been doing well in the squad, Phillips."

"Thank you, sir," Jake Phillips said.

The captain cleared his throat. "I like the work you've been doing with Mondello, he can teach you a lot." Jake didn't answer, just waited for the captain to get around to what he really wanted to say. "Lynch, too, he's a good man, bright. Senior man on the squad, but nowhere near as smart as Mondo."

"Mondo's got the vision, sir," Jake said, and the captain looked at him sharply. When he was sure that Jake wasn't joking he nodded, giving credence to a widely held departmental superstition.

"Seen it myself, Phillips, many times. The man's un*canny* the way he does that shit."

"Sir?" Jake said, and the captain raised his eyebrows. "I never did thank you for getting rid of Roosevelt." Jake shrugged. "As long as we're talking . . ." Jake was hoping that saying this would break the ice, make the captain feel more comfortable with him.

"Roosevelt's an asshole." The captain's tone was dismissive. "All he wanted from this squad was status. He'd been partners with Moore so long, Moore's death hit him as if he'd lost a wife." Royal shrugged. "Your report came out, shitting all over Moore; it was either dump Roosevelt or get rid of you. I know you run into him on the street all the time, but it's better than having to see his ugly ass in here every day."

"I wish I could have proven bribery charges on him. I know he was just as dirty as Moore."

"Knowing and proving, well, you know how it is. Rosy's happy in TAC; he's a boss there, God have mercy. You know he's retiring at the end of the week?"

"That's very good news, Captain."

"Too bad it wasn't him caught his lunch last year, instead of Tony Tulio."

"Roosevelt never worked hard enough on a case to pose a threat to anyone who could whack him out, Captain."

"You got a point."

And that was all they had to say to each other, the extent of their casual conversation. Jake fidgeted, resenting the smoke that filled the room, watching it swirl around the captain's head, caught in the breeze of the fan from the small window air conditioner.

At last the captain put his cigarette out in the large, brown round glass ashtray sitting on top of his battered desk and said, "Jake, I need to talk to you, and you have to keep it to yourself."

"All right."

"It's not that easy. I have to explain something to you first, then I have to ask you something. And I need the truth from you, Phillips. Plus, it can never get back to anyone on the squad."

"All right."

"Will you stop saying that?"

"Sir, I didn't say I'd answer your question, I only implied I'd hear it asked, and I'd tell you the truth, and that I wouldn't tell anyone you'd asked it."

"You college boys, you really get to me." The captain said, then sat back in his chair, lit another of his damnable cigarettes and took in a deep initial drag, looked at Jake intensely, and got down to the real reason he'd asked him into the office in the first place.

"I got a call, Phillips, in fact, I got three of them now, over the course of the last couple of weeks. Woman called me about her husband, complaining about him, through the proper chain of command. Happens more often than you'd think. Lawyers usually put them up to it. That way, if some brutal cop should hurt his spouse bad—or, worse, kill her—they can say the department was warned and that it's all documented. Then they got a lawsuit against the city." He paused, giving Jake the opportunity to respond, but Jake just sat there, sweating and choking from the smoke, his hands on the arm of the chair, legs crossed, looking at the captain with as benign an expression as he could muster.

"Problem is, Phillips, it was Sergeant Alex Mondello's wife who called."

"Come on."

"That's what I had to tell you. Now I've got to ask you a question. You're as close to him as anyone but Lynch, you been partnered together for months: You seen him exhibit any sort of strange behavior, anything you'd call bizarre?"

"No sir." Jake issued it as a flat statement, a total denial.

"Don't cover for him, Jake. I asked you because I trust you to tell me the truth."

"Sir, I almost left Homicide my first night because of Jerry Moore. You think I wouldn't come in here and tell you if Mondo was acting crazy?" Jake kept his face straight, didn't say another word. He now knew why the captain was acting so sheepishly; he'd wanted Jake to play the part of the lowest form of human life any street cop ever came across: that of informant. But it hadn't worked, Jake had told him the truth, and it wouldn't hurt his partner. Jake didn't know what he would have said if Mondo *had* been acting oddly.

"I heard a rumor he's screwing around with Elaine."

"Elaine?" Jake was shocked. Volpe was good-looking, around Mondo's age, too, but Jake looked at her as a colleague, sexless, as just another good cop in the Homicide squad room. She sure didn't flaunt her sexuality around, either, like some of them did. "I'd believe it about Sandy, but not Elaine. Sandy makes a point of telling uniform rookies that she never sucks dick on the first date."

The captain didn't seem pleased to get the information. "I want you to keep an eye on him, Phillips. I want you to watch him close."

"You want me to be a spy, you mean, a rat, Captain, is that what you're saying?"

"No, it's not. And keep that whiny-ass tone out of your voice when you talk to me, son." The captain wasn't sheepish anymore, he sat forward in his swivel chair and *glared,* used his Pall Mall as a pointer, sticking it out at Jake's face.

"If there's a man on my squad losing it, I need to know. I'm not talking about going to OPS or IAD or police boards or departmental hearings, or none of that shit, Phillips. I'm talking about keeping everything in the family, within the squad. If the guy's losing it, I can get him help before it goes too far. Before he winds up like Tony Tulio. You know how bad we'll look to the boys upstairs if we have two elite men freak out in just one year?" The captain wasn't the sort of man to often explain his motivations, and Jake sat up straighter in the chair, knowing he wasn't being chastised, it was in fact entirely the opposite.

The captain was opening up to him.

As if the Captain had read his mind, he said, "Phillips, I haven't told you everything that I've been told. I've known Mondo for fifteen years. I'd do anything I could to help him. Sheila Mondello's talking up some pretty serious charges against his character, and I don't think Mondo even knows what she has in store for him. And no offense meant in these politically correct times, but some lawyers have been known to put a woman up to lying so she can get the alimony raised, win custody, you know what I mean."

"Yes sir."

"So all I'm trying to do here is make sure that Mondo's covered. And I want you to help me out with that. I want you to keep an eye on him."

"Have you talked to him?"

"I didn't tell him everything she's saying, he'd probably go crazy if I did. For his part, he says she's nuts. He thinks she'll come around to her senses." The captain stopped himself, as if he'd betrayed a confidence. "That's not all he said, but it's all I'm telling you."

"She's coming to the fund-raiser tonight, I know that much."

"She's good at that social shit; she likes to go out a lot more than Mondo does. Besides, you know the deal, you don't bring your wife, don't bother to show up; mayor's orders. The man doesn't want the hoi polloi to know that there's an assassin stalking his ass."

"If there is."

"That remains to be seen."

"Is that all, sir?"

"Yeah, besides the fact that this conversation doesn't leave this room."

"It won't."

"It better not."

Jake got to his feet.

Captain Royal said, "You might not have noticed, Phillips, while you're out there fighting crime, but I've been grooming you since you put the finishing touches on the Collector murders last year. That was Tulio's crowning glory, and he wasn't around to see it closed out. You brought it to closure every bit as well as he would have. I've been pairing you with the best I have; I want to see you make sergeant before you're thirty. And I know you want that, too. It's good for a young man to have his ambitions. I don't want to have to rub that in, the fact that I've done a lot for you, but I don't expect to ever have my orders questioned again, *or* my motivations, you got me, Phillips?"

Jake stood in front of the captain's desk, listening, feeling happy inside. This was the captain he knew, the man was back, and Jake nodded his head in understanding, mumbled an apology—which was ignored—then turned and left the room just as Mondo, out in the squad room, was waving at him, yelling at him to get his ass in gear, they had a cold one out there getting cooler by the second.

"**OH, GODDAMN, LOOK** who's here. You see that son of a bitch? Jesus Christ." Mondo was shaking his head in disgust as he pulled the unmarked squad car up over the curb at the corner of Dearborn and Adams. Mondo drove right up onto the plaza of the Post Office branch, nosing the car up next to the yellow crime-scene ribbon. Jake looked over at the crowd of police officers inside the crime-scene perimeter, saw what Mondo was talking about, and groaned out loud.

Robert Roosevelt, big as life, was standing in the middle of the crowd of coppers, smoking a fat cigar. Holding court while they waited around for Homicide. Smiling. Roosevelt lifted his hand in the air in greeting when he saw Jake in the car beside Mondello. Left his hand up there and slowly closed his fingers and twisted his hand around, until only his middle finger was still sticking up. It looked like a branch sticking out of the side of an oak tree.

"You want me to handle this?"

"Come on, Mondo, you can't do that. I'll never get past it if you do. They'll think you're looking out for me on account of we're in love."

"You're a good-looking kid, I got to admit." Mondo put the car in Park and left it running so that the air-conditioning would keep the interior cold. "Way things are going at home, I might even make a move on you here pretty soon, now that you opened the door for it to happen."

Mondo got out of the car and Jake felt the heat from his open door drop over him like a wet blanket. Shit. On top of everything else— the captain, the heat, Mondo's problems at home and the stiff on the sidewalk—there was Roosevelt, now walking toward the car. Swaggering.

"Hey, Jay-key!" Roosevelt shouted it as Jake climbed under the tape and followed Mondo toward the body. "Big-time death squad crime-buster, how you *been*?"

"Get away from me, Rosy, I'm telling you." Jake walked around him, out of grabbing distance, pulling surgeon's gloves onto his hands, snapping them at the wrist.

"Aw, is that any way to treat the guy whose partner broke you into Homicide?" Roosevelt followed him, shouting now at Mondo. "What's the matter with you, Mondello, you go to nigger driving school? Pulling right up onto the curb like that, you didn't even signal your turn. Didn't you see all them ci-*vil*-ians?" Jake looked around, acutely aware of all the black faces beyond the crime-scene tape. Mostly black, city dwellers, in a neighborhood distant from their own on a hot Sunday afternoon. Now those faces, which had been enjoying the exciting break in their usual weekend lives, were glaring.

"Shit," Jake spat it out in a whisper. He wasn't responsible for this pig, Roosevelt, but he'd be damned if he didn't feel like apologizing to the crowd. He walked toward the body, and the uniformed officers parted for him. In a police department torn apart—like the rest of Chicago—by racial tension, Roosevelt could get away with his bigotry through light of the fact that he himself was black.

And big. A lot bigger than Jerry Moore had been. Which was saying a lot. Mondo and Jake together might be able to subdue him, if they both had their nightsticks out and at the ready. Otherwise the man would give them serious trouble. His claim to fame was the fact that he had more beefs pending at the Office of Professional Standards than any active officer on the department. He was proud of it, too.

"Got a big case here for you hotshot Ho-mi-cide boys, Jay-key. Type you don't see often; dead *white* guy. Maybe fifty—" Jake was kneeling down next to the dead man on the plaza pavement, on one knee, his tie over his right shoulder. He'd left his suit jacket in the car; it was too hot to wear it out on the street. Mondo had left his jacket in there, too; his long-barrel .44 Magnum seemed to hang halfway down his leg. He was the only cop Jake knew who could never properly cover up his pistol.

Jake tried to ignore Roosevelt's raucous voice. "—Pockets turned inside out, wallet missing. Right down the street from your new apartment, ain't that some shit?" Roosevelt had said it to show that he knew where Jake lived. Jake ignored it. His address and phone number were both listed in the departmental telephone guide, and besides, he wasn't hiding from anyone. Least of all from a crooked piece of shit like Robert Roosevelt, who was now saying, "Ain't that a bitch? Ain't *no* neighborhood safe, not even a good solid white 'hood like this one here."

"What you doing working Sundays, Rosy?" Mondo's voice had a jocular tone. Jake, looking down on the corpse, clenched his jaw, but kept his mouth shut. He flipped the trunk-blanket that someone had thrown over the corpse's face aside, looked down at what was under it. Jake knew his partner well enough to understand that he was going to give Roosevelt a ration of shit, and he was doing it to deflect the man's attention away from Jake.

The body in front of him was maybe forty years old, a white male, greatly overweight, nearly obese, the body soft and pudgy. His hair was mostly black, with single gray hairs here and there beginning to make their move. He wouldn't have to worry about that anymore. Jake stuck a finger into the man's soft belly, into his side, probing. He ran his gloved hands over the entire corpse, looking carefully, seeing only the blood that was now caked on the man's face. Under his nose, on his chin, on the side of his head where it had dripped out of his ears. The man's knees and elbows were badly scraped. There was a lump on the man's forehead. He was wearing a white cotton T-shirt, the type with a pocket, and light brown cotton shorts. He had white ankle socks on, and a pair of Nike Air 180 running shoes. There was a pack of Lucky Strikes nonfiltered cigarettes in the man's shirt pocket. Jake took them out, felt inside there, couldn't find a lighter or matches.

Mondo said, "What with the preseason football games, the pennant races heating up, I thought you'd be working one of your special security details for the bookies."

"You a funny motherfucker, Mondo." Jake risked a look up. Roosevelt was smiling, broadly, hands on his hips, his weapon riding high up on the right side. Roosevelt was dressed in casual civilian clothes. Unlike Homicide detectives, TAC guys didn't have to wear suits. "Make me laugh, thinking a man like me'd ever do no work for one of them swamp guinea, spaghetti-bending, dago mafioso faggots."

"Hey, *hey!*" Jake put the sound of command in his voice. "We got a body over here, you guys want to knock it off and show a little respect?"

"OOh-*eee!* Listen to this one. Wet behind the ears, still-suckin'-mama's-tit young pretty-boy motherfucker gonna give us orders! Mondo, what do you think of that? Shit, boy puts steel in his voice like that, it stiffens me up, makes me want to turn him out."

"How do you make it, Jake."

"I make it that whoever called us in was wasting our time."

"*I* called you in," Roosevelt said. "Called for the M.E., Homicide, and a bambulance, right by the book. What you got's a robbery-murder. Our ears still ringing from the last time one of us po' old TAC boys took one of your cases without calling you in. I ain't gonna let *that* happen again. You got you a homicide. Crime scene techs agreed. M.E. didn't say shit, but they never do; they ain't got no balls until they cut the stiff up and study it for 'bout ten hours."

"What we've got is a heart attack, Roosevelt." Jake could hear the uniformed officers grumbling among themselves. He knew that Roosevelt had cowed them, taken over and hadn't allowed any of them close enough to the body to destroy what he would have thought was a major crime scene.

Roosevelt raised his voice even louder. "Look at the man, pants pockets turned out, wallet's missing. Big-ass bruise on his forehead, his knees and elbows ripped. Blood coming out of his nose and ears, shit. *If* he had a heart attack, the killer give it to him while in the commission of a felony. That's a homicide, in case you ain't looked at the regulations lately, youngster."

"Eating too much gave it to him." Jake flipped the blanket back over the man's face. "Lucky Strikes gave it to him." Jake got up and pulled off the latex gloves, held them in one hand while he wiped at the dirt on his knee with the other. He turned to face Roosevelt, and raised his own voice a few decibels, to make sure that everyone could hear.

"Rookie two weeks in the Academy could take one look and tell you what happened."

"Yeah? So tell me, hotshot, what happened?"

"Man had a heart attack. Not being a doctor, I can't say, but I'd bet he's been lying here at least two hours. In that time, someone came along and mugged the corpse, took his money, his wallet, watch and ring—and his cigarette lighter."

"How'd he get that knot on his head?" Roosevelt was shouting now, advancing on Jake, his hands balled into fists. He wasn't used to being made a fool of on the street. Jake sneered at him, hiding his fear. "The blood from his nose and ears? How his fuckin' knees and elbows get all tore up?" Roosevelt was in Jake's face now. Jake stood his ground.

"He fell, you asshole. Hit his face on the pavement. Flopped around a minute, in pain, he didn't plan on dying when he left the house today, Roosevelt. Fact is, he'd probably still be alive if whoever came along knew big-time CPR instead of small-time robbery. Or if he'd used one of the quarters he stole to call your 'bambulance' before you got here." Jake turned to the dozen or so uniformed officers at the scene, inside the tape with them. He lowered his voice so the crowd outside the tape couldn't hear what he said.

"The perp's got a lighter on him, and hopefully the guy's wallet, I'd bet his watch and ring. Pawn shops aren't open today. With any luck, the lighter's engraved. The wife or whoever can ID the property."

One of the cops said, "What? What the hell are you talking about?"

"Shut up and listen," Jake said. He had a good feeling about this one. "Anyone got a camera? A video camera in the car? Start taking pictures of the crowd, shoot at them in general, not at anyone in particular. Then be ready. Whoever robbed the stiff'll run the second you snap his picture."

"What the fuck make you think the killer's in the crowd?" Roosevelt damn near screamed it, in anger. Jake suddenly didn't care about the man's size, was about to turn and punch him, when one of the officers pointed and began to shout.

"There they go!" Then, "Hey! Halt, right *now!*" Jake watched as half the uniformed officers ran after the two young men who'd begun running as soon as Roosevelt had stopped shouting. The others must have figured it was just too hot to get all sweated up. Jake turned to face Roosevelt now, glaring at the bigger man.

"You big, dumb, ignorant son of a *bitch!*"

"What you call me?" Roosevelt was moving in, crowding Jake, up close. He towered over Jake. Jake backed up two steps, reaching for his hip.

"You touch me, and I swear to God, Roosevelt, I'll shoot you where you stand." At that moment, Jake meant every word.

"How you gonna get to your gun if I'm pounding you into the sidewalk?" Roosevelt said it with a cocky tone, but he hadn't advanced any further.

"He won't have to; *I'll* shoot your ignorant ass. Now you back away from that man, right now, Rosy, I'm serious." As Mondo finished speaking, Roosevelt turned, slowly, to face him.

"You two bastards, you make me look bad in front of everyone, you think I'm gonna let you get away with this shit?"

"Can you imagine the killers, the dope dealers, the rapists who walked away the last twenty years, laughing about how stupid the cops are, because this stiff caught their case?" Jake was livid now, breathing hard, wanting to hit Roosevelt more than he'd ever wanted to hit another human being. Several of the uniformed officers were dragging the captured suspects toward the cluster of squad cars. The two young men were handcuffed behind their backs, fighting, not wanting to get into the cars. The crowd was muttering loudly, some of them shouting for the officers to let the two kids go, wasn't no crime to go jogging on a Sunday afternoon.

Jake said, "We're wasting our time here, come on, let the paramedics take this guy away." He said to his partner, "Violent Crimes
can question the kids; no way this is a homicide." Mondo was smiling at Roosevelt, as if he wanted to say more, but not here, not now.
Not in front of witnesses.

"That's right, both of you take your sad asses away from here."

As they were walking away, back to the squad car, Mondo
shouted over his shoulder, "When's the retirement party, Rosy? I
want to take an overdose of stool loosener, make sure I got a big box
full of what you're worth for you before you leave us."

"Man, *fucks* you," Roosevelt shouted, and Mondo and Jake both
responded in the way that they knew would most anger the man.
They laughed.

Just before he got into the coolness of the air-conditioned car,
Mondo raised his voice loudly, and shouted in high-pitched, ghetto
slang, "Rosy, yo, Rosy! You can just kiss *bofe* of our asses!" Then he
got in the car and shut the door, cutting off Roosevelt's shouted
curses.

THEY SIPPED AT large to-go cups of Dunkin' Donuts Dark Roast,
sitting in the living room of Jake's apartment, on the eleventh floor
of the Metropolitan Building, the only residential high-rise on this
entire square block of Dearborn. The Harold Washington Library
was directly behind the building, to the east. Jake's apartment had a
western exposure, with a view of the Sears Tower. What you could
see of it rising up from behind the triangular architecture of the
Metropolitan Correctional Center. Sometimes during the day Jake
could see the federal prisoners on the roof, leaning on the wire,

looking down. Other times he could hear them shouting things down at the pedestrians on the street. There was an all-night Standard station on the corner of Dearborn and Congress Parkway, with three pay phones that were always in use, attached to the eastern wall. At night, you had to pay up front for your gas, and the Middle Eastern guy who ran the place had to buzz you in to do so. Congress was always busy, but on the weekends it wasn't so bad. Jake had never in his life lived in a city apartment that was anywhere near as quiet as this one.

He'd pointed the bronze plaque out to Mondo, the one mounted on the wall, right inside the vestibule, telling whoever might be interested that the building had been accorded official landmark status. It had been built fourteen years before Jake's grandfather had been *born,* and at one time, for a few short weeks, had been the world's tallest free-standing structure. Jake's grandfather had died of old age, and this building was still going strong. Jake found that thought to be somehow oddly comforting. There were two closed-circuit cameras in the lobby, one on either end, and another one in the vestibule, too; a fourth by the rear entrance. Before moving in Jake had checked the place out, had discovered that in the entire eleven years since the place had been converted into living quarters, there hadn't been a single burglary in the Metropolitan Building.

Mondo listened to it all politely, but didn't comment on anything that Jake said about the building. His mind appeared to be elsewhere. He seemed relieved to get inside Jake's air-conditioned, two-bedroom apartment.

"It's big." Mondo looked around, at the spacious living room, the double-sized master bedroom. He stood in front of the large bay windows for a while, watching the late afternoon shadows lengthen as Jake set out cream and sugar and spoons on the table outside the small kitchen.

"We had to get the two-bedroom when we moved out of Roger's Park. The baby's getting bigger, she needs her own room."

"Her grandma's watching her tonight, you said?"

"Marsha's over there now, she doesn't see her mother much anymore."

"Your mother still alive, Jake?" Mondo asked, as he sat down at the table. Making conversation, but Jake felt there was something more.

He said, carefully, "Did you know my father?" and Mondo told him sure, everyone who was anyone on the department knew who Jack Phillips was. Jake let the silence lengthen, wondering how far he should go. Should he tell the man that he didn't go over to his mother's much because he couldn't justify visiting a house that had been paid for with dirty money? His father had taken every bribe ever offered him, with the exception of drug and Mafia money. He drew the line at that. But Jake couldn't respect the man's distorted sense of honor.

As a kid, he'd thought that all cops lived in large, rambling homes in the Beverly neighborhood. Thought they all bought new Cadillacs every year, shiny cars that they washed on Sunday morning, before loading the family inside them and driving off to church. He'd dressed better than most of his classmates, he went to private schools. His father had retired a patrolman, and when Jake had joined the force, he'd enthusiastically counseled Jake to do the same thing himself.

"You did good out there, with that heart attack."

"It's how my father went. I was there. He didn't clutch his chest and shake, then drop back on his bed. He flopped around on the floor, tearing everything up in the house, it was all I could do to hold him down, try to get him under control before the ambulance arrived." As for his mother, Jake hoped that Mondo had forgotten it, wouldn't mention it again.

Mondo had, or else he had simply chosen to once again let Jake off the hook. Mondo was an expert at that.

He said, "You were lucky, Jake, with an old man like you had. My father, he was no good. My mother was even worse." Mondo's voice trailed off, he wouldn't take that any further. "Me, I was in Nam, at the very end. I swear to God, I thought I'd found my calling." Mondo took a sip of his coffee and made a face; it was still too hot. He set it down on the table. "Seems like yesterday, but it was so long ago, Jesus, over twenty years now. Marine Corps. You in the Service, Jake?" Jake told him that he hadn't been. "I enlisted, you know, in the Corps. Wasn't drafted. Learned a real good trade over there, I'll tell you, prepared me for civilian life."

"What was that?" Jake asked, and his partner gave him a sad smile.

"How to kill," Mondo said softly. He looked off at the bay windows. "I got out, it was the early seventies, I had no skills, no trade, a high school education . . . Then I met Sheila. She was only a kid herself. Just out of high school and so impressed by the stud with all his medals." The sad smile was still on Mondo's face. Jake began to feel a little strange; this was the sort of discussion that was usually held late at night, in bars.

Mondo turned his head away again and for a minute Jake thought he was crying. Then he turned back to face Jake, and his eyes were dry. He said, "All these years, two teenage kids, and you know something? I never fooled around, Jake, not once, although I had my chances. I think she is, though, I really do. And I think I know who with."

Jake thought that silence would be his ally now, the man just needed someone to listen; he wasn't soliciting advice. Jake kept his face straight and he didn't move, sitting forward in his chair, his arms crossed on the table.

Mondo again looked around a little, as if the view were going to change, now squinting at the bright sunlight that was filling the room from the bay windows, Mondo's gaze taking in the two old wooden bleacher chairs Jake had bought for sentimental reasons when they'd torn down Comiskey Park. He'd had the chairs welded together, and they were now set up in front of the 19-inch color TV. There were red cushions covering the hard wood. There was a couch and a chair, and a bunch of baby toys lying around, on top of the furniture and all around it.

Mondo turned back to Jake and said, in a very quiet voice, "I envy you, you know it? This apartment, your youth, your future. The pictures of you guys all over the walls. Together. Happy. Touching and laughing. Christ." He spat the last word out, as if suddenly realizing that his own life had been wasted.

"We used to be like that, the two of us, Sheila and me, before the girls were born." Mondo paused, then snorted. "Last year, when I was going away to the FBI Academy training? You know what she said to me? 'What's your goal, with all that studying, to be a bigger cop?' Now I'm not good enough, the job isn't prestigious enough for her." Mondo said, "You watch her, tonight, at the mayor's fundraiser. See her smiling, laughing, like everything's all right between us. It makes me sick to my stomach, Jake, honest to God, sometimes I just want to—"

"Want to what?" Jake asked, and Mondo opened his mouth as if to tell him, when they heard the key in the door, then Jake's wife Marsha came in and said hi, and broke the solemn mood.

. . .

Mondo didn't stay long after Marsha came home, just long enough to drink his coffee, long enough so Marsha wouldn't feel that she'd rushed him off. He told them he had something to do before he went home and got his wife. Marsha wasn't in too good a mood. For that matter, neither was Jake. He was thinking about what Mondo had said, how it had once been the same way between him and his wife as it now seemed to be between Marsha and Jake. It nagged at him a little. Marsha had a Master's degree in sociology from the University of Illinois. Her plan was to go back and get her doctorate, as soon as the baby, Lynne, was in school. She'd chosen to stay home for the time being, but would she regret it later? Jake wondered about that, often.

Now he closed and locked the door behind Mondo and turned to Marsha, smiling sheepishly, a little embarrassed because she was looking at him strangely and he couldn't tell her what was on his mind. He knew she would ask; she knew him better than he knew himself, would be able to tell that something was wrong.

"What's the matter?" See? He knew it. Sometimes she was scary.

"I was about to ask you the same question."

Marsha shook her head dismissively, waved a hand in the air. "Nothing."

"Come on . . ." Jake said it to deflect attention from his own thoughts as much as to find out what was bothering Marsha.

"It's my sister, Betty," Marsha said as if it were nothing serious, picking up the empty Styrofoam coffee cups, stacking one inside the other. She had the sugar bowl in her other hand. She walked into the kitchen, and Jake followed her, bringing in the cream, the dirty spoons. He put the cream in the fridge, grabbed the dishrag off the faucet, went into the living room and began to wipe down the table. He knew that she'd tell him the rest when she got around to it. He felt Marsha's hands come around his waist as he leaned over, wiping, and he stood up slowly, the rag in his hand. She lay her head against his back.

"Your sister's always been a—" Jake stopped himself. He didn't want to make matters worse.

"A bitch," Marsha said. Jake turned around and hugged her, held her close, his chin on the top of her head. She was so petite, she seemed half his size. Jake was a big-boned man, yet slender, with thin, tight, hard muscles. The first time they'd made love he'd been terrified that he would crush her. He inhaled, deeply. He loved the smell of her long brown hair, so clean and fresh, as if she washed it every couple of hours. They stood like that for a time, enjoying the uncommon peace and quiet. It was strange to have the apartment to themselves like this.

"As soon as I got there with Lynne, Betty started in with her usual, 'So, you're still not working? It must be nice, staying home, watching soap operas all day' routine. Then she got on me about being married to a cop, how can I put up with it, don't I worry every time you step out the door. I told her I was doing all right until she opened her damn mouth." Marsha had been talking into Jake's chest; not complaining, not whining, just getting it all off her mind. Now she pushed away a little and looked up at him. Jake silently cursed her sister Betty; he could see the hurt in his wife's eyes. What Betty had said had hurt Marsha more than she was willing to say.

"*Then* she starts in on the city," Marsha said, "all the bums, all the crime. Wants to know why we didn't just get a Mail Boxes, Etc., street address, area code three-one-two remote Call Forwarding, wouldn't that meet the city-living requirements of your work? Then we could move back to the suburbs, where it's safe." Jake kept quiet. Marsha shook her head. "Mom said she heard that two winos had been stabbed on our block in the past month. Somebody told her that the office supply store down the street was held up at gunpoint. She was worried about us," Marsha said, justifying her mother's actions. She wouldn't ever give her sister that same benefit of the doubt. "She doesn't like the idea that the Pacific Garden Mission's only two blocks away, either."

Jake rubbed her back, wishing he'd been there. Then was glad that he hadn't been. There was no use in further alienating his mother- and sister-in-law. They'd wanted their little Marsha to marry a doctor or a lawyer, at the very least, an accountant. They'd told her repeatedly that if her father had still been alive he would have forbidden any union with a police officer. Jake's arguing with them would only confirm in their minds the faultiness of her choice.

"I was doing all right up until then, not paying much attention, playing with the baby because I knew I'd miss her tonight. But then Betty had to share her opinion that any woman who chose to raise kids in this city when she didn't have to just simply couldn't love them as much as the mothers in the suburbs do."

"Oh, for Christ's sake." Jake couldn't hold it in anymore. "What'd you do?"

"Nothing. And that's why I'm mad, I think." Marsha smiled. "I didn't want to upset the baby. She hardly ever sees us arguing, and she loves Betty, for some reason. She didn't stay long after that, just long enough to twist the knife a little. I wanted to lay into her, tell her there was more to life than the fast track, trying to break through the glass ceiling. More to life than safety, especially if the price of it was blandness and being bored. More to life than being single, for God's sake. She's always lorded it over me that she never got married, that she doesn't need a man."

"You don't, either."

Marsha smiled, lifted her head up, and pecked him on the cheek. "You're too humble."

"Does it bother you, staying home?"

Marsha made a contented noise, scratched Jake's back with her fingernails. "What time do we have to be at the dinner?"

"We've got a couple of hours yet."

"We walking?"

"Might as well, it's only three, four blocks away. By the time we walked over to the garage, we'd be halfway there."

"Come on, let's be decadent. You know how long it's been since we did it when it was still broad daylight? Let's make some hay while the sun's still shining," Marsha said, letting go of him and taking his hand. Jake dropped the rag onto the table and followed his wife into the bedroom.

The phone rang as they were dozing, and Jake reached over to grab it. Marsha looked at the clock and leaped out of the bed, saying "Shit!" and made for the bathroom. Jake said hello, and a man named Ryan from Violent Crimes introduced himself and told Jake that he was just making a courtesy call, to thank him for giving them the two solid slam-dunk pinches who had robbed the heart attack victim. Jake felt a flush of pride, and had a quick flash of insight into his father's past, and from there into his own present: he suddenly knew how his father had felt all those years, doing things for people, collecting debts that would someday be repaid if he ever needed them to be. It was a good feeling.

Jake said, "How's it look?"

"Murder probably won't stick, no matter what, but we have to wait on the medical examiner's report before the assistant state's attorney makes his mind up about it. But we recovered the jewelry, credit cards, over three hundred in cash, the guy's lighter—it had his name engraved on it, and the years he was in the Army, the platoon, company, battalion, the whole thing—all in their possession. All except the cash has been identified by next of kin."

"You ever find the wallet?"

"In the garbage can—get this, Detective—on the corner of the Post Office plaza, twenty, thirty feet from the vic. Had one of the kid's prints all over it. We got them both for strong-arm robbery, and, you ready? Robbing and defiling a corpse. That's if the M.E. comes up with a time of death that precedes the robbery. They better hope she does, or else they might even be looking at at least manslaughter; we might be able to pull that off, no matter what the lawyers say."

Jake thanked the man for filling him in, hung up the phone and lay back, relaxed and happy, his hands behind his head, looking up at the ceiling. He was smiling, listening to the rainlike sound of pounding water as Marsha took her shower. He was about to surprise her, join her in there, when he had a thought that jolted him.

Marsha had never answered his question.

LAURA BINGHAM NERVOUSLY listened to the man on the other end of the line, wondering how to respond to what he was asking of her, the guy's voice low and deep, as if he were trying to disguise it, the guy asking her all kinds of questions. Laura hadn't been warned in advance that a caller might try to pull this kind of shit.

Wouldn't you know it? Third day on the job, and some dumb, sick freak of a sex-line caller had decided she was dishonest.

Laura played dumb. "Sir, the price of the call all depends on the type of call you want," Laura tried to tell him, but he cut her off before she could recite her list of prices for types of call.

"What I *want*," the man said, "is your home phone number, where I can call you, where I can pay you *directly,* and not have to go through the agency; that way, dear, *you* keep all the money." Laura looked around, furtively. The other women—even the ones with calls—looked bored, disinterested. Even Diana, sitting right next to her, who'd gotten Laura the job. Nobody was paying any attention to her. Not even Al, who was down at the end of the room, sitting at his desk, looking in disbelieving, wide-eyed wonder at something written on a sheet of paper. She could see the ultra-white leather of brand-new gym shoes on his feet, through the kneehole in Al's desk. It was the only real desk in the room. The women had to sit at cheap, wooden prefab cubicles.

"I could get fired for doing that," Laura said, in her most sexy, throaty voice. She wondered if the calls were monitored; Diana had warned her that they might be. Even from the little she'd seen of the man, Laura wouldn't put it past Al to tape the phone conversations just so he could check up on the women, or maybe so he could take the tapes home with him, to listen to and masturbate over later on.

Already, after just two full shifts, Laura had learned more about phone-sex perverts than she'd ever wanted to know.

She looked at the bare, unfinished walls of the loft that Al had rented in the dingy office building in the far South Loop, at the eleven other women either talking into their headsets or waiting for the next call to come through to their lines, as the caller kept trying to con her into giving out her home phone number. At least the "office" was air-conditioned, thank God for that.

"We could get to know each other better, Lori, you and me," the caller said, calling her by the name she'd given him, the one that Laura had made up; none of the women used their real names when speaking with the freaks, except for Diana. Lori with an Eye, she'd told him. Was he going to try and get off without paying? Laura wouldn't say an unnecessary word to him until she was sure of his agenda. But she couldn't stay silent for long. Not with "time-is-money" Al sitting right over there.

Behind his back they called him Al the Pimp, even though he was actually some kind of lawyer in his nine-to-five life. Al was short and very skinny, with thick, dyed black hair that was far too heavily moussed. The overuse had backfired on him, giving his hair the ap-

pearance of just being dirty and greasy. He looked around thirty-
five, but who knew? Any man who dyed his hair could certainly be
vain enough to have had some plastic surgery. The women laughed
at him, loved to make fun of him, when Al was in the bathroom,
sneaking a drink, or after work, over a couple of drinks. The women
had decided that if Al'd been given a choice as a kid, he'd have
wanted nothing more than to grow up to be a mobster.

Even to Laura, after only a couple of days, that was obvious in his
swagger, in the way he talked and acted. Al waved his hands around
a lot and dropped his Gs when he spoke. Used a lot of "dese,"
"dems," and "dose." He was big on single-colored silk undershirts,
and thick gold chains. He'd tuck the undershirts into tailored silk or
linen pants, or, as he'd done today, into expensive, custom-fit
shorts. He wore hand-made Italian shoes, or else running shoes that
he never seemed to wear more than one time. With diamond pinky
rings on both slim hands. There was some muscle tone there, but it
was gym defined, the sort of muscles that looked pretty but weren't
necessarily functional. Not like Laura's husband, Bing, who'd never
lifted a weight in his life, but who could snap Al in two without
hardly trying. Her soon to be ex-husband, if Laura could get enough
money together to divorce him. She had other priorities to attend to
first, such as putting food in her son's mouth.

Al was looking back over at her now, frowning. Laura tried to
look intent. If she played this right, she might win his favor. The
thought of what that might mean was more than she wanted to
think about.

It wouldn't be that hard to do; for all his bluster, it was obvious to
Laura that inside, where it counted, Al was very weak. With his too-
slender waist, his short, skinny hands, and the booze that was on
his breath most evenings, it didn't take too long to figure out that Al
was, mostly, an act. That, and the fact that he sweated too much in
the air-conditioned room. Only nervousness or fear could make
such a skinny guy sweat so much.

But the women let him pretend that he was bad, and never made
fun of him when he was in the room, because Al was ruthless when
he wanted to be, and he threw his weight around often, maybe as a
form of compensation. Diana told Laura that Al fired women almost
every week, and she'd watched as he'd fired Desiree just last night,
when he caught her laughing into her headphone at what a caller
wanted her to say. Al, drunk, had thrown a hissy fit, had pulled the

headset right off Desiree's head, had thrown it to the floor, then he'd grabbed Desiree by her hair and had dragged her to the door, cursing her all the way. The pig. There were women in this room who would slash Al's throat if he ever tried that with them, and he knew it, and carefully picked the shots he took—and who he took them with—to prove to the other women that he was a tough guy. Desiree had been a mousy, frightened young white woman, just trying to make a few bucks in perhaps the one place in the world where her gorgeous, silken voice carried just as much weight as the two hundred pounds that were packed on her frame. That voice was Desiree's only skill. Laura could relate to that.

"Well?" the caller said, and Laura blinked her eyes in shock. She'd nearly forgotten about him. Decided she couldn't risk it. She knew that it was silly to try and picture what someone looked like from his voice, but he sounded like a professional, a businessman, someone who was used to getting his way. She'd bet he wasn't talking in his normal tone of voice. Maybe he was a lawyer, like Al. She didn't get paid if she didn't talk, so she opened her mouth to tell him she couldn't do it, but the caller spoke again before she could say a word. "I want—let's call them—special services—and I want a regular girl. You have just the sort of voice I'm looking for, Lori. I don't want to break you in, then get someone else next time I call . . ."

Maybe later, when she had more time on the job, when she had enough time under her belt and knew her way around, his offer might sound more appealing. He had that hypnotic, deep voice and a very deliberate manner of speaking; and she was in this for the money, after all. But at this point in her newfound career, Laura didn't much give a shit one way or another as to what this guy wanted. And she was about to tell him so, when she remembered Desiree. She looked up at Al. He didn't seem drunk tonight, but he was once more engrossed in his paperwork, so she lifted her hand, waved it above her head, listening to the man's almost mesmerizing, seductive voice as he continued.

"I will give you a lot more money than the agency pays you, Lori, in cash, tax-free, and you won't even have to give up your job. Just be home at certain specific times, perhaps once a week, maybe twice. I'll notify you beforehand to the times that I'll be calling."

Al looked up now, impatiently, pursed his lips, opened his hands outward, and shrugged his shoulders in an overly broad, Italianate gesture. Saying *What?!* without opening his mouth. Laura, determined, stopped waving, pointed a finger firmly at the bank of phones on his desk. Al squinted at her, as if trying to remember her extension, then he grabbed one of the three phones on his desk, punched a button, put the receiver to his ear.

"You don't want to give most of what I'd pay to some agency, would you, Laura?"

"What is it that you're looking for again?" Laura asked again.

"Are you dense, or just afraid?" The man's voice was growing impatient. "I told you already what I want, you slut, you fucking bitch!"

Al was looking at her with a puzzled expression; the guy was talking, what was the problem? He wanted to curse her—so what? Half the business was that, or the other way around, guys wanting to be cursed *at*.

Laura was staring at Al, hard. If the bastard didn't help her out here, if he hung up, she'd quit. But he seemed to be starting to understand. He sat back in his chair, nodding his head, making a fist out of the hand that wasn't holding the phone, then opening the fist quickly. It was a gesture her husband used to make to strengthen his hands. Laura shut her eyes briefly, until the caller brought her back to the reality of the present.

"You dense *bitch,*" the man shouted.

Laura at last saw comprehension dawn across Al's face. He sat forward, punched another button on the phone. Now he could speak as well as listen.

"Hey, hey, *ass*hole, what are you trying to pull?" There was a pause as the caller obviously took the time to comprehend what was now occurring. Al glared at Laura, made a stabbing gesture with his finger. Telling her to cut off the call, he had it under control. She looked at him and nodded, pretended to do what she'd been told. But she left the line open, mostly out of simple curiosity, wanting to find out for herself what Al was really made of.

"Who is this?" Al asked. "What the hell do you think you're doing, trying to hustle one of my bitches?"

Bitches? Had he just called her one of his *bitches?!* Good God almighty, if she wasn't desperate for money . . .

Laura heard the caller say, "Your name is Allan Beck. You are a small-time, one-man office, ambulance-chasing Jew. Your office is on Van Buren. Your single window faces the El tracks. Now, Al, would you like me to tell you your Social Security number?"

Shocked, Al paused, and Laura turned in her chair, watched him out of the corner of her eye as she pretended to look at Diana. Her downstairs neighbor caught on, looked over at the boss herself.

Al's tan seemed to have all of a sudden faded. Laura saw the fear on his face, could almost smell it flowing off him all the way across the room. She thought, Good for you. The guy on the other end, though, his voice was calm, relaxed. He was in control. There was a hint of threat in his tone, as if he knew he was holding all the cards. He waited Al out.

"Yeah, so you know my name. I'm looking at Caller ID, I know *your* name and number, too, tough guy."

"I've blocked the call. And if you curse me again, lawyer Beck, I will come pay you a visit sometime. At home. Want me to tell you your address?" Laura had to fight not to laugh. Al was truly squirming. When he spoke, it was in a high-pitched whine, his voice quivering with fear.

"Are you threatening me? Look, I'm running a legal, legitimate business over here—"

"You're a sleazy piece of trash, Beck." Laura heard the man laugh softly. Why didn't he just hang up? she wondered, then quickly figured out the answer.

He was enjoying himself.

Al, terrified now, trying to mollify the guy, said, "Listen, you can send in money orders, cash, whatever you want, and I'll find the girl to fit your personal desires, all right? Individually. I'll custom-call you, sir, you'll get exactly what you want—"

"See you real soon, Al."

"What do you mean? What are you saying?"

"I'm saying I'm going to cut your dick off, Beck, and make that bitch on the phone eat it. You tell her that for me, tell her that's the price she pays for sandbagging me, for putting you on the phone." The man's voice was now malevolent. This didn't sound like a fantasy. He wouldn't be paying a dime, but Laura would bet that he'd just gotten off. Laura, no longer thinking of her financial situation, pushed her four-legged wheeled desk chair away from her little cubicle.

"Wait a minute, *wait* a minute," Al was begging now, waving his free hand around in the air. It was trembling. Several of the dozen women in the room had by this time turned to look at him, were listening to the pitiful whimper in his voice. The caller gave a little knowing laugh, then gently disconnected the call.

"Wait just a fucking second, mister!" Al looked around frantically, and suddenly realized that he was the center of attention. Laura disconnected her line, removed the headset, and looked over at Diana. She felt light-headed, dizzy. Frightened. Diana looked back at her with compassion and understanding.

"Tough one?"

"Yeah, but he's hung up," Laura said, and shrugged, and Diana snorted, looking over at the boss, who was shouting, "I'll kick your goddamn ass all the way to Evanston, motherfucker!" Al stood, working himself into a rage, shooting furtive glances around the room, making sure that the women were still watching him, apparently stupid enough to believe that the women couldn't see him doing it. Sweat was pouring down his face in *streams*. "Do you know who you're talking to? Do you know who I *am?*"

"I know *what* you are," Laura said, to herself as much as Diana. She stood as Al slammed the phone down, stood with his hands on his hips, glaring down at it. "Asshole," Al said, to the phone.

"Asshole," Laura said, to Al.

"Hey, *hey!*" Al looked over at her, came around his desk as Laura leaned down and reached into the kneehole of her cubicle, picked her purse up off the floor. "Where the hell do you think *you're* going?"

"As far away from here as I can get, you phony, two-faced, cowardly son of a bitch." Laura glared at him, walked around her chair. She was five-feet-eight inches tall and weighed a hundred and fifteen pounds. Almost as tall as Al, maybe twenty pounds lighter. She said, "If you can't stand up to some freak over the phone, what are you going to do if he decides to show up one night?"

"The lines aren't listed, it's—" Al began to explain, then must have realized how he looked. He said, "Fuck this, I don't need this shit," and took a couple of steps toward Laura, who reached one hand into her purse and stood her ground.

"I'm not Desiree, Al, you move on me and I'll cut you."

"You don't have a knife," Al said, but his voice didn't carry much conviction, and he'd stopped moving, stood in front of his desk.

"You're right, I don't," Laura told him. "I've got a razor, though, and I'm not afraid to use it." Diana screeched in delight, and clapped her hands together. Several of the other women snickered, until Al leveled a glare at the room in general.

"Tell him, girl!" Diana said, totally unimpressed with Al's dirty looks.

"You shut the hell up!" Al was livid.

"Who you talking to?" Diana got to her feet, began to move slowly toward Al's desk. She was crouched over, her shoulders slumped. Her broad, muscular black shoulders stretched the material of her orange-and-green tank top. Laura had never seen Diana appear to be anything but happy before. She was stunned.

"You freak!" Al shouted. "You goddamned morphadite! I took you in, gave you a job, you and your girlfriend, and now you're gonna give me this? Go on, get out of here, both of you, get out before I call the cops!"

Diana stopped in her tracks at the thought. She began to laugh. "Call the cops?" Laura, in spite of her fear, couldn't help but bark a short laugh herself. The two women looked at each other, nodded, then gave each other a high-five. They turned slowly, as one, and, arm-in-arm, walked from the room, and were outside it when they heard Al yelling at the other ten women still in the room, asking if any of them wanted to join the two bitches he'd just fired.

ABI. AL BECK, Incorporated. It had seemed so easy, a First Amendment–protected, simple way of making a quick, tax-free buck. Things had a way of getting complicated on you, fast.

Al looked at the Caller ID readout on the phone he'd taken the call from, saw that the caller had indeed blocked the call. He was a careful man, the caller. And he'd done his homework. Al had paid a fortune to get into this business, what with incorporating, laying out the dough to rent and furnish this loft, the deposit for a dozen phone lines, and buying the headsets for the girls. Not to mention the insurance on the joint, both fire and theft, paid in advance for a full year, stipulations which the landlord had insisted on, as the building was in a pretty sleazy part of town. He had three phones of his own, with four different phone lines attached to each one, so that every call that came into the place went through one of the phones on his desk. He punched the proper button and the call was sent to one of the available girls before the third ring.

And what girls some of them were. Ugly? Christ, most of them could stop clocks. It was a good thing they worked at night; they got caught outside in daylight, they'd get stoned to death right on the street. Laura had been the exception, though, the prettiest girl he'd ever seen in the place in the year that he'd been in operation, and now she and that morphadite had run out on him. Ingrates. Just when he'd been getting ready to put the moves on Laura, too. This goof calls, some damn *freak,* and blows everything for everyone.

Al absently sent calls over as they came in, leaving what had been Laura's line untouched, the button still depressed, so no calls could come in over that line. He'd laid out enough for his technology, should he use it to call the guy back?

The man's call was one of maybe three a night that were blocked. Al didn't know if the other callers were unaware as to how they could block their calls, or if they just didn't care. But it was also one of two or three calls a night where Al had to step in, had to call somebody back, using either the readout from Caller ID or the Last Number Callback feature that he laid out $42.00 a month to have on each of the dozen separate lines. It was always a shock, when they heard his voice, those weak little men, cowering naked in their bungalows, thinking they'd gotten away with something slick, until he called and set them straight. For fifty dollars, a connection he had at the telephone company could tap into the line as Al hit the callback numbers, and in seconds she could give him the telephone number of the person who'd called. Al didn't have any idea how she did it. If it was an especially frightening call, Al would give the number to one of the cops who were bleeding him dry with what they charged; let them call and throw a scare into the sons of bitches.

But he didn't think he would need that tonight, not for this guy. In the year that he'd been in business—in the course of literally thousands of calls—he'd used her maybe thirty times, and only when one of the freaks had threatened to kill one of his girls.

But none of the previous callers had ever threatened *him,* had known who *he* was. Or what he did, or where he worked. Or, dear

Christ, where he *lived.* Al hoped that the caller had been lying about that one, just trying to con Al into backing down. He sure hoped that was the case.

But it wasn't the sort of thing you could automatically take for granted. Not from someone who knew your name, knew which direction your office window faced.

So, what could he do? How could he play it? Al knew that he wouldn't be leaving it alone. He'd have to do something. Before the guy came around and cut off his dick. Ten off-duty thieving cops couldn't save him if the man decided to come to Al's house, when he was sleeping. Al shivered.

He couldn't think about it anymore, or it might just drive him nuts. He had enough stress in his life already, what with the law office barely meeting expenses, the three ex-wives, the four ex-kids who were all within the next couple of weeks going to be needing tuition for their private schools so they wouldn't have to go to class with gang-banging *schvartzers* . . .

He should turn it over to one of his people, right now. Take a fifty out of his pocket, hand it over to one of the coppers, let them call the guy and raise hell. Maybe then he'd leave Al alone. But if he did that it would be a hundred dollars total out of his pocket. Fifty for the phone company connection, fifty for the cop.

Al decided to deal with the call himself. He'd do it, eat some shit here, then go out and get drunk to forget about what he'd had to do. The only problem with that was when Al got drunk, he got belligerent. And then usually wound up getting himself in trouble, sometimes serious trouble. Like last night, with that broad, god*damn.* If he hadn't been drunk he wouldn't have abused her, and thank God that she was a mousy type, because if she'd come back with the cops, or, worse yet, her lawyer, Jesus, she'd have wound up owning the place, it'd be Desiree, Incorporated. Al still wasn't out of the woods on that one, either, and he knew it.

Screw it.

Al reached out, grabbed the phone, lifted it and dialed *69. He heard the phone ring on the other end, once, twice. Al took in a deep breath, let it out shakily. He started as the phone rang a third time, having almost forgotten the reason why he was calling in the first place. He reached out in a panic, flipped the cards in his Rolodex, found Laura's number as the phone rang a fourth time, and the guy's machine kicked in.

"I can't take your call, leave a message," the familiar, terrifying voice said. Then a tone.

Al said, "Listen, pal, it's me, we just talked." He wanted to sound as tough as he could, didn't want this man to think he was some kind of a punk. But he'd be damned if he could get the quiver out of his tone of voice.

Al said, "I fired that bitch wouldn't deal with you, the customer's always right in this line of work." He flipped the Rolodex card back over, shoved the plastic cover back over the thing. Shit, he was talking to a *machine,* maybe the line was on voice mail. There was nothing for him to fear.

Al said, "You want to make a deal with me, or with one of my other girls, hey, I'm your man. You want to square things up, if you're really that upset, I can give you the broad's name and phone number. The address, I don't have. Just call the number you called earlier, ask for Al, they'll shift it to me, and we'll get everything worked out, all right?"

Al hung up, took a deep breath, then let it out slowly. The phone under his hand rang out, and he jumped. The guy wouldn't call back so soon, would he? Al didn't chance it. He depressed a button, sending the call over to one of the girls. A black chick this time, like that morphadite, Diana, or whatever the hell he called himself. He heard her voice, with its jungle accent: "ABI, may I be of service?"

MR. X LOOKED down at the answering machine, half a smile on his face, as Al's quivering voice came out of the speaker. He was tempted to pick up the handset phone and terrify the man some more, would have if he were in a better mood and didn't have a social function to attend in just a little while. He waited until Al ended the call, then reached out and rewound the tape. Automatic Callback didn't frighten Mr. X. He knew the number to ABI, should he want it. But he had no desire to speak to the woman any more, to that Lori, nor to Al. Lori had shown herself to be too dense for words, not the sort of woman he liked to dally with.

Mr. X sighed. It was always such a pain in the ass, but especially now, with all the problems he had, the pressure he was under, with all he had on his mind, he didn't need the complications, what he needed was a woman!

Mr. X was having a rare confidence crisis.

But he had to go slow, not rush into it; in spite of all the pressure, he knew how he had to play it. Because he'd had to go through this same, slow process every time he sought fresh meat. It frustrated Mr. X, this seeking of new women. He'd learned a long time ago, through trial and error, which numbers he could and couldn't call; 900 and even the 800 numbers were out, as the charges were billed to either your phone line or your credit card. Even though this phone number was not billed under his real name, it was still not the sort of risk that Mr. X was willing to take. He couldn't have a paper trail coming back to haunt him, ever, and he didn't want to blow his marriage, not, at least, right now. Although his wife knew of his predilections, predilections which simply appalled her.

He'd tried one time, after several years of marriage, to explain them to her, the things he felt he needed and which were lacking in their relationship. After a cozy and romantic dinner, where they'd both drunk too much wine. He sat behind a desk in his special "office" now, all these years later, and he closed his eyes and cringed at the memory of that night, of the way his wife's lips had twisted in disgust; the way her eyes had narrowed; the clinical way she'd observed him, as if looking at something repellant, something that slithered rather than walked upright on two feet. He'd tried laughing it off, shaking his head and grinning at her naiveté, at the fact that she'd seemed to believe him, but he knew that she hadn't been fooled. It was only recently, though, that physical intimacy had completely left their relationship.

The end had come slowly, his wife at first hesitant to bed down with him, constantly finding excuses not to, and he'd have to talk her into it, nearly plead with her for sex. When they did have sex though, Mr. X often liked to watch her, fantasizing about the acts she wouldn't even consider; when he looked down he'd see her watching him right back as he humped away atop her, that terrible, frightened look in her eye, as if she could read his mind.

Over the years their marriage had become pretty much of an accommodation to them both, and in the past few months they'd simply stopped having their infrequent, unfulfilling sex acts at all until, now, finally, they slept in separate bedrooms. He suspected that when the time was right for her, his wife would take the children and leave him.

Which was something he didn't want to think about right now. He had enough on his mind already. But the thought wouldn't leave his head; he pictured himself alone. He had to look on the bright side of it, or he'd crack up, he knew it. Had to find a positive in it all. It was what this room was for, solving all his problems in whatever manner he chose.

He told himself that he'd have her replacement in line before she left him, and that replacement might even be a woman who would do what he needed her to do. One who wouldn't balk at his desires. He believed he might even already have such a woman lined up. He smiled as he thought of the woman at work, how she came on to him when no one else was around, how he'd played with her a little bit already, just hugging, touching and kissing during secret, stolen moments away from the job. Would she ever be in for a surprise when she found out what he *really* wanted. But once you're naked in a hotel room, it's a little late to say no. That time was coming, too, he could sense it. Who knew? She might even like it.

As for his long-term lack of marital sex, Mr. X had owned up to the reality of it a long time ago, and had found other ways to satisfy his unconventional desires.

Phone sex.

It was expensive, but worth it. The stress in his life, all the terrible pressure, drove him to it. He didn't know what he would do if such help weren't available, what might become of him. He might even have to go out on the street and take what he wanted from hookers; who cared about them? The worst thing about the phone whores, though, was that after a time he grew bored with any individual woman, and had to find someone else, someone new and more creative, to satisfy his ever escalating demands. That or else they couldn't handle him anymore, like his wife; they had to find a way to diplomatically give him up, because he frightened them to death.

Mr. X liked the idea of that, of frightening them to death.

He sat in the tiny, private rented office that nobody but he knew about, the small, balsa wood desk, the large, comfortable chair, and the two telephones—one with a handset and one with a head-phone—hooked together to a single line that was connected to the answering machine were the only furnishings in the place. There was a roll of heavy absorbent paper towels in the top desk drawer. Lying next to a loaded, unregistered pistol that couldn't be traced back to Mr. X. The window air conditioner he'd installed hummed quietly behind him, blew cold air onto the sweat that was making his pleated white dress shirt cling to his back. In spite of the air-conditioning, he felt rivulets of sweat streaming down his back, and into the split of his chest, between his breasts, soaking his sleeveless undershirt. Mr. X checked his watch. He had to be somewhere soon, and his wife would soon be waiting for him to come home and get her.

He had time for one more call, if he could find a private number, not an agency like ABI, where the girls all sat in the same room and spoke into mouthpieces while they chewed gum, while those who could read thumbed through magazines to fight the boredom, wait-ing for their shift to end.

Mr. X looked through last week's edition of *The Reader,* in the Adult Entertainment section, trying to decipher which were the agencies and which the less-professional numbers. Voice mail screwed things up, too. He wanted to speak to human beings, not just to disembodied voices on phony phone numbers rented out at ten dollars a month. He'd placed small check marks next to the numbers he'd thought he should try. There were hundreds of ads in the paper each week, but only a few of them were new listings, and many of the ads were for escort services and the unacceptable 900 and 800 lines. Both types of numbers could record your phone number; blocking Call Forwarding didn't matter over those lines.

Mr. X recognized most of the ads right away, could skim past the ones that he'd used before or had previously seen and rejected.

The phone he used was unlisted, and not in his real name. He'd paid a deposit by money order to have the business line installed, and he paid the monthly bill the same way, and he never signed the money order. There was no way this phone or office could ever be traced to his real life.

Mr. X felt safe as he lifted the phone to his shoulder, dialed *67 to block any Caller ID that might be on the line he was calling, and punched in the last phone number he'd marked, the only new listing left that he hadn't yet tried. He heard it ring, then there was a sudden, loud screech in his ear, and a recorded voice spoke to him, in a near robotic tone. "The number you have reached does not accept blocked calls." Said as if chastising him.

Mr. X slammed the phone down in anger. He had an important political fund-raising dinner to attend, and there was serious work for him to do there. Now he'd be attending it in less than a stellar mood.

DETECTIVE SERGEANT ALEX Mondello turned to his left and then his right, checking out the hang of the rented tux in the half-length bathroom mirror, Mondo posing and admiring himself, the way men who don't often wear tuxedos inevitably do on the rare occasions when they dress up in one. It somehow made him look more debonair, more sophisticated and suave. He smiled smugly and in spite of his problems he let his imagination run free, imagined himself as James Bond, entering a casino. Which took a stretch of his imagination, as he was standing on the cord to a boom box that was plugged into the bathroom wall socket, and looking down at pink curlers that were in a container on the sink. A curling iron lay next to it. No wonder the electric bills were out of this world around this house. Mondo shot his cuffs, adjusted them, so his pride-and-joy dress-up diamond chip cuff links showed. His initials were spelled out on them. A long-ago gift from his wife. Oh, well.

He didn't look too bad for forty-two, there were no bulges at the waist of the tux, except where his pistol hung. Although he *had* paid exceptional attention to his wavy brown hair, in back and on the crown, using a special shampoo and a thickening conditioner; he'd blow-dried over the thinning spot. He held a hand-mirror up, moved closer to the light. He could barely see the thin spot now; it would be invisible in softer light. Thank God. He was one of the 80 percent of men for whom Rogaine was merely an expensive bottle of water.

He had never in his wildest dreams thought that thinning hair would bother him. Nor had he ever thought that turning forty would be a problem. Both of these milestones had, however, disturbed him far more than they should have. Maybe it was due to his growing sense of insecurity, the belief that had hit him like a baseball bat to the kneecap, a couple of years ago: Life was never going to work out for him the way he'd thought it would.

His marriage was in deep trouble, and his teenage daughters weren't growing into the young women that he'd always planned them to be. They in fact didn't even *like* Mondo, for Christ's sake, he could tell. It was coming up on the end of summer and had they voluntarily done anything with him since school had let out? Once in late May, then again in early June, he'd gotten three box-seat White Sox tickets for them, from a friend of his who had prime season tickets. The girls had gotten excited and thanked him both times, asked him if they could take the train to the game. The older girl, Ellen, thinking the extra ticket was for her boyfriend. Or pretending to. Mondo hadn't gone out of his way to promote any more tickets to sporting events. Which made them petulant, act hurt. Especially after their mother just had to tell them that he'd worked on the extra security detail at the Bulls home championship games.

Their mother's feelings for him—and her emotional makeup—seemed to be rubbing off on the kids.

He heard her now, his wife Sheila, in the other downstairs bathroom of their comfortable brick, four-bedroom East Side home, cursing under her breath because she couldn't find something in her bathroom. He stuck his head out of the bathroom he shared these days with his daughters, looked down the hallway but he couldn't even see her shadow. Mondo walked down the hallway, wondering where the girls were, and on into what had been, for most of their marriage, his bedroom. Now he lived down the hall, in what had always been the guest bedroom. The physical separation hadn't been overlooked by the girls.

Sheila was only half-dressed, in a black slip with a matching, lacy, low-cut bra. She hadn't heard Mondo enter the bedroom. She was in the bathroom, bending over, looking into the cabinet under the sink, cursing him under her breath. "Bastard moved *every-thing—*"

"What are you looking for?" Sheila jumped, smacking her head a good one on the edge of the sink. Mondo flinched and moved to comfort her, but she leaped to her feet and backed away from him, as if frightened of his touch.

"Leave me alone!" She was gently probing the top of her head with one hand. She didn't seem uncomfortable or self-conscious about the way she was dressed in his presence. Mondo stopped where he was. He tried again.

"What are you looking for?"

"Some fucking privacy, is that too much to ask from you?" There were maybe thirty quick responses that popped into Mondo's head, important and serious things that hadn't been anywhere near too much for Sheila to ask from him, things he had in fact delivered. But he kept his mouth shut, because he knew if he brought any of them up, that the argument would only escalate. He was dreading this dinner enough without having to attend it alone. He'd been ordered to bring his wife. Sheila had turned and was facing the mirror now, ignoring Mondo, biting her lips together and pushing them out into a pout.

"You want privacy, you should close the bedroom door."

"Nobody's home." Nobody? Is that how she viewed him these days?

Mondo said, "What if the kids came home? It's not a healthy thing for them to see, their mother undressed like that, young girls, competition and all, you know?" She glared at him briefly in the mirror, her nostrils flaring, teeth bared. The tips of her rich, shiny black hair barely touched her shoulders. She was thirty-nine years old, and looked ten years younger. Fuller in all physical ways than she'd been when they'd first married, but it was a mature fullness, a muscular richness, rather than softness or fat. Her scalp didn't have any balding spots that Mondo could see.

"You're *sick*," Sheila hissed, and Mondo shook his head.

"Look, we've got to leave in fifteen minutes . . ."

"Then get out of here and let me get ready." Sheila spoke to her own image; she wasn't looking at him now.

There had been more than one time in the past when the sight of her dressed like this had caused them to be late for one function or another, or to miss it entirely, as they rolled around on the bed together, laughing at their decadence. The remembrance of those times now brought a lump to Mondo's throat.

He said, "You look pretty good the way you are, you ask me," and Sheila stiffened, then gave him another withering glance in the mirror.

"Get out of here," she whispered. The disgust in her voice cut him.

He turned from her, took a step out of the bathroom, and heard her call after him, "Your gun's sticking out," and Mondo couldn't pass it up, he told her that wasn't his gun, he was just happy to see her . . .

Jake and Marsha walked arm and arm toward the hotel, from the north side of the building. On the short walk over, Jake had admired his wife, the way she looked tonight, the self-possession she managed to project. Even dressed in a sleeveless evening gown, carrying a little blue purse that matched her dress and shoes, she seemed to be in total control, not the least bit self-conscious.

She was doing a lot better than Jake. He felt like a fish out of water in the tux. It was the first time he'd worn one since their wedding day, and only the second time in his life that he'd even had one on. The rented shoes seemed too tight; he felt every eye on the street staring at him. Which wasn't much of an exaggeration. How many people had he ever seen walking around this part of town in formal evening attire? The elitist snobs at the private Standard Club, down the block from their apartment, wore them all the time, and they weren't very good examples of the sort of people who did. On Saturday nights, after a function, their obnoxious behavior was enough to make Jake glad that, unlike them, his daddy hadn't left him a million dollars when he died. They would stand under the awning, in the middle of the sidewalk in the front of the club as if they owned it, not budging even an inch as the red-jacketed Mexican attendants ran to retrieve luxury cars that had suburban stickers in the windows. You had to walk around them, or step out into the street, to pass. They acted as if normal people simply didn't exist, or if they did, they didn't matter.

"Having fun yet, Jake?" Marsha said it jokingly, she must have sensed his discomfort.

He was thinking that it was an honor to be on this assignment, but deep down, he now wished, for the first, that he *hadn't* been one of Merlin Royal's top three men.

"You ready?" Jake asked. He reached over with his free hand and touched Marsha's hand. She seemed to be having the time of her life, basking in the attention. The people on the street were wondering who they were, knowing they had to be somebody, because they'd been invited to the hottest party in town.

"Come on, Jake, lighten up, all right?" Marsha sounded as if she were teasing him, but he wondered if she were angry. "I'm going to be a doctor before I'm thirty-five; black tie affairs are going to be a part of our lives."

Oh, really? Jake thought, but didn't say anything. He just led his wife through the crowds of gawkers in front of the hotel, and had to flash his badge at the uniformed cops manning the barricades in order to get the two of them inside.

Sheila told him in the car that she wanted a divorce, and Mondo didn't say anything, he wasn't the type to beg. Her voice was calm and casual, as if throwing away damn near twenty years together was no big thing to her. Later on, he knew, he would just as calmly ask her why, even though he was already aware that it would be a useless question, as he knew what her answer would be. The same thing she'd been telling him for some time now.

He was inattentive to her needs. He didn't *share* with her. He was selfish and secretive and she knew he was sneaking around behind her back, having sordid affairs. When she'd first accused him of cheating, Mondo had been stunned. He'd tried, as was his way, to joke his way around it, asking her why in the hell would he cheat when he had a sex kitten like her at home, but Sheila wasn't buying a second of it, she *knew* he was fooling around.

He could have, and maybe he should have, as little as they'd been together lately. It had in fact been months since they'd done anything physical. Before he'd been banished to the extra room, she had tried to explain away their lack of intimacy by telling him it was all his fault, because he was never home. Or, when he *was* home, she'd work around that too, telling Mondo that his idea of foreplay was to ask her if she wanted to fuck. Tell him that that sort of thing didn't do much to turn her on. Then, last month, she'd asked him to move into the extra bedroom.

He had suspicions of his own as to why she was being so distrust-
ful, but he never acted on them, never tried to discover if his mis-
givings were fact. Because he suspected that Sheila was accusing
him of infidelity because she herself was having an affair, and she
felt guilty about it. It was the way she'd always acted, twisting things
around so that she was always blameless, blaming Mondo for everything that went wrong in her life as her way of justifying her own
shortcomings. If *he* was fooling around, she would reason, then it
was all right for her to cheat in return. It wasn't something Mondo
could think about for long, because he knew that if he did, the
thought would drive him crazy.

As far as he was concerned, they'd had a normal, happy marriage
until she'd started working again. Sheila was selling real estate
these days, pretty good at it, too, having gone to school to get her license and now working for that sleazy asshole, Jimmy Reed. REED
REAL ESTATE signs seemed to be sticking out of every third lawn in
their Tenth Ward neighborhood, and Mondo had been around long
enough to know that you didn't get that kind of special action without having first paid off the alderman. He swore if he found out that
Sheila was having an affair with Reed, he would pull the man's
toupee off his head and shove it up his ass.

Now Mondo drove down Lake Shore Drive toward the Loop, in
the darkening minutes of the scorching late-August evening, looking out at the lake when they were stopped at red lights, thinking
over what Sheila had said.

If she really wanted a divorce, what would Mondo's options be?
He couldn't fight it, that was for sure, nor could he battle for custody. The kids just plain didn't *like* him. And they worshipped their
mother, related far better to her. He loved them enough not to use
them as pawns in some game just to try to hurt Sheila.

So what he'd be doing, basically, would be starting all over again,
at forty-two years old. With a bald spot. The thought scared him; not
just the idea of being alone, but the fact that Sheila meant what
she'd said, that she no longer loved him, that what they'd once had
was over.

No wonder his hair was falling out. And not growing back.

"Are you sure this is really what you want?" he said at last, as
they drove down Balbo, heading for the Chicago Hilton and Towers.

"Our marriage is a joke . . ." The revulsion in her voice sickened
Mondo. Sheila was gazing casually out her window, not looking at

anything, he knew, merely trying her best to ignore the fact that he was even in the car.

What had happened to the girl he'd married, the one who'd been so impressed with the man he was? He'd feel her watching him as he'd left for work, in that first year of marriage, feel Sheila staring at him lovingly from the second-floor window of their hundred-and-fifty-dollar-a-month apartment down in the Hegewisch neighborhood. He'd turn and smile at her, and she'd seem to melt at the sight of him. Was this the same woman who had been the first sight he'd seen in hospital rooms, two times, after being shot? Mondo coming awake in great pain, tubes sticking out of him everywhere, to see her crying eyes shining at him, knowing as soon as he saw them that it would all turn out okay?

Now she only wanted him to hide his gun, as if the things about him which had once delighted her were now things of which she should be ashamed.

Mondo said, "I don't see anything funny about it, lately." Her iciness, her obvious dislike of him, Jesus Christ, was it unnerving. He understood what she was trying to do. She'd spent the past months looking down her nose at him, Sheila too good for him now, pushing and pushing, trying her best to make him leave, hoping that, with his Italian pride, she'd finally push him out of her life. She hadn't been prepared for him to try and wait her out.

So now it was out in the open, she really wanted a divorce. He wasn't the only guy he knew in this situation. He'd get used to it. He'd survive.

"If you don't agree, if you don't get out, and soon . . ." Sheila paused a second, as if she were afraid to finish the sentence.

"Yeah, what?" Mondo said. He looked over and saw her staring out at the solid block of police cars in front of the Hilton. The second she saw them, she relaxed, and a wicked look passed across her face.

"I'll tell everyone who'll listen that you sexually assaulted the girls."

Mondo was too shocked to respond. If he could have he would have pulled a U-turn right there on Michigan Avenue, kicked her out in the middle of Grant Park and driven back home, gotten his clothes and left, right now, tonight. But he was unable to. He could only drive straight ahead, toward the scene of the party.

"You hateful *bitch!*" Mondo whispered harshly, through clenched teeth. Sheila was smiling as if she'd won some sort of victory, looking out the windshield, as if she enjoyed his anger, fed off it in some way.

"The girls will back me up, and you know it; they'll do anything to stay with me. They really can't stand you, Alex." She spoke in a matter-of-fact voice, that half-smile planted on her face.

Mondo somehow managed to pull his car over to the curb right in front of the entrance without hitting anything, cutting off a taxi that honked at him in anger. He got out of the car, shaking, and was immediately approached by two of his colleagues, one of whom stopped and kissed Sheila on the cheek while the other one, his partner, Phillips, came over and stood next to Mondo.

"Hey, Sarge, looking good," the younger man said, and Mondo ignored him. He knew he'd hurt the kid's feelings, but he just didn't care. He was watching his wife. His wife and his ex-partner, Kenny Lynch.

The ice maiden was now all smiles. Looking at Kenny with obvious warmth and affection, hugging him and stepping back, holding onto his shoulders. Kenny's usually straight, all-business face was cracked in an uncommon smile. Mondo knew how much it took out of the guy to act like a human being.

"Don't you look handsome in that tux!" Kenny was about twenty pounds overweight, and mostly bald. He was holding a cheap cigar between his fingers. The top of his head was flushed. Sheila asked him, "Is Marie inside already?"

"She's waiting for you outside the ladies' room; there's an ashtray there, just follow the smoke trails. You'll find Marie in the middle of the fog." Kenny turned to watch Mondo's wife walk through the revolving doors. Mondo stared at Kenny's back, wondering. A valet came up, trying to take Mondo's keys. Mondo pulled them away.

Kenny walked over to Mondo, shook his hand briefly, merely acknowledging his presence. "How you doing, pal?" Kenny was squinting at something behind Mondo. He quickly looked back at him.

"Where should I leave the car?"

"Have Phillips move it up a couple of yards, and park it. I think that'll leave room for all the limos to get in and out." Mondo handed Phillips the keys, and the kid took them without comment, his face tight, controlled. Kenny waited until the kid was in the car before he said, "Mondo? Listen, I don't mean to be critical here, but your gun's hanging out of your tux . . ."

IT WAS STILL oppressively hot. Laura and Diana had decided to walk home, as it was still early, and besides, they were now both unemployed. Usually they took cabs together, back and forth from their building. They took them to work because they didn't want to get all sweated up when they were on their way in, then have to spend ten hours sitting in air-conditioning. They took cabs home because it wasn't the sort of neighborhood two women wanted to be caught alone in after dark.

Even now, with nighttime freshly fallen, the weasels were out there, watching. Seeing two stunningly beautiful women, one tall, slender and white, one tall, slender and black, the white woman dressed in loose summer shorts and a casual sleeveless blouse, the black woman dressed just as casually, but in clothing so tight that almost everything she had to offer showed.

"Hey, Ba—*bies!*" one of the guys in front of the tavern shouted at them, and they heard the others laugh. A little later on tonight—maybe three beers later—and "Ba—*bies*" would become "Bi—*tches*." Laura'd heard that word enough in the last three days to last her a lifetime.

The men in the neighborhood believed them to be hookers. Even if it was a fair assumption in a dense, sexist, and ignorant mind, the men still had no business harassing them. Diana simply ignored them; she'd been facing far more serious discrimination since she'd been a little boy, but Laura knew that for her this sort of thing would take some getting used to; these men always made her feel dirty, as if she were doing something to be ashamed of by walking down the street.

"We're lucky we're walking, rather than driving," Diana said. "You haven't been here long enough to have seen it, but sometimes, when a woman drives through at night? The animals actually throw their empty forty-ounce bottles through the windshield of their cars. It was a *big* problem earlier in the summer. It's some kind of tribal rite to them."

"I don't get it," Laura said. She was watching a very tall, nearly anorexic man weave his way across the four-lane street toward them. "The main police station's two blocks away." The man was ignoring the cars that were blaring their horns at him, his eyes glued on Laura. He changed course, walked diagonally directly through traffic, in order to cut the two of them off before they got to the light on the corner.

"The only time the cops come around here is when it's time to collect the bribe money from the tavern and the gas station. Or at Christmastime, two weeks before? This whole *block's* alive with cops, making jive arrests that you can buy your way out of for twenty dollars."

The man was right there. He looked as if he hadn't bathed or changed his clothing in several days; he was holding a bottle of cheap red wine in his hand.

"Hey, baby," the man said to Laura, now staggering over the curb and almost falling onto Diana, "you want to party with me?" He was grinning. The few teeth he had were an incredibly ugly dark brown. Diana put a cautionary hand on Laura's arm and tried to quicken the pace, but Laura shook her hand off and stood dead still on the sidewalk, staring the man down.

"Honey, everybody's watching," Diana whispered. She didn't have to tell Laura that, she could *sense* their eyes invading her body—all those men from in front of the tavern, all the guys wiping off their windshields or getting gas . . .

The man read her hesitation wrongly. He smiled and said, "Come on, babycakes," and waved a hand in a wide arc at her, beckoning Laura to come down the street. "I got a monthly room at the St. James. I got a fan, too, cool you off from all this heat."

"Well the saints be praised," Laura said, "my dream's finally come true. I've waited twenty-six years, my entire *life,* for some smelly, filthy wino asshole to offer to take me to his flophouse room and fuck me." The humor left the man's eyes, replaced by a flicker of something dangerous. Diana tried to pull on Laura's arm, but she was still having none of it. Laura took a step toward the man.

"What's the matter, bitch? You white ass too good for a black man?" Laura punched him on the side of his jaw just as hard as she could, and the shocked look on the man's face more than made up for the pain in her knuckles. She moved toward him, menacingly, but the blow had already made him lose his balance, and he staggered backward off the curb, trying to regain it, but instead fell hard to the pave-ment. A cab screeched to a halt, inches away from the man.

A number of sounds filtered into Laura's brain, as if from miles away: the sound of breaking glass, a cry of self-pitying pain, laugh-ter from the other tough guys and drinkers at the tavern . . . and Diana's voice, shouting now in her ear, "Come on, come *on,* god-damnit, we can't get stopped in this neighborhood, we *can't!*" and somehow Laura heard her, understood her, knew that what she was really saying was that *she* couldn't bear to be stopped.

Because the cops would soon discover that she was really a he, then Diana would be, at the very least, totally and publicly humili-ated. It wasn't something Laura could allow to happen to her friend.

Still, she stood there for a moment, looking at the wino, who was now sitting up, the man covered with blood that was pouring out of his hand from where the broken wine bottle had slashed him. Laura saw that it was a long, deep cut. She felt a moment's exhilaration, and she nodded her head at him, ignored the catcalls and the shout-ing and the laughter that the other men were now laying out. She looked up at Diana, saw the horrible plea in her eyes. As frightened as she was, Diana would still wait and risk arrest, rather than leave Laura here to face this alone.

Laura let out a deep breath, adjusted her purse across her shoul-der—the strap between her breasts and to *hell* with what these bas-tards thought—and stepped close to Diana. She grabbed Diana's elbow, and hurried down the sidewalk, away from the wounded man. He heard him shout after them, "Ya'll's dykes! You goddamn lesbians!" and then they were around the corner, heading for Michigan Avenue and the blessed anonymity the wide boulevard would offer.

"You want to stop for a drink?" Diana said, and Laura gave her a sideways look. "Sorry, I forgot."

"Yeah, well, drinking isn't in my plans."

"Bing did enough for the both of you."

"Still does, judging by the shape he's in when he calls in the mid-dle of the night." Laura shrugged. "He's not my problem anymore. Or, anyway, he won't be soon."

"Bing teach you to punch like that?"

"I taught myself, in self-defense."

"Come on, he didn't hit you, did he? Big old man like that, he'd kill you he ever punched you."

"Hit me?" Laura seemed shocked at the suggestion. "No, he never *hit* me." She thought about less obvious forms of abuse, and knew that she didn't want to discuss them, at least not now. She said, "But he came home drunk more than once and tried to force himself on me, and I punched him until he understood that I wasn't feeling very amorous."

"What'd he think, that you'd been waiting twenty-some years for some big, drunken white bartender to come home and throw a fuck into you?" Diana snorted, trying not to laugh. "I love that line, I got to remember it, the next time some playboy thinks I'm going to drop over at the sight of him."

"It just came into my head . . ." Laura smiled at the memory of the drunken man, the shock and fear on his face when she'd let him have it.

"Pretty good left hook, for a skinny little white girl." And that did it, the two of them were laughing now, losing it, leaning forward a little bit, holding onto each other for strength as well as for the welcome and nonthreatening awareness of each other's touch.

"You still got it for Bing, don't you?"

"I've known him ten years." Laura's voice was wistful, a little surprised. "I still don't see myself as being old enough to have known somebody for ten years. Except for maybe my parents, or the other relatives."

"You're twenty-six, that sure isn't old."

"I don't feel so young these days, I have to tell you, Diana."

"It's harder for a woman." Diana often made statements like that, and one of the reasons they were friends was due to Laura's attitude when she heard them. She didn't judge, like a lot of people did, didn't point out that, truth be told, Diana really wouldn't know what was harder for a woman. Diana had told her how most of her women friends reacted to her, and Laura had been disgusted to hear it. How could Diana ever refer to such creatures as her friends? She accepted the fact that Diana was a woman; at least in her mind, she was. Diana had spent the past three years living a total woman's life. Laura saw her as a woman trapped for a time in the body of a male. That wouldn't be forever, either. Diana was, financially, more than halfway to being able to afford the final, and to Laura's mind, drastic, operation.

"He was your first time, wasn't he?" Diana must be feeling unin-
hibited tonight; she generally never asked Laura such personal
questions. Quitting the job at the same time had brought them
closer together. Laura decided to answer her because of Diana's loyalty when she'd punched out the drunken pig back on South
Wabash.

"Yes, he was."

"You never forget the first time."

"I guess not." Was she waiting for Laura to ask about Diana's first
time? My God, Laura *couldn't* ask her that! She felt embarrassed at
the thought, and quickly spoke to cover it up.

"So what do we do now? The rent's due in a few days, my phone's
getting cut off tomorrow, my husband spends all his money drinking, and I'll starve before I go on welfare."

"You wouldn't let that child starve, and we both know that's true.
You'd sell your soul for him, so now you'll have to do whatever you
have to do."

"I will not go on welfare." There was no equivocation in her tone.
She heard Diana sigh, but wouldn't look at her. From the corner of
her eye she saw a well-dressed, distinguished man eyeing her
openly. She hated when they did that, and they did it all the time.
What the hell did these men think she was, a suit on a rack at their
tailor's?

"You understand what you're going through? Do you know what
you look like? I mean, Laura, do you *really* see how beautiful you
are?" Diana reached over and with long, slender fingers, squeezed
the hand that Laura had resting on Diana's forearm. "I see the magazines, I watch the TV shows. I don't know of *one* of those models,
those actresses, who look anywhere near as good as you."

"Oh, come on . . ." Laura was uncomfortable with such talk; she'd
never seen herself as any classic beauty.

"Come on, my backside. You've got those high, high cheekbones,
those deep brown eyes. Laura, when you look at men, they go swimming in there, I've seen them. You've got lips other women pay
thousands of dollars to get. And it's not like that body of yours has
any extra flesh on it."

They were coming close to their "apartment" complex, a six-story
building that had once been filled with workers but which the
owner had converted into residential lofts without city approval.

"What the hell is going on down *there?*" Diana asked, saving

Laura the trouble of finding a tactful way of changing the topic. Laura heard the horns beeping madly a couple of blocks up the street. She squinted. Saw the blue and red flashing of police car lights, saw tiny blue figures down the street, directing traffic from the middle of the avenue.

"Is there another movie being shot down there?"

"How about that?" Diana said, the sight putting her in a good mood. "You and me, a couple of young South Side girls, living here on Michigan Avenue, right in the middle of everything!" She didn't mention that their incomes, combined, weren't enough to pay the electric bill in the high-rise apartments just a few blocks north.

"You want to wander down there and see what's going on?"

"I should get up to Tommy . . ."

"Babysitter isn't expecting you until after two A.M."

Laura wasn't certain she was in the mood to be looking at all the rich folks in their finery, but Diana seemed to want to so badly, and Diana didn't like being on the street at night alone. So she said, "I guess we could."

"Come on, then!" Diana said, suddenly laughing again, and increasing her pace, heading toward the excitement in front of the hotel as if she were ten years old again.

MONDO SAT AT the table for six in the very front row of the ballroom, looking around angrily; the various loud voices occasionally digging into his brain through the plastic earpiece were really beginning to get on his nerves. The curly wire ran down into Mondo's collar. The mayor might have ordered all the cops here tonight to wear tuxes so they wouldn't draw attention, but Mondo didn't think the plan was going over real well. There were so many cops with earpieces in place that the dining room looked like a convention for the deaf. There was one good thing about it, though; it kept Mondo from hearing half the conversation at his table. He was drinking enough scotch to drown out the other half.

What kind of hypocrite was she? Look at her. She was leaning way over the table, showing everyone the top of her breasts, Sheila laughing and joking and smoking up a storm with Marie, white teeth flashing in an ever-present smile, the smile not even fading when she talked, which she did often. Sheila never smoked at home; Mondo never smelled cigarette smoke on her, either. So when had she picked up that habit? She was smoking a long, thin, brown cigarette, inhaling deeply.

Jake Phillips had been quiet throughout the evening, but Mondo had caught the kid looking at him strangely. He felt a little bad about that, seeing as how he'd bared his soul to Phillips just a few hours ago, and now he'd snubbed him. He'd tell him about it later, maybe tonight, maybe tomorrow. Let him know the score. Jake was a fast study, he'd put it together real fast. And he'd forgive him. He didn't want to alienate Phillips, not now. At this point, Mondo needed *somebody* on his side. Phillips's wife, Marsha, was a fresh-faced, pretty young woman who was enjoying herself immensely. She listened well, with an intent look on her face, as if she were enjoying the shit she was hearing. Good thing she wasn't a talker. A kid like that wouldn't get a word in edgewise between Sheila and Kenny's old lady.

The fourth man at the table, some slug who'd introduced himself as being from Area Four Violent Crimes, was openly leering at Sheila, and she wasn't saying a word about it. Neither was the guy's wife, for that matter. Judging from the way they related to each other, their marriage was probably as fun-filled as Mondo and Sheila's own.

The guy said to Mondo, "So you're Mondello, huh?" not bothering to take his eyes off Sheila's chest as he spoke. "I thought you was only a myth."

"He is," Sheila said.

"You gotta be an Indian, right?" The guy from Area Four looked over at Mondo now. "I read about them, how they can tell things, like you do. I hear you can just look at a guy and know if he's guilty or not." When Mondo didn't answer, the man only shrugged and looked back over at Sheila's chest.

Kenny wasn't paying attention to any of them. He was looking around casually but suspiciously, alert to every move in their vicinity. Doing his job. The death threats had been coming into City Hall since the announcement of the guest speakers last week, and if the mayor got shot, man, they'd all be handed their asses. At least they had lucked out and had been ordered to the big fund-raising dinner. Some of the detectives Mondo knew hadn't been so fortunate; they'd spent the past week walking around the mayor's Bridgeport house, in full patrolman's uniform, marching around the block at attention, day and night in the past week's record-breaking heat-wave.

There was only one thing to be grateful for; nobody had leaked the death threats story to the press. Yet. Which was why all the mayoral toadies were taking it so seriously. If it had been some attention-seeking slob, they figured, he would have called the reporters himself just to brag about his plan. The mayor hadn't even told the governor about the calls, as the man was from the other party, and couldn't be trusted not to let the cat out of the bag just to be a piece of shit. The officers involved in mayoral security had been ordered not to tell even their spouses about the threats; they'd been told straight out that doing so would immediately jeopardize their careers.

The mayor was sitting at the head of the room, a couple of feet above Mondo's head, on a raised dais, no less, and if the guy was worried at all then he was a better actor than he'd ever gotten credit for. Mondo briefly craned his neck and looked up at the man as the mayor laughed and joked, smoking a long, thick cigar. The governor's teetotaling wife sat at the mayor's left side, making a big production out of waving the smoke away, her face all scrunched up in a look that let her feelings about secondhand smoke be known.

Her wimpy-ass, blow-dried phony of a husband wasn't about to say anything to the mayor, though. Not tonight, at least. Even though they were still in deep negotiations with the Chicago Teacher's Union, trying to avoid another of the regular September strikes, and the governor should have been in the catbird seat with the mayor begging him for money. No, the mayor was doing the governor a rare but huge favor tonight, and he knew it, letting him mingle with movie stars and big shots, Democratic celebrities, and it was no secret that the governor's wife idolized Oprah Winfrey, who was scheduled to attend but hadn't yet shown up. Which was why the mayor was getting away with blowing smoke all over the governor's wife. The mayor's own wife was conspicuously absent.

"Suspicious male subject in jeans and T-shirt, walking toward the east entrance." The words cut through Mondo's thoughts, and he half-rose in his chair, looking around the immediate area. The mayor paid him no attention, and Mondo allowed himself a quick look around. At least twenty other men in the room were doing the same thing. He settled back down, slowly. Kenny looked at him, cynically. If it was going to happen, the attack wouldn't come from the front doors. No assassin was going to try to break into this room in regular clothing, without a pass to the high-profile black tie affair.

Mondo watched as the man was shown away from the ballroom by the uniformed patrolmen who were guarding the entrances, saw the guy patting one of the officers on the back in gratitude.

"He was just lost, relax," the relieved-sounding voice in the earpiece informed Mondo.

Christ.

The problem was, the phone caller could be almost anyone. Even one of the cops right here in the room, one who was dissatisfied with what the mayor had been doing throughout his term of office in support of affirmative action. The only things they were sure of about the caller was that he was white, and male. Which didn't mean that the assassin, if there was one, would necessarily be either. But if a professional hit had been planned, why the hell would the killer advertise?

It was exactly for that reason that several of the older coppers weren't taking the death threats very seriously, conventional wisdom among tonight's close-to-retirement attendees being to stand down, enjoy the evening out with your wife, have a nice dinner and a few drinks on the city, and try not to get drunk and fall asleep during the speeches. All the officers assigned to this detail were male and married, as the only communication equipment available was the old-fashioned type with the corded earpiece, not particularly well-suited to women's evening wear.

Someone would more than likely get caught soon while making one of the calls, then it would have to hit the press, and whoever the cop was who ran the caller down would become a hero for about two days. And that would be the end of it. They could go back to fighting crime instead of guarding fat-cat politicians and taking all kinds of shit from the assholes who ran his personal security.

In the meantime, Mondo had to sit at this table and pretend he was enjoying himself, while the same woman who, less than an hour ago, had brutally and coldly informed him that she no longer loved him and wanted a divorce, that she was going to tell the world that he molested his *children,* sat right beside him, from time to time patting his arm affectionately, so that nobody in the room would know that there was trouble in the Mondello paradise.

At least the dinner part of the evening was almost over. In a few minutes, the interminable speeches would begin. If somebody was in fact planning an assassination attempt on the mayor, Mondo hoped he'd try it before the speeches dragged on for too long.

He saw a tall, thin figure making its way through the crowd toward him, watched as a face came into view, and didn't try to hide his feelings when he saw that it was Jimmy Reed. Jimmy Reed, the Alabama country-boy war hero who'd made good, who'd made it to the big city thirty years ago by hitching a ride on a freight train, hungry and penniless, and who since then had turned himself into a millionaire maybe twenty times over. Jimmy Reed, who told the story often, to anyone willing to listen. Jimmy Reed, who had a long, thin, brown cigarette dangling out of the corner of his mouth.

Reed was wearing a custom-made jet-black tuxedo, and he had his usual smarmy smile in place, ignoring the look that Mondo was giving him, acting as if Mondo was his best friend in the world. Mondo knew when Sheila noticed that Reed was at their table. He caught her reaction in his peripheral vision, Sheila stiffening up quickly, then trying to act as if she hadn't.

"Alexander the Great, how you doing tonight?" Reed asked, leaning over with his hand out. Mondo sat back in his chair and crossed his arms.

"Come on, Sergeant, what are you upset about?" The bastard's smile grew broader. He knew how safe he was here tonight; this was *his* element, while Mondo's was the street.

"You get to sit in at a thousand-dollar-a-plate fund-raiser, rubbing elbows with people you'd never get a chance to meet in your real life, it should seem to you like you won the lottery, and there you sit, pouting." Reed leaned in a little closer. Mondo could smell Dentyne, and the heavy smell of scotch.

"Your gun's sticking out of the bottom of your jacket." Reed whispered it, conspiratorially. "Sheila tell you the news?" Mondo stiffened. Reed said, "Tonight's the night, the mayor's gonna announce I'm on his ticket, right in front of the governor and all these dozens of celebrities. I'm his man for alderman in the Tenth Ward, your very own neighborhood." Reed flashed teeth too white not to be capped. "Gonna vote for me?"

"You fucking around with my wife, you asshole?" Mondo whispered, finally getting Reed's attention. The man stood straight up, somewhat stunned for just a moment, before he caught himself quickly, turned the smile and the charm back on. He leaned in again and patted Mondo's arm and laughed, as if they'd just shared a naughty joke. Then he straightened up again.

"Why I'd be delighted to have that pleasure a time or two again, Sergeant, I do have to admit," Jimmy Reed said, and stepped right past Mondo, to shake Sheila's hand.

"And how are you tonight, Sheila?" He turned to the table at large, spoke in a loud, booming voice, making sure that he was heard beyond the immediate range of the table. "I've got me one-hundred-and-forty-eight people working for me, full-time, and *none* of them bust their tails like this little woman right here does."

Mondo felt Jimmy Reed's elbow dig into his back. That's it. He rose to his feet, saw the terrified look on Sheila's face, and he smiled at her, about to bust Reed's head open, when he spotted the man who was sitting just two tables over, watching.

Mondo froze where he was, still standing. Jimmy Reed had noticed him by now, had taken a couple of horrified steps away, was standing there afraid, looking at Mondo's face with anxiety.

But Mondo's crazed look wasn't for Reed, not anymore. Mondo slowly lowered himself back into his chair, his eyes narrowing, not looking directly at the man who'd caught his attention, but focusing in on him, watching his every move.

The fat man was wearing an ill-fitting tux and sitting not fifteen feet from where Mondo now sat, the man laughing and talking and drinking too much, appearing for all the world to be nothing more than a sad, rich loser. He had looked over at Reed's loud comments, then had dismissed him and turned back to the people in his own group. Mondo looked, but he didn't see a single earpiece at the table. Shit! The man was sloppy, a good fifty pounds overweight. He had three chins that jiggled every time he opened his mouth.

But his eyes, man, there was nothing he could do about them; you couldn't hide those type of eyes. Mondo had seen eyes like that before, oh, yes. Twice.

Both times he'd been shot, the shooter had had eyes just like this guy's. This was the assassin, Mondo would bet his life that it was.

JAKE **PHILLIPS SAT** at the table, quiet, taking it all in, not showing Marsha very much of a good time and feeling guilty about it. He was still smarting from Mondo's earlier snub; his feelings were stung. He didn't know if Mondo had done it on purpose, perhaps thinking he had to because he'd opened up so much to Jake earlier and now regretted it, or if the man had gotten into another fight with his wife on the way over here. Whatever the cause, it had been the sort of rudeness Jake would have expected from Robert Roosevelt, or from Roosevelt's late partner, Jerry Moore. Jake told himself to relax and enjoy the evening, try to have a few laughs with Marsha while they had a chance to be together, without the baby for a change. But he couldn't loosen up, couldn't forget Mondo's slight. Was that being shallow? he wondered. He wished he could talk to Marsha about it, get her alone and air it out. She'd probably tell him he was being juvenile. But still, the fact was, his feelings were hurt.

For the first time since Tony Tulio's death, he'd thought that he'd been on the verge of a close relationship with another cop. The sort of friendship he'd only dreamed about when Tulio had still been alive. With an older cop who cared about him, as his father had cared for so many young guys. He would show them the ropes, years ago, help them out, teach them how to act. Jake had gone out of his way to prove himself, and because of the way he'd done Moore after his death, a lot of the cops in the Death Squad had been wary of him, mistrusting.

But not Alex Mondello. Mondo had always seemed to be on Jake's side. And now Mondo had cut him down, insulted him, had treated him like a rookie. In front of everyone outside there watching, hundreds of people behind the barricades had seen him treated as if he were nothing more than a carhop in a monkey suit.

He felt Marsha's hand cover his own, and he smiled automatically, turned his hand around so their palms met and squeezed, lightly. He looked up and winked at her, saw that despite her fixed smile, Marsha was bored to death. He understood, he hadn't been a lot of laughs tonight, but then again, he hadn't been invited here to enjoy himself. He was about to lean forward and say something nice to his wife, when something happened that he must have missed, because Mondo was now standing up, his face flushed and angry, looking ready to fight, and some aristocrat with a wig on his head was backing away, appearing afraid. Jesus. Was this the guy Mondo had told him about, the one who was fooling around with Sheila? "Mondo . . ." Jake said it warningly, but now Mondo was slowly lowering himself back into his seat, staring with grave intensity at somebody at another table.

Mondo was now grateful for Jimmy Reed's presence. Reed was leaning over the table, had stopped pushing his luck. He was saying something to Kenny; Mondo could hear Kenny's bored voice answering in monosyllables. He felt Kenny's eyes on his face, and he nodded almost imperceptibly. His ex-partner was too much of a professional to turn and look at the man. Mondo himself was observing the man from a spot directly below Jimmy Reed's chin. Mondo smiling now for camouflage, as if Reed's wit and wisdom were more than he could handle. Kenny would know what was going on; Mondo's gift of sight was legendary throughout the entire department. Jake Phillips was looking at him, Mondo could tell. Good, the kid was paying attention.

Mondo was in his element, his *glory*; he knew he was onto the right man, knew that this was the potential assassin. He would have bet his pension right here on the spot that the man was the one making the calls, that if Mondo went over to him right now and confronted him, he'd come along peacefully and make a full and complete confession, maybe even start bawling in relief when the cuffs were slipped onto his wrists. Even if the man clammed up and didn't cop to anything, a voiceprint would prove Mondo right. There were only two words stopping him from going right over to the table and pinching the man:

Probable cause.

No judge would want to hear about Mondo's gut feelings, about his gift, his sight. Nor would they listen to his story about the sort of eyes that had glared at Mondo the two times he'd been shot. He'd have to watch and wait, while Kenny did his own thing, never losing sight of the man. He'd follow him right into the toilet if he had to, because there was absolutely no doubt in Mondo's mind that he was looking at his man.

He heard Kenny excuse himself, saw him rise from his chair, blocking Mondo's view for just a second before he hurried out of the way, heading for the nearest exit. Kenny would check the man out quickly as he passed the table, would go out the door and to the covert command post set up in a smaller conference room. He'd find out who the man was from his seating assignment, make sure he was a properly invited guest. He'd be checked out from the photo ID books at command post, which had pictures of everyone who'd been invited to the bash. If he wasn't righteous, Kenny would come back, and he wouldn't come back by himself.

Mondo didn't think about that now, though, he was searching the man's fat body with his eyes, trying to find a suspicious bulge, anything that would give him reason to go over and make the pinch. He couldn't wait for the man to make his move, for one incredibly important reason.

Once you've been shot and nearly killed, it becomes vital to your life that it never happen again. And it had happened to Mondo, twice. He didn't want to find out if the third time was the charm. He wasn't about to give the man a chance to pull his piece.

Mondo saw Jimmy Reed's head turn toward him, heard the man's voice come at him, sounding more like a trained stage actor than a backwoods Alabama hillbilly, Reed speaking with barely a hint of a Southern accent.

"Tux fits you pretty good, for a style ten years out of date; where'd you rent it, Sarge?"

Mondo heard the words and the accompanying, uncomfortable laughter from the rest of the table. He heard them but he couldn't make sense of them, he had just a vague sense that he was being spoken to. Mondo's hands were in his lap. His right was inching toward the holster at his side. He was fighting a growing sense of fear, the slight panic edging up his spine. He felt sudden quick pains in the left side and in his upper right arm: the places he'd been shot before.

He wouldn't do anything. He'd just keep his eyes on him, let Kenny take care of the pinch if it happened. Kenny and about twenty other cops; if they came they wouldn't be playing around, they'd come in hefty number. All Mondo had to do was keep his eyes on the guy, that's all. Kenny would make sure that Mondo got his share of the credit, would tell the bosses and even the mayor himself that Mondo had spotted the fat man.

As long as the fat man didn't get up and walk toward the dais, everything would be just fine. There was no reason for him to do so; the mayor was elevated, an easy target, just a couple of short feet away from the fat man's table. Mondo prayed that he wouldn't get up. He didn't want the man to be in any way mobile. Fat or not, a moving target was hard to hit.

There was the sound of feedback, then a hush fell over the crowd, as the mayor's voice came to them through dozens of speakers that were hidden in the recessed ceiling.

"Good evening, ladies and gentlemen, and thank you so much for coming tonight." Mondo watched the fat man take a deep drink from his glass, watched him reach up with a napkin in his free hand, watched him wipe the sweat away from his face, even as he drank. Was the man having second thoughts? Was it a fantasy gone awry?

He heard the tinkling of the ice in the man's glass. Mondo focused in on him with an intensity beyond profound. He believed he could hear the man's heart beating in his chest, so in tune was he with the fat man. He knew exactly when the fat man was going to look over at him, knew it before the man even was aware of it himself, and Mondo was looking at Reed and smiling when the man looked over, heard Reed whisper that he'd better be getting back to his table. Saw Jimmy Reed's finger stroke Sheila's shoulder for only a single, yet possessive, erotic-charged second.

To hell with them both. They deserved each other.

Mondo looked back at the fat man, who was now looking up at the dais, engrossed in whatever it was the mayor was saying. He might be waiting for a signal, for some red flag that only his psychotic mind's eye would be able to see rising.

"I don't remember the last time I saw so many of Chicago's movers and shakers in one room." The mayor paused. "It might have been at my inaugural!" There was polite laughter and scattered applause throughout the huge room. Mondo didn't bother to join in.

Mondo saw Kenny enter the room from an entrance way off behind the man, Kenny standing with a contingent of other officers. The man obviously hadn't checked out. Kenny was waving his hands around, telling the officers how best to approach the fat man.

The mayor's voice began, then stopped for a second, he'd obviously noticed Kenny and his crew. Then Mondo heard him start to speak once again.

"So now that you've eaten your thousand-dollar rubber chicken—" There was more laughter at the old, dependable joke "—we can get on with tonight's festivities."

Kenny was no more than a hundred feet away from the man now, the other officers circling around, coming from different directions. Mondo hadn't noticed how huge the room was before just now. The social climbers, unaware of the death threats, were starting to notice that something was wrong. There were at first disquieting murmurs, then a sudden scream of panic as some rich matron saw a drawn weapon and shouted: "My God, they've got guns!"

There was immediate pandemonium as people leaped to their feet and began running for the exits. Mondo rose, still the closest officer to the man, stepped onto his chair and then the table to watch him as people ran by.

The man suddenly seemed to deflate, as if he knew they were on to him. He was no longer sweating, didn't seem at all nervous. Mondo watched in fascination as the man shrugged his shoulders and struggled to his feet. Mondo took one short step and leaped as the fat man drew his gun.

He flew over people, above their heads, Mondo's hands empty, his arms wide, wanting only to grab the man's head, slap at his arm, somehow divert his aim. He felt a bright flash of pain as their foreheads connected, then they were falling to the ground, Mondo's hands searching frantically for the weapon, as he saw red-and-white flashes in front of his eyes. He felt his forehead swelling, felt his pulse pounding in the growing bulge. The fat man was squealing and squirming around beneath him, and he couldn't find the fucking gun! Mondo pulled a hand free and punched blindly, again and again, knowing he was connecting with the man's head only due to the sudden sharp pain in his fist.

He felt hands grabbing him, pulling him away.

"No!" Jesus, what were they doing? The guy still had his gun!

He felt abruptly weak at the exact moment that he heard the roar of the pistol, Mondo fighting to get away from a bunch of grabbing hands and then suddenly all the fight drained right out of him. There was no pain. That wasn't a good sign. He tried to stand, but the guys holding him were pushing him to the ground. He let them. He felt someone fall on him, felt a dullness in his chest where the guy's torso landed. Then the side of his head seem to come alive with pain; there was a red-hot stinging in his ear. Mondo cursed, wanting to get back up, wanting to see Sheila, to see his kids, Jake, Kenny, somebody, anybody but this raging swirl of legs in front of his eyes.

Then whoever was on top of him was getting off, thank God, and looking down at him. Mondo looked up and saw Jake Phillips, his face worried, Jake worriedly stroking Mondo's brow. The noise all around them was incredible, but he heard Jake's voice clearly.

"How bad is it, partner?"

"I think he got me in the ear."

"You're forehead's all fucked up, Mondo, you sure you didn't get hit there?" Mondo was touched at the worry that was stamped on Jake's face, and so obvious in his voice.

"I headbutted him, that's all, after I jumped. The bullet got part of my ear."

"Concussion?"

"I don't think so. I can hear you okay—there's only one of you." His sight was good enough that he could see the would-be assassin being carried away by four uniformed officers, the man cuffed at the wrists and ankles. The man was passive, not giving them an argument now that he was unarmed.

Jake said, "You're bleeding pretty good from your forehead and ear. Lay back, I'll get a stretcher in here for you."

"Like hell you will." Mondo pushed at the legs milling around him. "Get the hell out of my way!"

He sat up, and didn't feel dizzy. He looked up at Jake and squeezed his eyes shut as blood ran into them. He swiped at it with the sleeve of his rented tuxedo. He opened his eyes and saw Kenny standing behind Jake, a worried expression on his face.

"I'm not going out of here in a stretcher, Jake, not with all the cops in this room, I'd never live it down."

"Take my arm."

Mondo grabbed onto him, felt people ease away from him as he slowly got to his feet. He moved his head slowly, saw that the mayor and the governor and the governor's wife were nowhere in sight. None of them could have gotten hit—or could they? The bullet had only grazed Mondo's head; that wouldn't have even slowed it down, and it had to have gone off somewhere.

"Who else got hit?"

"Uniform behind you, but we think she's okay, she was wearing her vest. She'll have some broken ribs, heavy bruising, but she should be all right."

"Thank Christ."

Jake moved him through the crowd slowly, raising his voice and shouting for the coppers to make a hole while Mondo leaned forward so that the blood from his forehead would pour onto the carpet instead of into his eyes.

"You all right, partner?"

"I'm okay, partner." He'd never called Jake that before. Then again, Jake had never thrown his body over him before, risking his own life as he used himself as a shield just in case the fat man with the gun got off another shot.

He felt Jake suddenly jerk him sideways, and the dizziness hit him then. "What the hell are you doing?" Mondo stopped and pulled away, stood wobbling for a second, then looked up angrily, to see what Jake had been trying to avoid.

Sheila was right in front of him, being held tightly by Jimmy Reed, Sheila crying into his chest. Reed's face was chalk white with fear, but he was repeatedly kissing Sheila's forehead, making little shushing sounds. There was nothing innocently comforting about the way that Reed was holding her. They didn't even notice that Mondo was there. Without thinking about it, Mondo pushed at his wife, and as she fell back, he struck out blindly, punched Reed hard, the blow landing right on the bridge of his nose. As Reed fell back Mondo hit him again, catching him high up on the side of his head. Reed grabbed Mondo's arm and fell backward. Mondo felt his sleeve rip; Phillips was hanging onto his arm for dear life, with Sheila somewhere behind them, screaming now in fright. Mondo pushed Reed away, stood there, wobbly, as the man tripped over his own feet, and fell to the floor. Reed's head bounced off the heavy carpet, and his toupee went flying. Mondo turned in rage, saw his wife staring at him with a hateful glare that was painful for him to look at. For one brief but intense second, Sheila's eyes locked with Mondo's.

Then Mondo turned away, breaking the stare. He looked down. "Get me the hell *out* of here, Jake," he managed to wail, and Jake wouldn't even look at him, not wanting to witness his partner's public degradation. He just grabbed Mondo's arm and led him out of the now nearly silent ballroom.

THEY'D WORKED THEIR way to the front of the crowd and now stood there, the two of them gawking at the celebrities who were arriving fashionably late. Laura and Diana were leaning on the blue police barricades, ignoring the stares of the uniformed officers who were, as cops were known to do, openly gaping at the two of them. Laura thought that it must have something to do with being able to carry a gun. That might give a man a reason to think he could behave as he pleased, no matter how rude or revolting that behavior might be.

Diana was in her glory, not afraid of the officers now, as she had been back on Wabash. Back then, when Laura had punched out the wino, the officers would have come as enemies, would have seen Laura and Diana as hookers. Here, they were just men in uniform with sexist attitudes. Diana knew exactly how to handle that type of animal.

Suddenly there were people running out of the hotel, dashing madly into the crowd of unwitting uniformed cops who seemed shocked to see them coming.

"What's going on?"

The crowd behind them got pushy, and Laura felt herself shoved into the blue police barricade. It gave a little, then pushed outward and to the side, one end pointing toward the hotel entrance. The crowd surged forward again, and Laura stepped forward—it was that or be pushed to the pavement—as the barricade fell over. She looked quickly to her side, but Diana wasn't there. The cops weren't paying any attention to the gawkers now, were moving rapidly toward the well-dressed crowd who were rushing out of the hotel, trying to find out what was going on. Some of the women were screaming.

"Diana?" Laura said, fearfully.

"Right behind you, honey," Diana said. "What the hell's going on?"

"Somebody said someone's in there with a gun."

The crowd had formed itself around them, pushing and shoving, mixing with the rich folks, and the cops suddenly noticed that the barricades had collapsed.

"Everybody back!" one of them shouted, and Laura felt a strong hand on her shoulder, looked over and saw an officer on the other end of it, getting forceful.

"Hey . . ." He came to life, spreading his arms and stepping forward, shouting right into Laura's face.

"Get back, all of you, everybody back!"

Laura was being jostled from both ends, pushed from behind and shoved from the front, hearing Diana behind her, cursing at someone. When the officer eased up a little, Laura stepped to the side, away from the crowds, and into the hotel entranceway. She felt Diana's hand on her arm.

"My lord," Diana said.

"Come on, let's get out of here before they start swinging their clubs." The crowd was unruly now, cursing and jeering the officers who were trying to push them back, away from the hotel. Men in tuxedos and women in evening gowns had filled in the space around Laura and Diana, hiding them from the officers' view. They caught quick, panicked snatches of conversation, society people talking, buzzing among themselves, having found themselves in an uncivilized—and therefore unthinkable—situation.

"He had a gun!" a woman said to them, her eyes open wide, aghast.

"Don't often see one of *those* things from the backseat of a limousine, do you?" Diana said.

"Diana . . ." Laura said it warningly; this was no time for class conflict.

"Make a hole, come on, goddamnit, get these people the hell out of the way!" It was a gruff voice, coming from just inside the hotel. Laura turned and looked, saw that a short, stocky, mean-looking man was pushing his way through the crowd. He was followed by a handsome young man in a tux, who was half-pushing a wounded man ahead of him, guiding him through the crowd. They stood still right outside the entrance, waiting for the mean-looking cop to return. The young cop looked as if he were welded to the older man. The wounded man was tall, muscular, with wavy brown hair that was—along with most of the rest of him—soaked with blood. He had a huge welt in the middle of his forehead; Laura knew just by looking at it that he'd be needing stitches, at least. He was holding his tuxedo jacket up to his left ear. The society folks around them stepped back to get out of the way of the two men, who were obviously cops. Laura could see the taller man's gun hanging down from his right side; there was a badge hanging from his belt.

"Jake!" Diana screamed, and the man turned his head, surprised, to look over at her. He nodded, almost in a bored manner, then looked away. "Hey, Mondo," Diana yelled, and the wounded cop looked over, as if disoriented, half-nodded, as if trying to place her in his mind. Another man, older and slim, holding what looked like a hairpiece in his hand, staggered out of the entrance. A very attractive older woman was helping him along. He was bleeding from his nose; the side of his face was all puffy.

When he spotted the bleeding cop, he began to shout.

"You motherfucker, you cock*sucker*! Do you know who I am? I'm the next goddamned alderman in your ward!" The bleeding cop took a step toward the man, and the man who seemed too young to be a cop got between them and pushed the bald man away. He said something to him, and the woman grabbed the bald man's arm and hurried him back inside the hotel. The bleeding cop looked straight at Laura now.

"Where's the goddamn ambulance!" she heard the stocky cop shout. Where had he come from? There was pandemonium all around them, as cops fought with the citizens who had battled their way closer, wanting to see what was going on. The stocky cop came over and said something to the other two men, then walked straight ahead, toward the curb, shoving anybody who got in his way out of it. He soon disappeared into the crowd again.

"What happened to you?" Diana said, and the cop looked at her.

"I cut myself shaving," Mondo said, and now he *was* smiling, looking at Laura rather than Diana. "Hi." He seemed almost embarrassed. Laura saw that the younger man was looking at his friend in near awe. He shook his head, then looked away.

"Uh, hi," Laura said, suddenly embarrassed herself. What were you supposed to say to a man in this sort of situation? He was right there, inches away from her. Smiling. Laura reached out and touched his arm. The young cop looked at her warningly, and she pulled her hand back. "Are you all right?" she asked, softly.

"Jesus, you're pretty," the cop said, and Laura was stunned by the comment. She looked at the blood flowing from under the tuxedo jacket, onto the cop's white shirt. Then looked back up at him, not knowing what to say.

"Did you at least get to finish your dinner before it happened?" she asked. Then the other cop was back, bitching as he grabbed the tall cop's free arm, and told him that he'd drive him over to North-western Memorial in his own vehicle as he pulled the tall cop away without preamble into the dent he'd created in the crowd of so-cialites, gawkers and cops.

"What was *that*?" Laura asked, and Diana looked over at her, slapped her on the arm.

"Which one? The younger cop's a cool head. He helped me out last year, got me out of what could have been serious shit." Diana paused, as if wondering how much she should say. "I was working the streets back then. Maybe someday I'll tell you all about those days. You see him?" Diana was angry. "He didn't even recognize me."

"No, not the younger man. The guy with the blood, the guy I talked to."

"Him, it all depends on who you ask," Diana said. "Some say he's a legend, others call him a monster. That's Mondo, and he's got the Sight. The word is, he can tell if a man's a killer just by looking him over. He's the meanest, baddest cop the city got, if you happen to be a bad guy; but if you're straight with him and in serious trouble, if you should ever need an honest cop? That's the man to call."

"How do you know all these cops?" Laura asked, before she real-ized that she probably didn't really want know the answer.

"My God, he was gorgeous," Laura said, and Diana grabbed her arm and told her to come on, they had to get the hell out of there be-fore they got themselves arrested.

"Don't see much of that on the East Side, do you?"

"Men with guns?" Laura said, and shrugged, dismissively. "Fist-fights, usually, most weekends at Bing's father's tavern, that's about it."

"Look at it, ten o'clock at night, and the night's alive." Diana seemed somehow sad. "Where I grew up? The streetlights were al-ways shot out, and the Gangster Disciples ruled the block. Stood there before the cops ever heard about crack, and sold the shit to anyone passing through. That was before the gangs became politi-cal, convinced the dumb, white liberals that they were a force for good and worthy of their guilt money. There wasn't anything like this, back then, though. I never dreamed it could be like this."

"You sound like you're from Iowa."

"That's me, a conventioneer's dream." They walked away from

the hotel, on the other side of Michigan Avenue, only a block or two
of Grant Park left before they came to their apartment building. Behind them, the crowd had found its way into the street. Horns
honked in a continuous flood of noise that would have sounded
right at home to a New Yorker, but which was highly uncommon in
Chicago.

Diana's beeper went off, and she reached into her purse and shut
it down by feel, then pulled it out and held it up to the light. Laura
saw her smile. "Night won't be a total loss."

"Diana, come on, you said you didn't want to do that anymore."
There was a hint of exasperation mixed with disappointment in
Laura's tone that she couldn't hide.

"Only now and again, and only with the generous ones. No
freaks." How strange that sounded to Laura, but maybe not to Diana.
What would the average citizen say if you asked them about it? A
transsexual taking outcalls from an escort service—somebody
wanting to pay her for sex—and the transsexual saying, no freaks? It
was too much for Laura to think about at the moment.

"Here we are. You send Mrs. LaRitcha home, but don't go to bed. I
won't be late, and I want to talk to you when I get back."

"I won't ever do that, Diana, just don't even bother trying to talk
to me about it again."

"Just stay up, all right? It's got nothing to do with any of that."

"How do you know you won't be late?"

They stood in front of their building, by the tavern that took up
most of the lower floor, Laura digging into her purse for her keys,
wondering what Diana wanted and too afraid to ask because she
suspected she already knew. So instead she'd asked the safe question. And was sorry she had after seeing the ineffably sad look that
passed across Diana's face. Someone in the tavern was knocking
hard on the window, trying to get their attention. They could hear
male voices calling out, drunkenly shouting out things that were
blessedly muffled by the large plate of glass. The two of them ignored it.

"It never lasts too long, Laura," Diana said, in a very soft voice.
"My clients are mostly confused; once it's over, they get disgusted
with themselves, they want you out of their room."

"Diana, I'm tired."

"All right." Diana was exasperated. She turned to Laura, angrily.
"You remind me of a man, sometimes, with your impatience. I want

to tell you a few things, what I am, what I'm like, when I get home. Then I'm gonna make you a proposition, honey. After you really know me, I want to know if you still want to go into business with me, just the two of us, work our own damn phone-sex lines and keep all the money for ourselves instead of turning it over to men."

"What?"

"Which word didn't you understand? Hell, we don't even have to wait until the ads get into the papers."

"Why not?"

"I stole some of Al's files, snatched files on twenty of his best callers; we can use them for a start." Diana hugged Laura quickly before she could respond, then pushed away, waved her hand in the air, trying to get a cab's attention. A Checker cab pulled to the curb.

Laura watched her get into the cab, heading north, on her way to the escort service's offices to meet her driver rather than returning the beep and making him have to drive all the way down to the South Loop. The key to the outer door was in Laura's hand. The assholes in the tavern knocked again, harder, on the glass. She could hear the male voices, louder now, shouting at her. Without looking, Laura gave them the finger, heard a bunch of surprised, beer-filled male voices raised in locker room laughter and shock, then she walked over to the door and let herself into the building. The first thing Mrs. LaRitcha told her was that her husband, Bing, had called, twice.

BING WAS LYING on the pool table doing sit-ups with his legs straight out, unbent. Big Bing watched him, along with the rest of the Sunday night crowd, from behind the bar in Bing's Bar, the tavern he owned on 101st and Ewing. There was a pretty good crowd tonight, as there was on most nights. In addition to the usual nightly regulars, the softball team the bar sponsored was sitting at a bunch of tables, pouring pitchers down. The crowd was almost exclusively male.

Big Bing reveled in the crowds; in the way they deferred to him, listened to his stories of the good old days without acting as if they were bored. The only regulars Big Bing didn't get along with were the two young punks sitting over at the table in the corner, waiting to talk to his son, with their dirty T-shirts and shorts, their baseball caps worn backward. He'd known them both since they'd been shitting their pants, and they'd been bad news even then. Big Bing figured it wasn't genetic, because their mother was a wonderful woman, or had been, until she'd grown too feeble to take care of herself and had to be taken to a home. Due mostly to their economic circumstances, the two of them were only semiregulars; small-time hustlers, bad influences for his kid, but then again, he was a full grown man now, and you couldn't tell them what to do forever, now could you?

Big Bing had a look of not-too-subtle contempt on his face, but the look wasn't directed at his son, or even at his son's friends. It was intended for the trendy young kid standing at the bar, the new guy, who was doing his best to fit in yet didn't have a clue as to how he could become one of the boys. So he'd decided the best way to do it was to get drunk. And from there, it wasn't hard for Little Bing to talk him into a bet.

Little Bing, who was three inches taller and seventy pounds heavier than Big Bing, was pumping out his two-hundredth sit-up, and it was obvious to anyone watching that it was getting pretty tough. He had worked up a good sweat, even in the heavily air-conditioned tavern. The deal was, he couldn't rest for more than a second at a time; those wide shoulders could only touch felt for a brief count of one-Mississippi. Bing's face was bright red, he looked ready to throw up, but still, he somehow struggled up into a full sitting position. "Two-*hun*dred!" Bing shouted, his face set in determination, as he fell back onto the pool table, began to struggle for 201. His cigarettes had fallen out of his shirt pocket, were spread out all around him and on the floor around the table.

The kid at the bar had a guarantee in his voice when he said, "He'll never make two-fifty." The newcomer had his face set in a way that made Big Bing want to punch it: the classic young drunk's face, lips pursed, eyes narrowed, with an expression that was a pretty equal mix of cocky and ignorant. The type of kitten who turned into a lion after drinking six ounces of scotch.

"Whattaya got left in your pocket, sonny boy? I'll match it out of the register. You got to give me two to one, though." Big Bing said it, looking over at his son. He made sure that he looked half-worried when the kid turned to look at him.

"You nuts? The guy won't make two-fif*teen,* for Christ's sake, let alone two-fifty. Look at him. He's too big, too out of shape. He can hardly breathe now."

"Put your money where your mouth is, or shut the fuck up." The newcomer glared over at Bing, challengingly at first. Bing Junior, voice straining, shouted out two-hundred-and-one! The old man was glaring back at the kid, prepared to leap the bar and slap him silly if he got too far out of line, and to hell with the bet. The kid must have sensed this, even as drunk as he was, and decided the only way he could teach this old man a lesson was to take his night's profits away from him. He reached into his pocket and angrily slammed a folded wad of bills down next to the original bet.

"Two-hu-nd-red and *two!*" Bing expelled air on the "two," as if he were a balloon that had been blown up and let go without the neck having been tied.

"There's three, four hundred there. You count it. Straight-up bet, though, forget the two-to-one bullshit."

"All right, you got a bet." Big Bing counted out the money, and announced the total to the bar. "Three-twenty-eight." He went to the register and punched up the No Sale, counted out the bills, turned with them and added them to the stack as his son counted off two-hundred-and-five. "That all you got, sonny?"

"For the moment, unless you got a cash station," the kid said, now standing with his back to the older man, his elbows on the bar, talking dismissively over his shoulder as if to an underling. "In a minute, though, I figure to have over a thousand in my pocket. And I'm buying the house a round the second this guy scrubs." He paused for a second, then added, "Down the street, at Rukavena's."

Oh, this one was a cutie.

His attitude matched his clothing: he was wearing oversized khaki shorts with a loose shirt that was maybe eight sizes too big. The shirt was out of his pants, hanging halfway to his knees. He had super-dark Ray-Bans pushed up into a curly head of hair that had gotten that way in a beauty parlor, the curls coming close but not quite covering up a big bald spot on the crown in back. He hadn't shaved in a couple of days. Said he'd come in to watch the Sox game, but had spent most of the night trying to kiss up to the regulars who, out of habit, had ignored him. Feeling out of place, with his ego whacked to hell, he'd been ripe for the picking when Bing had come along, and eager to prove himself a sport when Bing had told him he could do two-hundred-and-fifty sit-ups at once on the top of the tavern's pool table.

"Two-hundred and *eleven*!" Bing was expending more energy than he had to now.

Big Bing yelled out, "Five-twenty-eight, that's every dime he got!" and watched his son go to work. Then having to rub it in, Bing Junior turned his head slowly to look at the goof in the clown outfit, letting a big, slow smile spread across his handsome face.

"You should'a got his car keys," Bing said to his father. All of a sudden he didn't sound so out of breath.

Big Bing said, "Forget about it; who wants a Volvo? Besides, it's probably leased."

Bing, God bless his heart, he'd always had a flair for the dramatic. He lowered himself quickly, hands crossed on his wide chest, and knocked them out one after another, his eyes never leaving the wannabe player's face, Bing counting the sit-ups off, shouting them out as if he were in the Marines. Big Bing saw the kid's shoulders stiffen, watched him come slowly off the bar to stand with his fists ready, the kid starting to breathe as heavily as Bing had been pretending to. At the same time Big Bing noticed that most of the regulars in the crowd had begun to not-so-subtly close in on the kid. If this idiot made a move, he'd lose more than his money tonight. The kid turned to face Big Bing.

"You hustled me." The outrage in his tone was the object of great amusement in the tavern. Big Bing waited until the laughter died down, heard the phone ringing behind him, but let it ring.

"Hustled you? What hustle?" The words weren't out of his mouth before the kid made a grab for the money, but Big Bing had been expecting it, had the ice pick in his hand, down under the bar. He brought it up and around and down as fast as he could, stabbing the pile of money right through the middle. The kid had pulled his hand back fast, was now holding it to his chest, clutching it with his left as if he'd actually been stabbed. The only sounds in the tavern were the kid's heavy breathing and the ringing of the phone . . . and Bing, counting them out, now up to 238.

"The bet," Big Bing said, "was that he could do two-hundred-and-fifty situps. If he does 'em, that money's mine. If he don't, it's yours. And that's that." He turned his back on the kid to answer the telephone, not concerned for a second that he'd make another play for the money.

The crowd in the tavern helped Bing with the last ten situps, counting them out as if counting down the seconds on New Year's Eve. "*TWO-FIFTY!*" There had to be twenty-five voices shouting it, none louder than Bing's, who was still grinning at the mark, now shaking his head at the kid's stupidity. He got off the pool table, widened his eyes in mock fear at the mark's intimidating glare. "I'll bet you're the terror of the corporate racquetball team. But you know something? You ain't shit to me."

Walking toward him, making conversation, Bing said, "You like that thing I did, like I was constipated, around two-hundred? It's easy, you know how to do it. Just hold your breath for a few seconds and strain, turns the face red, makes the sweat pop out." Bing rubbed his backside, up high. "It's tougher as I get older, though. I won't be able to take a bath for a week without the damn thing burning."

"That's *bull*shit!" the kid had finally found his voice. Bing's grin grew wider as the group around the tavern laughed loudly at the young man's outrage, which only caused to further stoke his anger. The young man stood as tall as he could, swaying a little, and pointed an accusing finger at Bing. "That's fucking illegal! I've got friends on the force, you better not take my money!"

Friends on the force? "Ooooh," Bing said, and dropped the smile. The kid had no idea how much money they paid out every month so the force wouldn't even come *around*. And Bing had no intention of telling him. Bing moved his hand quickly, right past the man's shoulder, as if grabbing at a summer fly, and the young man flinched in fear. Bing looked at him as if surprised, then patted his shoulder in a reassuring manner. It had just been a teaser, Bing letting the kid know where he stood. He frowned when he saw the icepick sticking out of the pile of money. "Jesus, Pa, that's a little melodramatic."

"He was about to rabbit with the dough." Bing got a kick out of it when his father talked like that; like a gangster in a black-and-white movie from the forties.

"Rabbit?" Bing repeated. He pulled the icepick free. Counted the money out into two even piles. The kid with the Ray-Bans in his hair at ten o'clock at night was eyeing it, as if wondering if he should try once again to rabbit with the cash. Bing didn't return his look. "Put this back in the register." He pushed half the money toward his father. Put the rest of it in his pocket.

"What about my cut?"

"You my manager now?" His father was incensed now, Bing could tell.

"I hadn't backed your play, he'd'a seen through the game. What, you don't get drunk one night, you forget your place?" Bing reached into his pocket, trying to act resigned and angry. He'd only taken it all to get a rise out of the old man. He peeled a hundred dollars from the pile, dropped it onto the bar.

"Here, you happy now?"

"You're fuckin' A right I'm happy now, shit. What do you think I'm running here." Pa was playing to the crowd as much as he was to Bing, and Bing let him. It was good to see the old man show some life. He looked over at the kid, who didn't seem to know what to say.

"You still here?"

"I got a right."

"Not without money, you don't. You're a vagrant now, that's all. You leaving peacefully, or should we call our 'friends on the force'?" Bing stood there smiling at the man, acting casual but acutely aware of the looseness of the man's clothing, knowing from experience that the gang-bangers had invented that style of dress in order to hide lethal weapons. He didn't know if this kid knew that, but wasn't taking any chances that he might.

"I'll be back," the young man said, but it didn't come off as threatening, it sounded more a petulant whine than menacing words of vengeance.

"Don't come with the second team," Bing said, knowing he wouldn't be back, but letting him save whatever face he thought he could.

The kid wasn't out the door before the place broke into applause. Bing took his bow, winked over at his father, and walked over to the little round table where Rafe and Tony were waiting.

• • •

He sat down at their table and pushed their pitcher of beer away from him, so he wouldn't have to smell it. Bing lighted a cigarette and sat back in the chair, grimacing and rubbing his stomach, dominating the table through sheer size as much as through force of personality. Both were things he tried to downplay; in fact he went out of his way to do so. Like now, with Rafe and Tony watching, Bing was acting as if he were in pain.

"Hurts like hell. Time was, the bet was five hundred sit-ups, you guys remember?"

"Shit." Rafe spat out the word, looking over at his brother Tony instead of at Bing. Tony was smiling broadly; he'd always enjoyed the games Bing played, and besides, there was something he needed Bing to do.

"I got the money." Bing's lips turned down in distaste before he could stop himself. He acted as if it were part of the grimace, kept rubbing his belly, then put both hands on the table. "You still going to do what you said?"

"Maybe," Bing said, dragging the word out, trying to act reasonably and give them the impression that whether he did it or not would be due to the way they'd behaved. "Your mother still in the home?"

"She was, until this morning. The diabetes finally got to her. She can't see for shit. They took her to South Chicago Hospital this morning, had to take off one of her legs. It looks like the other one might have to come off, too. If she makes it through the next forty-eight hours. That's in the hands of God."

"Ah, shit."

"Nothing for it," Tony said, and shrugged. "She got old, man."

Bing remembered their mother, Mrs. O'Conner, who wasn't a day older than his own father. He looked over at his pa, watched him laughing it up with his cronies, the old man with one foot up on the backsink, his elbow resting on his knee, a half-empty shot glass in his hand, a cigarette dangling from between his lips. During the time when the old man wasn't working, he wasn't really alive.

"So, you gonna do it? We ain't gonna get a better opportunity," Tony said.

Rafe said, "We told the nurses we was only going out to get a bite to eat. We got to get our asses back to the hospital pretty quick."

"You don't finish this pitcher of beer, you hear me? Those beers are all you have tonight."

"That's funny, I thought our daddy died twenty-two years ago."

"I'm serious, Tony. You want me to do this, I'm in charge." Bing was looking for a way out as much as anything else, not wanting to do the thing he'd said he'd do. The fact was, he'd been drunk when he'd said he'd do the job for them. A simple job, too, that any dummy could have handled. But the O'Conner boys were as stupid as they came, and if they tried it themselves, they'd get caught. They were smart enough to understand that much.

"All right, you're in charge." Shit. Bing had to find another tack.

"You got the money, you said? Didn't take it out of any of your mother's bank accounts, out of somewhere the cops could trace?"

"We took it out of—" Rafe began, but Tony shut him up with a glare.

Tony said, "We got it, and it can't be traced back to us. It's all green and it folds, what else you need to know?"

"When you got so tough, that's what I want to know." He stared at Tony O'Conner, wanting to know, too, when he'd gotten so cold-hearted and devious, but not about to ask. "How much you bring?"

"What you said, five grand." Tony made a point of looking around, and Bing felt something placed in his lap. Tony looked back at him. "Don't shove that down the back of your pants, you're likely pretty raw down there right about now." Bing fingered the manilla envelope, made as if he were rubbing his stomach again, and shoved it down into the front of his pants.

"You can't have cleaned the place out—"

"We didn't take nothing out of there."

"Nothing? Not the TV, the VCR? A favorite pillow, nothing?"

"Swear to God."

"All right." It was all Bing could do not to sigh. He'd said he'd do it, and he'd never broken his word. But it had been a long time ago and they'd all been dead drunk. Still, he had to keep his word, he didn't even want to think of what might happen if the rumor was spread around that he didn't keep his word. He looked over at his father again, saw that the old man was no longer smiling, seemed to be chewing someone out. Some poor sap who had probably made the mistake of ordering a drink when the old man was in the middle of telling one of his stories. "You guys go on, get back to the hospital, right now. I'll take care of it, but I'll have to wait until you've been back at the hospital for a couple of hours."

"But you'll do it tonight?"

"Tonight."

"How you gonna do it?" Rafe wanted to know, and Bing saw Rafe jump as Tony kicked him under the table.

"Go on, and do me a favor, tell your mother I send her my best."

"She won't be able to hear me," Rafe said. Bing had to fight the urge to kick the man himself.

"Tell her anyway," Bing said, then got up, grabbed the pitcher, and walked it over to the bar.

His father said to him, "You ready, or you still on the water wagon?" and Bing just shook his head without looking at the man.

He was looking at his reflection in the back bar, his mind a thousand miles away from the East Side gin mill. He was wondering how long his father had, and what he would do when the old man died. He'd be thirty-seven on his next birthday, and it wasn't too far in the future. He'd never held a regular job in his life, had just tended bar here and now and again bounced in the joint as needed. He didn't even get a piece of the place, he just got a salary; he didn't even know if his father had left the tavern to him in his will.

What if he hadn't? What if his father's disappointment in him had led him to leave the bar to one of his friends? What if he lived another ten years? Bing would be middle-aged then, and what would he have?

The same as he had now: nothing.

What he hustled and the ten an hour his father gave him for tending bar. Four hundred a week minimum, tax free, and how long did that last? Bing liked to play the ponies and he had a drinking jones and he knew it. He was never more aware of it than he was right this second, with his blood *screaming* for a drink, and not beer, either, but a shot of the hard stuff, the brand didn't matter, he craved anything that had a high enough alcohol content. Bing could taste it, feel it going down, burning his mouth and his throat and warming his belly, the warmth spreading outward until it was just a glow that would seem to fill him.

His wife had left him behind his drinking, though. The drinking and the gambling, the staying out late at night. The last straw had been when she'd learned about his one-night stand with a girl who'd seduced him on the pool table after the joint had closed for the night. He'd lost the best thing that had ever happened to him, and what could he do about it, who could he talk it over with? His father? Not a chance. His father held women in low esteem, didn't seem to even need their company since Bing's mother had died, nine years ago last Thanksgiving Day. Where had the time gone? It seemed he'd just yesterday been a kid. He still acted like one, too, didn't he? Doing sit-ups on a pool table to clean out some young stud who thought he was a tough guy. Pretty soon, before he knew it, he'd be like his old man, and there was no doubt about what *he* was. A washed-up drunk who didn't have a whole lot to live for. Just the hours he spent behind the bar, and even then he wasn't much company until he had a few drinks under his belt.

Christ.

Bing closed his eyes tight, shook his head, trying to get rid of the ugly thoughts.

As if he didn't have enough on his mind, he'd agreed to do something ugly. Had in fact now been paid cash up front to perform the ugly act. Which meant he'd have to do it. He wished he'd get his return call, right here, right now, at the bar. He'd called the AA people at their Central Office number Friday, and here it was Sunday, and no one had called him back. Maybe they didn't care as much as they liked others to think.

Then yet again, maybe they did.

Maybe it was like Bing had once thought, they had some sort of magic wand they waved at you, and when they did, the pain went away. A lot of the guys in the bar had gone to AA at one time or another, though, and it hadn't seemed to have done much for them. Maybe there was some special words you had to speak, maybe they—ah, maybe hell.

They'd call or they wouldn't, and Bing would drink or he wouldn't. He didn't see how he'd get through what he had to do tonight without a drink. And seeing as how they hadn't called, well, if they could hold him up for two days, he could hold them up for a couple more, too. Another day or two, it wouldn't matter, would it? He'd have one, maybe two drinks, just enough to loosen him up, to get him through what he had to do.

He waited until his father stopped talking before saying, "Pa? Set me up, would you?" And he saw the gleam come into his father's eye, the all-knowing look that settled on his face. His father thought he knew Bing's secrets. It made Bing want to punch him.

"Thank Jesus," his father said. "You been acting like a goddamn school kid ever since that woman left, and now you even went on the wagon. What'd you do, read one of them fucking self-improvement books?" His father was pouring the whiskey into a double shot glass, backing it up with a glass of iced tap water that he'd brought over with him. He topped the drink off with a practiced twist of his wrist. Bing wasn't sure that he could pick up the drink without spilling it. "You figure you stay sober, think pure thoughts, she'll come back?" Bing dreaded what he knew would be coming, a heart-to-heart with a drunk who thought he knew everything there was to know about any subject, the education gleaned from his years of standing behind a bar.

His father was walking away, then stopped, as if he'd suddenly remembered something. He turned back to Bing.

"By the way, she called."

"Laura?" Bing had forgotten the drink.

"Yeah."

"When?"

His father had to think about it. At last he nodded. "While you was doing the sit-ups, but after the sucker gave up the last of the moolah—" Big Bing shook his head in disgust and said, "Fuck me," but he said it to his son's back, as Bing had ignored the drink and was racing to the back of the tavern, heading to the stairs that led up his apartment, not about to use the house phone to call the woman who'd broken his heart.

AFTER THE GUNSHOT rang out and the mayor's life had been saved, Mr. X got out of the fund-raiser just as fast as he could, considering the circumstances. He'd lost track of his wife after the fistfight, had left her somewhere in the frantic crowd. He'd gotten his ass out of there and had been taken to the hospital, and after being taken care of there he'd come here, to his "office."

He'd gotten here all right, had driven over and parked the car, gotten into the building and into the elevator, and anyone who'd been watching wouldn't have given him a second glance. Only he was aware of the turmoil within, the turmoil that threatened to destroy him if he didn't do something about it quick.

The first thing he did, after locking the door behind him, was to collapse against it, with his back to it, slide down to a sitting position and shake, crying hard. After a time, he felt better. At least less humiliated. He wiped at his tears with the sleeve of his tuxedo shirt, sniffed, got himself under control. Still, though, he sat there.

His wife would be on her own now, and to hell with her. To *hell* with her! The stress, the fear, the pain of the night had been too much for him to handle, and he couldn't bear the thought of her seeing him when he was weak. It wasn't the sort of thing she would ever let him live down.

So he'd snuck away from everybody and come here. To his safe haven, to the one place on earth where he felt that he could truly be himself, or, for that matter, where he could be anyone he wanted to be, and do it in absolute safety.

Mr. X soon found out that he'd been wrong about that. Because when he got to his feet and walked over to his desk, he noticed that the message light on his answering machine was blinking.

Uncharacteristically shocked, he stood and looked at it for a minute. Who could have possibly called? The machine was here for only one reason, so Mr. X could tape his phone conversations and relive them at a later time. He had never given this number out to a single living soul. So who the hell could have called? It had to be a wrong number.

But it wasn't a wrong number. It was Allan Beck.

Drunk, too, by the sound of him. Slurring his words and trying to get back the manhood he thought he'd lost in their last conversation.

"Hey, Mr. Big Shot," Al Beck said to him. "That's right, I know who you are. You want to threaten people? You're so big on knowing shit? Let me tell you what *I* know, you freak." There was a slight shift in Beck's voice, a subtle but mocking tone that Mr. X found so insulting he felt degraded in his own little room. "No, maybe I won't tell you. At least not everything." He'd said that as a bluff. Even as surprised and confused as he was, Mr. X could figure that one out. Now the little man could pretend that he knew more than he did. Beck coughed a couple of times. Mr. X could hear loud background music and the clamor of boisterous laughter. The little bore was in a tavern.

"Just let me say this. I know who you are, I know your phone number and address—" Beck read them off to him, and the address and phone number were correct; the number was listed under a false name so he didn't have that right. "—and I can have ten guys down there, anytime I want. So, you want to fuck around with me? You want to put dicks in people's mouths? Take mine in *yours,* and suck it, honeyboy, while it's still swinging from the vine. I bet you'd like that, wouldn't you, freako? I got friends at the phone company, and in plenty of other places, too. So take your threats and stick 'em in your ass. I hear from you again, and your ass is mine." There was more, but Mr. X didn't hear it, because he grabbed the answering machine off the desk and smashed it against the wall.

Mr. X was enraged. He overturned his desk. He shouted on the top of his lungs, screaming curses in a voice that would have caused Al Beck to pass out in terror at the very sound of it had he been within range.

He'd kill him. He'd kill him. He'd fucking *kill* that little maggot!

Did he know who he was dealing with? Hadn't he learned anything from talking to him earlier? Mr. X was breathing heavily, his hands were so tightly fisted that the muscles of his forearms trembled.

He stood there for a minute, remembering who he was. A man used to pressure, a man who *had to be in control.* Who was Al Beck to fluster him? he asked himself. A no one, a nothing. A small-time Jew lawyer who wanted to be a player. Mr. X would play with him. He'd have to now. That, or leave this place right now, tonight. Get out and never come back, before Beck made good on his threat.

Because if the little bastard ever came here, or sent someone around, taking pictures, it would be over for him. Mr. X couldn't survive the scandal. He would not back down from such a man, could never let the Al Becks of the world push him around or force him to turn tail and run.

He set his desk back upright, replaced his phone. He disconnected the phone from the now useless answering machine, plugged it directly into the jack and picked up the pieces of the machine. Mr. X pulled out his chair, sat down, and forced himself to take several deep breaths and blow them out slowly, calming himself, relaxing. When he thought he would be able to talk, he reached for the phone and dialed the number for ABI, cleared his throat while the phone rang, setting his tone deep, deep, as deep as he could get it. No one would ever recognize him through the sound of his phone-sex voice.

"Al Beck, please?" The woman who answered seemed taken aback that someone had called for the boss.

"Uh—I'm sorry, he's not here," she said, then made somewhat of a comeback. "May *I* be of service?"

"I'm a friend of Al's," Mr. X said. "What time will he be back."

"I'm not sure, but he's always back before two, that's when we close up, and he's the only one with the key." The woman sounded bored now, but not bored enough to insult someone who could be a friend of the boss.

"I know, I know, time is money, and I hear other phones ringing. I'll call him back later." Mr. X hung up.

He sat back in his chair, staring at the ceiling, thinking.

As a young child he'd often fantasized about murdering someone, had lain in his bed playing with himself, visualizing what he would do to people once he got old enough. *If* he got old enough. Then, later, as a young man, he'd had the opportunity to do it for real. And more than once.

It had been better than he'd ever dreamed.

But now he didn't know if he could take the chance. He wasn't worried about the morality of it. Morality was something he'd always believed was for other, weaker men.

His problem was getting caught. Mr. X couldn't deal with prison. He couldn't lose all that he had, not after all that he'd done to put himself where he was today.

He sat back, thought about his dissolving marriage for a minute. He could live without her, too, no problem. He felt better about that, for some reason. He could live without the kids, too. It wasn't as if he'd ever been a part of their stupid little lives. It was always Mommy, Mommy, Mommy. The children always avoided him. Daddy was only there to write the goddamn checks when they needed something. It would be embarrassing, but it wouldn't hurt him or his career. He would move out of the house, and soon. He might even move tonight. No later than the weekend. He'd been humiliated tonight, publicly, in front of everybody at the fund-raiser. Made less powerful in the eyes of people to whom the illusion of power was all.

But he could live with that.

What he couldn't live with was being threatened. And never, ever, *ever* by a little piece of shit like Allan Beck.

Mr. X had booze mixed with painkilling drugs in his system. There were more pain pills in his pocket. He had to think this through, calmly, lucidly. He couldn't allow the effect of the drugs and the drink to lower his inhibitions, not over something this important, when the stakes were so high. He wouldn't use drugs as an excuse to commit a violent act for which he might have to suffer at a later date, sober. So he had to think it over before he acted.

But he had to admit, the idea was intriguing. He hadn't killed in so long, in years. He realized now—and not for the first time—how very much he'd missed it.

So what was the downside?

He was in a position to know from personal experience that police were, as a whole, far from stupid. He knew that some officers were stupid, lazy, and corrupt, but others were fearless and dogged. They took everything personally, and their egos were large. Large enough that they couldn't rest until they solved criminal puzzles to their personal satisfaction.

So would a man like Beck have any friends like that in the department? Not likely. He might be paying someone off so he could operate, and he might even have cops on the payroll. Mr. X wouldn't be surprised to discover that off-duty female cops worked the phone lines. Some men liked the fantasy; being arrested and brought to task by leather-clad women with badges. But he couldn't see a man like Beck having good friends in the upper echelons of the Chicago Police Department. Or even low ones. Any police officer involved with Beck would be in it for the money, and from what Mr. X knew of the man, there wasn't a whole lot of that to be had.

So, where did that leave him? What could he do? Even if he went after the man, he'd have to somehow ensure that Beck hadn't given out the information he'd learned to anyone else. There was the phone company connection, too, he had to think of that. Although that didn't pose much of a problem. If Beck died, the last thing his connection at the phone company would do would be to confess to taking money—and Mr. X was certain that the connection was a paid informant—from Beck in return for handing over legally classified, private consumer information without a signed court order. The connection would be fired, might well go to prison.

He held his arm straight out in front of him, looked at his fingers. They were steady, unshaking. He couldn't believe how he'd lost it earlier, how he had ever behaved like a whimpering, sniveling coward. Making the decision to kill Beck had brought him back to who he was. And what he was.

Who would miss someone like Beck? No one, that's who. And he couldn't see the cops making too much of a stink over the death of a sleazy lawyer who ran a porno phone line on the side. They might even have a party to celebrate the guy's demise. He knew that normally his inclination would be to wait a few days, to think things over, and if he still thought that killing was the only answer, then he'd go out and make his move. But it had been so long, and he'd been so humiliated tonight. He felt the urge to kill, the need, in his blood. The longer he waited, the more time Beck would have to brag on his toughness, to tell people about Mr. X's office and how he'd been put in his place. The assassination attempt on the mayor would be on the front pages of both papers, and the lead stories on all the local TV news programs. The death of a shabby South Loop lawyer wouldn't even get a play.

So it had to be tonight. And he knew where the man would be right after two in the morning. Mr. X checked his watch. Twelve-fourteen. He noticed that his fingers were trembling, but with anticipation, not fear, and that his spine was tingling the same way it had so many years ago when he'd been scheduled to go out on patrol, knowing that before it was over he would either die or take another man's life. Suddenly, the decision made, Mr. X felt incredibly calm, as if nothing could hurt him. Not losing the children, not losing his wife. Nothing could hurt him. He now had the emotions of a boulder in the rain.

And he was stiff, too, as hard as that boulder. Mr. X laughed out loud. He picked up the phone, took a couple of deep breaths as he blocked Caller ID, then dialed a number that he had once called frequently, but hadn't called in some time. The woman he was calling wouldn't be happy to hear from him, and he wouldn't leave a message on her machine if she didn't pick up. Fortunately for him, she wasn't talking with a client at the moment.

"Tina's Talk Line, this is Tina . . ." Tina somehow always managed to sound as if she were licking her lips at the same time as she spoke. She had a low, deep, provocative voice, one that he loved to hear when she became terrified as she envisioned the terrible, morbid images he invoked in her mind.

"Tina, this is X."

"Dear God." There was no disguising the fear in her voice, the shock over the fact that he was calling again.

He hurriedly said, "If you hang up, I'll come over; you know I have your address."

"Mr. X, please, I thought we had an understanding."

"We did. Things have changed. I have a fifty-dollar bill in my hand, and I'm addressing an envelope to you right now."

He could hear her crying over the line. The sound filled him with joy.

"*Please—*" It was an animalistic wail for mercy. He laughed, actually chuckled into the phone. "You don't know what you did to me," Tina whimpered, and Mr. X touched himself, lightly. Just ran his fingernails down his zipper, teasing himself.

"Your imagination is too strong. You must have an artistic soul."

"Please, Mr. X, I just got over the nightmares. I almost quit the business. I had all these images in my brain, seeing myself the way you said you'd do me—" Tina stopped herself, more than likely having realized that she was playing right into his hands.

"You fear me, Tina. And you have good reason."

"*No*! Goddamnit, you *prom*ised!"

"I am putting *two* fifty-dollar bills into the envelope now, Tina." There was a long pause; he could hear her sobbing. Mr. X knew she was his. He told her to wait while he got undressed, and he wasn't at all surprised that she was still on the line after he draped his bloody tuxedo and underclothing over the back of his leather chair.

Mr. X closed his eyes and smiled. When he spoke, his voice was deep and low, a hissing, guttural sound; what a snake might sound like if it had the powers of speech.

"I am coming through your window now, Tina, there's a knife in my left hand."

"No!" Tina's plaintive keening was, to him, symphonic. Mr. X held the phone to his undamaged ear and began to stroke himself with the other while he spoke to hopeless little Tina, telling him what he was going to do not only to her, but to her terrified young daughter.

"Hı." **BING SPOKE** the word softly, but he put everything he had into it, trying to convey the depth of his feelings, his longing, into a single, mournful syllable.

"What did you want, Bing." There was no forgiveness or understanding in Laura's voice tonight. Bing fought the impatience and anger he felt at her dismissive tone of voice. If he was ever going to get her back, he'd have to prove to her that he'd changed.

"I just wanted to talk to you. It's been a long time, Laura."

"Not long enough."

"Come on, Laura, please." Something in his voice stopped her, he could tell. Maybe he was getting through to her. He'd keep calling until he did.

"Bing, you have to stop this. I left you. It's over. I'm never coming back, Bing." The last sentence was said very softly.

Maybe she didn't believe it, either.

Bing, desperate, played his hole card. "I haven't had a drink in three days and two nights. I don't know if I can get through tonight without talking to you, Laura."

"Call AA, they have—"

"I did." Bing cut her off. "I called them Friday and they never called me back, now it's Sunday and I'm going crazy and I miss you and my son."

"He's fine, you know that, you know I'll take good care of him."

"I know you'll try, but in that neighborhood, who knows?"

"I'll take care of him." There was a sternness in her tone now that made Bing back off.

"All right, but still, he needs me, Laura."

"He needed you for the past eight years, and what did he get, Bing? What example did you set? When he did see you, you were either drunk or too hung over to even look at him." She paused, and Bing could picture her sitting there thinking of the past, the way he'd hurt her and their son, Tommy, and he knew that if she dwelled on that she'd hang up on him, so he hurriedly filled the silence.

"Laura, please, I've changed."

"Give me a break."

"Give me a *chance*."

"Bing, we've been over this a hundred times; it doesn't do any good. You're embarrassing yourself and trying to make me out to be the bad guy."

"Listen, it takes two to wreck a marriage."

"No, it just takes one. And you did it."

"I was wrong. I mean it, you have to listen to me."

"No, you're wrong there, too, Bingo old boy. I don't have to do anything anymore but take care of my kid."

"He's my kid too, goddamn it!"

Laura hung up on him then, and not angrily. Bing only heard a soft click. Bing held down the button, looking at the phone, then punched in her number again and let it ring for a long time before Laura finally picked up.

"Bing, *stop* it! Tommy's asleep!"

"Let me see him, let me see you. I got a right to visit my kid."

"The judge didn't think so, did she?"

"That bitch, if she'd been a man, I'd have gotten visitation."

"You're a convicted felon, Bing. You only see Tommy when I can supervise the visit." She'd calmed down some, thank God. But that didn't mean she'd calmed down because she was enjoying the conversation. It could be just the sort of attitude some other women could have talked her into having, a game they'd made her play, being the calm, above-it-all wife, the voice of reason. He knew guys at the bar whose wives were in Al-Anon, and to hear them tell it, such women would live forever; as long as there was one drunk left whose life they could make miserable, they'd hang in there.

Bing proceeded with caution.

"So give me a supervised visit."

He must have been breaking down her barriers. She didn't reject him out of hand, as she'd done so often in the past, nor did she hang up on him. Bing's heart filled with expectations of a reunion. She'd loved him for a long, long time, had done everything to make him happy. She couldn't have gotten so cold so fast.

Could she?

"Bing, let me ask you a question." There was a quietness in her voice he didn't like, almost a calculation. If he were talking to a man, one of his friends, red flags would have been flying, he'd have suspected that they were wanting something Bing might not want to deliver.

"Sure."

"Do you believe you owe me? That what you did to me was wrong?"

"Owe you? Christ, only my life. You were the best thing that ever—"

"Save it, Bing. Now listen to me carefully, pay attention, all right? Do you or do you not figure that you owe me?"

"How much do you need? Hell, I'm broke." Bing believed that she would come back sooner if he didn't give her any money. There was five hundred–some dollars in his pants pocket, and another five grand stuck down his pants, under his shirt, but he wouldn't give her any of it, it wasn't the way to win her back. Still, he found out quick that he'd asked the wrong question, because now the calmness was out of her tone; suddenly, Laura was mad.

"Listen, you son of a bitch, I haven't asked you for a dime, and I could get it from you, too." He'd like to know how, seeing as he was technically unemployed. Laura said, "I haven't asked you for anything, and I'm not about to, either. But if you want a visit, you want to see me, you want to see your son, you have to do something for me."

"Anything, Laura, you name it."

"How about a B and E, would you do that for me, Bing?" Laura asked.

Jake walked into the apartment and Marsha was right there at the door, still dressed in her evening gown, an anxious look on her face.

"How's Alex?" she asked, before he could pull his key out of the lock. He nodded reassuringly, feeling tired. He closed the door behind him and double-locked it. There might not have ever been any burglaries in the building, but there was no use in taking chances, and no percentage in being a fool.

"He's all right, physically, at least. No concussion, nothing like that. The bottom of his ear took a load of stitches, part of the lobe's gone." Jake walked into the kitchen and got a beer out of the refrigerator, twisted it open, went over to the old bleacher chairs, and stopped. He handed Marsha the beer, and when she took it he picked up the chairs, carried them over to the large bay windows, set the chairs down in front of them. He took his beer, touched Marsha's hand, and led her to her chair.

They looked out at the Sears Tower for a while, silently holding hands. At the mesmerizing, steady blinking of the lights atop the two tall white antennas, the sight nearly hypnotic in the surrounding darkness of the night. Jake felt close to her, strongly connected. His insecurities of the afternoon now only faded memories. Action had pumped him up, taken away his fears, and left him little time to dwell on them. He squeezed Marsha's hand.

Jake said, "In honor of the occasion, they had Mondo in one of the private VIP rooms, so he didn't have to sit and wait with the rest of the people in ER." Jake sipped his beer, closed his eyes tight, shook his head to try and clear it but it didn't do much good. He felt all choked up, and for reasons that were far greater than the attempted assassination, or even Mondo's shooting. "He told me all about it in the room, while we were waiting for the doctors. Sheila told him in the car, on the way over to the *dinner,* that she wanted a divorce. She told him that if he balked, she'd tell the judge that he was molesting his daughters."

"My God. She's some kind of player." Marsha was angry. "Did you catch her at the dinner? Hanging all over that man? Thank God we don't socialize with other cops and their families."

"They think I'm arrogant because we don't. They think we're stuck up because we went to college and most of them didn't. These same guys, they snort and slap their knees when blacks say that white people don't understand their problems. Then they only hang out with their own kind themselves. I ask them why, guess what they tell me?"

"Because nobody else understands them."

"You're the psyche major; isn't there some hotshot term for that?"

"Sure," Marsha told him. "Ignorance."

"Not that we socialize with a whole lot of *non*-cops, either."

"All we need's each other," Marsha said. She took her hand back, and Jake looked over at her, saw her looking out the window, but he knew she wasn't seeing anything.

"What's wrong?"

She didn't answer for a second. "Why were we there tonight, Jake?" When he didn't answer right away, she said, "It was more than just extra security, wasn't it?" Her voice was very soft. Still, Jake kept silent. Marsha said, "Did you find out anything about the man with the gun?" She didn't have to ask him that one twice.

Jake hurriedly said, "Oh, yeah. He sang like a little birdie, wanted to know what he'd done wrong. Why had they stopped him from performing a public service? They came right to the hospital to tell us. To tell Mondo, rather. They didn't seem to care either way if I found out what happened." Jake finished his beer, thinking about the sick little fat man, grateful that he had his sickness to expound on in order to distract Marsha from her earlier train of thought.

He said, "The guy, he was from South Chicago, born and raised. Lived with his parents, cared for his mother for years after his father died. Worked at the mill until it closed, off his folk's pension and their Social Security after he got laid off. His mother died a couple months ago, and he found out he couldn't get anything for his house. Blamed the mayor for the way his neighborhood went to hell in the past twenty years. They said his house was filled from top to bottom with newspaper clippings, crimes in the neighborhood, promises the mayor had made and never kept."

"He was stalking him?"

"In his own way, he wasn't dumb. They take pictures, videos and stills, of every public appearance the mayor makes, did you know that?"

"It makes sense, they do it for the president, I know."

"Big-city mayors, too, these days. They went back six months, this guy isn't in any of the shots. And you know what? If he hadn't shot off his mouth, gotten on the phone and started making threats, he would have gotten away with it. Now they got him on voiceprints, too, as if they needed more evidence of first degree, attempted." Jake paused. "I imagine he wanted to get caught."

"What did you say?"

"When?"

"Just now." Marsha was looking at him, oddly. There was controlled anger on her face. "*What* phone calls?"

"Death threats."

"Death threats." Marsha whispered the words in disbelief. She said, "I *knew* it."

"It wasn't in the papers, nobody leaked the calls, thank God." The words sounded weak even in Jake's ears.

"Thank God? You *knew*?" She stood now, with her hands on her hips, looking down on him.

"Nobody really took it seriously."

"Of course not. That's why there were an extra hundred cops and their wives at the dinner tonight, getting a free ride at a thousand-dollar-a-plate banquet, because nobody took it seriously." Marsha turned her back on him, her arms crossed now. He watched her, looked at the tension in her body as she stared out the window.

"Come on," Jake said. He got up, took two steps, and gently touched her upper arms from behind. She shook them off.

"You should have told me, Jake, I had a right to know. If there was a chance that there was going to be gunplay, I had a right to choose whether I went or stayed home."

"Nobody got hurt."

"You knew and you didn't tell me. We weren't supposed to ever be closed off to each other, remember?"

"We were under orders to keep our mouths shut."

"That sounds familiar. Ever study history? At Nuremberg, they made that sort of statement all the time."

"Marsha, what are you so upset about?"

"What am I so up*set* about? I could have gotten killed! Lynne would have been without her mother because *you* were under orders not to tell me what was going on!" She turned to face him now. "I should have been allowed to make that choice, Jake, and you know it."

"I couldn't tell you, Marsha, my job was on the line."

"Funny, all this time I thought I'd married a loving, sharing, sensitive man. I didn't know you were just another closemouthed, job-scared cop."

"Come on . . ."

"What's the matter? Figure the little woman couldn't have handled the news?"

"Marsha—"

"Marsha, your ass," Marsha said, and began to walk out of the room.

"You'd have gone anyway, and you know goddamn well you would have!" Jake shouted after her.

"That's not the point, Jake, and *you* know goddamn well it isn't."

And then their bedroom door closed behind her, and Marsha was out of his sight. Jake looked down at the chairs, had to fight the impulse to pick them up and toss them out the window. He kicked at the beer bottle and missed.

"Shit."

It was her sister's fault. What Betty said had bothered her all day, had boiled around inside her until it spilled out over the top. Naturally she had to take it out on him, because she hadn't had the courage to stand up to her successful older sister.

It was an interior argument that lasted for about as long as it took him to think it.

It wasn't her sister. It wasn't her mother. It was him.

What Mondo had said earlier that day now echoed in Jake's mind. How he and his wife used to be like Jake and Marsha. Happy. Smiling. Touching. Jesus Christ.

But he wasn't Mondo, and Marsha wasn't Sheila. Not by a long shot. And Jake wasn't about to let their relationship dissolve, as Mondo had allowed his to. Not over macho pride. Nothing was worth that, nothing was worth losing Marsha over.

He stood looking out the window for a minute, while he calmed down, thinking about what he should do.

Mondo had stormed out of the hospital as soon as the doctors had finished with him, and when Jake had asked him where he was going, his partner had told him that he wasn't sure. "I don't have a home anymore," were Mondo's exact words.

Jake turned away from the window, looked at the large picture of the three of them on the wall. A slash of light from a streetlamp illuminated Marsha, who was holding Lynne, the two of them smiling broadly for the camera, Lynne holding out a baby fist in greeting. Jake's image was in shadow. What was this, an omen? He looked away from the window, and over at the bedroom door. She'd still be too angry to discuss it, he'd bet.

Jake went and got another beer, then came back and sat back down in the chair and looked out at the city lights.

BING HAD TWO drinks, that was all. Double shots of bar whiskey that his father had the nerve to charge him for. He washed them down with ice water, then spun around without a word, got off the bar stool, and walked out of the joint. He wouldn't take his car, he didn't want anyone to see it, to grab the license plate number while he was inside the house, working. Besides, he wanted the fresh air, the time, to clear his mind. It wasn't every day that you found out that the woman you loved was a whore.

Inside the envelope Tony had given him, along with the money, was a key. To the back door of the O'Conner household. Bing stayed off Ewing Avenue, walked down dark side streets, the whiskey, like an old friend, comforting him. The inner warmth was welcome. Bing was sweating in the evening humidity. He ignored the mosquitoes that attacked him in swarms, the bugs drifting over from the lake a few blocks away. Bing turned into an alley and came up to the house through the back.

The O'Conner house had a five-foot Cyclone fence surrounding the backyard, and Bing easily leaped it, crouched next to the side of the empty garage and listened. Nothing. Not a dog barking, not a neighbor calling out who's there. All he heard was the humming of several window air conditioners. It wasn't the sort of neighborhood where central-air units were the norm. Bing stood up and hurried to the back door, got into the house and stood in the dark for a minute, letting his eyes adjust to the darkness.

He was in the kitchen, right where he wanted to be. He'd earn five thousand dollars tonight for five minutes of simple work. He had to keep telling himself that, had to remind himself that it wasn't really a crime. If there was anyone to be blamed, it was the real estate slobs who'd scared off all the good people, or the fat cats who owned the mills and let them close down. As for himself, all he was doing was ripping off an insurance company, helping a couple of friends to get back on their feet. The company would pay right off, too, with the rightful owner of the house in the hospital, dying. It would be a public relations disaster if they decided to fight the claim.

Still, the thought of destroying the place gave Bing pause. He'd played here as a little kid, all the time, had run up and down the basement stairs, slamming the door and waking Grandpa O'Conner, the old drunk who slept on a cot downstairs. Which would put the old man in a foul mood; he'd chase them through and out of the house, cursing.

And what about the people next door, Jesus, what if the blast killed one of the neighbors on either side? The houses were pretty close to each other.

It wouldn't happen, that was all. It just wouldn't happen.

Bing walked purposefully toward the stove, used the quilted potholder that was hanging on a nail beside it to turn on all four burners, halfway. As they came to life, he blew out the flames, then twisted the knobs all the way open. Bing stood in the sudden dark, hearing the hissing of escaping gas. The stove faced the backyard; the bulk of the blast would blow out that way. Nobody would get hurt, it would all be okay. Bing bent over and opened the oven door, leaned his head in, and blew out the pilot. Then he stood and used the potholder again to turn on the oven. He hung the potholder back on the nail, then walked away from the stove. Bing reached into his pants pocket and took out a stainless-steel Zippo lighter.

Bing went into the living room, away from the stink of natural gas, opened the lighter and pulled the wick out as far as it would go. He thumbed the lighter to life, watched the extra-long flame leap toward the ceiling, then placed it down on the coffee table. By the time the gas made it all the way into here and found its way to the flame, there'd be enough natural gas loose in the house to blow this place to hell.

Unless the cord on the refrigerator was frayed, and it cycled on while he was in the house, causing a spark.

Bing had heard of a man who'd had a gas leak in his house on a Saturday night, who'd found out about it after coming home from a long evening in the gin mills. He'd discovered his problem when he'd put his key in the lock; the tiny spark caused by the friction of steel on steel had been enough to ignite the gas and blow him to pieces, along with the entire house.

Scared now, smelling gas, Bing hurried through the house, and went out the way he'd come in. He retraced his steps through the alley, hurried down the side streets. When he got to Ewing, he fished in his pockets, got the car keys ready before he got anywhere near his car. His car was parked in front of the tavern. The temptation to stop in would be great. So Bing stayed focused, thinking of Laura, thinking of Tommy, thinking of anything but of whiskey. He'd had two drinks, that would hold him, until after he saw Laura and heard her proposition.

He'd had two drinks.

Bing stopped in front of the tavern and thought about that. He'd have to go inside; he needed some gum to cover the smell of whiskey on his breath. While he was inside, he would have one, maybe two, that was all.

"You sleeping?"

"You know better than that." Jake had opened the door just a crack, stood in the triangle of light that came in from the living room. He entered the bedroom, left the door open, went over and sat down on the edge of the bed. He reached out a tentative hand and touched Marsha's hair. She let him. She was on her side, facing him. She was looking up at him. He had trouble reading her expression. Did she feel betrayed, used?

Jake said, "I spent twenty-two years living with a man who never told his wife a word about his business. As long as he paid the bills, she never asked any questions, either. She'd get into his life from time to time, get mad at him? *One look* from him, that's all it would take, and I swear to God, she was so cowed that she'd clam right up." He paused, and she didn't say anything. Good. He was afraid she might think he was bragging, or wanted that sort of life for himself.

Jake said, "I'm ashamed of the way I acted tonight. I'm sorry, I should have told you. I didn't keep it from you for the reasons you think, Marsha. When I told you we were going, you were so excited and happy, I couldn't tell you I was going to look out for an assassin, I couldn't do it." Jake stopped again. The hard part was coming up.

"I wanted you to think I was as good as any of them. As good as the celebrities, the stars, the politicians. I don't know. It's hard to explain. I've never been around anyone in my life I felt I had to impress. I've got my degree. I could go teach school, I could do a thousand things. I think we both know why I decided to be a cop."

Jake flashed her a sad smile, and stroked her hair again. She let him.

He said, "But I want to impress *you*. I want you to be happy. I know what I took you away from, Marsha, the life you were leading. What you could have had if you hadn't married me. You're not the only one Betty shoots her mouth off in front of. I spent half of last Christmas Eve—every time you left the room—hearing about all the men whose hearts you broke when you married me. Rich men, successful men."

"Don't talk like that." Marsha's voice was soft. Jake felt himself relax.

"I behaved in a way I never thought I would tonight. I was secretive and mistrusting. I've always told you most everything, Marsha, I've never held much back. I've always talked to you, and you've always helped me. You didn't marry a cop, you married me, Jake, the guy who loves you." He was stroking her head constantly now, back and forth, front to back, smoothing it, his large hand covering most of her scalp and forehead. His touch was gentle and loving. "And tonight I behaved like the one man I've spent most of my life resenting. I'm sorry. You're right, I should have told you. I should have given you the choice."

"You know something?"

"What?"

"I would have gone anyway."

Jake looked at her sharply, saw the smile on her face.

"Now why don't you get out of that tuxedo, take a shower, and come to bed? No matter how much you socialize at night, you've still got to get up and go to work in the morning, hotshot."

"What time are you picking up Lynne?"

"I'm not sure. I'm gonna sleep late, I'll tell you that. Then maybe I'll laze around all day, watch soap operas, eat bonbons, you know, the usual."

"I know." Jake bent over and kissed Marsha's forehead. As he was pulling away she reached up and grabbed his face with both hands, held him there and kissed him full on the mouth. When she pulled back, he saw that her eyes were afire, blazing at him.

"You'll *never* be like your father, or like Alex, either, Jake."

"I know," Jake said again, and then he was holding her, his face deep in her shoulder. He whispered it a third time, "I know."

THE TWO COPS walked into Bing's bar at one-thirty in the morning, acting the way cops do, looking around at everything with no expression on their faces and pretending they hadn't noticed that the place had fallen silent. Big Bing watched them, not bothering to conceal his contempt. One of the officers was black, the other was white. They were dressed in casual summer clothes, jeans and short-sleeved shirts. The guns and cuffs and badges attached to their belts, along with the portable radios in their hands, were the dead giveaways. The black officer came over and sat at the bar, a ways down it from where Big Bing was standing. He looked around casually, at the mirror, at the whiskey on the shelves, at the white painted walls; his gaze proceeded over to the hallway that led to the back room, where the toilets and more pool tables were, along with the stairs that led to the two apartments above.

The softball players had left; most of team had to get up for work in the morning. Their tables hadn't been cleaned off; empty beer mugs and pitchers and overflowing ashtrays littered the small tables. A cadre of hard-core drinking regulars were still at the bar. The black cop finally looked over at Big Bing, saw his expression, and for the first time, smiled.

"Get a little service down here, bartender?" he asked. Big Bing grimaced and shook his head. He picked up a filthy, soaking bar rag and threw it hard to the floor, just to be doing it, to show his displeasure. He took his time walking down to where the black cop was sitting. The white cop had disappeared, somewhere in the back.

"Where'd your partner go?"

"He had to take a whiz."

"This look like a gas station?"

"It's an *awful* hot night out. I'll have a short beer to cool me off, while we're waiting."

"We were just closing up."

"I'll leave when the rest of the crowd does, don't worry." The cop smiled again. He had a knowing smile, one that somehow bothered Big Bing. "I'm not going to rob you. I just want a cold beer."

Big Bing now smiled himself. "On duty, huh? You one of them closet cop alky-haulics we're always hearing about?" Big Bing raised his voice so no one in the place would be deprived of his wit. "Citizens of Chicago can sleep better tonight, knowing *you're* on the job."

"You saying you won't serve me, is that what you're saying, bartender?"

"That's what you're *trying* to get me to say, isn't it, Officer?"

"Now, why would I do that?"

"Get the EEOC in here, the Civil Rights Commission, get Jesse Jackson marching outside with pickets, try and close me down for not serving one of your types."

"You mean cops?"

"You know good and goddamn well what I mean." Big Bing took out a water glass from under the bar, shoved it under the tap, and made sure it was at least half foam before he put it down in front of the cop.

"That's two-fifty."

"For this?" The cop looked like he was having a good time. He lifted the glass to the light, squinted at it a little while, then shrugged and sucked away some of the foam. He put the glass down and reached in his pocket, pulled out a wad of bills that were held together by a gold money clip. The first bill on the roll was a hundred. He peeled it off with—Big Bing had to admit—a certain dramatic flair, and laid the bill on top of the bar. "Better break this up. These prices, I'll be needing the change."

"I ain't sure I got that much change in the till."

"Better have, seeing as I offered you legal tender." The cop said it in an offhand way, not threatening. He looked around.

Big Bing said, "Do me a favor, don't go falling in love with the place."

"I kind of like all the pictures of the dogs playing poker. It gives the joint a certain ambience."

Big Bing was offended. "I put those pictures up in nineteen-fifty-eight."

"Been in business that long?"

"Since before you were born." Big Bing put his foot up on the back bar and leaned forward, sneaking a glance around him to make sure he still had his audience. "Back then, the nig—I mean the *coloreds*—they all stayed north of Sixty-third Street and west of the expressway. Knew their place back then, if you follow." Big Bing leaned back in case the cop tried to hit him, but the man appeared to have been highly amused by the remark; in fact, he laughed out loud.

"Itty-bitty little old man bartender, talking shit, listen to you." He shook his head, still chuckling, and drank down the rest of his beer. "You didn't happen to see the O'Conner boys in here tonight by any chance, did you?"

"Who's that?" Big Bing was having a pretty good time himself, now that he was sure that the big tall cop wasn't going to try and hurt him. "Mishonerboys, you said? I don't know anyone by that name."

"How about—" the cop made like he was thinking "—Norman Bingham, Jr. He's your son, isn't he?"

"You got a warrant allows you to come in here asking all these questions?"

"Is he your son, or isn't he?" The cop wasn't fooling around anymore, he was staring at Big Bing in a way that made Big Bing squirm a little bit.

"I got a son by that name, sure, my only kid. Ain't seen him in, I don't know, gotta be ten years. I think he's in the Foreign Legion."

"Old man like you at home, I'm not surprised to hear it. But it's not true. He was paroled into your custody in 'ninety-one. That wasn't ten years ago. Did a couple years for attempted arson. Before that, he went away for burglary. So, what're you saying; that he got tired of this enchanting lifestyle and ran off to France?"

"Wasn't me what run him off, it was what happened to the neighborhood. All your Mexicanos, your niggers moving in." Big Bing looked around, then looked back at the cop. "What happened to your partner, he fall in? Or maybe he's back there earning a few bucks, if you follow. You hear all kind of things about you tough guy flatfoots, how it's all an act and you gotta do strange shit to, let's say, ease the tension."

"Know were I can find your little boy, outside of some Middle East trouble spot?"

"No idea." Big Bing was a little nervous now. "Look, I'm trying to run a business here, and in case you ain't noticed, three customers left since you sat your ass down on my stool. Now if you ain't got a warrant, I'm gonna have to ask you to leave."

The cop was looking past Big Bing's shoulder, and the old man looked around in time to see the white guy shake his head, his lips pursed. He looked back at the black cop, who was getting up off the stool.

The black cop said, very softly, "Don't need a warrant, I guess. It looks like Norman isn't home."

"You went into his apartment? You went upstairs without a warrant?!" Big Bing was standing back now. He punched at the air in frustration. "What right you got to do that? I thought I fought a fucking war to keep you Nazis out of America!"

"You were turned down for service; psychosis mixed with paranoid schizophrenia, if my memory serves. That would have been around nineteen-forty-two, right after you got out of the Bridewell, after you beat the rap for killing your first wife." The cop looked at his partner. "Everything come out okay?"

Big Bing stood there staring at them, trembling with rage, afraid to open his mouth because these two men now were deadly serious. The white guy was looking at him as if he were automatically suspected of murder just because he was standing behind the bar.

"You give my partner a hard time while I was going pee-pee?" The son of a bitch that he was, talking like that with a mean look on his face. Making fun of Big Bing right in his own gin mill.

"Both of you sons of bitches get out of my tavern, right now. I'll be down at headquarters tomorrow, you can bet your ass on that, come into a man's place of business, harass him, tell ugly lies on him in front of everybody, go through his apartment when he isn't looking. You'll both be walking a beat in Hegewisch before I'm done with you."

"You sure you can't get me Sixty-third Street?" the black cop said, as he picked up his hundred dollar bill and put it back with the rest. He took his time, made a big show out of it, then looked back up at Big Bing. "That way, I can stay in my place."

Al stood at the bar in the happening North Side tavern, his hip cocked, one foot resting on the six-inch-high rail that ran all the way around the horseshoe-shaped bar, wishing that he didn't have to leave. Pearl Jam was playing on the turntable; earlier, the DJ had run a collection of U2's greatest hits. Robert Roosevelt sat next to him, and Beck thought he was only on the stool so that everyone still in the place would know that he was taller than Al, even sitting down.

Which didn't bother Al as much as it usually would have; he wanted this big side of beef with him tonight. Especially after Rosy had shamed him into calling the disturbo on the phone and telling him off.

"What, you scared?" Roosevelt had asked, as if it were a rhetorical question. Huge black buck, he looked like a retired defensive lineman. He always had that look on his face that told you he thought he was a better man than you. Al generally hated to use him, and in fact hadn't called him first. But Rosy was the only officer Al knew who was willing to come out late on a Sunday night for a fast fifty bucks, plus all he could drink, in exchange for his personal protection. So Al was stuck with him.

Al didn't mind the expense. The more he thought about the guy who'd called, the more afraid he got. Until Roosevelt started in. He said, "What's he gonna do? Man calls phone-sex lines. Those ain't tough guys, those are pussies. Bullies. Stand up to them, they fall to their knees in fear and blow you. You start letting dudes like that back you off, though, and the next thing you know, you're in Boystown, turning tricks for *them*."

Or, "Big, tough Al Beck, what happened?" He'd actually made a grab at Al's balls, which Al had barely escaped from with an inventive side move. "You lose something down below there?"

So Al had accepted the challenge, had called his contact at the phone company from the pay phone over there on the wall, and found out that—thank God—she was on duty tonight. Then he had her connect him to the loft, where Chantell was holding down the desk. Chantell had followed orders, she hadn't disconnected the freako's line. He'd had her press the proper buttons while the telephone lady was doing whatever she did, and next thing you know, she was giving him a phone number, which Al had written down on a sheet of paper out of Rosy's notebook. She'd reminded him that she'd be expecting the cash in the mail, no later than Tuesday delivery.

And Al had called, with Roosevelt and half of the young bar patrons listening in and cheering him on. Which had led him on to greater vocal heights than he'd at first thought he'd attempt. It had in fact made him feel better, for a while, but there was still a doubt niggling at the back of his mind: the man knew where he worked, and had said he knew where Al lived.

"Incorporation papers, that's how he knows. Nothing to it," Rosy had told him. "Anyone wanting to can find out who owns ABI, or any other corporation; it's all a matter of public record." That knowledge, too, made Al feel somewhat better, even though he believed it to be an invasion of his personal privacy. The guy could well have been bluffing about having Al's home address. About having his Social Security number.

If he hadn't been before, Al was sure of it now, three sheets to the wind on a Sunday night, with a nine o'clock court date in the morning. He didn't give a shit, he was having a good time. Even more of one since the little blonde across the bar from him had told him that she might be amenable to working an extra job for him, talking on the phone lines. But not ten hours a day, she'd said, and never on Friday and Saturday nights. She said she was an actress. "I think, done right, it can be made into an art form," she'd told Al, with a straight face. She was almost as cute as Laura had been, though she was with a guy right now. But Al could tell by the way she kept shooting glances his way that she wanted to blow the guy off.

"You gonna make your move, you better do it soon, it's getting close to closing."

"I can't tonight, I got to close the shop."

"Get her to meet you later, one of the four o'clock joints, what are you, afraid?" Al looked over at the girl, sitting there wearing a man's plain white cotton undershirt that was a couple of sizes too small. Even in the dim light, he could see her nipples all the way over here. She had to be impressed with him. How could she not be? He was an Italian-looking, well-muscled man, and obviously important. The fact that he had his own personal armed bodyguard was proof of that importance. Rosy's pistol rode on his belt on the right side, the weight of it pulling down at his designer jeans. He wasn't wearing his badge on his belt. He got a lot of looks from the people in the bar, but nobody had called the cops.

Al borrowed Roosevelt's notebook again, and wrote down his own name, then his work, loft, and home phone numbers, tore the page out of the pad, and, holding it in his hand, picked up his drink and finished it. He grimaced as he put the glass down. The glass had been nearly full. He winked at Rosy. "Watch this," Al said.

He walked all the way around the bar, and he had the girl's attention before he was halfway there. And that of the man she was with. Al could feel Rosy watching him; he didn't fear the boyfriend. He stopped at the couple, waved at the bartender, told her he himself'd had enough, he had to go, he had business to attend to, but to give them both a drink, on him. He smiled away the girl's thanks; the guy she was with didn't say anything. Al looked over to make sure that Rosy was still watching. Rosy gave him a little fag wave, using just his fingers.

"Here're my numbers, you want to talk about that—job offer."

"She doesn't want to do that, pal," the man with her said, and the girl turned to look at him. Al took the opportunity to sneak a look at her equipment.

"You don't speak for me, Barry." The woman's tone held barely controlled rage. "How dare you pretend to?"

"Mariah, I'm warning you."

"What?" Al said, "What's your warning, ace?"

"Lose your trained gorilla, and I'll show you or what, shorty."

"Gorilla?" Al raised his voice. "You calling my bodyguard a gorilla?" Al looked over, but Rosy was now nowhere in sight. Shit! He put the piece of paper on the bar, then smiled as confidently as he could at Mariah.

"I'll be at one of those numbers all night, you want to talk."

"She doesn't want to talk to you, I told you that, you dwarf!"

Al smiled. Patronizingly. As if the man were just drunk and didn't know what he was getting into, nor important enough to waste his time with. Mariah told him again that he didn't speak for her, who the hell did he think he was? Al noticed for the first time just how big the man was. He said, "I've got to go. Business." And began to swagger away.

Barry shouted at his back. "Got to collect the night's earnings from your bitches, pimp?" Al stopped, without turning, then shook his head and continued to walk away.

As he walked out the door he heard Mariah arguing loudly with Barry, but forgot about it when he saw Rosy sitting in the car, which was idling at the curb. The side window powered down. Rosy, prick that he was, was smiling his self-satisfied Rosy smile.

"I'll follow you to the loft," Rosy said.

"I thought I told you to wait."

Rosy acted as if he hadn't heard him. The window powered up, and Al, still smarting, walked around the car, got into his own, started it up, and angrily pulled away from the curb.

"**W**HAT ARE ALL those papers?" Bing said. He was standing just inside the door to Laura's apartment, not sure yet if she was going to invite him in. She'd told him to come over, but now didn't seem very happy that he'd shown up.

"I thought you hadn't had a drink in three days and two nights." There it was, out in the open. Bing had to fight down a sarcastic response. He reached for a cigarette, and Laura told him not to smoke here. Bing pulled his hand back.

"The AA people never called me back."

"And it's too much to expect you to do anything tough all on your own."

"I only had two drinks."

Those words told the entire story of Bing's relationship with his wife.

"Can I see Tommy?"

"No. Sit down."

The loft was bigger than he'd expected, wide, the space taking up at least a fourth of the entire floor. There wasn't much in the way of furnishings. A ratty, used couch; a couple of folding chairs that were opened up on the floor in front of an old portable TV set. There were built-out areas in both far corners, obviously the bedrooms. He saw the door to the bathroom, open with a bare-bulb light burning inside, next to one of the closed bedroom doors. Laura had buzzed him in without asking who it was; a breach of security he wanted to mention. Maybe later he'd say something. After they broke the ice a little.

Bing sat down in a straight-backed steel chair, at an old Formica kitchen table. The stove was ancient, Bing noticed that right away. The refrigerator was one of the old-fashioned types that didn't even have a separate door for the freezer part. He could hear the machine cycling on and off. And it was very hot in here, man, he was burning up, even with a standup room fan over there, the fan just blowing hot air around and making a lot of noise.

Laura sat down herself, was looking at him in a way she never had before, not even when she'd left him. Back then, at the beginning of summer, she'd at least acted upset, had packed and walked past him, looking at him with eyes red and swollen from crying.

Now it was like looking at a dummy in a department store window.

"So, how've you been?"

"How've I been?" The question seemed to cheer her. "Let's not talk about how I've been, let's talk about how things are going to be from now on."

"All right. How are things going to be from now?" He hoped she understood how reasonable he was being. Bing was very conscious of the fact that he towered over her, that he dominated even this huge room with his size. Bing sat up straight, liking the feeling. He could use a little more of it, a confidence booster, right now.

"I'm going to be getting a hundred dollars a week, every Friday from you, for a start." She held up a hand to stop him from complaining. "That's a fourth of your legitimate income, and we both know, with all the scams and hustles you pull, that you make way more than that. Prorated, you owe me, let's call it twelve weeks back child support. And I swear to God, if you balk about paying me, I'll not only take you back to court, but I give you my word as Tommy's mother, you'll never see that child again."

"You're gonna blackmail me?"

"Fuck you, Bing. I could get a lot more than that out of you without even half trying. And a bonus from the IRS for turning you in, and an even *bigger* bonus from them for turning in your father, for paying you cash under the table."

"Laura, I didn't come here to fight."

"No, you came over here to win me back, but that's not going to happen, Bing. Let's clear the air, right up front, how it is between us. I spent eight years of my life married to you, and now it's over. In those eight years, Bing, I did everything I could to make that marriage work. I waited for you when you were in prison, living in that rattrap above the tavern with my son, waiting tables and tending bar downstairs, slapping your best friends' hands off my ass, hating every minute of it but having to do it, because that skinflint bastard father of yours charged me and his grandson rent. I cooked for you and I cleaned for you and I read every stinking sex manual ever written for you, trying to be what I thought was a good wife, trying to keep your interest. And Bing, the fact is, you treated me like shit. And now, believe me, Bing, it's over. I'm not ever coming back. Not ever. You just have to get that through your head." Laura paused. "What did you expect, you were going to come up here half-drunk and I was going to swoon and see the error of my ways?"

Bing couldn't think of an appropriate response. He sat there with his mouth open wide, suddenly feeling short of breath, as if he were starting to suffocate.

Laura said, "Let me tell you something else, while we're talking. If I could have afforded an unlisted number, you never would have found me. It is absolutely, without a doubt, over between us, Bing. You have to accept that before we go one step further."

"So what am I doing here?"

"Negotiating. You're the father of my child. I don't want to deprive you of seeing him, unless you leave me no other choice. Now, we can be civil to each other, Bing, or we can play hardball. That's up to you. You want to play hardball, and I guarantee you you'll lose. I'm holding more heavy bats than the Toronto Blue Jays, and you know it."

Yeah, Bing thought. Not to mention the balls she was holding. "I got to go." Bing began to rise. His head was spinning. Who was this woman doing all this big-time talking? This wasn't his Laura.

Who was talking at him now with cold, hard steel in her voice. "Sit your ass down, Bing, I mean it. Right now. Sit down. You get up and leave, and I'll never speak to you again in this life." Bing slowly lowered himself back down into his chair. He couldn't look at her, so he looked down. He thumbed through the papers on the table.

"I'm taking that money from you and putting every dime of it into an account for our son. Five thousand a year, it'll pay for his education."

"You plan on sending him to Harvard? I don't think he'll pass the entrance exams."

"You son of a bitch. That was a cheap shot, you bastard." Laura saw Bing sitting there, smugly, and fought the urge to just reach over and punch him. She said, "He's going to need an education to make it, Bing. If anything happens to me, who's he got? You, your father? A couple of major role models."

"We made out all right."

"Sure you did. Do you agree to that, to the hundred a week?"

"I'm a little short on the back pay."

"I can forgive that, write it off, but you have to do something for me."

"The B and E you mentioned."

"It's a fifteen-minute walk from here, the corner of Twenty-first and Wabash, third floor, three-C. It should be a piece of cake for a man of your skills. It's less than a mile from where we're sitting, you won't even have to drive over, you can leave your car wherever it's parked. The phone lines close down at two, and after that, nobody's in the building until the following morning at nine. I want you to get two things, well, three, really: first, the little plastic-coated cards, with Lori on one, that'll be mine, and Diana's name's on the other one, she doesn't care who knows her name. Take them out of the Rolodex."

"Twelve hundred, just for that?"

"And something else. There's more that I need from that Rolodex, some other cards, all right? There'll be mens' names on most of them, with phone numbers, and a bunch of letters that probably won't mean much to you. B and D, S and M, things like that. I want you to take two, three files—remember, they're on index cards, Bing—out of every letter of the alphabet, no more than that. I don't want anyone noticing that any of those files are missing."

"What are they, phone-sex freaks?"

"None of your business what they are. Just get them and bring them to me. Tonight. That and my own card, and Diana's. You do that, Bing, and I forgive the twelve-hundred."

"When do I get to see my kid?"

"He's got day camp until five every day—"

"Goddamnit, Laura, you know what kind of perverts run those camps—?"

"—and you can see him anytime after that, as long your breath doesn't reek of booze—or those cheap mints you suck on to try and cover up the stink. You can see him one hour at a time, for a start. And you don't ever show up here drunk. You take him near that tavern, and I swear to God, all privileges are revoked."

"I live above that tavern. I can't take him there, where can I go?"

"Grant Park's right *there,* Bing." Laura waved her hand at the wall. "You can pick up a football, a baseball, and a couple of mitts, whatever. Try playing a little catch with your son for once in your life. There's maybe fifty miles of lakefront to walk around, there's museums and movie theaters and God knows how much else. This isn't the East Side, Bing. There's more to do here than watch dirty videos when you think your wife's sleeping. You don't take him to the tavern, and you keep him away from your father. That's not negotiable."

Bing looked at her, giving her his most soulful, lost, little boy look. He knew it wasn't working when Laura rolled her eyes. He reached out for her hand, and she pulled back, out of reach.

"I love you, Laura. I love you. I can't—I can't make it without you."

"Bing, you're just going have to learn how to," Laura said. She stood up. "Now go get me what I need, and don't you come back here without it."

"Why you need Diana's card, too? Do you think that your hanging around with someone like Diana is good for the kid?"

Laura's eyes narrowed, then flashed angrily. In a barely controlled voice, she said, "Let me tell you something, Bing. Diana's shown me more love, kindness and friendship in three months than you did in ten years. Another thing that's not negotiable: *I* decide how Tommy is raised."

"What am I then, just somebody to pull you out of the jackpots you get yourself into?" Laura was still standing. Bing didn't feel so big anymore.

"Say the word, and I'll get somebody else to do it. I was just trying to kill two birds with one stone; get the papers I need, and clear the air between us, find a simple way for you to see our son without going through any more lawyers or any more of our constant telephone battles."

"Who you gonna get to do it, one of your phone-sex boyfriends?"

"That's none of your business, either. Now, are you going to do it, or aren't you?"

"You were a phone-sex whore." Bing whispered it as if he couldn't believe it. "And now you're going to try and tell *me* what's right for my kid?"

"No, the judge already did that. All I'm trying to do is look out for you a little bit."

"If I commit a felony for you."

"Don't look at it that way, Bing. Consider it payment for all the years you spent screwing me around."

"You drive a hard bargain."

"I don't have any other options."

"Yes you do. You could come back home, you could give me another chance. I promise you, Laura, I'll change!" Bing looked up at
her. Laura's expression hadn't changed one bit. There was not even
a crack in that icy exterior. "Make a list of what you want, I'll do it!
Write down a list of the things that I do that you want me to change.
I know how much I screwed up, and you have to know how much I
love you; I'll do anything, anything, just come home."

"I am home, Bing. And I don't have time for this anymore. Are
you going to do it, or not?"

"You listen to me, Laura, goddamnit!"

"Don't raise your voice to me. I won't tell you that again, either.
I'm not about to ever let you curse me or browbeat me anymore,
Bing, those days are long gone."

Bing rose to his feet just as there was a hesitant knock at the door.
He looked over at the door, jealous already, knowing in his heart
that it was one of Laura's boyfriends. "Is that why you were rushing
me out? You have somebody coming over?" He made a move to the
door, but Laura ran over there and beat him to it.

She opened it, and Diana walked in.

"Hi . . ." she said. She seemed depressed, then she spotted Bing
and sniffed the air suspiciously. But she didn't say anything.

Laura said, "You've got one hour, Bing. That's all. If I don't have
what I need, right here in my hand by then, I'll assume you didn't
accept my offer, and I'll get somebody else to do it. He won't be
hard to find."

"I'll bet."

Diana didn't say anything to him, not hello, good-bye, not a word.
She looked down at her feet as Bing walked through the door, Bing
now resenting the both of them, wanting to strike out at Diana, but
if he did, he knew, Laura would never talk to him again.

So he just stormed out, marched down the filthy tile hallway to
the stairs, and took them three at a time, down to the entrance hall
and out the front door. Bing stood on the sidewalk for a second,
looking around, getting his bearings in an area of the city that was
totally foreign to him. He felt humiliated by his begging. And emas-
culated by the way Laura'd treated him. He heard the loud music
and convivial voices raised in laughter coming out of the tavern that
was built into the first-floor part of Laura's building. Bing touched
the money in the envelope under his shirt, fingered it, wanting to go
inside and spend some.

He'd do it, too, when he got back, if the place had a four o'clock license. He should be done with the little job at the phone-sex place in a couple of minutes. He had decided to do as Laura asked. He felt that he had no other choice. It was the only way he knew to stay on her good side, and he had to do that, if he was ever going to win back her love.

And when he finally did, man, was *she* ever going to have do some changing. Three months without him, and she'd turned into the biggest bitch he'd ever run across in thirty-six years of life. It was the nigger guy with the tits, he bet, Diana's influence that had turned Laura into a ballbuster, Bing believed that in his heart.

He left his car where it was parked, at the curb down the street, a block and a half away. Bing walked past the tavern, crossed Michigan Avenue and went down a block to Wabash. Bing thinking one hour, my ass. All he'd need was a couple of minutes.

BING STOOD ACROSS the street from the corner building, in the deep alcove of an abandoned office building, checking the place out. He could go in through the fire escape, no problem. It ran right across the windows of 3-C. Laura hadn't said anything about the joint being alarmed. He was on Wabash, a mere block away from Michigan, but a world away from the high-priced clothing and jewelry stores, the high-priced hotels, the water tower . . . all of that was a lot further north. The sidewalk in front of him was caved in; the street filled with trash, newspapers and empty beer cans, bottles, with dust everywhere. He'd been eyed suspiciously when he'd passed the tavern, the guys outside probably thought he was the man. It relieved him to think that; if they thought he was the man, they wouldn't mug him.

Bing knew the right windows without having ever been inside, he could see lights up there, in 3-C. He could also see the top half of women in there, walking around, the women cut in half because the lower part of the six windows was frosted. There was a huge window air conditioner stuck into the bottom half of the middle window, dripping condensation in a steady stream, down onto the sidewalk.

Bing slunk back into the shadows as a car came down Twenty-first Street, the bright headlights sweeping over his corner hiding place. The car pulled to a stop at the broken curb, right in front of the building. Even in the dark, Bing could see that it was a Lexus. He watched as a second car turned the corner, this one an American car, looked like a GM, a Chevy or a Pontiac. It pulled up close to the first one, right up on top of the back bumper, and the little guy in the dago-T who'd gotten out of the Lexus had a heart attack at the sight.

"What the fuck's wrong with you! Goddamn you, back up!" The driver in the second car didn't pay him any attention. The second man got out of his car, and Bing could hear him laughing, asking the much smaller man, what, are you *always* such a chickenshit, or did it just come over you tonight? Like it was a running joke between the two of them. The man in the second car was black, and about the same size as Bing. The gun on his hip made him even bigger. Bing watched as the little man pulled out a ring of keys, and waved a hand at the big black guy, saying something to him now that Bing couldn't hear. The two of them walked inside, and Bing had an idea. He came out of the doorway, walked across the street and stood at the front of the building, then waited.

Just a few minutes later he heard them marching down the stairway, a bunch of women gabbing among themselves, happy to be getting off work. Bing backed up to the corner, pulled out his keys, and began to walk quickly toward the building, reached it just as the women came pouring out of the door. He had a key ready, as if he were going to unlock the door. He stepped back, being a gentleman, but hung onto the door handle so he could walk in after they were all out. Bing kept his head down, but said hello, in a friendly way, so they wouldn't pay him any attention, just another pussy hound artist, going to his studio in the middle of the night. He let the door close behind him before he risked a close look at the women. Dear God, they looked like a bunch of cleaning ladies, just getting off work at one of the larger office buildings. Some of them middle-aged, a lot of them dumpy. Most of them ugly. And men called them up wanting to fuck them? If only they knew. When you were dealing with guys like that, though, you never knew, they probably wouldn't care what the woman looked like.

Bing turned and climbed the steps, took them fast, to the fourth floor. He didn't want the Mafia type and the big nigger to even suspect he was in the building. He stood on the fourth-floor landing, breathing hard, wishing he'd stopped for a half-pint, when he heard the door to 3-C slam shut downstairs, then the sound of male voices raised in what could be argument or kidding around.

"That shit ain't funny, Rosy, anymore. How long you gonna keep it up? You waiting for me to bust out laughing, I ain't gonna."

"I was just wondering if you was scared that the man was inside, hiding, waiting to cut your little wee-wee off for you, that's all. What's wrong with that? Want me to run through the building, check all six floors for you?" Bing prayed that the mobster would know that he was only kidding; he himself could tell from the sound of the black man's voice that he was only busting the Mafia guy's balls.

What had Laura gotten him into? Had she done this to set him up, to get him killed? Dear God, after all these years of being a small-timer, now he was mixed up in the major leagues, with the Mafia, no less.

Bing heard the white man's voice. "Come on, goddamnit, let's just go."

"Am I off-duty, or what?"

"In a minute. Let me get to my car."

"Reason I ask, if I'm through, I want to get paid."

There was the sound of their footsteps, echoing up to him from further and further down the stairway. Their voices were fading, getting harder to hear. Bing breathed a sigh of relief. He tiptoed down the stairway, wanting to get in and out as fast as he could, too impatient to even wait for the men to get out the front door.

The wooden door to 3-C was a joke. Bing luded it and was inside the place in about five seconds flat. The light from the streetlamp on Twenty-first Street gave him enough illumination to work by. Bing hurried down the aisle, past a bunch of cramped cubicles that had phone headsets laid on the small desk part. The entire place reeked of cheap perfume. Bing began to feel sick to his stomach.

The Rolodex was right where Laura had told him it would be, on the desk, a huge, strangely shaped thing, with a large dust cover protecting it. Bing flipped the blue plastic cover up and squinted at the little cards, found that the thing had already been flipped to Laura's card, the card right there in front of him, as if the Mafia man had just tried to call her. Maybe he'd tried to call her and convince her to come back. Maybe he didn't like people quitting on him.

And maybe Laura was having an affair with this little sawed-off runt. Goddamn her. The way she'd acted, he wouldn't put it past her. God*damn* her cheating ass.

Bing thought about her with part of his mind, while he flipped back, looking for Diana's card. And found it. He tore it out, shoved both cards into his shirt pocket, behind his cigarettes. He flipped the Rolodex back to A, and began to snatch the cards that Laura wanted.

Just a couple of months without him, and she'd turned into a slut. He'd bet she was selling more than her voice over one of those headsets. Or even worse, giving it away, to that little runt in the silk undershirt.

Bing snatched four or five index cards out for each letter of the alphabet, just ripped them out of the Rolodex without looking at them. He'd check them out more carefully when he was safely in his car; he wanted to see if anyone he knew was perverted enough to call a place like this.

Bing had about twenty of the index cards in his hand when he heard the voices on the stairway.

Bing pushed the drawer shut and nearly panicked, looking around for another way out of the place. The voices were close; the one he recognized as the little guy's was talking, it sounded as if he was pleading. There was another, deeper voice, a white guy's voice, telling the little guy to shut his fucking pussy little mouth, right now. Bing didn't hear the black guy's voice. He didn't have time to make it out the window to the fire escape. He threw himself to the floor, the cards clutched in his hand, shoved them down into his back pocket and crawled toward the cubicles.

He had barely gotten behind them and curled up into a fetal position when he heard the key in the lock and, a second later, through the kneehole of one of the cubicles, saw three pairs of legs come walking past him, into the room.

• • •

Bing tried to breathe through his mouth, tried not to say a word. He had no idea what he'd stumbled onto here, whether it was a mob turf war or a street tax problem, like the ones in the old days when automobile chop-shop operators who didn't give a piece of the action to the mob were getting blown up in their cars every other week. Whatever it was, he knew for sure, he didn't want any part of it.

He still hadn't heard the black guy say a word. The white guy— Al—was still begging the other man for mercy. He was crying, his words barely understandable.

"Oh, please please please please don'tkillme don'tkillme don't-cutoffmydick," the words all ran together, in a stream. Bing closed his eyes, heard a smack and then heard Al scream, then he heard the sound of a body hitting the floor. Al was whimpering now, his head only a few feet away from Bing's, turned his way. If Al opened his eyes, they'd be looking at each other.

The sound of a gunshot drowned out Al's whimpers. The noise was incredibly loud in the enclosed room. Bing flinched and shut his own eyes, his ears ringing, and he heard the sound of a heavier body hitting the floor.

The black man with the gun.

Bing opened his eyes, but from where he was lying he could only see the black man's legs. The room seemed suddenly filled with smoke that had a sharp, pungent odor. Bing thought he might pass out from fright. He was scared to death, looking under the desk at Al, who now was curled up into a ball and had his hands up over his ears.

"Sit up, Al," the other voice said. He was incredibly calm, as if he'd done this before or else had rehearsed this moment to the point of perfection. "I said sit *up!*" Al's whimpering grew louder, then leveled off. Bing watched the man, wondering why he didn't shake into little pieces. He'd never seen anyone literally shaking as badly as Al.

"Okay, okay, okay, okay, I'm sitting up," Al said, and somehow made it. Now Bing could only see his legs, his butt, Al's waist.

"Do you remember what I said I'd do to you, lawyer Allan Beck?"

"*Noooo*—" Al screamed it.

"*Do you!*"

"I remember, yes, I remember." Al was having a hard time breathing; the words were still all jumbled together, hard to make out. The floor seemed flooded with his tears. Bing smelled shit. He didn't

know if it came from Al, or from the dead black guy. He didn't
move, he lay there terrified. He was shaking pretty good, himself.

"Well, I'm not going to do that."

"Thank *God*, oh, thank God, thank you, thank you, dear God,
thank you."

"As long as you don't lie to me." Al whimpered that he wouldn't,
several times, over and over. The man asked Al for the name of the
telephone company worker who'd given out his phone number, and
Al didn't think twice about it, told the man her name was McKenzie, Annette McKenzie. The man asked Al if he'd told *anyone* his
name, or given out his address, and before Al could answer he
stopped him, told Al to take his time, make sure he thought real
hard. Al waited a few seconds so as not to piss the guy off, then told
him no one, absolutely no one. Only he and Rosy, over there on the
floor, knew his name, his address, and his telephone number.

"Did you write it down?" the man asked, and Al swore to God
that he hadn't, that he'd dialed direct as soon as Annette had given
him the number. Al swore he was only trying to scare the man, to
frighten him off. He didn't deserve to die for that, did he? The man
told him to shut the fuck up, in a distracted manner, then there was
a silence.

The guy must have decided that he'd wasted enough time, because without warning there was another shot, and Al fell hard to
the floor. Bing couldn't take it anymore. He was afraid he would
start keening aloud. He bit his tongue so he couldn't, covered his
ears with his hands and cowered there, but for some reason his eyes
wouldn't close, wouldn't follow his commands to do so.

The guy who'd shot Al and the black man knelt down beside Al's
body, and Bing felt himself stop breathing altogether. All the man
had to do was turn his head, and that was it, he'd spot Bing. Bing
got a good look at him as the man twisted Al's head from one side to
the other—what was he doing in a tuxedo?—then gave it a little ugly
extra twist and pushed it away from him. Bing saw the man rise,
saw the bottom of his legs, walking away from Al. Bing prayed that
the man wouldn't bend over the black man, too, that he'd just leave,
get the fuck out of there before Bing couldn't control himself and
shouted or cried or screamed.

The legs moved away, Bing heard his footsteps above the ringing
in his ears. He heard the door open, then he heard it close. Bing
prayed to a God he'd long ago abandoned, asked Him to do him a

favor, to please not let the man with the gun come back. He lay
there for a while longer, trying to get himself under control, then
wondered if maybe anyone else might have been working in the
building tonight, someone who might have heard the shots, and
called the police. Or maybe one of the guys from in front of the tavern had heard it, it had been loud enough. Bing wouldn't be surprised if Laura had heard it, up in her loft.

He had a flash then, a thought that came into his mind, unbidden.
He saw Laura and Diana in bed together, naked. That had to be it,
why she wanted Diana's card, too. They were carrying on, and the
boss had fired them for it, and Laura had sent Bing over here and
nearly gotten him killed, just to help Diana.

The thought gave him the strength he needed to finally get up off
the floor. Bing forced himself to stand on legs that didn't want to
hold him up. He looked around, saw the telephone on the desk,
thought about calling the cops for about three seconds, then ran out
of the room and down the stairway, through the front door and
around the corner without thinking about it again.

His car's driver-side window had been smashed out; the stereo had
been stolen. Bing didn't care. In fact, he was glad that the thieves
had left the door unlocked when they'd escaped, so he wouldn't
have to try and slip the key into the lock with his shaking hands.
Bing jumped into the car, somehow managed to get the key into the
ignition, then put the car in drive and sped away from the curb,
spraying gravel behind him.

He forced himself to calm down on Lake Shore Drive, to go the
speed limit and to stop at all the red lights. Bing didn't want to get
stopped, didn't want any cops to see him in this condition. If they
saw him, they'd immediately know that something was wrong, and
it wouldn't be long before they'd find out what it was, considering
the state he was in. He gulped huge drafts of air into his lungs from
the wind that was streaming in through the broken window. He
slapped at the shattered fragments of glass, got them off the door,
out of the window slot, so no passing cop would spot them and
think that Bing had stolen the vehicle.

He reached for a cigarette, felt the two Rolodex cards in his shirt
pocket, pulled them out and abruptly threw them out the window,
as if they would contaminate him. He tried to force himself to calm

down, did his best, but calmness wasn't there, would not be there for him for a while.

Somehow, some way, Bing made it back to the tavern.

He parked the car right in front, used his key to get inside, then went straight to the bar and poured himself a drink without locking the door behind him. He poured the drink down, sucked it into his system. Bing smacked the glass down hard on the bar, made a guttural, near-orgasmic sound as the booze spread through his stomach. He poured himself another, drank it down, then fought nausea because he hadn't poured himself any water, there was nothing to take the smell, the bite of the cheap whiskey out of his mouth and nose.

Bing grabbed the soda nozzle, pressed the button down, and drank directly from the Coke spray. He got Coke all over his face, his hands, and his clothes.

His clothes.

Had he stepped in any blood? Dear God, had he left a footprint in there for the cops to find? Bing made a frightened sound, then hopped onto one foot, holding his other foot in his hand. He twisted the sole of his shoe up, so he could see it. The sole was clean. He repeated the procedure with the other foot. No blood that he could see. Thank God. But there wouldn't be any, would there? He hadn't stepped around the other side of the cubicles, had no desire to see what the killer had left behind. He'd run right to the door, opened it . . .

Opened it . . .

He hadn't been wearing gloves. It was a simple job; no one was ever even supposed to suspect that he'd been in there.

His prints would be on the doorknob. And on the clear blue plastic cover of the Rolodex.

The phone rang, and Bing almost leaped out of his skin. It had to be Laura, checking up on him, seeing if he'd done what she'd asked of him. Had she known about the hit, and set him up? Was he supposed to have been inside the place at two, when the hit man came calling? That would kill her two birds with one stone, wouldn't it? She'd get rid of both guys who'd been bothering her, Bing and Al. No. She had changed, but she'd never be able to do that. He couldn't bring himself to believe it. He'd simply stumbled into the middle of, and witnessed, a mob hit.

He thought about not answering the phone, but the old man's

bedroom was directly above this spot. Drunk, passed out on his bed, fully clothed, he might not hear it ringing. But then again, he might. And the last thing Bing wanted to do tonight was have a heart-to-heart chat with his father. Bing took several deep breaths, walked over to the phone and lifted it to his ear.

"Hello?"

"Hi, yeah," a surprised voice said to him. "I'm trying to reach—" Bing heard a rustle of paper. "Norman Bingham, Jr." Was this a cop? Bing didn't think so. Cops were never this polite.

"What did you want?"

"Hi, Norm, my name is Johnny, I'm returning your call from AA."

"Oh, God."

"What's wrong, you been drinking?" Then Johnny started talking quickly, as if trying to convince Bing that it wasn't his fault if Bing was, indeed, drunk. "I called you several times Friday and Saturday night, and hung up when I found out it was a bar. I thought it was a joke, you know? Drunks do that all the time, and I wasn't going to play into it. But it bugged me, Norm, I gotta tell you, and I couldn't sleep thinking about it, that another alcoholic might need help, so I called again. Norm? Are you all right? You want a couple of us to come over and talk to you?"

"You got the wrong number," Bing said, and hung up. He closed his eyes tightly, fighting tears, and turned, reaching blindly for the bottle, when a hand grabbed his arm. Bing looked up, terrified. A huge black man held Bing tight, pulled him in to him as another man leaped over the bar and grabbed him from behind.

"Norman Bingham, Jr.?"

"Yeah, yeah, what's this all about?" Bing was in shock, had they found him out already? The fear was mixed with relief; for a terrifying second, he'd thought it was the big dead black guy who'd grabbed him.

"You're under arrest."

Bing exploded. "For *what?!*" They had him spread-eagled over the bar now, pulling his wrists back, slapping on the cuffs, tight. Bing felt hands patting him down, felt the index cards he'd forgotten about being pulled out of his back pocket. He heard them get slapped down on the bar top, next to his wallet and money.

"For attempted first-degree arson, and conspiracy to commit arson."

"What?"

Bing felt hands pulling at the envelope stuck down his pants, heard it being ripped open, heard the cop whistle and say, "Bingo, Bingham."

The other cop said, "Don't play dumb. We tried to look you up earlier, but, bad luck for you, we got to your partners first. They rolled over on you, Bingo, both of them. And now we got the payoff, and the key to the old lady's house. Come on." Bing was pulled roughly to his feet. The black cop stepped back, took a wad of money out of his pocket, riffled through them and put two single dollar bills atop the bar. He put the bills back, jiggled some change, then dropped two quarters on top of the dollar bills. He grabbed Bing's arm without explanation and pulled him roughly toward the door.

"Trying to burn down an old woman's house while she's lying on her death bed, what the fuck's wrong with you? Whatever it is, you'll have plenty of time to fix it. Cause my man, you're going down for a long, long time."

LAURA SAT AT the table, feeling blue. Diana seemed to be even more depressed than Laura. It wasn't much of a surprise, seeing as what she was saying. Laura looked down at the financial assistance papers from Chicago State University, thumbed the edges of the papers absently, as Diana poured her heart out to her, telling her things Laura wasn't at all certain she wanted to hear.

About a man named Roman, who used to fight on TV; about a scam they used to work on the Halsted Street hooker stroll. Diana would pick up a trick and have him pull around in the alley, then this Roman guy would come out of nowhere, beat the shit out of the trick and take all of his money. How, on the very night that she'd finally talked Roman into giving her a full half of the proceeds, the trick had turned out to be a suburban police officer, and Roman had beaten him senseless, then broken his arm as he'd been handcuffing him to the steering wheel of his four-wheel-drive pickup truck. How Diana had run out of the alley and down the street, with all the money in her hand, not even thinking about what Roman would do to her for it until later, when she came to her senses.

Which was something she didn't have to worry about long, because Roman had been killed the very next day, along with two Chicago police officers, in the house of one of the cops. One of the cops, at least, had been killed with the gun that Roman had taken off the suburban cop.

Diana told Laura, "That's how I met Jake Phillips and Mondo. Jake ran me down during his investigation, and he'd been partnered with Mondo, who I guess was pretty close to this dead cop, Tulio. Jake was so handsome, so young, so innocent, and he didn't treat me like a suspect, didn't act like I was some freak he had to run and wash his hands with disinfectant after he talked to me." Diana took a small, feminine sip from a glass of wine, her legs crossed at the knee, Diana hunched over, running her index finger around the outside rim of the glass. Laura watched her, feeling sorry for Diana. She'd been in a pretty tough situation herself, but Diana's story made Laura feel as if she'd spent the last eight years of her life living on Sunnybrook Farm.

"I'm gonna tell you something I've never told anyone else before. I was a street hustler, sure. Started when I was young, just a little girl, in fact, fifteen. Sure as I knew what I really was inside. I went out on the streets for money. Where else could someone like me make the kind of money I need to get fixed?" She told Laura how she'd always hated cops, especially the ones who came around looking for her specifically, after they got off duty, cops who knew she still had a dick; that's in fact what they'd been looking for. But cops in general, as well—she hated them. She'd never seen one of them, in all the time she was growing up, who didn't treat her people as if they were dirt beneath their feet. Even the black cops—in fact, they often were worse than the white ones, who treated the ghetto as they would the darkest jungle, with a mixture of awe and fear. She told Laura that when the two cops—Phillips and Mondello—had come to her, she'd expected them to roust her, put her in a jail cell with a bunch of violent felons, then listen to her scream as she was raped into confessing to them whatever it was that they wanted to hear. She told Laura how surprised she'd been that they'd treated her with respect.

Diana said, "But after that, after talking to those two cops? I quit the stroll. Gave it up. Started working for Al, and just did outcalls, now and again. And when I get enough money together to stop being a half-and-half, to finally get everything done? I'll tell you something. I'm gonna do what you're doing. I'm going back to school and get away from this nasty part of life forever. If I don't get AIDS first. Or beaten to death by some freak."

Laura didn't say anything, just picked up the wine bottle and re-filled Diana's glass.

"I've been grateful to those men for a year now. I almost called them up, more than once I started to, just to let them know that I'd gotten off the street, that I was trying to change my life. Tonight, when they were outside the hotel? I could tell, they didn't even recognize me."

"You don't know that, honey, come on, remember, one of them was shot in the ear."

"No, there was no sign of recognition, none." Diana shrugged. "Doesn't matter, it's not like I was trying to impress them. I just wanted them to know, I thought they might care, at least Jake. I'd bet he'd care."

Laura reached over and touched Diana's hand, caught it on the tabletop and gave it a firm squeeze.

"*I* care."

"I care, too," Diana said, and squeezed Laura's hand back. She looked up. "So now you know the score, it's not just phone calls, or outcalls for an escort service. It was a little heavier than that. I've got more arrests than you've had birthdays."

"But that's over now, right?"

"For over a year."

"Did anyone ever die, anyone you—did that thing with with that Roman character?"

"Only customers I had might have died didn't die by Roman's hand."

"What?"

Diana smiled. "They died of ecstasy."

"Oh," Laura said, picturing it. She smiled.

Diana said, "You still want to go into business with me? 'Cause I could pay off your phone bill, get some extra phone lines installed tomorrow. I know a guy that can get it done, who can bypass all the paperwork, and it won't cost us anything." Diana smiled, ruefully. "Well, at least not much. We could call it Laura's Love Line. We'll do it up all classy, use our real names, what do we have to hide? We'll put ads in the paper and everything. I been thinking, we cut-rate it? Some of the lines charge three to six bucks a minute, and men pay it just to have women talk dirty to them. You and me, we do it for a dollar a minute, cut the throats out of *all* the competition. Ten-minute minimum. Cash, check, or money order only. No credit cards, no billing. No more turning tricks for me, either."

Laura told her that she was way ahead of her, that Bing was steal-ing some of Al's files for them—Laura wanting to match what Diana had stolen, so they could start out as even partners—even as they spoke. He was getting their Rolodex cards for them, too. Diana looked up, shocked, astonished that her friend had done that for her without hearing the whole story. She suddenly noticed that they were still holding hands. She squeezed Laura's in delight.

"We get voice mail for when we're out, sleeping, or busy; get Call Forwarding so you can come down and talk on a line at my place when Tommy's not at camp or in school. But here's the deal, here's the kicker. We do it for one year, not a day longer than that. We don't get lazy, we don't get used to it, fall into the easy money trap. We'll do what we have to do until the time comes when we've got the money to do what we *want*. Then we close it down, retire the best phone-sex line Chicago ever had. How's that sound?"

"You think we'll make that kind of money? That we can do it for a year and retire?" Laura seemed doubtful, but Diana's smile grew broader.

"You kidding me? The two of us? We sell cheesecake pictures, too, dirty panties if we want. I wouldn't be surprised if we can quit after six months."

"All we need now is for Bing to come through."

"No, we don't even need him. I was *wondering* what he was doing here. We've got my files for tomorrow, and I'll get the ads in the pa-pers, and we'll move ahead from there, even if Bing doesn't come across." Diana reluctantly let go of Laura's hand and stood up, hold-ing her wine glass in one hand. "But I appreciate what you did."

Diana said, "I want to get up early in the morning and get things started. And you have to get up and make Tommy breakfast, get him off to camp. Come down as soon as Tommy's gone. Now come on, stand up."

"What?" Laura hadn't realized how tired she was. The wine had mellowed her out some, too. She got to her feet. She didn't feel so blue any more. Diana picked Laura's wine glass up off the table, then handed it to Laura, solemnly.

"Here's to Laura's Love Line," Diana said, and Laura repeated it, then they touched glasses and finished the wine, looked at each other, and smiled.

HE WAS SLEEPING, soundly. So soundly that when Marsha shook his shoulder, Jake Phillips nearly leaped out of bed. He heard her voice, in competition with an insistent chirping that sounded like a canary on crack, singing rap. "What!" Jake opened his eyes and found that he was sitting up in bed, looking around. The sheet was down around his waist, his skin felt cool and clammy. He must have been having a nightmare; thankfully, he couldn't remember it.

"Your beeper . . ." Marsha sounded a little angry. Jake looked over at the nightstand, felt around for his beeper, found it and shut it down.

"Damn it!" He still felt shaken; he was sweating heavily. Marsha touched his arm.

"Are you all right?"

"Bad dream. I think." Even though he couldn't remember anything about it, the nightmare still had a grip on his feelings. Jake tried to focus his attention on the oversized red numbers of the bedstand digital clock. The digits seemed to swim into focus. Jake saw that it was five-fifteen. He felt the rustle of the sheet, then one of Marsha's hands, gently rubbing his shoulder. She could go from hot to cold, fast. She had resented being awakened by the beeper, but now she was concerned about his nightmare. Jake appreciated the gesture, and patted her hand.

He got out of bed and went into the bathroom, carrying his beeper. He squinted with the knowledge of pain to come, then flipped on the light. The digital readout was almost impossible for him to make out, with the cobwebs still in his head, the loginess, the emotional upset he was still feeling. What could he have been dreaming about? It must have been a really bad one; thank God he couldn't remember. Jake shook his head, then gave up trying to see the numbers, put the beeper on the back of the toilet, and turned on the cold water nozzle in the sink. He let it run a few seconds, working himself up to what he was about to do, his hands on the sink, rocking back and forth a couple of times.

Jake took a breath, then stuck his head under the faucet. "Shit!" He was shocked and angry, but he let the water run through his hair and down onto his face. It got into his ears. He hadn't realized he'd been so tired. When the rare call came in the middle of the night, he was generally awake and moving after the first beep. Not tonight.

He knew that he'd been wearing himself down, burning the candle way too brightly. Grabbing four, five hours of sleep here and there when he could, trying to be an ace homicide bull and an attentive husband, a loving father, all at the same time. Jesus *Christ,* but he was tired. At last Jake shut off the water, stood up, dried his head with the bath towel, then picked the beeper up again.

It was Captain Royal's direct office number. Captain Royal? At *this* time of night?

Jake hurried out of the bathroom, grabbed his robe off the end of the bed, then went out into the living room, sat down on the couch, near the phone. He'd left his beeper in the bathroom. He dialed the captain's number from memory.

"Phillips?"

"Yes sir."

"You awake?" It was why he'd beeped, rather than called on the phone. He'd wanted to give Jake time to wake up. Jake was thankful that he had.

"Yes sir," Jake said, then held his breath, waiting. Out of a clear blue sky he began to worry, and he stopped thinking for a second, letting his brain work things out on its own: Something was fighting to get in.

The captain didn't say anything right away, and Jake thought he knew, from the captain's tone, what was wrong, there was no doubt in his mind. A picture flashed into his head out of nowhere, and Jake suspected that he knew now, with crystal clarity, what his nightmare had been about.

He had a sudden vision of Alex Mondello sitting fully clothed on a toilet seat in some seedy motel, still wearing the tattered tuxedo, his pistol in his mouth, his thumb on the trigger—oh, Lord, that was what he'd been dreaming, that was his nightmare, he knew it now, Mondo was dead. Jake began to shiver.

The captain said, "Get down to Twenty-first and Wabash, right now. You meet me there."

"Sir?"

"What?"

Jake hesitated, then blurted out, "Can you tell me what this is about?"

"Not on this line." Royal paused, then spoke in a low, grim tone. "We got a dead cop. A dead cop you threatened to shoot about twelve hours ago, you and your partner both." The captain hung up at the same moment that Jake sighed a huge, involuntary sigh of relief.

"They can't be serious," Marsha said. She was sitting in her summer ESLEEP gown, on the closed toilet lid, her hair in disarray, pillow lines on her face. She was moving her bare right foot around the small puddle of water that had cascaded off Jake's hair. She didn't seem upset about it being there; rather, she seemed to be playing with it. "Did you do it?" Jake, tying his tie, shot her a quick look in the mirror. Marsha looked up and met his gaze. She let out a small, embarrassed laugh. "Oh, come on. I know you didn't kill him. I meant, did you threaten him?"

"I know what you meant." Jake had made a comeback. The call had awakened him more than the cold water had. Thinking of Mondo dead, seeing it so vividly in his mind, had wiped away all traces of tiredness. He finished with his tie, splashed on just a tiny bit of cologne, then picked up the brush and tried to straighten out what holding his head under the sink had done to his hair. He hadn't taken a shower, but his last one had been less than four hours ago, so he didn't feel grungy. The wet hair would give the brass the impression that he had showered, anyway.

Jake knew the brass would be there, maybe the mayor, too. A lot of dignitaries always showed up whenever a cop got shot. Maybe not the mayor, though. After the assassination attempt, he'd probably gone out and gotten drunk. Jake didn't blame him. He hoped the man had. There'd be one less boss he'd have to convince that he hadn't shot Robert Roosevelt.

Jake said, "It's so unusual to get called out at night. I mean, there're eight guys on nights now in the Area. The only time I get beeped at night is when something comes up in the course of an investigation that's relevant to something I'm working on." Jake impatiently pulled at his hair, slicking it straight back. For a moment, in the mirror, he looked like an old man; it was the way his father and grandfather both used to comb their hair. Marsha touched his hip, around back, and let her hand linger there, her fingers deftly avoiding his pistol. She stroked Jake's lower back. Jake knew there was no getting around it.

He told her, "The dead cop's name is Robert Roosevelt, he used to be partnered with a man named Jerry Moore."

"I certainly remember Moore."

Jake nodded at the soberness of her tone; he'd almost quit police work over Moore. He said, "Roosevelt's cut from the same mold. Big, mean, brutal guy, was set to retire sometime this week. He's the type of old-timer who went into mourning, who wore a black armband when Miranda came into effect. He's hated me since I signed the report that said Moore was crooked, on the payroll of an outfit punk named—"

"Alleo, I remember." Marsha finished it for him, rushing him.

"Every time he saw me, he had to give me a hard time."

"He busts your balls, you can say that to me." Jake looked down at her. Marsha wasn't smiling. He continued as if she hadn't said a word.

"He goes on about my age, my hair, my clothes, whatever he can. Part of it was just him being who he was, part of it was resentment. The guy didn't like me."

"Jake . . ."

Jake put the brush down, held out his hands and helped Marsha to her feet. He put an arm around her, from the left, so his weapon wouldn't be in the way. He walked her to the bed, sat her down, then went back and turned off the bathroom light. His jacket was on the back of the straight-backed reading chair that was in front of the window. Jake picked the sport coat up, swung his arms into it, ready to go.

He said, casually, "I ran into him today, working a heart attack he called us out on, right down the street. It turned out to be obvious that it wasn't a homicide after all, but Roosevelt responded to the call, for TAC, and a guy like him doesn't do anything unless he absolutely has to, so he called us in. I didn't even see his partner; he must have been in the coffee shop." Jake crouched down in front of his wife, put both hands on Marsha's knees, to help keep his balance as much as to offer Marsha reassurance. "He did something really dumb, and I cursed him out, and he made a move on me and I told him that if he took one more step, I was going to pull my piece and shoot him. He made some wisecrack, then Mondo said he'd shoot him, too." Marsha seemed appalled. Jake quickly shook his head, trying to make light of it.

"It happens all the time in the department, Marsha, believe me, when a bully copper comes on too strong with a guy smaller than he is. Nothing ever comes of it, nobody ever gets in trouble."

"But now Roosevelt's dead," Marsha said. "Does that happen all the time, too?" She quickly added, "You were here all night, I can tell them that. And you know how the Rat Patrol is, the Internal Affairs people and those others from the OPS. Don't you try and convince them of your innocence." Marsha seemed angry now; she was giving him advice. Jake was smiling at her having called Internal Affairs the Rat Patrol, and she saw it and took his smile the wrong way.

"Don't you dare make light of this, you know better than I do how those people treat other cops. They just want to close the case out and make their rank, so they can stop being rats. If they even suspect you, Jake, if they treat you like anything less than the man you are, you tell them all to go to hell, you call a lawyer right away, or call me, and I'll get ahold of one. You promise me."

"Marsha, would you stop?" Jake snorted a laugh that didn't ring true. "You're worrying a lot more than I am. Don't. If the Captain heard about it, it just means that somebody beefed. Probably Roosevelt himself, it was the type of guy he was. Royal's probably more worried about the press picking up on it than he is about whether I shot Roosevelt, he knows better than that."

"Or Mondo."

Jake hesitated a second too long before he said, "Or Mondo."

He pushed off Marsha's knees, got to his feet. "You call me and let me know what's happening the second you know what's going on, Jake, I don't care what time it is. You call me. Don't forget." Jake told her he'd give her a ring just as soon as they read him his rights, but he didn't think Marsha appreciated the joke: She didn't laugh, or if she did he didn't hear her before he left the apartment and carefully locked the door behind him.

There was a young woman standing right outside the Metropolitan Building's double glass doors. The woman well-dressed, holding a little boy's hand. The child was three or four, and dressed well himself, in a short-sleeve Bears Starter shirt, with good tennis shoes on his feet. The young woman was in her late teens on the outside, and very attractive. As Jake passed her she said, "Sir? Could you help us? Would you have a bus token you can give me?" Jake, preoccupied, shook his head. "Could you please loan us fifty cents, then?" She was smiling now, humbly. Jake began to walk toward the new Chevy Caprice with the "M" license plates that he'd left parked a few doors up. He heard a male voice, shouting, and turned to see a young man with his head sticking out of the doorway of the deli that occupied the corner of the building. His WEST SIDE baseball cap was tilted far to one side.

"Goddamnit, what's wrong with you, bitch, can't you learn nothin'?" The young man was yelling at the young woman. "Get in they faces, block them, goddamnit, I can't come up—" He spotted Jake watching and turned stone-faced. "What *you* lookin' at, you suit-wearin', baby ignorin', ugly white motherfucker?" Jake began to walk toward him, pulling back on the hem of his sport coat. He knew right away when the young man spotted the belt badge, could tell just from the look on his face. The kid tried to duck back into the doorway, and Jake began to run, put his hand on his weapon.

"Hey!" Jake moved hurriedly past the woman, who now seemed frightened. The little boy had begun to cry. Jake spun into the deli doorway with his pistol half out of its holster. He moved so that he could see both the man and the woman without giving his back to either. The man stood there, angry, insolent, glaring at Jake even after Jake took his hand away from his weapon.

"What, it against the motherfuckin' white man's law to stand here and wait for a *bus?*" The woman had turned her back on them now, was in fact standing right next to the bus stop sign. The man crossed his arms and went into the street lean. A skinny young man with dark blue tattoos on both tight biceps. Jake imagined Marsha coming out of the building, with Lynne in her stroller. He saw Marsha smiling then stopping, showing compassion for the woman who was in a fix. Perhaps reaching into her wallet to hand her a dollar . . .

Then he imagined this loser coming out of the doorway and hitting Marsha over her head, then taking her purse.

Jake said, "Listen to me," softly, and the man spat on the sidewalk. Jake grabbed him by the front of his shirt and shoved him hard against the deli's front door. The glass rattled, but held.

"Man, what's wrong with you, what you doing?" The kid was outraged. He wasn't so insolent now, the attitude gleaned from prison or the street or from watching rap videos was rapidly fading.

Jake said, "Listen to me, can you hear me all right?" The man nodded his head. "That's good. Because it's important, and we will never have this conversation again, you need to know that." Jake leaned in closer, until their faces were inches away. "I can reach into your pocket, and I'll find a sap, a knife, something that you use in robberies, so you won't mess up those fine hands, or to instill terror into the hearts of the white oppressor; I know how it goes. Now, son, I can lock you away on that right now, and my word alone as a police officer would be enough to put you and your woman together in the deal, and to get that poor young kid put into the custody of the DCFS. I could maybe even get the paperwork lost, so you won't see him for a year or two."

"I never seen that bitch or her baby before in my life—" The man was getting some of it back. Jake had been talking too calmly.

"Shut up!" He shouted it, and the man obeyed. Jake whispered now, venomously. "You get off Dearborn, and you *stay* off Dearborn. I see you on this street again and I'll lay every unsolved crime committed in this district in the last six months on your ass, you know it can be done. You don't care about the kid? Then listen to this: I'll lock *your* ass away in the County jail until Christmas, you believe me?"

"Yeah . . ." Jake thought he finally had the young man's attention. Jake let him go. He stepped back. The woman and child had disappeared.

"I can't make you stay out of crime, and I can't get you off drugs. And I'll never convince you that the white man ain't your enemy. But I guarantee you, I give you my fucking *word,* I can keep you off Dearborn, from Polk Street to the end of the line." Jake paused. "I mean it, playboy."

"I hear you." The young man shoved his hands down in his pockets, and Jake stepped aside to let him pass. He watched him turn past the low cement wall at the corner, watched him bop his way up toward State Street. When he turned onto State Street, Jake finally let himself relax. Feeling vaguely ashamed, he walked over to his car.

20

HE THOUGHT ABOUT it in the car, driving the mile-and-a-half over to the scene. Not about the young man and his girlfriend, or of the robbery scam they were working, though it wasn't a bad one when you thought about it, better than most he'd seen. A well-dressed woman with a kid in expensive clothes; she wasn't doing anything wrong, was simply asking for a token, how was she supposed to know that the stringy young ex-convict standing over in the corner meant somebody harm? She thought he'd been waiting for the bus, too. But Jake didn't dwell on that. He was too busy thinking about what Marsha had said to him last night, when she'd been angry.

She'd called him a loving, caring, sensitive man; even angry, she'd thought that of him.

What she hadn't said was that there were no secrets between them; Marsha knew better than to ever assume that to be the case.

Jake kept his share of secrets; there was plenty he didn't tell her. And not all of the secrets concerned deranged assassins stalking public figures, either. Jake could never tell her about the things he saw in the course of his average day. They weren't things she'd want to know about, either. He could never bring himself to tell her what men were capable of doing to one another. And when a child was killed, forget about it; he would pretend he knew nothing about the murder if she asked, even when the squad he was in was working the crime. Particularly when the victim was a little girl, like Lynne.

From time to time Marsha would sit him down and talk to him, about his job, the way he felt about it, her eyes locked on his, Marsha watching. Then, there was no use lying. She'd be checking him for signs of burnout, for stress, in a way that no partner could ever see. Sometimes living with a psych major could be a royal pain in the ass, as Marsha would scrutinize him carefully every time he got a little more quiet than he usually was. But he appreciated what she was doing, how much she cared for his well-being, how much Marsha loved him. Even while, on another level, he resented her analyzing him, he never doubted the depth of her love. He loved her just as much in return. He'd do anything for her.

She'd told him, more than once, that he didn't have to work. That Jake could quit the department and return to school and get whatever degree he wished. She didn't especially care for him being a cop; something else they didn't have in common with his colleagues. Most cop's wives seemed to love the department as much as their husbands did, or at least they pretended to. Jake didn't understand why, but Marsha thought it had something to do with the power involved, with being insiders, not to mention the fact that they never got traffic tickets. Cops don't ticket other cops. Or their wives.

Maybe someday Jake would take Marsha up on the offer, but not right now. Jake suspected that she might even resent the fact that he hadn't quit the force and stayed home with Lynne after the baby's birth, to free Marsha's time, so she could go on with her education. It wasn't something he could do. He wasn't cut out to stay home and watch kids, no matter how much he might love them.

Although he would act overly proud, and would never tell her the truth, it was a great relief to Jake, as it probably would be to most people, to know that his welfare and that of his loved ones didn't depend on his take-home pay.

There'd been enough money left for Marsha in a trust fund from her father for the two of them to live in splendor without either of them holding down a job.

It had at first been a bone of contention between them, early in their marriage. Marsha had grown up being spoiled rotten while— after having left home—Jake had gotten used to doing without. She'd sneak things into the house that they really didn't need; luxuries to keep up with the Joneses, he'd say they were. Now they'd come to the point where her money almost never came between them. She used it for things she thought were important, and Jake never argued with her about what she decided was significant. The way he saw it, it was Marsha's money, not his, and surely not *theirs*. It was the way he felt, no matter what she said about it. Hell, Jake had never even *met* Marsha's dad, the old man having died several months before the two of them had met, in college. Even though Jake might have debated as to whether the Infiniti in the garage down the street was a necessity, he sure had to admit that he enjoyed driving it when they went out. The brand-new dark blue Chevy he was driving now wasn't all that bad, though. And the Infiniti didn't have a police radio mounted inside it.

Marsha knew as well as he did that he had been destined for a career in police work, and although she worried, he didn't think she would ever tell him to quit; Marsha would never force Jake to make such a radical choice.

He knew what his choice would be, though, if she ever did. Which was another thing he hoped he'd never have to tell her. If it came down to it, he'd choose Marsha. There was no doubt in his mind, and he hoped there was none in hers.

Jake pulled to the curb out on the street, at the address the captain had given him. He knew he had the right place when he saw what seemed to be the entire neighborhood standing outside the building, talking to the assembled reporters. Jake got out of the car, his jacket open, so the uniformed officers could see his belt-badge and would allow him access. He ignored the reporters, ignored their questions, and put a hand up to his face to block the sudden bright light of the TV cameras that turned toward him. He lowered it when he realized that it was a criminal's move, more apropos to a suspect than a homicide detective.

The cop guarding the door said, "Third floor, Detective," and Jake nodded his thanks. He entered the building, bypassed the elevator, and slowly climbed the stairs. He found Captain Royal standing in the third-floor hallway, his left hand bunched up into a fist, punching the wall with it in a distracted manner as he awaited Jake's arrival.

"**Y**OU HEAR ABOUT Jankowiscz?" Royal shook his head. "No, you wouldn't have, you were sleeping when I called." The captain's voice was low, nearly a mumble; Jake had to lean forward to understand what he was saying. He could smell the man's sweat. Even this early in the morning, it was very hot and sticky. There was the smell of stale beer in the hallway, mixed in with the smell of cheap cigars. The captain was smoking, crowding Jake; he didn't give Jake much room to maneuver. "Dirty bastard, I never did trust him." Jake waited, fear beginning to creep up his spine. The captain was glaring at him, standing there blocking Jake's access to the crime scene. Besides the fear, Jake felt, for the first time in years, intimidated.

They stood at the end of the hall, at the top of the stairwell, over to one cobwebbed corner, under a broken lightbulb that was hanging down from the third-floor ceiling by a frayed black cord. Cops were going in and out of 3-C—two doors down from where they stood—in a steady stream. Jake didn't see any brass. His back was against the wall, one shoulder nearly touching each juncture of the corner. He felt trapped. Were the IA boys down there? OPS? The captain was keeping him from 3-C for a reason. Was he about to get accused? Was the captain trying to break it to him gently?

"Two, three hours ago, Jankowiscz's out on the street, off-duty, out drinking. With his girlfriend—his wife's at home, with the kids, he told her he was working. Girlfriend's husband confronts them out in the street. *He's* drunk, too. Jankowiscz tells the responding officer, later, that the man came at him with a knife, what else could he do? He shot the guy, six times, with his off-duty piece, a small .38 snubbie. RO goes over to the man, and sure enough, he's holding a knife, still clutched tight in his right hand. The girlfriend's in hysterics, her husband, her husband! But she pulls herself together enough to talk to the RO, and she backs up Jankowiscz's story."

Jake fought his fear and tried to be a part of the insider cop gossip. "That's it, he's in divorce court, even if the press doesn't get wind of it."

"They already have, and divorce court's the least of Jankowiscz's problems."

Jake swallowed. "Sir?"

"RO does it right, by the book, makes all the proper calls like he's supposed to. Paramedics come, do a quick vital-signs search, then they wait for our detectives to come along and check the corpse, just in case. Well, this time, there was a 'just in case.'"

"What happened?"

"Husband had his own piece, a little baby twenty-five semiautomatic, in his left-hand pants pocket. Turns out, the man's left-handed. He had his left hand in his pocket when he approached them, more than likely just about to shoot right through the fabric. One homicide detective looks another in the eye and asks him why would the deceased come at him with a knife in his one hand when he got his other hand on a pistol in his pocket, hammer back, safety off."

"Oh, no."

"Oh, no is right. If Jankowiscz had waited two more seconds, he'd have been justified, if he'd survived. Now it's at the very least manslaughter, maybe even Second Degree."

"He break?"

"The girlfriend did. Johannsen and Rucker got her in a room, told her that it was the last chance she was gonna get, come clean now, tell the truth, she didn't do anything, why should she go down with Jankowiscz? Told her if she didn't, they'd convince the assistant state's attorney and the press that she'd *paid* Jankowiscz to kill her husband, that it was a hit, and she'd be ruined, even if she didn't go to Dwight's Women's for the rest of her life, which she would. She tells them about how her old man had followed them, how Jankowiscz shot him when he saw him running toward them, then planted the knife in his right hand, you know."

"Yeah."

Captain Royal said, "There's a lot of resentment on the squad, Jake, against you." Jake started at the change of topic. The captain dropped his cigarette down on the filthy tile, then stepped on it. "I'm not telling you anything you don't know. Young man like you, already a homicide bull, while there's plenty of people who've been waiting twenty years to get into the squad, but for one reason or another can't get out of uniform. Even I hear the rumors, the way it's rationalized. How it's your father's friends looking out for you, your wife's parents' connections, whatever."

"My wife's—" The captain's glare cut Jake off before he could finish the sentence, but still, he wondered: Who the hell knew about his in-laws?

The captain stood there for a moment and looked at Jake, sizing him up and perhaps even trying to see if he'd gotten whatever moral there was to get out of the Jankowiscz story. The captain decided to tell him, in case he hadn't. At least he gave Jake an overbroad hint.

"There'll be a lot of bad press coming with this Jankowiscz business, added to this," he nodded his head at the door to 3-C. "We're gonna come out looking pretty bad before the night's over. Jankowiscz, he had a lot of friends in this squad, too, throughout Homicide altogether, truth be told."

"Who found the gun? I'm surprised it didn't disappear."

"Lorenzo Gonzales found it."

"He's a good man." Jake was wondering if Gonzales resented him, too, knew about his in-laws' money. He wondered if Mondo did.

"He'll have a bad name by this time tomorrow."

"But he has enough time in the department to bear the weight, is that what you're saying?"

"Do you think you do?"

"Me?" What was this man getting at? And why was he constantly changing the topic? Jake said, "Captain, I don't worry a whole lot about the opinions of other people, you know that."

"Seems to me you shared that thought with me once before, about a year ago."

"Captain?" The combination of the story, with all its implications, Jake's tiredness, and the captain's attitude all gave Jake the courage to ask, "What the hell is this all leading up to?"

"I have reason to believe your partner might be responsible for those two deaths in there." The captain's look didn't leave room for argument, or even discussion. What he hadn't said, however, was that he also suspected Jake. Just Mondo. A good sign. Maybe the captain wasn't going to arrest him after all. Although Jake couldn't be sure; he couldn't judge by the way the man was acting. The captain said, "I hope to God I'm wrong, but there's some evidence."

"Sir?"

"Wait 'till I'm finished, then you can talk." The captain turned and glared at a detective who'd been walking up behind him. Jake hadn't even heard his footsteps. The detective stopped dead in his tracks, and the captain turned back to face Jake. Now he was nearly whispering.

"Mondo's the most popular man in the entire Homicide division. They know how good he is, and he hands the glory around. It's one of the reasons I paired the two of you up in the first place. He's connected to everybody in Homicide, and everybody likes him, respects what he can do, too. I knew if they saw you with him, and if he likes you, then you'd be in. His liking you took a lot of the heat from the Moore thing off your shoulders, too, in case you hadn't figured that out." Jake nodded.

The captain said, "It hadn't been Gonzales out there, tonight, with Jankowiscz? I don't know what might have happened." The captain reached into his shirt pocket, pulled out his pack, shook out a cigarette and lit it up. He showed respect this close in, blowing the smoke away from Jake. Jake noticed that the captain's left hand was still balled into a fist. He was tapping it against his leg. "Maybe the knife would have disappeared, maybe Jankowiscz would have gotten a chance to change his story." The captain took a deep drag on the Pall Mall, then threw it against the wall with anger that didn't enter his tone when he said, "Who knows?"

The captain said, "I've got three six-man squads working under me. A lot of people, a lot of responsibility. I don't talk with the guys like I used to when I was a lieutenant, when I was working the street with them; I'm a boss now, they don't know if they can trust me like they used to. But I have a pretty good idea of what's going on in the squads, who I can trust and who I can't." The captain said, "You're my Lorenzo Gonzales, Phillips. I don't think you'd bury evidence to save anyone, not your partner, not me, not anyone."

"Thanks," Jake said, stunned.

"But I might."

"What?!"

"And don't thank me yet. I want you to go out there and find Mondo, right now. He's not home, I called. Can't blame him, either, after what happened at the dinner last night. Don't look surprised, shit, the superintendent woke me up to tell me about it. Called back an hour later to tell me about Jankowiscz. Then an hour later, *this* happens. Two of these men are in my command, and the third one was until just a year ago. It looks bad right now, Phillips, my ass is on the line. I've always suspected that Roosevelt was dirty, and I told you before, I never trusted Jankowiscz. But Mondo, I'll never believe Mondo's over the edge. The thought of *two* renegades is too much for me to consider right now. And one killing the other, well, it smacks too close to the Tulio thing for me."

The captain turned the full force of his personality on Jake now. He said, "Phillips, you go find me Mondo, and then you find me the truth. Find out what happened. If he killed those two men in there, he's got to go down for it, Phillips."

Jake didn't know what to say. He'd been expecting to be accused himself, and now it seemed as if he was in charge of the investigation.

"But if he didn't, I don't want his good name ruined, not over a piece of shit human being like Robert Roosevelt."

"Captain, I'm sorry, but you lost me."

"We got two scenarios, Phillips, as far as I can see." The captain turned, looked behind him to see if anyone had snuck up on them. He turned back, moved in even closer. Jake could smell stale cigarette smoke on him, on his clothing, the smell mixed with that of his sweat. He felt nauseated. The captain held his left hand up, shook the fist right under Jake's nose. "Either Mondo killed them both, or somebody wants it to look as if he did." Royal opened his hand. There was a single cuff link shining in his palm. "This is Mondo's, isn't it? You tell me if it's not."

Jake looked down at the letters *ALM,* spelled out in diamond chips.

"It's his. I noticed them earlier tonight, at the fund-raiser."

"All right." The captain closed his fist up again, suppressing the evidence. He put his fist in his pocket. When it came out it was an open hand.

"For the time being, I'm running this one myself. Lieutenant Francis is on his way in right now, and I'll have to give it to him later on today, maybe tomorrow, whenever the bosses give me enough heat, or the union finds out and kicks me in the ass. I got at least that much time to look into this closely. I find out anything else, I'll disclose it. And then we've got to run him down like a goddamn dog." The captain shook his head, sadly. "I don't want that to happen. I've been his friend for fifteen years." He paused, then said, reluctantly, "I owe him."

"That's it? All you want me to do is find Mondo?"

"That's enough, Phillips, and you do more than find him. You find him and you look him in the eye, and you ask him straight out if he did it." The captain shrugged. "Maybe you been around him long enough that some of his Sight wore off on you. I want you to come inside here, get the lay of the land, the feel for what happened. I want you to familiarize yourself with the case and the victims, then get back to the office and start running him down," the captain said, then turned, about to head back into the scene of the double homicide, until Jake called his name.

The big man turned back, slowly, almost reluctantly. As if the movement were difficult for him. Maybe it was, with one of his hand-picked squad members already having committed murder tonight, and another a top contender to have committed a brutal double.

Jake whispered it. "What about the cuff link?"

"What cuff link?" Captain Merlin Royal said, then turned around and lumbered away, leaving Jake, open-mouthed and astonished, staring at the sweat stain that made the captain's shirt stick to the middle of his broad, arched back.

MR. **X** WAS wide awake, lying tense on filthy rented sheets, arms crossed on his chest as he stared up at the ceiling. His mouth was open, though he was unaware that it was, and his eyes were glazed over. He was breathing shallowly though his mouth. Tears rolled down his cheeks, wetting the pillow. The sounds of the television set from the room next door intruded into the silence of his own bedroom, but he paid it no attention; his mind was elsewhere, seeking solutions.

What had he done?

What had he done?

Dear God in heaven, what had he done?

It hadn't turned out as he'd thought it would, nothing did, ever, did it? Now that he thought of it, the truth of his life was clear: Not once in his entire life had things worked out as he'd planned them. Oh, he'd done what he'd set out to do, and he'd succeeded; everyone who knew him viewed him as a success in his real life.

But he was a failure, a loser. He'd always suspected it, the little voice in the back of his head was never silenced, always talking, telling him what a loser he was, how stupid, how clumsy, how ugly, how dense. Most of the time he could disregard it, having direct evidence that the voice was wrong, that he was none of those things.

But reality had come crashing down around him tonight. There was no way he could justify what he'd done this evening. He'd killed. In cold blood. Brutally. Twice.

What bothered him the most was that he'd planned it out so carefully, and he'd stuck to his own script, even after he'd discovered a second player in the game, the black man with the gun who'd recognized him on sight. In his mind, earlier, in his office, he'd seen the ending differently: He'd walked away from the killing as coldly as he'd walked into it, then he'd go to his office and make a phone call, to let off the steam. From there he'd go to a hotel somewhere, take a long hot shower as he remembered the thrill of the moment. In his fantasy he fell immediately to sleep.

In his fantasy he didn't lie there shaking, trembling, wondering what mistake he'd made that would bring the law to his door. And bring his world to an end. He didn't even have the gun he'd used, couldn't use it to kill himself here in the anonymous bed. He'd thrown it in the river as he'd crossed it, heading here; he'd had the presence of mind to remember to do that. He should have known better, should have thought to keep it. He had another one at home, but he couldn't go there . . .

He couldn't live with this. This fear. The torment that overwhelmed him, now that the effects of the painkilling drugs were out of his system, now that he'd sweated out the booze. He'd thought about it, fantasized about it, and it had always gone so *smoothly*. He'd never planned on his own cowardice coming back to haunt him, had in fact completely forgotten about the days he'd spent, back in 'Nam, after patrol, curled up in a ball in his hooch, crying. He'd romanticized it for so many years that he'd blocked out the terror of later.

Well, he was remembering it now.

Mr. X pulled the second pillow over his head and bit down on it as hard as he could, trying to keep from shrieking right out loud.

"Mommy, I'm sorry . . ." Mr. X moaned in a child's pitiful wail, and saw the woman in his mind.

Heavyset, looking down at him, her face so full of disgust that it shamed him beyond words. He closed his eyes, and imagined the beating, getting what he deserved because he was such a terrible little bastard, only getting what he had coming to him. See what he made her do?

He took deep breaths, and found himself, after a time, beginning to calm down. He even started to think that with luck, it might be all right.

They wouldn't find him, they wouldn't find him. Would they? No, he was Mr. X.

Having experienced firsthand what he'd spent the last several years instilling in others, using the telephone as his instrument of terror, Mr. X was able, unlike some of his victims, to let it go, and sleep.

Jake was getting bleary-eyed from lack of sleep. Squinting down at the tiny printing in the telephone book wasn't helping matters, either. He thought that before the day was done, he'd have a callous on his index finger. He'd started using the eraser end of the pencil to punch in numbers. He'd get through today, that's all he had to do. Then he could sleep for the next two days if he wanted to, as Tuesday and Wednesday were his "weekend" days.

Chicago had had a busy night, as far as the division's work was concerned; it was late summer and hot weather did that to people, made them kill each other more often. There were four two-person teams working nights, and for most of the time that Jake had been in the room, he'd been alone. During the few occasions that tired officers had wandered in from the street, the topic of discussion hadn't been Mondo. Roosevelt was a major topic, and not one cop offered sympathy. A couple officers even told Jake that they'd seen it coming, always knew it would someday happen. And when Roosevelt was bounced off the grapevine, it was due to Jankowiscz's murder of his girlfriend's husband being given higher priority. Can you believe it? Can you fucking believe it? were the words most often spoken. Jake wondered if some of the men were worried because it might well have happened to them. Fidelity to one's spouse might be the rule of thumb around here, for a while, at least. Jake tried to ignore the one detective who tried to lay the bulk of the blame on Gonzales.

Elaine Hoffman, though, didn't want to talk about Roosevelt. Or about Jankowiscz. Or about Gonzales. Elaine wanted to talk about Mondo.

But not in front of her partner. Jake could see her looking at him, out of the corner of her eye, glaring at her partner, willing him to go take one of his lengthy breaks in the cafeteria. At last, her partner got up, stretched, and silently left the room before she looked over at Jake.

"I heard about what happened at the fund-raiser last night." Her voice was low, and she tried her best to act in a nonchalant manner, not knowing how much, if anything, Mondo might have told Jake. "How's Alex, is he all right?"

"I guess. We went to the hospital together, and I waited with him until he was patched up."

"I don't mean that, I know that." Elaine was impatient now, she kept looking at the doorway, as if expecting her partner Andy to return at any moment. "I mean about—you know—what happened with his wife."

Jake looked at her, glad for the break from the phone book. He'd never known how many hotels and motels there were in the downtown area. He had called maybe half of them already. None of them had an Alexander, or an A, or an Al Mondello registered. For all Jake knew, Mondo had paid cash for the room and had signed the register under an alias. Elaine was looking at him in a guarded way, and he felt a stab of sympathy for her, felt his face go red. She was worried about what he would think of her. He wasn't used to that around here.

He said, "It's over between them, I know that for a fact, Elaine."

"Thanks," Elaine nearly whispered the word, then seemed ready to say something else. Then she appeared to think better of that. She looked down at her report. Jake heard Andy's footsteps, and looked down. Black letters were swimming around on a yellow page. He blew out his breath, looked up over at the table in the corner. The coffeepot was empty. Andy was sitting across from Elaine now, back at his report.

Jake said, "I'm going down to get a Coke, you guys want anything?" Andy shook his head without looking up from his report, and Elaine waved a negative hand in the air. Jake left the book open on his desk when he left the room.

• • •

"You want to hear something? You are not going to believe this," the Criminal Investigations detective in the cafeteria said to Jake. Jake couldn't remember his name. He was a big white guy who liked to kid around, with a senior partner who was black and just as big, but a more laid-back individual who had a wicked but very dry wit. What was his name? Thomas? Tomlin? Something like that. Jake was picking his coins out of the changer when Tomkin—that was it, Terry Tomkin—came into the room, excited. From the way the man was acting, they must have just pinched John Wayne Gacy all over again.

"FBI's investigating these two East Side punks for bank fraud, and they ain't happy about it, as usual, on account of it's not exactly what you'd call a real high-profile media-type case. These winners are never gonna make the Ten Most Wanted list. All they did was, they forged their mother's name to a check, for—you ready?—*five grand.* And they think they won't get caught. Thank God the bad guys are dumb, you know it? Otherwise we'd be overwhelmed. Bet the teller who cashed it got fired." Tomkin was wearing jeans and a thick white shirt with the sleeves ripped off. He had bulging, well-defined arms, and a beer belly. Tomkin looked more like an ex-biker than a cop. He got a cup of coffee out of the machine, then came over and stood next to Jake.

"Greatest paper trail–hunting motherfuckers in the *world,* they claim they can't find these two slobos, but still, they run a computer check. Get this: both kids are on probation, so what they got is a state violation. They can get *us* to run down the punks for them and pinch them, then *they* can step in and file federal charges. Lazy pricks, the address for both of these degenerates is right there on the sheet. Agent-in-charge says to my captain—you aren't gonna believe this, with a straight face, he says—'We have sources who have informed us that both subjects have recently moved.' So the captain sends us over to the house, just for the hell of it, at start of shift. He wants to embarrass the FBI more than anything else, show them how easy it is." Tomkin looked around the empty room. "Come on, Jake, let's sit down."

Had Jake spoken a word yet? He wanted to get back to his Yellow Pages, but he remembered what the captain had said about how many people in the department already resented him. There was no use in alienating Tomkin, not over five quick minutes. He told Tomkin he could use a break. He sat down, and Tomkin pulled up a chair, turned it around, straddled it with his arms around the back, his coffee in his right hand. He looked at the NO SMOKING signs on the walls, then shrugged, and fired up a cigarette. He kept it cupped in his hand, ready to drop into his coffee cop if a ranking officer came in.

Tomkin said, "We go over to the mother's house, last known address for both of these punks, and we can smell gas before we even get up the porch stairs."

"Gasoline?" Tomkin shook his head.

"Natural, like there's a gas leak in the house. We ain't got time to even call the emergency number, the smell's so strong. And we got all the right in the world to try and save whoever's in there. So Billings, my partner, what's he do? He smiles at me, like a cat, runs up to the door and puts his shoulder to it, *Bam!* the door explodes like it was never there in the first place. Now, I'm right behind him, against my better judgment. I don't want no *parts* of fire." Tomkin paused to sip his coffee and to take a drag off his cigarette. Jake thought he understood why the man was so excited; it was the way you got after having faced down death, seen it up close. After the Collector had been shot, with Jake right there in the middle of things, it had taken him two or three days before he'd stopped bouncing off walls.

Tomkin said, "We're in the house, Billings is running through it, following his nose, and there's a *lighter,* a fucking Zippo, on the coffee table in the living room, burning away."

"Arson."

"Guess how."

"Gas? I don't know. What'd they do, loosen the gas valve in the basement? The last arson I worked, a guy stuffed a load of toilet paper into the toaster, and pushed it down. He had no idea how fast his kitchen would burn, or else he didn't care. Two of his three kids died of smoke inhalation, his wife was burned over fifty percent of her body, and our guy, he's outside when we get there, crying into his hands, sobbing about how he'd tried to save them, how he hadn't meant for anyone to die. Slam dunk."

"Why didn't he save them?"

"That was the plan. Let the fire get going good, then save everybody's life, be a hero standing out on the lawn in his underwear when the firemen got there. He watched too much television, I think. Probably planned to sue the toaster maker as well as collect the insurance money. Smoke filled the house, got in his eyes and he panicked. We found the two little kids hiding in the closet. Holding hands."

"Oh, dear Christ."

"We didn't even have to chase down his job record, his bank statements, nothing. We had a confession out of him two minutes after we got there."

"What happened to him?"

"He's doing two life terms in Stateville, consecutive. He begged the judge to give him the death penalty, but the judge wouldn't do it."

Tomkin snorted. "Fucking lawyers."

"No, the judge told me off the record later that he wanted the guy to serve his time in the general population. He didn't want him isolated on Death Row somewhere, getting fat, alone in a cell all day. He wanted the guy to spend the rest of his life getting sodomized by guys who got kids at home and worry about them."

"The jailhouse moralizers, think they're better than some other convict who done something worse than they did." Tomkin said, then said, "No, it wasn't a toaster in this case. What the guy did, he blew out all the pilot lights on the stove, then turned the jets up high. Put the Zippo on the coffee table and flicked it on. Stupid bastard that he is, that was the dead giveaway."

"How's that? What else should he have done?"

"Nothing. The house would have filled up with gas, and when the hot water heater popped on, ka-*boom*. Anyway, we catch up with the guy in the bar he lives upstairs of, he's in there crying like a baby, drunk, probably been told we're looking for him. He's got an IROC out front, with the driver's window bashed out. Unemployed bartender, driving a twenty-thousand-dollar pussy car."

"You got the other guys? The brothers who robbed their mother?"

"We finally ran them down over at the South Chicago Hospital. You want to hear what princes these are? They forged their mother's check that morning, while she's in surgery, getting one of her legs chopped off. The old lady ain't supposed to make it through the night, and these two can't wait a couple of days to inherit, they got to rip her off while she's thinking they're in the chapel, praying for her recovery."

"They cop to anything?"

"Oh, you should have heard them." Tomkin put his hand to his chest and twisted his face into an exaggerated display of outraged innocence. " 'How could you do this to us? Harass us at a time like this! Can't you see our mother's dying?' " Tomkin dropped the pose. "Like either of them gives two shits. But to answer your question, no, nobody's copped to nothing, not yet. We told both interested parties that the other ratted them out, but I don't think they believe us." He shrugged. "Not that it matters. The torch bearer, he's got a prior, did time once before for attempted arson. We search him, guess what we find? Five grand cash, in a manilla envelope, stuck down the front of his pants. Next to his heart, I guess. He had a key to the old woman's back door in his pocket. He can't explain the key, doesn't have any idea how it got there. As for the cash, he says he won it on the Daily Double out at Arlington this afternoon, but couldn't tell us the numbers. Guy says he's been drinking all night to celebrate and can't remember. You should see him, how slick he thinks he is. Doesn't want a lawyer, tells us he's done nothing wrong, why should he need a lawyer? He has no problem talking to us, as long as it'll clear up this little misunderstanding. He's been around the block a few times, this kid has." Tomkin drank down his coffee, made a face, and sucked in on his cigarette to chase the rancid taste away. Jake had heard of juries who'd acquitted over far less believable stories than that. And there was something about the entrance that bothered him, something he remembered from school; a precedent, perhaps.

Tomkin said, "He keeps trying to cut his own throat, though, the guy. Has to work 'nigger' into every sentence, just to piss Billings off. Smart move." He dropped his cigarette butt into the empty paper coffee cup, shook it around a couple of times, then held up his hand, as if Jake had been about to interrupt him.

"Wait, it gets weirder. We found a bunch of little Rolodex cards in his back pocket, still in their little blue covers, like he ripped them out of the Rolodex. Maybe he got them at Arlington, too. Either way, he ain't telling us where he got them from."

Jake perked up. "What kind of Rolodex cards? What was on them?"

"Names, then a bunch of sex abbreviation shit that anyone else looking at them's supposed to be too dumb to figure out. W.S. for water sports, shit like that. Shit that any twelve year old these days can figure out."

"Could I take a look at this guy?" Jake had to hide his enthusiasm; he didn't know Tomkin well enough to confide in him, not yet.

"Sure. He's in our interrogation room. In the pink one, down in Investigations."

JAKE LOOKED IN through the two-way glass at the sort of man he'd seen before a time or two in his life. An aging jock, who hadn't come even remotely close to fulfilling his teenage daydreams. He'd have been a football or baseball star in high school, and would have been living off the glory of those times ever since, for twenty years or more. The man was large, going a little flabby, with the red face and veined nose of a veteran alcoholic. He held a filter-tipped cigarette in the hand that was cuffed to the heavy wooden table, would lean down into it to take a drag, as if it were some kind of reminder, the man forcing himself to suffer for his stupidity in getting caught. He was in profile to Jake, shaking his head often, cursing himself silently, his lips moving without sound. Jake watched him suddenly slap hard at his thigh with his free hand, putting all he had into it, the man leaning so far down on the backswing that his forehead nearly touched his knee.

Jake wasn't the least bit tired anymore.

He said, "We got sound in here?" Tomkin threw a switch. The man was sobbing quietly. Jake watched his shoulders shake. He had to be careful here, he knew. This guy was their prize, something every veteran detective yearned for; the vehicle they could use to stick it to the FBI. He shut off the sound switch. He said, "Can I get a look at those cards you were talking about?" Tomkin told him sure, still acting very friendly, smoking all he wanted to now that he was back on familiar ground. Even with the door open, the little room was filled with cigarette smoke. Jake waited until they were out of the viewing room, then said casually, to Tomkin's back, "You guys hear about what happened to Robert Roosevelt yet?"

The plastic-covered Rolodex cards were in a brown, lunch-sized paper bag, along with the other personal effects that had been taken off the suspect's person. Jake carefully dumped the bag on the desk, not wanting to dislodge them any more than he had to. The manilla envelope with the five grand inside lay on the desk, the flap opened. Jake hadn't even looked at the denominations. Billings said, "Watch it with that envelope now, Detective Phillips, we counted it all, three times."

"Why isn't it in an evidence bag?"

"We ain't got a crime, yet. Still waiting on an ASA to call and okay charges."

"Attempted arson, right?" Jake didn't look up from the desk. He was pushing the Rolodex cards away from the other things, using the eraser end of a pencil. He could feel Billings staring at him. The man was sitting at his desk, leaning back in his chair, casual, but Jake could feel his tension. He was obviously aware that something other than arson was on Jake's mind. His partner hadn't seen it, which wasn't surprising. It was hard to make intelligent impressions when you never shut your mouth. Maybe Tomkin had a drug problem, dropped white crosses, or snorted crystal meth, something. A minute ago Tomkin had taken a newspaper and gone off to the bathroom to hide; he and Billings would be off-duty as soon as they got approval to charge this Norman Bingham character.

Jake said, "Where're the evidence bags, Billings?"

"In Tompkin's top drawer, that desk right there. My partner may not like it, you going through his things." Jake looked up at him, saw the man's lazy smile, Billings sitting there patient, waiting, secure in the knowledge that Jake would have to go through him if he wanted a shot at his suspect.

"I'll make it up to him." Jake opened the drawer, got out a plastic evidence bag, opened it, then used the eraser to push the Rolodex cards inside. He didn't seal it. He wanted to have them dusted for prints first.

"So what's our torch got to do with Roosevelt?"

"Friend of yours, was he?" As he spoke, Jake watched Billings closely, trying to think of ways he could break his news to the man. Billings's smile faltered at Jake's words, then he got it back, and slowly shook his head.

"My, my, my. Jake Phillips. Heard a lot about you since you been a detective. Never heard you were stupid, though, nobody ever said that." Jake waited. "Nobody ever told me you thought all the black cops in the department looked, thought, and acted the same way, either."

"I don't think any such thing."

"You work with Mondo?" Billings was acting surprised. "Man should have taught you how to speak. You should hear yourself, you

sound like a damned schoolteacher. 'I don't think any such thing,' "
Billings mimicked. He snickered. "Far as Roosevelt goes, I wouldn't
drink with him if he owned the last brewery on earth. That answer
your question?"

"Everyone who knows him pretty much feels the same way. We've
got cops downstairs from every district in the city, from far suburban departments, wanting to help catch whoever shot the brave off-
duty cop. Nobody from this building volunteered, though, not even
from his own TAC unit."

"Man was dirtier than a child molester's soul."

"I think your torch in there may have killed him."

"What?" Billings sat forward. He'd lost his laid-back composure.
"What do those index cards have to do with Roosevelt?"

"They found Roosevelt in a phone-sex office; he was working security for the man who owned the company. Which suggests the
man might have had a problem with a caller, had someone threatening him."

"Or else he was one of those ego-trippers, got a hard-on from having a big black buck like Roosevelt drive him around, guard his
body for him."

"Maybe." Jake felt he'd made it clear that he disagreed with
Billings's assessment. He said, "The Rolodex on the dead man's
desk was open. The cards inside are exactly like these, see-through
blue plastic and all."

"That's a yuppie thing, they all got that glare-killing shit on their
Rolodexes now."

"Yeah, but how many of them have phone numbers and sexual
preferences typed on them? No, we run a print check on these, I
guarantee you, they'll have Allan Beck's fingerprints all over them."

"You know, for a college boy homicide bull, you're not too big of a
shit stain."

"Thanks."

"So what are you saying, you want our man?"

"I'm saying your entrance might not hold up. You didn't have
John Doe or no-knocks, either, all you had were two guys who were
suspected by the FBI of cashing a bad check, possible probation vio-
lators with a small-time warrant over them, that's all you had. Two
guys with their mother in the hospital, maybe dying. How'll that
look when it comes to court? The media gets ahold of that, it's over,
and you know it. And these guys, you know better than I do, they
love going to the media, posing for pictures with their sad-ass faces,

look at me, the poor victim." Jake said, "Your smelling gas isn't a good enough reason to kick down their mother's door, either. The smell could have been coming from anywhere, and even a retardate lawyer knows it."

"Judgment call."

"Maybe, maybe not. You'll more than likely wind up getting written up, though; it's not standard procedure, you're supposed to call the gas company right away on something like that. You get them to turn the gas off first, *then* somebody goes in. They'll say you endangered the safety of the rest of the neighborhood residents."

"You think our pinch won't stand up, is that what you're saying to me?" Billings seemed interested, rather than angry. A cop who'd been around long enough and was smart enough to know that pride and ego didn't do you a lot of good when it came to learning things. It could hold you back if you let it. Billings would know that if Jake could tear down his pinch, any first year lawyer from the public defender's office could do it, too, and do it a lot better. And he might even suspect that Jake was looking to hand him something much better.

"I don't think it will. And I think you do, too."

"So you want to talk to my man in there before the ASA finally gets his ass out of bed and decides to return my call. You want a murder charge on him." Billings was thinking, and Jake watched him. The man's sober face determined that he was no longer kidding around. He said, "But if the arson won't hold up, what about the murder? Fruit of the poison tree don't care where it drops; if we lose the arson, we got no probable cause to go after Bingham at all, right? I mean, if we can't use the lighter or the money we found on him, we can't use the Rolodex cards we found in his pocket, either, can we? And if we try, and it's thrown out, another cop killer walks." Billings paused and looked at Jake. "Roosevelt was a dirty pile of shit, but there was still a badge stuck into it."

Jake was glad that Tomkin wasn't in the room. He didn't want a witness to what he was about to say.

"Detective Billings, that would be entirely up to you. Your partner said the man assaulted you when you came in, that you entered the tavern after you noticed the door was open. *And* there was an IROC with a broken driver's-side window sitting out at the curb, right in front. I don't think even the dumbest judge wouldn't look at that as probable cause to enter the premises."

"Wait a minute, let me get this straight. You want me to change the report, say we were in the neighborhood and saw the broken glass in the car, the open tavern door, and we went in and got assaulted by the guy?" Jake didn't say anything. Billings thought it over, not at all offended, then said, "That still might not cut it. I mean, we were in the guy's father's tavern, he had a right to be there, didn't he? Even with the door unlocked and wide open."

"Not at that time of night, he didn't. In the first place, the tavern door had to be closed and locked by two. That's the law. In the second place, he didn't give you time to discuss the matter, tell you who he was, he just attacked, right? In the third place, Billings, you had an outstanding warrant on a couple of neighborhood punks who were known to frequent the tavern. Tell me you don't have a snitch in the area who told you the two guys hung out at the joint."

Billings's smile returned, and spread, lighting up his face. "Man, you are something else, Jake. No wonder Mondo likes you. Air-tight, isn't it? Waterproof. If we change a couple of words in a report . . ."

"No, let's not go that far. I don't want any part of changing a report. Write *another* report, hold off on getting ASA approval for the arson or the murder charge, though, and let's keep the arson on the back burner for now. We can always try to reinstate. But this way we got him coming and going. We hold him three days for questioning, seventy-two hours; we've got enough evidence to do that, on the double." Jake paused. "The five grand seems high payment for a simple arson in a run-down neighborhood."

Billings looked up sharply. "I see where you're going, Jake, shit, you think the five grand was payment for killing the guy at the phone-sex office. Roosevelt was a bonus; he just happened to get in the way."

"Down payment, at least. It would even be fun for the money man. Hand some local tough guy chump five grand all at once, watch his eyes bug out."

"You don't think he got it from the two brothers?"

"I'm saying it's worth a shot to talk to him, try and find out. And if he didn't get it from them, Billings, if my theory's right, then we've narrowed the field, even if the guy doesn't talk."

"What field is that?" Billings was sitting back again now, enjoying himself. He was looking at Jake far differently than he had been earlier.

Jake said, "Anyone who hated Allan Beck bad enough to kill him had to know this Bingham from somewhere, and know him well enough to trust him. It would tell us that the killer either lives on the East Side, or hangs out at the tavern."

"So you want to talk to the man before we charge him? *If* we charge him?"

"I'd like to take a shot, yeah. What about your partner, though, you think he'd mind?"

"That big old talky white boy? He'll do what I tell him, trust me. I been carrying him on my shoulders for so long now that he'll be happy to do whatever I tell him. But what about our man in the room? You want to tell him he's off the arson hook?"

"Maybe later," Jake said, rising. "There's no sense in giving him a false sense of security."

When the door opened, Jake saw Bingham wipe quickly at the tears on his face, as if nobody would be able to see him. He was smoking another cigarette. Between this guy, the captain, and Tomkin, he'd be lucky to get through the shift without a headache. And if the smoke wasn't enough by itself, the small room reeked of alcohol. Bingham was sitting up now, looking at them, mournfully. Billings and Tomkin entered the room behind Jake. Tomkin shut the door. Jake knew he'd been wise to keep his suspicions to himself at first, not to share them with Tomkin; he'd have never gone for the deal. But Billings had been smart enough to know that he might have messed up, and he was also smart enough to know that it was best for him to cover his ass. A solid case with a conviction beats sitting around cursing lawyers and the system after your pinch walks away, laughing at your stupidity.

It may not be by the book, but as far as Jake was concerned, it all came down to something a woman had said to him, a year ago nearly to the day. A woman who'd been lying on the floor, after she'd shot herself in the arm. The woman who'd killed the Collector. Jake had looked around the room and had figured out that she'd set the killer up, had killed him in cold blood. He'd leaned down until his mouth was next to her ear, and he'd asked her one question: Why?

"Sometimes you have to do bad things in order to get a good thing done." She'd whispered it. It had been Tony Tulio's philosophy, and now, it seemed, Jake had taken it for his own.

Jake took two small steps and was in front of the table. He pulled out the second chair, but he didn't sit down. He lifted his foot and set it atop the chair, then leaned his elbow on the knee, getting comfortable.

"Who are *you* now?" The man shook his head, as if surprised that he was still in custody. "You come to apologize? Man can't even take a drink in his own father's tavern without getting attacked."

"These officers attacked you?"

"Hit me repeatedly in the stomach with their fists." It was as if he were reading it off a trial transcript from a police brutality case.

"Why'd you fight them?"

"They tell you that?" He shook his head. "Jesus Christ. And even if I had, can you blame me? I'm alone, with my Daily Double winnings down my pants, I turn around in my own father's gin mill, and there's this big nigger looking me in the face, don't bother to tell me he's a cop until I'm across the bar and they're slapping the handcuffs on me. Shit, I thought I was being kidnapped, until we got down here to the station." He shook his head again, in case Jake missed it the first time, then patted at his cigarettes. The pack was empty. Bingham looked up. "You got a smoke?"

"I don't smoke." Tomkin told him he had Marlboro Lights, and Bingham called him My man.

Jake took his time. He knew what the man was doing. He was getting his story straight right here, saying it aloud to see how it sounded. Or how it would sound, later, when he was laying it on a judge. Jake waited until he got his cigarette burning—Bingham leaning over into Tomkin's lighter, taking a few puffs and then sitting back—before he said, "My name is Jake Phillips, I'm from upstairs."

"Upstairs?" Bingham seemed almost bemused. "What the hell is upstairs? Are you a boss, you mean? Jesus Christ, will *you* at least listen to me? All right. I had the best day of my life at the track, I go out and have a few drinks, somebody busts out my car window and steals my radio, my tapes, and my fucking cigarette lighter, and the next thing you know, I'm arrested for attempted arson. These jamokes here won't listen to reason. I swear to God, I should shut up right now, before you guys charge me with the crucifixion of Jesus." He said it, but Bingham didn't shut up.

Instead, he said, "Tell me, Mr. Detective Phillips from upstairs, what are you guys more interested in, finding criminals, or just closing out cases?" Bingham was half-smiling, as if he couldn't believe any of this.

Jake said softly, "Don't lie to us anymore, all right, Norman? We have witnesses who can place you at the scene, fingerprint evidence, we've got you cold. All that's left for you is a deal."

"Lie to you about what? You haven't asked me anything yet."

Jake asked, "What were you doing on Twenty-first and Wabash at two-ten this morning?" and touched a nerve; Bingham turned white. The cigarette fell out of his fingers and rolled away, and he couldn't bend down far enough to retrieve it. The single handcuff held him back. When he sat back up, he was breathing very hard, shaking his head now, but no longer in a kidding manner. Now, Bingham was in awe.

"That's it, fuck this, I ain't saying another word. Charge me, print me, take my picture, do whatever you got to do, but I am not saying one more word, not now, not ever, not to anyone, that's it."

"I understand, and that's your right. And when you're arraigned, the judge will be happy to appoint you a lawyer." Jake paused for effect, then said, "Who'll tell you where you stand, and he won't lie to you, Norman, he'll tell it like it is. He'll advise you to talk to us, to make a deal. Only by then, we might have made a different deal with whoever it was paid you to kill Allan Beck; by the time you come to your senses, it might be too late for you. We've got your prints all over Rolodex cards that were stolen from the scene of a homicide. We'll get your prints from the scene, too, you know we will. And where'd you get the five grand? You find it in a desk drawer there? Or was it a down payment on the hit?" Bingham was looking at the wall, his face stone-still. His cheeks were trembling. Jake wondered if he were about to start crying.

He took one more shot.

Jake said, "Your lawyer'll tell you your only way out. Plead, but by then we won't let you, 'cause we'll have you dead to rights. A cop's dead, Norman, don't you understand that? We're doing you a favor here, giving you one chance to save your own ass. This is a capital offense we're looking at, death by lethal injection." Jake lowered his voice. He said, "We know you didn't realize there'd be a cop there, Norman." Jake took his foot off the chair, took one step in the tiny room and was standing in front of Tomkin. He made a motion with his hand, and Tomkin handed him his cigarettes and lighter. Jake walked back to Bingham and put them down on the table in front of him.

"Go ahead, light up, you won't be smoking for a while. There's no smoking in the County now, and it'll take, what, a year or two at least, for your case to come to trial."

He watched Bingham light a cigarette, saw how badly the man's hands were shaking. He may still have a chance with the man. He held the cigarette in his free hand this time. He closed his eyes, tight.

Jake said, "And we know you didn't do it out of spite, out of anger or meanness. Somebody paid you for that hit, Norman, set you up for the fall, too. Why cover for him now? Why let *him* off the hook? Or her. If it was a woman, Beck's ex-wife, don't let chivalry stand in your way. A vindictive female can use you bad, Norman, as bad as any man. You can cop a plea right here, right now—and I'll bet the state's attorney will back me up on this, I give you my word as a man. You tell me who paid you to kill Allan Beck, and I'll get you immunity from prosecution." Jake stopped, and waited. He could see the man was thinking hard. Bingham's brow was knitted, his eyes still shut tight. He was jiggling his feet up and down. At last Bingham opened his eyes and spoke.

"I want to cop, all right, to the attempted arson. That's where I was at two-ten, setting that up."

"What arson would that be?" Billings said, as if he were interested. He ignored his partner's surprised grunt.

"The O'Conners' house, I did it, I was there at that time, I want to make a statement. Get me a tape recorder, a piece of paper to write it down on, whatever you use, get it. I'm confessing."

"I don't know what the hell you're talking about. And if I did, if there had been an attempted arson? Well, the officers who were trying to serve a certain warrant at that address would be prepared to state in court that the crime occurred before midnight. It had to, as they were at the residence at a little after one. The house was already filled up with natural gas by then."

"Oh, this is bullshit, this is so much bullshit."

"Talk to me, Norman," Jake said, in close, and Bingham slapped the table hard with the palm of his free hand, sending ashes everywhere.

"Get me a fucking lawyer, right *now!* I ain't saying another goddamn word, I mean it."

Jake believed him. He shrugged, he'd won them and lost them before. And they still had a case, a good one, against this guy. There were a few things niggling at him, but they could be thought about later. "You want me to take him upstairs, or do you want to process him down here?"

Both Criminal Investigations detectives seemed stunned by the remark; they would have been expecting Jake to take full credit for the pinch himself. Billings recovered first. "Man killed a po-lice-man?" Billings put ghetto slang into his tone. "You bet your ass we want him down here. Shit, we broke the case, didn't we? And I got on my best red T-shirt, show up pretty on the television news." Jake smiled, wished them luck, and walked out of the room to go beep the captain and tell him what had happened.

HE DIDN'T HAVE to beep him. The captain was in his office. Talking to Jake's immediate superior, Lieutenant Brian Francis. Brian wasn't backing down from the captain, either, he was in the man's face, waving away the cigarette smoke while the captain glared from his side of the desk and used his cigarette as a pointer, making his case as he shouted back at Brian. The room was busy now, with phones ringing and the day-shift cops hurrying in or out, talking on the phones, or just looking over the night reports, at things they'd have to follow up on. Jake went to his desk and waited.

After a minute, Brian stormed out of the room, and came right over to Jake, in a hurry and mad. Other detectives had noticed, and had stopped what they were doing to watch. Brian Francis had a rare case of the ass, and they knew such states didn't come to him easy or often. They wanted to know what had caused it.

Brian said, "Let me tell you something, Jake. I don't care *who*—"

"Brian, don't say it!" Jake held up his hand. He stood up. "I've heard my father's name mentioned three or four times since yesterday afternoon." Brian was looking at him, shocked into silence by

Jake's impertinence. "I've busted my ass for you, and you know it. Whatever I've gotten around here, I've earned. I haven't asked for any special favors, and everybody else in this department likes to mention my father a lot more than I do. Don't bring him up, Brian, I mean it."

"—or what." Brian was his calm self now, thoughtful, watching Jake closely.

"Or I'll have to ask for a transfer out of the best job I ever had." Brian nodded, liking the answer.

"You could have said, away from the best *boss* you've ever had." Jake noticed that the other detectives had gone back to work. He felt relief. Brian sat down on the edge of Jake's desk, motioned for Jake to sit down. He did. When Brian spoke, his tone was low; it didn't carry past Jake's desk.

"What are all these private meetings with the captain about, Jake."

"Brian, he called me into his office yesterday, I didn't go to him. And he called me at home this morning, beeped me, woke me up. I haven't approached him personally since last year, and I was new then, I didn't know any better, I hadn't met anybody except Moore."

"Welcome to Homicide," Brian said sarcastically, then paused. He nodded. "So you're not gonna tell me?"

"Brian, it's got nothing to do with the squad, or anybody's performance."

"Personal problem?"

Jake paused. "Not mine."

"The captain's an administrator. You're supposed to report to me."

"I wasn't reporting to him, Brian, and I wouldn't do it, either. I think you know that."

"All right." Brian seemed himself now, resigned that Jake was standing up and wasn't going to tell him what he was doing with the captain. "But if you're lying to me . . ."

"I'm not." Jake's voice was ice, his expression tense.

"I know, I know," Brian said, defusing Jake's anger, "you close the cases, you've earned it all on your own, blah, blah, blah. So, tell me, what have you done for me lately?"

"Not much, I guess." Jake paused, watching Brian watch him, with some humor in his expression; he suspected something good was coming, but he couldn't know how good it was. "I just spent the last hour and a half solving Roosevelt's murder."

"You *what?!*"

"*PHILLIPS!*" The captain was standing outside his door, shouting. "Get your ass in here." He looked at Brian Francis. "If that's all right with you, that is. Can I speak with one of the men under my command, Lieutenant?"

Jake rose, heard Brian talking from behind him as he walked to the captain's office. "You know I was right, Merlin, you're as big on the chain of command stuff as anyone." Brian's tone was conciliatory. He was a smart, savvy cop, a man who tried to use reason rather than intimidation to his advantage. Then Jake was at the door, and the captain stepped inside. He closed the door so hard that the glass in the top half shook.

"Sit down."

"Captain—"

"Sit your ass down." The captain sat down himself. When he spoke again, his voice was low and a little apologetic. "Nobody's putting you in the middle of anything, nobody's gonna accuse you of anything. Not as long as I'm in charge of this squad. So, did you find Mondo, or what?"

Jake told him what had happened in the last two hours. The captain's expression grew brighter and brighter as Jake spoke. The captain had smoked three cigarettes by the time Jake was done, and he hadn't interrupted once. When Jake sat back, the captain took his turn.

"He turned silent when you mentioned Twenty-first and Wabash, eh? That's it, that's it right there; the news hadn't even hit the news radio stations at the time he'd got picked up. He knows we've got him, hell, the Rolodex cards are as good as a confession. It's closed."

"Captain, wait a second. He's being held for *questioning.* A lot of this still bugs me, sir. It doesn't make any sense."

"Yeah?" The captain said it tentatively. He didn't care what was bugging Jake.

Jake hurriedly said, "The cuff link, for one. And the weapon wasn't found, though they haven't searched his apartment yet, or even his car, for that matter. And why were his prints all over a lighter in a house on the East Side? He could have had his car broken into, and someone stole his lighter, then used it in the arson, but who needs a lighter that bad? They're seventy-nine cents at White Hen. I mean, is this guy a one-man crime wave? You ever heard of an arsonist/hit man before?"

"I've heard of people who'll do anything for money, I've heard of that. And don't forget, I'm not on the street, but I'm still a cop, Phillips. Now that it's their case, not ours, we're out of it, but I can still call down there to Criminal Investigations, make a few suggestions. Have them check whatever body of water this Bingham drives past to go home, the weapon'll likely still be laying on the silt. There's a few other things I can do; I want to think about them first."

"Captain, come on, this isn't closed yet." Royal ignored him.

"You go home and get some rest, Phillips, I already squared it away with Lieutenant Francis. You got Tuesday and Wednesday off, so we won't see you back here until Thursday. By then, your conscience should have had time to calm down."

"Captain?"

"Don't say it, Phillips." The captain held his hand up, warningly.

Jake said it anyway. "Captain, what about Mondo's cuff link?"

"I don't know what you're talking about, what cuff link? I asked you that question twice now. Mondo's off the hook, and a man's in custody, on *evidence,* Phillips, he's not some warm body we snatched off the street, you lucked into him."

"Captain—"

"He could have grabbed it from outside in the street after the problem at the Hilton. What is that, half a mile, less than that, from the scene? Mondo's clothes were torn apart, he'd thrown a bunch of punches, the cuff link—and I'm not saying there is one—could have fallen off anywhere, and this Bingham grabbed it and planted it on Beck to throw us off the scent. Now that's all I'm gonna say about it, get out of here, go home. I got a double homicide to put to bed."

"Yes sir."

Jake got up, wondering where he should go next. Home . . . or to Brian Francis, give it all to him and see what he thought about it. Tell him about the cuff link, too. Jake didn't want to be a party to the suppression of evidence; the captain had to know that much about him.

But he'd given the captain his word, earlier. The man had trusted him. And he hadn't said anything, but it was clearly understood between them: Jake's clearing Mondo so fast meant that the captain owed him.

Owsies. The coin of the realm. Jake was collecting them this morning, big-time.

He hoped that collecting them wasn't going to get a murder suspect tied down to a gurney in the execution room at Pontiac.

He walked out of the captain's door, paused and looked over at his boss, Brian, who had a phone stuck between his shoulder and ear and was looking over at Jake with an astonished, wide-eyed expression. Jake raised his eyebrows and pointed a finger into the middle of his chest—You want me?—but Brian was just looking, didn't want to talk to him. He shook his head and waved Jake away with an expression that told him there were no hard feelings. Jake would bet his pension that Brian was on the phone with somebody from the Criminal Investigations Division.

Jake walked out of the squad room, then turned around. He went back to his desk and picked up the open telephone book, saw what page he'd been on, where he'd stopped. He closed the book and left it on his desk, nodded at Brian, and left.

He didn't go home. He instead went downstairs again, where the Criminal Investigations squad room was nearly empty. Everyone was out working or else out in front of the building, posing for the TV cameras and talking up their quick work in finding the policeman's killer. The few people who were there didn't pay Jake any special attention when he sat down at Tomkin's desk. He searched through Tomkin's drawers until he found the man's Yellow Pages, then opened the book up to the proper page, ran his finger down the margin until he came to the last motel he'd checked. Jake picked up Tomkin's phone and punched in yet another number.

LAURA KNOCKED TENTATIVELY on the door to Diana's loft, feeling nervous. The harshness of morning sunshine had given her a different perspective on things. She wasn't so sure anymore that she wanted to go ahead with this Laura's Love Line deal. The door

opened, and Diana was standing there, a cordless telephone handset in one hand and the doorknob in the other. She whispered "I'm
on hold," then let go of the door and waved Laura inside. She
walked back over to her little low-slung couch and sat down, patting the seat for Laura to come join her.

Diana put her feet atop a coffee table, drummed her fingers on the
arm of the sofa, waiting impatiently for whoever was supposed to
pick up. Laura saw that there were several sheets of lined paper on
the table, with numbers written all over them. Next to the paper was
a stack of 3 X 5 index cards that she had stolen from Al's Rolodex.
Laura knew where'd they come from, even though Diana had
stripped them of their glare-proof blue plastic covers.

At the far end of the loft—which was twice the size of Laura's—a
slender, wiry black man was on his hands and knees, running thin
gray wire along the baseboard. He had on a short-sleeve green work
shirt and matching pants, and a green baseball cap with the brim
turned backwards. Already, at ten-fifteen, the back of the shirt was
stained with sweat. He looked up quickly and nodded once at
Laura, and she waved a hand at him, not wanting to speak on the
chance that Diana's connection might be made. The man was back
at work before Laura lowered her hand.

It was a relief to be in Diana's loft. It was comfortable in here,
quite cool. Diana had two air conditioners hung in opposite windows, which were now quietly humming away. Laura looked at the
man, slightly confused, but she was aware enough to know that she
really didn't want any explanations as to why the man was sweating
so heavily.

Instead she joined Diana on the couch, as Diana suddenly leaned
forward and lost all evidence of impatience as she spoke in a low,
throaty voice.

"Mr. J. B. Tucker? This is Diana, from ABI." Diana stopped short,
then waved a hand in the air. "No, no sir, it's nothing like that, I as-
sure you. I didn't tell your secretary who it was for a different reason." Diana listened again, and leaned back. "Mmmmm. You know I
love it when you talk like that. I've *missed* you so . . ." She turned
her head, and winked at Laura. "The reason I called, J.B., is to tell
you that ABI has been overcharging you. And, the truth is, you can
do a lot better with a different service, a new one called Laura's
Love Line. I know, J.B., *nobody's* heard of it yet, it's brand-new.
That's right, in fact, you're the first man we're recruiting, and for

you, J.B., for a limited time, it's only one dollar per minute." Diana paused, and held the phone away from her ear. Laura could hear a man's voice, exclaiming happily on the other end. Diana put the phone back to her ear and said, "You have a pen in your hand, I hope—rather than something more interesting?" She leaned forward and picked up one of the sheets of paper, squinted down at it. She read off a number.

"That's Laura's direct Love Line, and," she read off another one, "that's *my* direct line. For prepayment only. We accept cash, check, or money order, which can be sent to, you ready? Forty-seven West Polk Street, apartment one-zero-zero-three-zero-zero." She listened as the man repeated the address and numbers. Diana said, "J.B.? Tell all your friends; they're not going to believe what we can do for them. As for you, I can't *wait* to get my lips on you again, baby. Oh, don't you worry, J.B. We know ex*actly* what you want." She listened again. "Today, at noon? That's fine. Honey, don't worry about it. I'll trust you for the money—no—I said don't you worry about it. Just send it to the address I gave you sometime today. You want me, or Laura herself, to sort of break her in?" She nudged Laura in the ribs. Laura waved her hand in the air and shook her head insistently. Diana's voice was so convincing. "Oh, J.B., I can't wait, honey, I just can't wait for noon." Diana hung up without another word. She turned to Laura.

"How about it? I've been on the phone since nine this morning, soon as I got back from the Dearborn Station. I been calling the men who like to get their calls at work, gives them an extra kick. They can pretend they're bending some uppity female supervisor over the conference table, showing her who's really the boss. Some woman who got the promotion the man believes *he* deserved. You ever get one of those?"

Laura was acutely aware of the man laying down the telephone wire. "I only worked two and a half nights."

"Oh, honey, we're gonna get rich. Every single one of these males believes they're the first one I called." Diana said, "So, Bing never did show up?"

"I didn't hear him if he did. The wine must have gotten to me, I passed right out after you left."

"Good thing, too; you needed the rest, the hours you been keeping." Diana said, "I stole your phone bill off the counter last night; it's been paid. And don't say a damn word about it, it's been done.

That's your private line, nobody can get the number." She said, "Starting at eleven, we've both got voice mail, and you've got to record your personal message pretty soon. Two different three-one-two area code numbers, one for each of us. We have the calls forwarded directly from voice mail to our phone numbers, yours or mine, either number, either one of us can do it from either line, if we want. We have our own pin numbers for access, codes to turn Call Forwarding on and off. It cost more, but it's worth it, if one of us is busy or out. We screen the calls if we want to, even. We don't have to call anyone back we don't feel like." Diana was acting like a little kid.

"Oh, by the way, say hello to Milton. He's been here since six A.M., God bless his useless heart. He's gonna take care of the extra four phone lines, run them free of charge. He's even hooking us up with MCI, undercover, so we never have to pay another long-distance phone bill."

"Hello, Milton," Laura said, and the man with the phone wire looked up and nodded again before returning hurriedly to his work.

"Milton's shy, he don't say much around strangers." Diana was aggressive now, making fun of the man, Laura could tell. What was wrong with her? This man was giving them hundreds of dollars' worth of work for free—not to mention free long-distance service. "But he can't shut his mouth up when I get his sorry ass alone." Laura looked at Diana, worried, but Diana waved her off.

"Milton paid to get my Adam's apple shaved. Helped out with the collagen and the breast implants, too. Didn't you, little Milton?"

"Yes, mistress," Milton said, and Laura understood. She sat back, shocked. Diana was into more than Laura could ever imagine. She hoped she wasn't getting the both of them into more than they could handle.

"I've had a busy morning," Diana said. "Was over at the all-night Walgreen's up at Michigan, got two more phones, two headsets, one for each of us, so we don't have to hold phones to our ears all the time. Got a box over at Dearborn Station, what it is is a P.O. Box that's a real street address, you hear me give it out to J.B? Thirty a month. That's only six hours' work per year. Not too bad, eh? And it's a legitimate tax deduction." Laura didn't think she'd ever seen Diana so happy, so excited and wired. The woman was *alive*.

"Called half the men who take calls at their business lines, and some of those who live alone and don't want to pretend that we can't find out who they are. While I was at Dearborn Station I had Otis—he runs the Mail Boxes, Etc. there—fax ads to the *Reader, New City,* and the *Sun-Times* newspapers. Cost twice as much as putting it in writing and mailing it in, but we have to get into this week's issues. We can get into tomorrow's *Sun-Times,* Wednesday's *New City,* and Thursday's *Reader.* Put it all on the MasterCard; by the time the bill comes due, we'll have enough to pay it all off without interest charges."

"Diana?" Laura wanted to ask her if she'd taken something to help her stay up all night. She was jittery, couldn't seem to calm down or be quiet.

"You think I'm high, don't you?" Diana was grinning at her. She reached out impulsively and pulled Laura to her, hugged her to her chest. "I'm just happy, sweety, I can't remember the last time I was this happy." Diana let Laura go, then smiled at her, and raised her voice. "Have *you* ever seen me this happy, Milton?"

The man stopped working, giving it serious thought. "Well, there was that time in Cozumel when—"

"*Shut* up, Milton," Diana said, and Milton immediately did so, lowered his head, and went back to work. Diana patted Laura's leg. "We're gonna make it this time, honey. I won't be a half-and-half much longer. And you won't have to worry about pigs like Bing not coming through for you. A month from now, there'll be dozens of men—*hundreds*—who'll do anything you want them to do, the second you give them the word." She handed Laura one of the sheets of paper. She used the tip of her pen to point each separate item out to Laura as she explained what it was.

"This is the address of our box, where the men can send the money. On top of that is the voice mail number, the pin number and access code, and instructions on how to activate the Call Forwarding to your home phone number. You can Call Forward one line from your home down here, or both of them, if you want; Milton's taking care of that. I can't believe it," Diana's tone suddenly softened, she was looking into Laura's eyes, her voice held a tone of wonder. "I just can't believe we're in business for ourselves." She shook her head. When she spoke now, she was her bubbly, manic self again.

"I already wrote down what I want you to say on voice mail—you ready for this? Tell me what you think." Diana lowered her voice, made it husky and seductive. "You've called Laura's Love Line, where we *al*ways know what you want." She smiled, seeking approval, and Laura told her that sounded fine. Diana said, "Then you give the prices, tell the mark to leave a message and number. Laura, honey, believe me, we'll have them eating out of our hands."

Laura looked at her, and forced a nervous smile.

"I'm ready to go upstairs now, Miss Laura, if you don't mind. I can lay the lines up there, be out of your way in about an hour."

"Why, thank you, Milton," Laura said, and smiled, and was surprised at the tears that sprung into his brown eyes. She felt her heart sinking, wondering how long it had been since someone had spoken to him with respect. And wondered again if perhaps Diana might be getting them in way, way over their heads. She didn't know if she was ready for this.

But now didn't seemed to be the proper time to burst Diana's bubble.

So she said, "Come on. Let's go upstairs."

"Don't forget your answering machine," Diana reminded her, pointing at one of the Walgreen's bags next to Laura's side of the couch. Diana was already punching in another number before Laura and Milton got out the door.

IT HAD BEEN announced as an interdepartmental joint operation, because the public would fall for that, and would not have any idea how much bad blood there really was between various divisions within the Chicago Police Department. They wouldn't know how jealously high-profile, media-involved cases were guarded, how hard positions of stature were fought for when the press got ahold of a big one. The public was aware of the ongoing animosity between the department and the FBI—television had let them in on that poorly kept secret—but what they didn't know was that the department was hardly the smoothly running, intercooperative machine they imagined it to be, everybody working toward one goal, under one boss.

The Chicago Police Department, as is every big-city department, is in fact one huge bureaucracy. And, like all bureaucracies, there is intense insecurity, particularly at higher levels, where performance or lack of it has to be explained away to superiors. Who held the purse strings. And made promotions. Or withheld those same promotions.

So it was only within the department itself that there was amazement over what Jake had done. Homicide bulls just don't *do* such things, give away solid pinches to general run-of-the-mill detectives. Jake sat in Tomkin's chair, while Tomkin himself—just back from his first French-kissing date with all the local media—stood next to it, glad to give it up to the man who had made him a star. Jake had made him a local hero; it was the least he could do in return. Jake was talking to his new best friend, Detective Lionel Billings, just talking out loud more than anything, reading over the inventory reports of what had been found on the persons of the two dead men, the cop and the sex-line operator.

"Your captain called down. I don't remember him ever offering us assistance before."

Jake looked up from his reading. "It was his officer who was killed. He didn't care who got the credit." Jake said it, knowing better. Billings's look told him that he wasn't bullshitting him, either. Tomkin might believe him. But Tomkin didn't count. Jake knew without doubt that by this time tomorrow morning Jake Phillips would be a Chicago Police Department legend. As his father had been before him. Billings and Jake had done the work, but it would be Tomkin who would spread the word, who would tell everybody what had *really* happened. He was already anxious to give anyone who would listen the insider scoop. Jake was made and he knew it.

But he had to get rid of certain doubts in his mind, or he would unmake himself, without hesitation or deliberation. His mind was made up about that. It was the only way he could justify setting Norman Bingham, Jr., up. He would have to prove the man's guilt beyond a shadow of a doubt—at least in his own mind—before he'd be able to rationalize away what he'd done.

"You guys get anything out of Bingham after I left?"

"Had to lock him up for his own good. Guys downstairs found out we had the cop killer, they wanted to come up and 'question' him themselves."

"He get hurt?"

"We've got forty bosses standing in line waiting to interview this guy, get the details from him, Jake. They all think they're Columbo, three minutes with them, he'll cop. Won't be any small-time investigators like us near him now. He's gonna fry, and the poor boy just doesn't know it yet."

"I asked if he got hurt."

"Relax, would you? He didn't get hurt. Not much. He's in lockup, waiting for legal appointment. They probably made him king of the place by now."

"Or queen," Tomkin interjected, smirking.

"No, not that guy," Jake said. "He'll be king. They think he killed a cop."

Billings looked up when Jake said the word "they."

"Besides, he's too big to get into a fistfight with, unless he shows himself to be chicken, and judging from the scars on his face and hands, I don't think he's afraid to fight." He looked briefly at Tomkin. "You have any idea how many guys Roosevelt railroaded? Planted drugs on? No, Bingham'll make out all right in there. It's in court where he'll have his problem. If we get that far."

"Get that far? What are you talking about? We got him dead to rights, the guy's dead meat." That was what Jake was afraid of, but he kept his doubts to himself.

He looked back down at the inventory report, then said, "What's this about a single piece of notebook paper, with numbers written on it?"

"I can find out."

Tomkin whispered, "Speaking of railroading . . . Choo, choooo."

"Don't you *ever* say anything like that again." Jake spat the words out sharply. Billings was staring at his partner. He asked him if he had a sudden desire to wind up with Bingham as his next-door neighbor, 'cause that's what would happen if the truth ever got out.

Jake had to sit and think about that one. He had never taken it that far, hadn't looked beyond the immediate results of the arrest, or at the other implications, what could happen to him, to his career and to his family. A year ago, if you'd told him he'd soon be doing the things he'd done today, he'd have looked you in the eye and worked up all his self-righteous indignation when he told you you were a liar.

And now here he was, setting people up. Telling honest police officers how to go about lying in order to entrap a suspect.

Yeah, okay, but not any innocent people, just a guy who had it coming. And there was evidence against him. He *had* been in the loft, his prints were all over the place, on the door, the wall molding, the smooth plastic surface of Al Beck's Rolodex cover. The report was right there in front of him. It wasn't as if he'd planted evidence on Norman Bingham. The fact was, with the sort of crooks they were cranking out today—bigger, smarter, and with better lawyers than ever before—you had to sometimes throw that book away, and come at them with both barrels blazing.

Didn't you?

But Jesus, weren't things moving too fast? What if the guy worked for Al Beck?

"Can I get that piece of paper?" he asked, and Billings turned to Tomkin.

"You want to make up for your stupidity? Go get Beck's belongings bag. The locker's open." Jake watched Tomkin walk away.

Jake said to Billings, "Do you trust that man? Is he going to put us in a jackpot?"

"He'll be fine. Now that he knows the consequences. Tomkin, he's a survivor."

"You getting tired?"

"I'm wide awake, wired to the gills." Billings yawned, though. "Won't be able to sleep, even if I was tired. Family be calling all through the day, forget a man works nights, 'cause they don't. Can't blame them. They'll have heard my name on the radio, or seen me on the TV news at noon. They'll be proud. I figure the bulk of the calls will come after four, though, after it hits all the local newscasts. Then I might even hear from my son."

"You got a son? How old is he?"

"Seventeen. Hear from him at Christmastime and on my birthday, usually. Or when he needs tickets to some sporting event and thinks his daddy's a broker." The pain in Billings's voice was difficult for Jake to listen to. He wished he'd never asked the question about the boy. "He's in a gang," Billings said. "I try to talk to him, try to set him right; he tells me the nation's his family, all the family he *really* got. Say it in a way where there's no point arguing."

"He'll come around."

"If he lives long enough."

Tomkin put the bag in front of him. "Here you go." Thank God.

Jake used his concentration on the contents of the bag to cover his embarrassment, shoving the wallet aside, the folded bills, the change, Beck's keys. He stopped when he got to the piece of notebook paper with a phone number written on it. Beck had doodled all around it, stars and arrows, lightning bolts, as if the number were something special, some sort of prize. Tomkin told them that it was time for him to hit it, and Jake told him good-bye, heard Billings merely grunt. Jake grabbed the phone, then put it back.

"What you want to bet Tomkin's heading to the nearest cop bar? You're gonna have a lot of friends after today, Detective Phillips."

Jake ignored that, and said, "If this is a suspect's phone number on this piece of paper, we don't want to scare him, do we? Tell him who I am, what I am."

"Suspect?" Billings was surprised again. "I thought we *had* the suspect." He shook his head, slowly. Then must have decided to go along for the ride. "Better way is, go through the phone company." Billings had his game face back on. As if Bingham wasn't in custody, as if they'd never discussed his personal torment. "This is a murder investigation, and I'm the detective who solved it." Billings smiled. "I can find out who owns that number in about five seconds."

"Would you?" Jake pushed the piece of paper toward Billings. Then said, "And could you turn your head away while you do it?" Billings didn't ask any questions, simply looked to the side and closed his eyes. As quietly as he could, Jake picked up Allan Beck's ring of keys and put them inside his jacket pocket. He grabbed a little phone book out of Beck's wallet, put it in his pocket.

"And if you can get me a couple of those crime scene stickers, I'd appreciate it, Lionel."

"Man, you do keep those wheels spinning, don't you?" Billings was dialing a number on the phone. He said, "You want some company?" And Jake told him he appreciated it, but Lionel should go and get some sleep, as he had a couple of stops to make before he took this thing any further.

HAD SHE DONE it right? Laura wasn't sure, it seemed so complicated. There was so much to do and learn: recording the voice mail
and answering-machine messages; turning the Call Forwarding on,
dear God, trying out the new lines, memorizing the number. Technology could be scary.

She picked up the old phone and dialed in her voice mail number, the number to Laura's Love Line. She was so excited when she
heard the new line ring that she actually clapped her hands. She
hung up, went over to the small table and looked down at the headset that was plugged into the answering machine, using a double
jack with the second line plugged into a regular-type phone. She'd
done it that way so she could unplug the headset easily when her
son was home. Voice mail would be turned on then, she wouldn't
need the machine. Or the double line: two separate phone lines
hooked into one number. That was strange. She could be talking
with one client on the phone while another call came in. Three bar-
bers, no waiting.

She had to remember to take out the message tape, too, the one
on the new answering machine, when Tommy was around. Or anyone else, for that matter. She was glad that these were unlisted numbers. Now Laura put the headset on, adjusted it to fit her head. She
fidgeted with the single black foam earpiece, twisting it, making the
set form to the curve of her ears.

The phone rang, and Laura jumped. Almost fearfully, she pressed
the headset button which activated the line.

"Hello?"

"Is this Laura?"

"Yes it is."

"My name's—Mike."

Laura waited until she was sure he was through speaking before
she said, "Hi Mike." There was an intense, uncomfortable silence.
Laura knew that men who called such lines didn't want the burden
of having to think for themselves. She flexed her fists, then loos-
ened them.

Laura closed her eyes and enticingly said, "Is this your first time calling my love line, Mike? Let me tell you a little bit about it."

There were three private security guards to get past, standing right by the front door, as if waiting for the siege. Another guard, an older man, sat at a desk in the middle of the hallway. Jake walked past the first three with his coat over his arm so he wouldn't have to explain his business to any four-buck-an-hour rent-a-cop. He pressed the elevator button, then carefully looked around. The security guard at the desk suddenly sat a little taller, then nodded to Jake, one cop to another. Jake nodded back, just as professionally. He saw the man start to rise, but the elevator doors opened, and Jake quickly ducked inside. He stuck his thumb into the Door Close button and held it there, pushed the button for the floor above Allan Beck's with his free hand. Jake got off on the tenth floor, looked around until he spotted the fire stairs, walked down them one flight, to Allan Beck's floor.

The floor looked exactly like the one right above it, with lots of tall, wide, glass windows that had Con-Tact paper covering most of it. Some of the doors had black lettering on the top half. He hadn't known that any office buildings still had so much *glass*. Of the six offices on the floor, only one of them didn't have something covering the glass. It stood empty; a communal conference room.

Beck, for his part, had expressed his individuality by having all his windows painted black. Plain white lettering spelled out his name on the office door. ALLAN BECK ATTORNEY AT LAW. A small card, protected by thick plastic and inserted into a cheap plastic cardholder next to the door, informed the caller of Beck's hours and gave out his office phone number. From the hallway Jake could hear a small but insistent chirping, coming from somewhere within Beck's office.

The door wasn't sealed. No crime had been committed here. Jake doubted that any police officer had even come by and looked around, seeing as how the case had already been officially closed. Jake fished out Beck's keys, and it took him fifteen seconds to find the right one and get himself inside.

He locked the door behind him and stood there, breathing stale, fetid air. The room was almost unbearably hot. Jake looked around. It was a sad place, and desperate. This office could be one of two things: the starting point for a young beginner working his way up and confident that he would get there, or the last refuge of a pitifully descending loser, a burnout.

Beck had been on his way down. It was easy to figure that out. He had been forty-three years old, if he were going to make it big, he would have done it before now. Other evidence of his decline was in abundance.

There were good mini-blinds on the windows, but they didn't quite match the frames; two sticks of solid leather furniture, the legs of which were now scratching the shit out of the uncarpeted wooden floor. The carved wooden desk was large, it took up half the room; a leather swivel chair was behind it. A Bang & Olufsen Copenhagen phone sat atop the desk, attached to a machine.

This had all been good stuff at one time, expensive furnishings that were out of place in this room. Beck would have seen himself as being out of place here, too. Jake could imagine what he told himself, how he justified being forced to move into this tiny space. How he'd move into Sears Tower once the phone-sex service took off in a big way.

There were no law books anywhere that Jake could see, no air conditioner in the windows.

There was a loud, ascending rumbling that turned into a gigantic roar as the El crashed by outside the window. Jake went to the window and separated the mini-blinds with his fingers. He looked down at the El tracks. He grabbed the drawstring and pulled the blinds open. The sunlight didn't do much to improve the quality or the mood of the room. There was a soft beep every ten seconds. It was coming from the answering machine. Jake walked over and hit Rewind, then Play, stood breathing the stagnant air through his mouth as the machine began to dispense a message for the late Allan Beck.

"Allan? Are you there? This is Mariah . . . Umm, I called the other number," the woman giggled. Jake didn't need his degree in criminology to figure out that Mariah'd been drinking. "And all I got was a sexy black chick telling me I'd called ABI, and could she serve me? I'll call your home number next, but in case I can't reach you there, I *do* want you to call me." Mariah gave out her phone number, then there was a pause, then the woman laughed. "Barry was *so* pissed! I blew him off, what does he know? I had to wait to go out until he finished watching the fucking preseason football game on cable. Anyway, call me, I want to discuss your job offer. You know what convinced me to take the job? The way you handled that creep on the phone. My present boss wouldn't have had the balls to do that. I know, because it's Barry." Mariah hung up. A female computerized "voice" replaced hers. "Two-thirty-eight-A.M.," the voice said, then the machine beeped, and fell silent.

Jake reached for the phone.

THERE WAS A very light knock on Laura's door, but it was loud enough to startle her. She got off the couch slowly, and moved quickly to the door. The man on the phone continued talking; he hadn't seemed to have heard anything.

It was Diana, grinning at her from the hallway, hunching her shoulders and making funny faces. Laura waved at her admonishingly, put a finger as close to the mouthpiece as she could get it and shook her head, then waved her into the loft. She went back and sat down. Diana closed and locked the door then joined her, now silent. They sat like that for what seemed to be forever, until the man on the other end said, "So? That's it! What do you think, Laura?"

Laura made herself sound convincing. "That might just be the most beautiful poem I've ever heard in my life." Diana stuck a finger down her throat. Laura had to close her eyes for a second.

"You mean it?" Laura grimaced. That was Bing's favorite line when he was fishing for her approval.

"I never say anything I don't mean." Diana covered her mouth with her hand, made as if she were laughing.

"Laura?"

"Yes, Harold?" She didn't care what he wanted to ask her, or how long it took. The clock was still ticking, and she was having fun, watching Diana's act.

"Will you . . ." She heard him half-sob, through the Walkman-like foam earpiece. Laura lowered her voice and spoke to him, trying to drag him out.

"Will I what, Harold? Please, you can always share your thoughts with me."

"Will you tell me you love me?" Harold's voice was a whisper. Laura made hers match it.

"Of course I'll tell you that, Harold, because it's true." Laura paused, then whispered, "I love you, Harold, my poet."

"Oh . . ." The single word was filled with ecstasy. Harold thanked her, softly. There was a soft click on the line. Laura turned off her headset.

" 'I love you, Harold,' " Diana mimicked. Her grin now split her face. "I knew you were a natural for this, I knew it all along."

"He's sweet, but it's somehow very sad."

"Yeah? You'd prefer some motherfucker telling you to eat his shit? I just got through with one of those; it's why I came up, I needed contact with someone human. Next time, he pays double." Diana sighed.

"Somebody put our number onto a computer bulletin board."

Diana rolled her eyes. "I heard. Over and over again, I heard."

"We're going to make it, you know it, Diana? I really think this is going to work. What have we been at it, five, six hours? I've taken a dozen calls, and it's a hot summer afternoon. Most of them are sweet, too, it's different than working for Al. But so many of them are sad."

"We'll get a million calls from first-timers, sure. The secret is in keeping most of them, to always keep them coming back. But don't you go romanticizing any of this, Laura. Men like Harold aren't sad, believe me. They're happy. They get someone they can bore to death for a bargain-basement dollar a minute. Get told they're loved. Come on, don't be a fool. Harold's probably got a wife's so sick of his poetry she'll kill him if he tries to read her one more lousy verse. He'll have half a dozen kids he ignores, claiming his creative, artistic temperament doesn't leave him time to be a daddy. It's the way he is. Now he'll smile all the rest of the day, trying to imagine what you look like. And a picture of his mama will form in his mind."

"Diana!"

"I mean it, and I'll bet you it's true. I been at this game a lot longer than you have. But you know what? I don't think I'm as good. I might have broke out laughing at little Harold's request for *love.*"

"I *did* laugh at one man. He told me he was wearing a rubber suit and had an enema nozzle up his ass. I couldn't help myself."

"He told me." Diana's voice held irony. "Who you think he called after you made fun of him? Guys like that, they're why we got the answering machines and the voice mail. To screen out the weirdos."

"You think that's weird? What's weird about it? It's funny, it gave me ideas, but it's not at all weird." Diana looked at her long enough to figure out that Laura was putting her on.

Laura took off the headphones, then harshly rubbed her ears. "My phone's been ringing since the second I hooked it up. I'll tell you what gets me, though, is the messages some of them leave when I'm on the second line. The rudeness, like they're talking to their whore. I'll tell you right now, the ones that don't have manners? I'm gonna hang right up on them."

"You wait for manners, honey, you'll starve." Diana paused. "You call Mrs. LaRitcha?"

"She'll be here at seven. I'll turn off the voice mail when Tommy gets home at five, and collect the messages when I come down to your place. Now, I can switch my voice mail line over to your second line, is that right?"

"To any line you want, Laura."

Laura stood up. "I have to return some of these calls." She walked Diana to the door, but didn't open it. She said, "We're taking all these calls without payment. I don't know about that, Diana."

"I do. I'll bet you every single one of them pays up, too."

"What if they feel guilty after they're done? What if they decide not to pay once they get their rocks off?"

"This ain't real life, honey." Diana put her hand on the knob, then unlocked the dead bolt. "This is *fantasy,* and you're Sandra Dee, Sun Kitten to their Moon Doggy. Remember, the Harolds of the world call us so they won't have to get involved with a real woman, so they can fall in love with their daydream. They'll pay up, and not because they're really nice guys, but because *they want to call again.* And that's the secret." Diana opened the door, stepped through it, turned, and pulled it most of the way shut before looking through the small wedge of opening.

"Always keep them coming back for more," Diana said, and closed the door behind her. Laura threw the dead bolt and thought about it, as she walked over to the answering machine to see who else had called.

JAKE SAT ON the side of the bed, looking down at the phone. His hair was still wet from his shower. The apartment was empty; Marsha must have gone to pick up Lynne from her mother's. Jake knew it was silly, but he didn't like it when Marsha spent a lot of time at her mother's Lake Forest estate. He liked the woman well enough—his mother-in-law was as kind to him as any multi-jillionaire could be expected to be—but he felt that Marsha might be tempted to make comparisons when she came home from a North Shore mansion and looked around their apartment. Yet Marsha had been raised in that environment, and didn't mind living here with Jake. At least she never said anything to him. Their first apartment in Roger's Park had been much smaller than this one. But both apartments could easily fit inside Marsha's mother's master bedroom. Christ.

Physically, Jake was feeling a lot better. The shower and a quick sandwich, shaving and brushing his teeth had helped. His mental and emotional states, however, were entirely different matters. Even if she'd been home, he wouldn't have told Marsha anything about the case; he would have been too ashamed of what he'd done to have her know anything about it. He'd called and told her that he wasn't in any trouble, that he was working the Roosevelt murder, but he'd told her nothing more. The thought of keeping it from Marsha bothered him, on some level, made him feel as if he were somehow betraying her. He'd always admired Tony Tulio, but now he was having second thoughts. From where he was sitting, the man all of a sudden didn't seem like much of a hero anymore. Everybody thought they had the cop killer, and they could well be correct. Under any other circumstances, Jake might think they did, too.

But he'd been there. He'd set the wheels spinning. He'd suggested to two detectives that they lie in order to make a stronger case.

What had Billings said? The detectives wanted a shot at the cop killer. Boy was going to fry and he just didn't know it yet. There was in fact very little physical evidence, but Bingham would now go down. It was a cop-killing case, and the judge would know that, would look out from his perch and see a thousand reporters hanging on his every word.

Jake had done that, put Bingham in that position. It was what would make him a star, a legend in police circles.

But the question that was niggling at Jake's mind was this: What if Norman Bingham, Jr., hadn't killed Beck and Roosevelt? It was dumb, and Jake knew it. What little evidence they had against the man was strong; certainly enough for a good prosecutor to get a conviction if Bingham wouldn't plead out and decided to go to trial. Bingham wasn't setting any major precedents, either—he wouldn't be the first hit man to deny that he'd pulled the trigger. But everyone was so anxious to close the case that they weren't looking beyond the one suspect. Jake could tell himself that he'd also suggested they hold the man for questioning, but he'd known as he'd said it that the brass would descend like vultures. Still, if there was someone else involved, his trail was growing colder with every second they spent on Bingham.

There were so many loose ends, so much that didn't make sense to Jake. Not just Mondo's cuff link, the missing weapon, or any other physical indications, but something far more esoteric, and something far more important, as far as Jake was concerned, because it was personal and entirely instinctive.

Jake didn't *believe,* deep down in his heart, that Bingham had pulled the trigger.

Jake had nailed his first potential killer when he'd been two weeks on patrol, and he thought about that now, how he'd *known* what was going on when nobody else—in a roomful of veteran cops—seemed to be paying attention.

A woman and her daughter had been killed by a drunken driver, and the rookie Jake and his Field Training Officer had been the first to respond to the scene. To this day Jake didn't know how he managed to keep from throwing up; he'd seen plenty of films before, but he'd never seen anything as bad as that car wreck. They'd caught the driver at the scene, and Jake had been given the assignment of processing him. The older cops didn't want any part of the drunken son of a bitch.

Jake had been trying to get information from the man, but it wasn't easy, because the drunk was acting the way drunks do; belligerent and surly one minute, while the next minute he'd be remorseful, that or full of self-pity. Jake had looked up and noticed a man standing just outside the low swinging wooden squad room doors. The man was well-dressed, holding a Bible tightly in both hands, looking around wildly before finally asking a question of a detective who'd happened to be passing by. The detective looked at the man, shrugged, then pointed over at Jake.

The man looked over, and his eyes locked with Jake's. Jake's prisoner, cuffed to the heavy desk, was complaining that he had to go to the bathroom. The man with the Bible was then stepping into the squad room, letting his thighs push the low-swinging doors open. Cops were milling all around, not giving him the time of day. Jake's prisoner was grabbing at Jake's sleeve, asking Jake didn't he hear him? Jesus Christ, he was gonna piss his pants, when Jake pulled away from him and was running toward the man with the Bible just as the man was opening it up, determined, not about to let Jake stop him.

Jake didn't even have time to pull out his service pistol. He ran full into the man, body-tackled him at the waist, dragged him to the ground as surprised cops scattered. The Bible went flying. It opened as it hit the floor, and a .38 snub-nosed pistol fell out of pages that had been cut down to size, to ensure a perfect fit.

The man with the Bible had been the victims' husband and father, come to seek his vengeance.

And no one had known it but Jake.

He'd played it down, and the other cops had let him, Jake putting it down to the hyper-vigilance involved with dealing with his first major felony arrest. Somehow he'd just known that the man was guilty. The look on his face wasn't the sort you'd see on a man used to carrying a Bible around all the time.

But what he'd done had earned him a promotion to a special detail plain clothes unit at the age of twenty-four; his father's connections hadn't hurt him any, either.

What it came down to was the fact that Jake had saved a drunken driver's life. But the husband had ended up serving more time than the killer, and for his part, Jake had never forgotten either lesson, and thought he had simply put them into practice, earlier that day.

His heroism and insight had put him on the fast track, but he'd thought about it over the years, and had come to a decision: If he was able to do it all over again, Jake would have let the mourning relative have his shot at his family's killer.

Up until just this moment, Jake had been certain that he would have. Even if he'd known up front and he couldn't plead ignorance after the driver had been shot down. What he was wondering now, as he sat on his bed, was if he could have lived with that. Judging by the way he was feeling now, he was by no means sure that he could.

There was something else niggling at him, besides the big, dumb ex-jock they had in custody. Besides the ex-jock whose head would soon be spinning when the department sent their best interrogators up against him and his sorrowful court-appointed lawyer, neither of whom would know what had hit them once the badgering began. The ex-jock who'd be signing a confession just to get them all off his ass.

If Norman Bingham, Jr., *hadn't* killed Beck and Roosevelt, then who had?

Jake got off the bed and got dressed quickly, in a hurry now to get out of the apartment before Marsha got home with the baby. He looked at his watch and cursed. Time was passing, and Marsha would want to leave in the early afternoon, because they turned the Sheridan Road southbound lanes down to a single lane at three o'-clock. He didn't think he was going to make it.

Marsha said, "So I'm at my mother's, and she's smoking one stinking cigarette after another, a filter tip, using a long gold holder, you know? It's kind of her trademark. She's holding the baby on her lap, tickling her, and I try not to worry about Lynne breathing in all that smoke, I mean, we live on Congress Parkway, one of the busiest streets in the whole city. What kind of disgusting fumes drift up to us from all that traffic? Anyway, my mother's telling me about this guy who'd been at her country club Saturday afternoon. You know how she talks, with that high-pitched nasal voice." There was no response, and Marsha looked up, wondering where he was in his mind—was she boring him? If she was, he'd never tell her; he was far too kind to do that. So she continued, trying to talk in her mother's voice as a sort of informative entertainment.

"He keeps going on about all the money he has, how much he's earned since he got out of college five years ago, what his father left him, where his house is, how many bedrooms it has, how many cars he drives. Jesus *Christ,* what a simpleton." Marsha reverted to her own voice again.

"So I'm sitting there listening to all this, nodding, waving smoke away from the baby's face, as she tells me that she finally has enough when they're in the grill later, having a drink, and this young guy's giving everyone stock market advice. She's appalled because he's handing it out to *stock brokers,* and to other guys who've been buying and selling stocks since before this kid was born. So Mom says, she goes, 'I finally walk over to him, he's standing right in the middle of the bar, with his audience bored to tears, and I say to him, Son, how much are you worth? I mean everything, not just liquid. He hems and haws, has to think about that one, how big a lie to tell. Finally he says to me, "I can't be sure, but it has to be three or four million by now." I say to him, let's just call it an even four million. By this time I'm reaching into my purse, and I grab a quarter. He looks down at me, he can't figure me out. He tells me, Okay, let's call it four million.' "

Marsha said, "Mom says to me, 'I hold the quarter up in front of his eyes, and shake it a couple of times so there's no doubt he knows what I'm doing. I tell him: Four million? I'll flip you for it.' " Marsha paused, and again there was no response. She didn't look over at him, in fact she closed her eyes. In her mother's voice she said, " 'He freaks out. He laughs, and I have to tell him I'm serious. He says, Everything? And I tell him yeah, the whole four million, and I'll add a hundred thousand 'cause in case you win you've got to do something else for me. I tell him, If you lose, it doesn't matter, because you won't be around here anymore, anyway. But if you win, you've got to promise that *you'll shut the fuck up about how much money you're worth.*' " Marsha opened her eyes. She said, "I can picture her saying it, just like that."

"Then what happened?" He responded? The Sphinx responded? Well, what do you know?

"I guess everyone in the bar cheered my mother on, went wild, applauding, and they knew she was serious, that she'd have to make some serious financial maneuvers to get it, but she'd never miss the four million dollars. Can you imagine that? She said that the kid fell apart, started shaking, even. She didn't say another word to him, just went back to her chair and sipped her drink. He left right away, and she doesn't think he'll be back anytime soon."

"Marsha?"

"Hmm?"

"Do you know how resentful you sounded when you were telling me that story? Do you think you might be jealous of your mother's money, her lifestyle? Do you miss living like that, with all the ostentation, the glitz and glitter?"

"None of the above. It's not that, really." She had to pause. "I don't think. I mean, I went away to school and chose to live like a pauper for six years, I didn't want anyone to know that my father owned more department stores than Marshall Field."

"But that was play-acting, wasn't it. This is real, this is your life now." There was no reproach in his voice, and she looked over to examine his expression. He didn't seem angry. Or in any way upset with her. Maybe he understood, maybe she *could* talk to him.

"All right. I don't want to sound like a snob, here. It's just that we live so far below our means. I mean *way* below what we can afford. I have to sneak in anything that isn't a necessity; I have to live within some stupid budget, we don't have to do that, it's dumb. There're no complaints about the new car every year, though, or the Christmas presents, are there?" Marsha snuck another look. His expression was unreadable. "I may sound like a spoiled brat, but who's really play-acting? I mean, come on, it's a fact, I have money."

"That your father left you."

"And my mother didn't get hers from slaving in the coal mines, either. Or my sister." Marsha was snapping, and she knew it. She had to calm down. She said, "We *all* got it from my father, and I don't resent it that he was rich, either." She sat forward and leaned toward him, wanting her words to have their desired effect. He raised his eyebrows at her sudden movement, but otherwise he sat quite still.

"I know what I do resent, though. I resent having to live like this, not being able to go back to college, not being able to hire a nanny to watch Lynne while I'm there."

"That was your decision, though, wasn't it? Nobody forced you into it."

"I know." Marsha sat back, defeated. Then had a thought. "But there's a certain manipulation there, isn't there? I mean, not right out in the open, but more subtle. When you love somebody, you don't want to ever hurt them, to bruise their pride." Marsha was on the verge of tears. She said, "And what would happen if I changed my mind? If I *did* hire a nanny and went back to school?" Marsha paused. She had to finish it, had to say the word she had never verbalized before. She said it all in a rush. "Would it cause us to get a divorce?"

"I know what *will* eventually cause a divorce."

"What's that?" She wasn't sure that she really wanted to know.

"If you keep holding all this in, if you don't tell Jake how you feel."

"But Doctor, I can't tell him, he's an Irish *cop*, for Christ's sake." The doctor smiled, and nodded his head officiously. He closed his notebook, and put it on the little table next to his chair.

"Next session, we have to discuss your telling your husband about our therapy." He smiled. "He's a cop, he'll find out sooner or later." Marsha got off the couch, pulled at her clothing to get the wrinkles out. "And Marsha?" She stopped, almost at the door. The doctor said, "You were absolutely right about resenting what he did last night. He had no right to withhold something that important from you."

"Doctor, I don't know what I'd do without these sessions right now."

"You'd be fine. My question is, do you think you might convince Jake to come in with you for a session?"

"Not in this life," Marsha said, then said, "See you Wednesday, Doctor."

ANNETTE MCKENZIE WAS frightened, in fact she was terrified. That was obvious to Jake as he walked past her and on into her apartment. She had stepped back in a hurry, although she hadn't invited him in. He turned to her, motioned for her to close the door.

She did. Then stood there in a very light, nearly see-through robe that fell to just past her knees, the woman holding it closed with both hands, at the neck and breast. Sleep was in her eyes, and her face was lined; her jet black hair was in total disarray. There was a shapely body enclosed by that imitation silk robe. She appeared to be in her mid-thirties, somewhere in there, but who knows? He probably looked a lot older than he was when he first got out of bed, himself.

Annette was the first to break the heavy silence. "Boy, you better really be a cop," she said. She wiped at her eye with one hand. He noticed that it was shaking.

"I showed you the badge, and besides, I'll bet you've been expecting me." He wanted her afraid, but not afraid that he was a home invader with a phony police badge. He wanted her certain that he was the law, and that he was about to come down on her, hard. Jake pulled out his wallet. The movement made her flinch. He flipped out his photo ID. "Here, take a look." She inched forward, peered down at the ID, then looked back up at Jake.

"You look familiar, do I know you from somewhere?"

"No."

She was looking at him oddly now, with the sort of expression on her face that told him she almost wished that he wasn't a real cop. A burglary or armed robbery would be a terrible thing, but she could replace whatever he robbed. A cop was a different matter. A cop could destroy her life.

He didn't go out of his way to disabuse her of the notion. He got right down to business without any more formalities.

"You took a call last night at work from a man named Allan Beck." Annette McKenzie's mouth dropped open wide; she visibly sagged. He hid his glee. He had her. He said, "You understand that selling legally privileged information is a violation of state and federal law? Do you have any idea how much trouble you're in?"

"Wait a minute, hoo boy, fuck this, calm down, Officer," she said. She staggered over to a couch and flopped down. She put bare feet up on the coffee table. He looked at her legs, then quickly looked away.

"Is your husband here?" She looked up quickly.

"He's working!"

He shrugged. "He'll find out soon enough."

He could see her thinking. He watched as her eyebrows knitted together, as she frowned down at her hands, as she brought one hand up to her mouth and began to worry a nail. She said, softly, "Am I under arrest?"

"No."

"All right." Annette McKenzie looked up at him, shaking her head. "I know why you're here." There was a tone of deep resignation in her voice. Resignation and regret.

"Do you."

"I heard about it on the radio when I got off work, you know, what happened to Al and the cop. I took three Darvons to get to sleep. I figured if they came, it would be the FBI."

"They could still get here."

"But you didn't say anything to them yet."

"No."

She looked up sadly. "Why not?" She nearly whimpered it, thinking she knew the answer. Then he understood, and was taken aback. He lost his sense of cool.

"Hold on, now, let's just wait a minute, goddamnit, Ms. McKenzie . . ."

"You work for Al Beck, right? You're one of his famous payroll cops?"

"No, I'm not. His Rolodex has been impounded; there are detectives going through it right now. Any police officers he's been paying off will be getting a call soon enough. And I'm not one of them."

She seemed puzzled. "Then what are you doing here?"

"Look, let me tell you something. I don't care about your personal relationship with Al Beck. And I won't tell your husband about it, either, it's none of my business." He could tell by the way she looked up at him that he'd hit a nerve. "All I care about is the name and address you gave to Beck last night."

"How do you know he called me?"

"Knock it off. I'm a cop. He called you, we both know it, and neither one of us has time to play games right now, Ms. McKenzie." She looked away, shaking her head, seeing her way out, and wondering if she could trust him. He said, "We know you took the call. Now what I want is the name of the man he called. The address, too, if you have it."

"And you couldn't get them from somebody over at Ameritech?"

He didn't answer that one. Instead, he said, "I won't tell your husband. He won't hear it from me."

Annette sat a little forward on the couch now. Her robe was open at the top. She had lost some of her sleepiness. He could tell what Al Beck saw in her.

She said, "You think this man killed him. But his name was on the radio, I don't remember it, but it sure wasn't the name of the man I gave Al."

"What was that name?"

"Can you wait a minute?" She got up and pulled the robe tight again, then began to walk out of the room. He began to follow her, then stopped himself. What if she was going to the bathroom?

She wouldn't be calling 911, she couldn't do that, she wouldn't cut her own throat. Unless she was tired of the game, of all the time waiting for the knock to come on the door. A thought struck him, hard. One he hadn't even considered in all the time since he'd seen Beck's body.

This woman loved him; somebody loved Allan Beck. How strange.

And then she was coming back, holding a small, cheap, steel filing box in her hands. Jake looked at her with a different eye now, knowing things about her, wondering about her. When she got within a couple feet of him she stopped, shyly looked down.

"Am I in any position to make a deal?" Her voice was small.

"No."

"Then take this," she held the box out to him. "Take the whole damn thing. It's a list of every number I've ever run down for Beck, the phone number, address, and names of the callers, too. I don't keep it at work for obvious reasons; I leave it here to make sure he pays. I usually only gave Al the number, 'cause the name and address cost more, and he was a cheapskate." She looked at him, stricken, having spoken ill of the dead. "It was a business thing, Officer. It had nothing to do with he and I. I charged him a flat fifty for a phone number, seventy-five for a number and name, and another twenty-five for the address. He rarely took more than the number."

"I see."

"Do you?" The woman looked around, forgetting about the robe, or at least giving the impression that she had as she waved a hand around the room. It was clear, though, that Annette slept in the nude.

"Look around you," Annette McKenzie said. "See what I've got to show for eleven years of marriage? See any baby pictures on the wall? Any bronzed fucking shoes? No, all you see are his goddamn bowling trophies. Come around at night and you'll see all the empty beer cans. Look around before you judge me, all right?"

"Ms. McKenzie, all I want is the card from last night, that's all."

"He didn't even pay me for it yet."

"Maybe it's in the mail, but I wouldn't suggest you cash a check from him, if it is."

She opened the steel box, and took out the first card. She handed it to him, and he looked down at it, compared it to the name and address that Billings had given him, and put it in his inside jacket pocket. Annette said, "You weren't kidding, were you, putting me on? I mean, you're not gonna arrest me now that you've gotten what you wanted?"

"Arrest you? No. I'm not going to arrest you." Jake looked around, wondering how to tell her what he'd really come here to say. Wondering if he even *should* say it. He had no proof, had no reason to terrify her more than he had.

Still, he had his suspicions, and this woman had a right to know.

He said, "Ms. McKenzie, the man we have in custody at the moment might not be the killer; he's being questioned right now, and that's all. If I got your address, and it wasn't that hard to do, then whoever actually killed Beck might be able to get it, too."

"My God." She was hanging onto the top of the robe for all she was worth now, walking backward until the back of her legs hit the couch. She let herself fall back into a sitting position.

"I don't want to frighten you, but—"

"Why would he want me, why would he want to kill me?"

Jake touched his sport coat pocket. "This isn't the name of the man in custody, Ms. McKenzie." Jake didn't tell her that it was indeed the same name as the one he'd gotten from Billings.

"Then you have to help me!" She was panic-stricken, staring up at him. Wanting Jake to protect her, to save her from harm. He'd seen that attitude before.

"There's no way we can guard you. I can't even take you into protective custody."

"What's that, jail?"

"It's a long shot, but you should know: The killer might be looking for you."

"See what you get? See what the fuck you *get*?" He heard her repeat it, strongly, as he walked toward the door. "See what the fuck you *get*?"

It was time for Jake to find Mondo.

DIANA LAY ACROSS her couch, looking idly up at the ceiling as the voice in her ear spoke what he probably thought were filthy words, Diana answering him in kind without even having to think about what she was saying; Diana speaking by rote, without having to formulate any specific response. She'd been there so many times before she could do it in her sleep.

But could Laura? Diana had been certain that she'd be perfect for this work, right up until the moment that Laura'd said she'd felt sorry for Harold the Poet. You could like them, you could be sensitive toward them, but there was no room for pity in this business, none at all.

And Laura might just be too well intuned to freaks like Harold the Poet, that was worrying Diana just now. Because she'd gotten two threatening phone calls herself, one right before she'd gone upstairs, and one right before this call, and she didn't know how Laura would act if the man had reached her line instead of Diana's.

She could hear the caller's passion escalating now, the guy about ready to shoot his load. "*Talk to me,*" he was whispering harshly, and Diana did, loudly, whisper-shouting into his ear. She heard him gasp, heard his breathing suddenly stop, and she kept talking until he gasped again, then he spoke in a washed-out whisper.

"Thanks, Diana." She heard him take a deep breath. "I'll put the envelope in the mail as soon as I leave work."

"Thank you, hon. Talk to you soon." Diana disconnected and had barely had time to shake her head and smile when her line rang again, and she flipped the headset back on. "Laura's Love Line, Diana speaking . . . Oh, hel-*lo* Wentworth, I'm *so* glad you called . . ."

Laura answered the phone on the second ring, and spoke into the tiny mouthpiece. "Laura's Love Line, this is Laura . . ."

"Yeah? Well, let me tell you something, Laura, you just stepped into a pile of shit."

"Oh, did I?" The man's voice was harsh, guttural. A tough guy was on the line, one who seemed to want her to walk around in his feces. She'd had more bizarre requests. "Ohhh, look, it's squishing through my toes!"

"No, you don't get it, honey. Just shut up a minute and listen. I already talked to the nigger."

"What?" Laura concentrated. What did this man want?

"You heard me. You're cutting into profits of people who don't like that to happen to them. Who don't let it happen, ever. You're playing fucking games with people who are very, very serious, do you understand?" Laura felt a tickle of fear rising. At the moment, she didn't trust her voice. Fortunately, he didn't wait for her to respond.

"You don't know what you're into, so we're gonna give you one chance, you dumb cunt. One chance, that's all anybody ever gets from us. Cut off the line, right now. Disconnect it, this is the only warning you're ever gonna get."

Laura forced herself to say, "Or what?"

"Or *what?* Jesus Christ, try and be nice to you fuckin' bitches . . . All right, you want to know 'or what?' Or else we'll run you down, find out where you live, then come over there and give you a double massterectomy with a razor blade, do you understand *that?*"

Laura could feel the pounding of her pulse behind her eyes. She was terrified, knowing now exactly who it was she was dealing with. The outfit. But she couldn't let this man know that she was afraid. Men such as this fed off fear, were nourished by it. She had to stand up to him.

Laura said, "I understand it's a federal law to communicate threats over a telephone wire, you son of a bitch."

"Hey—!"

"And if you want to talk to me or my partner, it's a dollar a minute, cash, check, or money order, motherfucker."

"You listen to me!"

It was getting easier. Maybe because it was only over the phone.

Laura said, "No problem. Me and the FCC. I'm taping this conversation, tough guy, you have anything else you want to say?"

There was a pause, then a click. Laura disconnected the line, sat back, and thought about what had just occurred, shaken. When the phone rang again, she tore the headphone off and threw it on the floor, stared down at it as if it were alive and about to bite her as she allowed the machine to pick up the call.

"Lady, do you have any idea how many calls we got like this today?" The homicide detective's voice sounded weary and bored. Not, however, angry.

Laura gave it another try. "Sir, this is an emergency. It really is. I need to talk to Detective Sergeant Alex Mondello, to Mondo. The papers didn't mention his nickname, did they?" The man didn't answer for a moment. Laura hoped she'd gotten through to him.

"Look, no offense, but *everybody* wants to talk to Mondo today, and I'd bet there's maybe around a hundred reporters in this city who know his nickname. He's on medical leave until he recovers from the shooting, and that's it. Now if you want to leave a name and number, I'll put it with the rest of his messages."

"I don't *want* to leave—" Laura forced herself to calm down. "This can't wait, he's ex*pec*ting this call. I'm not asking you where he is, or what his beeper number is. But he'll want to talk to me, today. All I'm asking is that you beep him and give him my message." Laura had to think fast to remember what little information Diana had given her. She lowered her voice, as if frightened that someone might hear her. "It has to do with Roman, with his death last year." The detective on the other end seemed interested now.

"Lenny Roman?"

"And Tulio."

"Tulio." She could hear him scrambling for paper now. "What did you say your name was?"

"It's—tell him it's Laura. Tell him we talked—" shit, would he remember? "—last night, outside the Hilton and Towers. Tell him we talked about his finishing his dinner—he'll understand." Laura hoped he would. "And this is an emergency, all right?"

"I'll see what I can do. Give me a number." Laura gave him her regular home number, rather than the number to the love line. The detective hung up. The phone rang under her hand. Laura, expecting Bing, and his excuses, answered curtly. "Yes."

"Honey, did that ignorant son of a bitch call you yet?" It was Diana. Her voice was low, and Laura saw through it; Diana was probing. Well, she'd let her probe.

"The one who's going to cut off my tits if I don't disconnect the number? Yes, I heard from him." She fought to maintain her cool, to act as if the call hadn't bothered her. "It was probably Al, for God's sake."

That stopped Diana. She said, "Uh, Laura?"

"Yes?"

"Are you watching the early news?"

"Are you kidding me? I've been on the phone nearly nonstop since eleven o'clock this morning."

Diana's voice turned cold, hard, and businesslike. "Listen to me, honey, this is important. You turn the voice mail on, Laura, right now. And leave the TV off. I'm on my way up." Diana hung up without any further explanation.

The tiny, bald, Jordanian man was having trouble explaining himself. He was flustered, angry, but too frightened of the law to articulate it very well, in a manner Jake could understand. Jake could only imagine what would have happened to the man back home if he dared to criticize one policeman to another.

"This man, he show my cousin his badge, he has the car outside, the obvious police one, with the green license plate numbers and the small antenna. My cousin, he was overjoyed. Finally, someone from the law comes here to stay, to help us!" The motel was on the near South Side, out of the Loop, but not at all far from where Beck and Roosevelt had died. Jake checked his watch, impatiently. It made the man so nervous that he spoke faster, reverting to his own native language. Jake held his hand up to stop the man, to calm him. The gesture had the opposite effect. The man shouted, "I have called and called and called with my complaints! The police, they do nothing! And now, at last, they come, but the man they send is drunk!"

"Sir, don't worry, I'm not here to cause you any more problems."

"We call the police every *night!* Someone wants to sell drugs in one of my rooms, someone else wants to bring in prostitutes. I cannot have this." The man was shaking his head. "I cannot have this in my place of business."

"So what did the policeman do?"

"Do? I have complaints coming in from all night! Perdeep, my cousin, he gave your officer the room for *free,* as long as he parked his car right there—" The man pointed out the back window, to-

ward the parking lot. Mondo's car wasn't in a regular parking space,
it was pulled over far to one side, where anyone driving in and out
would have to spot it, even if they could manage to get around it.
"—where everyone can see that yes, the police are here!"

"Sir?" The man didn't give Jake a chance to ask his question.

"Perdeep say, he say the officer, he go out, then come back, then
all night long, there are complaints. Many complaints, as to the man
shouting all night, screaming!" The motel owner shook his head. "I
cannot have this in my place of business."

"Tell me what room he's in and I'll get him out of here." Jake said
it all in a rush, before the man could continue with his tale of woe.

"Two-nineteen. Please, get him out of here."

Jake turned to leave then paused, turned back to the little man.
"Have there been any problems today? Or were they all last night?"
The motel owner appeared sheepish now, as if he were caught red-
handed.

"Sir, I have not very much business during the day. Except during
the lunch hour. My business is most all at night. But no, there have
been no complaints today. Please, you must understand. I cannot
have men screaming in the rooms as if they are dying. I am sorry,
but I cannot afford to lose all my customers." The man had to screw
up his courage in order to say his last words. "This policeman here,
he is very very bad. Very bad for my business."

Jake pounded on the door, again and again. He couldn't hear a television or radio, nothing, no noise from inside. He would have heard
it if there were any. The place was cheap, the walls thin. He put his
ear close to the filthy glass of the picture window, and listened. He
lifted his fist, pounded on the glass. Then again. At last, he heard
the squeaking of bedsprings.

"Mondo! It's me, Jake!" He shouted it so Mondo wouldn't shoot at
him through the window. Jake pounded on the glass again. "Mondo,
come on, wake up!" Jake's beeper went off, and he reached down to
shut it off. The door to the room opened. Mondo was in the doorway.

"Jesus Christ, what do you want?" Mondo said. He staggered back
into the room. Jake could smell the stench of the room all the way
out on the concrete balcony.

When had Jake seen him last, fourteen, fifteen hours ago? Already, Mondo looked like a derelict. He was still wearing what was

left of the bloody, torn tuxedo shirt. His wound had bled in the night; the large bandage covering his head was stained with blood, at the ear. Mondo said, "Fuck." And fell back onto the bed. He groaned as he bounced, twice.

Jake closed the door behind him. The room reeked with fetid breath, sweat, and the foulness of stale booze. There was an empty bottle of Pinch scotch on the floor, beside the bed. A large, red plastic ice bucket was beside the bottle. There were three cans of Coke inside the bucket. The pop was surrounded by small fragments of ice, floating in what had already melted. The bucket had overflowed onto a carpet so threadbare that Jake could see the light brown coloring of the wood underneath. God, it looked like plywood under there. Mondo reached a shaking hand into the bucket, pulled out one of the Cokes, and somehow managed to open it. It fizzed all over the badly stained sheets. Mondo poured the Coke down in one drink, then threw the can away from him. Mondo uttered a long, relieved, almost painful sigh, then burped. His eyes were watering so badly that Jake at first thought he was crying. Mondo swiped at them with the back of his hand.

"Have a good time?" Jake asked him.

"What are you doing here?" Mondo asked again.

Jake said, "Take a shower and get dressed. We'll talk then." He saw the look that Mondo was giving him. "It's important, Mondo. You might be in trouble."

DIANA LOOKED AROUND the loft for any signs of Laura's new occupation which she might have forgotten about. The new phone was turned off, the voice mail turned on. She'd taken both tapes out of the machine, just in case Mrs. LaRitcha got curious about the

new equipment and decided to listen in. She'd hidden Laura's
headset in the dresser in her bedroom. She'd have to come back up
here in less than an hour and wait for Mrs. LaRitcha, who didn't
have her own key. She'd offered to stay with Tommy until seven, but
even as upset as she was when Diana had told her about Bing,
Laura had exhibited the good sense to tell Diana to stick to the
phones, they needed the money. They could earn Mrs. LaRitcha's
babysitting fees in five minutes of work per hour. Laura had a good
business head on her shoulders.

Diana left the apartment and jiggled the door behind her, making
sure that it was locked. She walked down the steps toward her own
apartment, thinking about her friend Laura, hoping nothing she
would say or do would bring the cops calling around the lofts, just
when things were staring to look up. Dear God, not now.

The first thing the tall detective told Laura was that she didn't have
the right to visit Bing. Her husband was being detained for questioning, that's all. He hadn't been charged with anything yet, he
wasn't in the County, where visitation rights were liberally pro-
vided. The detective who told her this was a big man, as were most
of the men in the room. Laura was surprised to see how big most of
them were. She felt as if she were standing in the lobby of a hotel
where a visiting hockey team was checking in.

But she was in a detective squad room, and she knew it. There
were perhaps twenty desks in a room too small for them all. Pictures of unsmiling, mostly black male faces were Scotch-taped to
every wall. There were no other women in the room. But she
wouldn't be intimidated by their open stares, or their leering. To
hell with them. She had to speak to Bing.

The detective was smiling at her, trying to intrigue her, to beguile
her with his charm.

Laura didn't smile back. Instead, she said, "Fuck that, he's my
husband, and he's got rights, and you can't take them away from
him, no matter *who* you think he's killed." Behind her, she heard
snickering. Somebody made an off-color wisecrack. She didn't pay
any attention to it. The detective's smile had slipped; his arrogance
and anger had replaced his studied counterfeit charm. He opened
his mouth to speak, when there was a loud wolf whistle behind
them. Laura nodded.

"See? Even ignorant, lazy, doughnut-chomping, stupid-ass cops can figure out that I'm attractive. How'd'you think I'll play to the cameras? Go out there in tears, in front of all those reporters in the press room, and cry about how I can hear my husband screaming in pain right now from the torture."

"Lady, you don't want—"

"Don't you lady me, you Dirty Harry clown. My name's Mrs. Bingham. And I'll see you on the ten o'clock news." She turned to leave, and saw that a black man had come out of the only private office in the room. He was leaning against the door jamb. The sleeves of his white dress shirt were rolled up; she saw he was wearing a tie. Every other detective in the room was dressed in casual clothing.

This had to be the boss.

"There some problem?" The man spoke slowly, in a low, calm voice. He was tapping his lower lip with a pen. He was eyeing her, but not in a sexual manner. He seemed to be studying her as if to see if she carried any weight she could one way or another use to squash him.

The detective spoke up quickly. "No, Lieutenant, I think it's all under control." Laura shot him a withering glare.

"My name's Mrs. Laura Bingham. I understand you have my husband in custody. I was just telling Mr. It's-All-Under-Control here that if I don't get to see my husband, and I mean right this minute, then I'll have no other choice than to go to the press and tell anyone who'll listen that you're torturing him into a confession." The lieutenant looked at her, taking in what she was saying. His eyes slowly grew wider. He stared with undisguised hatred at the detective who'd been speaking to Laura, and the man looked away, with a smug look on his face. Laura looked at him and noticed that the detective was trying to hide a smile.

The lieutenant said to Laura, "Come into my office, if you would, please, Mrs. Bingham," and Laura tossed her head, throwing her hair back, glanced triumphantly at the first detective, and ignored the low chuckles and catcalls from the other detectives in the squad room as she walked past them all and on into the boss's office.

As soon as Mondo headed into the shower, Jake went back to the door and opened it wide, then walked back and sat down on the bed, picked up the nightstand phone. He dialed 9 for an outside line, then he dialed the number that was displayed on his beeper. It was an in-house department number, but he didn't recognize the extension. It wasn't Homicide, so neither Brian nor the captain was trying to get in touch with him.

It was Billings. They spoke for several minutes, and Jake was thanking him as Mondo came out of the bathroom, dripping water, a thin, soggy white towel barely wrapped around his waist. Another was slung over his shoulders. He had taken the bandage off his head, had washed and combed his hair. His ear was stitched, heavily. There was fresh blood oozing from the top, leaking from around the stitches. Mondo put the towel to his ear and held it there. "Who was that?" He looked over at the door. "Jesus, you're gonna air-condition the entire South Side."

"Leave it open, Mondo." Jake looked at Mondo's gun, lying next to the phone on the nightstand, dominating the thing. He gestured for Mondo to sit down in the single plastic chair, away from the bed. Mondo remained standing.

"What do you want, Jake? That hillbilly filed charges against me, didn't he?"

"Sit *down,* Mondo." Mondo sat. Jake looked at him as he would any suspect. There was no warmth in his stare.

"Come on, Jake, goddamnit, knock it off." Mondo's voice was weary. Jake was surprised at the man's muscle tone, the shape he was in at his age. Tight stomach muscles curved up into a strong chest; Mondo's shoulders were wide. Even without the gun, Mondo would give him trouble if he wanted to. "I was looking at people like that when you were in kindergarten, for Christ's sake." Mondo leaned his head back. It touched the wall. He quickly pulled it away, then winced. "At least hand me a Coke, would you?" Jake leaned over and grabbed one, without taking his eyes off Mondo. Mondo accepted it, popped the lid, and this time took it away from his lips after only drinking half of it, burped loudly, then raised it again and finished it. He raised his eyebrows at Jake.

"All right, kid, here's the deal. Tell me what you're here to tell me, or get the fuck out of my room, right now. I mean it."

"Al Beck got killed last night." Jake watched closely for any sign of recognition from Mondo at the mention of Beck's name. Mondo only looked puzzled.

"Who the hell's Al Beck?"

"He ran a phone-sex service from a place right down the street, almost on Cermak, at Twenty-first Street."

"So what? You woke me up for that?"

"Robert Roosevelt was with him." It took Mondo a couple of seconds to understand what Jake had said. Then, there was no mistaking his reaction; Mondo was either shocked to the core, or he had missed his calling and should have been an actor. Jake said, "Roosevelt was providing private security for the guy, for Al Beck."

"No shit . . ." There was wonder in Mondo's tone. Cop killings, in his world, were supposed to be unacceptable occurrences, no matter *who* the cop was, or how badly he'd behaved in his career. "Jeez . . ." He looked hard at Jake. "They get the shooter?"

"How do you know he was shot?"

"Oh, knock it off, for God's sake. Nobody was taking out Roosevelt with his hands, or a knife—" Mondo stopped speaking, and his expression changed, he grew suspicious. Then angry. "Is anyone accusing me of . . . ?"

"It'll go a lot easier if you talk to me first. Where were you at two o'clock this morning, from two to say three."

"Right here, I never left the room."

"You brought the bottle with you?"

"No." Mondo wasn't angry anymore, he was trying to prove his innocence, and Jake knew it; it gave him an advantage. Mondo had been a cop long enough to know the ropes. If the brass thought he'd done it, he had to establish an alibi immediately, eliminate himself as a suspect before he ever got downtown, or else things might get out of hand, quickly.

He said, "I parked the car and checked in, but I was too drunk to drive anymore, and I knew it. I walked down the street, to the liquor store on . . ." Mondo paused.

"On what?"

Mondo looked up at him. For the first time, he seemed afraid.

"On State and Cermak."

"A block-and-a-half away from where Roosevelt and Beck were killed."

"I didn't do it, Jake." He paused again, not wanting to ask the next question, but having to. "Are they looking for me? Am I a suspect?"

"The captain found your cuff link at the scene."

Mondo grabbed for his wrist before he realized he was wrapped in a towel. "Jesus, he couldn't have! I wasn't there." Mondo's face was white, his eyes searching the room as he tried to remember where he'd placed his cuff links.

"It was from the set you were wearing last night, Mondo, take my word for it, I saw it. Diamond chips, spelling out your initials."

"Jake, quit playing games! Are they looking for me, goddamnit!"

Jake said it softly. "No."

Mondo seemed to collapse in the chair. He leaned forward, and had to get on his knees to be able to reach the ice bucket. He grabbed the last Coke, sat back down, and leaned forward, rubbing the Coke over the back of his neck. He suddenly looked up at Jake, his eyes narrowed. He stared at Jake with suspicion.

"But you were, weren't you, kid? You were looking for me."

"I had to know, Mondo. For my own piece of mind."

"Do you know now? Are you certain? I mean, there aren't any more tricks you want to pull, any more questions you want to ask me?" Jake didn't answer. Mondo stood up. "Good. Then you're still the junior man on this team, partner. You run down to Woolworth's on State, get me a cheap pair of size thirty-six pants, a short-sleeve shirt," Mondo stopped, closed his eyes to think. "A toothbrush, some toothpaste, a razor, some foam." He leaned past Jake and grabbed the single pillow, turned it upside down and shook it. His wallet fell out, along with a bunch of bills. Mondo handed Jake some money. "Some clean underwear, too, Jake, top and bottom. I wear undershirts, large." Jake smelled Mondo's rancid breath. Mondo leaned back.

"And get me some mouthwash, too. Scope, no, Listerine. I got scotch germs to kill. And some bandages, some large bandages, I want to cover this ear."

"Anything else?" Jake stood, squared his shoulders, and stared at Mondo straight on. Mondo's eyes were still wet, and red, but they were alert, smiling at Jake.

"Yeah, as long as you're so hung up on Cermak Road, stop there on your way back, too. Get me some White Castles and a couple of large Cokes, to go. Some fries. And get whatever you want for yourself."

"We won't have time to eat."

"Why not?"

"There's a suspect in custody, and he's supposed to give a statement in one hour, accompanied by his attorney. I understand his wife showed up and talked him into giving a statement." Mondo stepped back. He flopped down in the chair. He reached down to where he'd set the Coke when he'd stood up, popped it open and drank it down, absently. He squeezed his eyes shut, rubbed at his stomach. He let the can fall to the carpet. He looked up at Jake.

"You've got a suspect in custody, and you come in here like Eliot Ness, acting like I'm an hour away from an indictment. You tell me why."

"I'll tell you all about in the car, Mondo, on the way in."

"You do that, Jake." Mondo was talking to Jake's back. "And leave the door open; it stinks like shit in here."

"**W**OULD **YOU PLEASE** sit down?" the lieutenant had said to Laura. She'd taken a seat, playing it cool. There was chilled air blowing from the wall vents; she was comfortable. She would see which way he wanted to play before she put on the tough girl act for him. He wasn't smiling, he wasn't pandering, either, though; just looking at her through deep brown eyes, slender arms crossed atop the desk. The lieutenant had perfect posture: He reminded her of her high school math teacher.

"I'm Lieutenant Nance. And I'm going to tell you what that was all about." Laura didn't respond. Nance nodded. "That cop you were talking to? He's a white, Irish Catholic, Emerald Society poobah, marches in the parades; he's connected all the way up into the mayor's office. And he's ten years older than me, been in the department six years longer than me." Nance nodded and looked at Laura. She stared back at him, coolly, listening.

"He resents that I'm his boss, that I got promoted over him, that he's not even a sergeant. He can get called back into uniform for traffic duty on a whim, any major accident. He's gotta work swing shifts. I'm college-educated, he's got a high school GED he picked up in the Marine Corps. So what he was trying to do, he was trying to make me look bad. You understand?"

"Are you apologizing to me?"

"I'm telling you how it is, that's all, I didn't do anything to apologize for. Now, your husband is being questioned in a very serious crime."

"I'm aware of that." Laura put just a slight snip in her tone.

"I'm sure you are. The problem is, we can hold him seventy-two hours, then we have to charge him or cut him loose. Are you aware of that?"

"I am now."

"We have strong evidence tying him to the murder of a police officer, Mrs. Bingham. Fingerprints and other evidence. Glass from his broken car window was found less than a mile from the scene of the murder." Laura had to fight to maintain her composure when he said that. Her look slipped, she knew, the facade of cool disinterest momentarily dropped. The lieutenant didn't seem to notice, however, merely looked at her as he had before, without any slick narrowing around the eyes.

"It's a capital crime. The State will seek lethal injection if he's convicted."

"Lieutenant?"

"Ma'am?"

"Why are we talking?"

"On account of your husband isn't. There've been teams of detectives trying to talk to him for hours, and he just sits there shaking his head, holding his head in his hands. When he's in his cell, between sessions? He goes right to sleep, Mrs. Bingham. That's not the sort of the thing an innocent man facing lethal injection's prone to do."

"Did it ever dawn on you that he might be tired?"

"It crossed our minds." The lieutenant let two seconds pass. "It appears that he did have a kind of busy night."

"And you want me to get him to confess?"

"I want you to get him to talk to us. I can put you alone in a room, unmonitored. He'll be shackled, for your safety, but nobody'll be listening in to your conversations. I want you to talk to him, that's all, Mrs. Bingham." He gave it the two-second wait again, then said, "And if he talks to us, if he tells us the truth, I can promise him, get in writing, that he won't be put to death."

"Let me see him."

Nance stood up. He was reed-thin, with a slight mustache. Laura thought he must be trying to look older than he was. He walked over to a coatrack and removed a heavy tweed sport coat, with patches at the elbows. She'd bet there was a pipe in the pocket. She sat there as he first lowered then buttoned his shirtsleeves, then put on his jacket. He opened the door for her. Laura said, "Can you get me a pack of Marlboro Lights? He'll be easier to talk to if he's smoking." Nance smiled.

"That's the brand Fleming smokes. The detective who gave you the hard time. I think I can get some from him," the lieutenant said. "In fact, I'm sure I can."

Diana was shaken, but not over what had happened to Al, the cop, or to Bing. She'd been watching the TV news when the call came in, and she'd muted the set, then answered the phone in her sexiest, most seductive voice.

In the year that she'd made her living taking phone-sex calls, Diana thought that she'd learned all there was to know about the sort of men who used such services. She'd spoken to transvestites, cute little angels who merely wanted to play dress-up, talk girl talk about what they were wearing in their boyish, little-girl voices. They were so cute that if they'd been in the room with her, Diana would have hugged them. She'd spoken to men, who, like Harold, had wanted to read her poetry. Men who were seeking advice on how women wanted to be treated on dates. And there were many others, so varied and yet so alike. The fact was, most of the callers were sweeties. And most of them were married. And looking for something they couldn't get within the parameters of their marriage. Basically sweet guys who wanted the sort of things they were afraid to discuss with the missus, things they thought were perverted, but which to Diana were old hat.

There were very lonely men, and those types often were older. They were at the very least old-fashioned, and they talked to her as if they were courting. She would coach them as if they were on a first date. "Frank? Ask me if you may have a kiss." She'd say it and they'd swoon.

There was all-night Mike, who would call different numbers, and talk to the girls all night, running up the bill as he looked for friendship, and that was it, that was all he wanted, somebody he could talk to. He was sweet, too; he claimed to own his own business and, unlike most callers, he liked to talk about himself. Such men were looking for friendship, for a connection with another human being. Many wanted to meet after work, get to know each other outside of the woman's work environment, establish personal contact of some sort. They were hard to dissuade. Others, she'd taken a liking to. They would ask for Diana personally. When they didn't call, she would miss them. Their needs were so slight, their guilt so heavy.

And then there were the weirdos.

At Al's place, on her little cubicle desk, she'd kept a baby's water cup, the type with three holes in the little plastic drink-top. She'd kept a little tin cup there, too, with a layer of Reynold's Wrap covering the bottom. Some freak wanted toilet sex? She'd hold the mouthpiece to the tin cup, pour the water into it, lean down and tell him that she was pissing all over his face. They loved it.

Sometimes it was funny, other times it wasn't.

Some men wanted to play daddy-daughter with you, wanted you to talk in a little girl voice, tell you what day of the week panties you had on. Diana always hung up on such callers. Others liked you to pretend you were wearing mules, to clip-clop all over them, to make them jerk off in the toe holes. Or they wanted you to throw fruits and vegetables at them, corn or potatoes or bananas or whatever. Others wanted you to wear a mink coat, wanted to jerk off into it. Guys like that were off the phone in minutes. Most of them were polite and businesslike after it was done, wishing her a good night, telling her how good she was. The disturbed callers didn't bother her; she'd seen and heard it all in the time she'd been around.

Such as the time, early on, when the caller had told her about his sister. How'd he'd killed her and left her in the kitchen, in the deep freeze. He'd wanted Diana to pretend she was freezing to death, to shiver over the phone and beg him to let her free. She had to promise to do anything he wanted if he let her out. Then she had to follow through, pretending at first that she didn't like it, then warming up to him, getting all turned on, as his natural charm and lovemaking abilities wore away at her terror of certain cultural taboos.

And, always, there were the pedestrian callers who thought they had dark secrets. The guys who wanted to dominate you, they were maybe 15 percent of the callers. Then there were the guys who wanted to *be* dominated. Most of the calls, 60 percent or more,

wanted that. Power men, high-profile guys, under stress and wanting the release without having to lose their tough-guy images to the
real women in their real lives. Some of them were pathetic, some of
them were creative. But basically, they were all alike, pitiful and
cowering, strong on the outside, made of jelly where it counted, and
terrified that the outside world would see through their tough fa-
cades. Diana had taken calls from men whose lifestyle mistresses
had ordered them to call. The dominatrix had been on another line,
coaching Diana in the best ways to humiliate their sex toys.

Laura had told Diana that the worst part, for her, was when the
men came over the phone, making their coming sounds. Such
sounds were music to Diana's ears; she would exult in the power
she held over the puny little men she'd always been so jealous of,
with their natural-born appendages, their swinging apparati. Their
guilt or joy afterward, the promises to call back, the begging to meet
her, to get to know her when she was off-duty.

Diana had no doubt in her mind that every one of them thought
that if he could only get her alone, she'd fall head over heels in love
with them. Lotharios with imaginations. Too much imagination,
most of the time.

In the year she'd been talking to such men, she'd heard it all.

Or at least she'd thought she had, until tonight, when this Mr. X
motherfucker called up, in a hurry, promised to send her fifty dollars for ten minutes, as a getting-to-know-each-other present, then
proceeded to whisper the most ugly, nasty things to her that Diana
had ever heard in her entire life.

Which was saying something.

Diana listened though, and didn't interrupt, shivering, cowering
inside, breathing hard as he vented his sickness all over her, as he
made her skin crawl and she had to fight the urge to vomit. He
sensed it, too, told her to go ahead and puke. Told her things she
would never relate to another living soul, not even to Laura, late at
night after drinking wine.

A thought struck her, sudden and sure.

This man must never speak to Laura.

He was calling her a nigger now, but that was the least of his in-
sults. All Diana could do was look at her watch and count down the
seconds, say the things he wanted her to say until his ten minutes
were up. Five bucks a minute, girl, she repeated that to herself, over
and over as she listened to him and said the things she knew he

wanted her to say. It wasn't hard for Diana to do. She was terrified.

The monster fed off that terror, it sent him soaring on to new heights.

Now his voice was growing louder, he was shouting, and it was suddenly familiar.

My God, my dear God, was it somebody she knew?

Diana thought about it as the man on the telephone climaxed, thought about it because he was saying the most horrible things, terrible things, acts of violation that the most perverted mind had never dreamed of. *Who was he!* Dear sweet Jesus in heaven, did this man *know* her?

She heard him moan, then nearly whimper. He breathed heavily, three times, then he spoke to her, quietly and calmly.

"Your cash will be hand-delivered to the given address in an hour. I may be calling back later tonight. You were a stopgap. I'll be wanting to speak with the white woman later."

"Mr. X!"

"What." Diana felt herself deflate. Words would only fail her.

"Uh—thank you. You're a very generous man." She heard him chuckle, then heard him say that she'd be hearing from him again.

LAURA RESENTED THE fact that she wouldn't be able to witness the questioning of her husband, because if it hadn't been for her, Bing probably wouldn't even be giving them a statement in the first place.

She thought about that now, as she sat in an uncomfortable, molded plastic chair, one in a chain-linked group of them that were set over to one side of the interior police station lobby. Thinking—even focusing on her anger—was a welcome distraction for Laura.

Around her, pandemonium reigned. People, most of them black, ran in and out of the building, shouting, screaming, cursing at the uniformed officer who stood solitary, stoic duty beside the building's metal detector. He seemed not to notice their curses. He seemed to be an Epcot Center robot, pointing at the machine and telling people what to do without any conscious thought. Laura focused her eyes on him, allowed her mind to wander.

She had gone into the attorney's conference room, and Bing had been so happy to see her he'd tried to leap to his feet to hug her, until the chains attached to his wrists and ankles—the handcuffs were bolted to the heavy desk—forced him back into his chair. Laura tried to ignore the bruises and welts that covered Bing's face and arms. His face lit up as she handed him the cigarettes and lighter, and Laura sat patiently, watching, as he anxiously worked one out and fired it up, having to bend way over to reach the filter, sucking smoke deep down into his lungs. He took several drags quickly, in a hurry, sucking until the glowing tip of the cigarette was as long as the filter, then he dropped it to the floor and stomped it out, lit another, and smoked it a bit more leisurely. After his second drag, he looked up and smiled at her.

"Boy, Laura, can you believe this shit? No smoking in a lockup. If that was public knowledge, Jesus, half the crooks in this city would retire." He was acting as if they were discussing an upset in a baseball game.

"What are you—?" Laura was about to chastise him, then thought better of it; this was no time to start an argument.

"What they do is, they lock your ass up for a couple of hours, then drag you in for questioning again, with a pack of smokes on the table between you. I bet they get half their bogus confessions from nicotine freaks."

Laura leaned forward and spoke softly, earnestly. "Bing, what *happened*?" Bing shook his head back and forth.

"You don't want to know, Laura." Oh, didn't she? Laura had to fight to control herself, to stop from slapping him across the cheek. He was locked up, accused of a double murder, facing the death penalty, but he was patronizing her, treating her with condescension. "The old man got me a lawyer, he's on his way right now. He had court, or he'd'a been here by now." Bing leaned over and

sucked on the cigarette some more, appearing depressed but trying
to act unconcerned, for Laura's sake. "Man, do I have a hangover."
Laura decided not to comment on that statement.

"Why didn't you call me?"

"They monitor the calls, I didn't want you saying anything that
could get you in trouble." Laura had to let that one pass, too, and
waited a few seconds before she trusted herself to speak to him.

"Bing, this is serious."

"Don't I know it." His handcuffs were snaked through a thick
metal ring that was welded to the center of the ancient steel desk.
He only had an inch or two of play on either side. Bing hung the cigarette between his lips then spread his fingers wide open, then shut
them tight, over and over again. He was unconsciously, nervously
doing his hand exercises. Laura had to close her eyes for a moment.

"Bing?"

"Yeah?"

"Did they find the cards with my name on it, or the one with
Diana's?"

Bing looked at her as if she had acted on her earlier impulse and
slapped him.

"No, don't you worry. *Your* ass is covered. And your girlfriend's."

"That's not why I came here, Bing."

His silence spoke for him, eloquently.

"Bing, you have to talk to them."

"You watch me talk to them. Go sit with the cops behind the mirror they think I'm too dumb to figure out is a hunk of two-way glass,
and listen to what the hell I got to say to them. I'll tell them *shit*."
Bing grinned. His teeth seemed red. How badly had they beaten
him? "My lawyer, though, *he's* got something to say. He's bringing a
camera, he wants pictures of these marks."

"And the cops will say you fell down the stairs, or resisted arrest,
or that the bruises were already on you when they arrested you.
Bing, you can't afford to outsmart yourself this time, you have to
talk to them." Laura looked at him, closely, seeking any sign of his
understanding. Bing's hands were shaking; his right leg was jigging
up and down, compulsively. He was blinking rapidly, too. Every one
of these symptoms could be attributed to the sudden rush of nicotine into his system. Laura tried again.

"This isn't some small-time East Side con, Bing—a *cop* got killed.
I know you didn't do it—"

"Well, Jeez, thanks a lot."

"God*damn* you, would you quit pretending that this is some *game*? Bing, they want to strap you to a gurney and shoot chemicals into your veins! They want to kill you, don't you see that?"

"The charges will never stick."

"Bing!" Laura shouted, and at last Bing's face betrayed his concern. He appeared, for the first time, worried. He was now a whiny, lost little boy.

"Goddamnit, Laura, what do you want me to do? Tell them the truth, that I was there robbing the place for you? Then what? They bring you in and charge you as a conspirator, or even claim you ordered the murder. Look, they got evidence against me, fingerprints, shit, I was *there*—"

"But you didn't kill them, Bing, I know you didn't kill them."

"Yeah? You, me, and God in heaven. So what? You think these guys give a shit? What does it matter who killed them? They're blaming me, Laura, and I can't tell them what really happened."

"Well, I can. I can tell them what I know." Laura said it and Bing lunged at her, but the handcuffs held him back. Laura reared back in her chair, frightened now. He had dropped his facade. Now he was showing his terror. And his anger.

Thank God she'd left him. Laura admonished herself for thinking that at a time like this.

Bing hissed, "You stupid bitch, for once in your fucking life, quit thinking you're some kind of a player and pay attention to what I'm telling you. This is a man's world we're in now, your attitude ain't shit in here. You think I'm not telling them what happened because of what might happen to *you*? Are you that goddamn stuck-up? Don't flatter yourself. I mention your name, or if they find out about you on their own, what do you think will happen to Tommy? You think they'll hand him over to my father? Or to your mother? Like hell. He'll go to a State home."

"For *what*? I didn't do anything!"

"Haven't you heard a word I've said? They won't give a shit about what you did or didn't do, or say, or what you were or weren't involved in. These are *cops,* Laura, they don't care about truth, they just want to look good in front of their bosses, shit. There's a million reporters watching everything that happens on this case, and the cops have them convinced that they have their man. And they be-*lieve* it. They're not even looking for anybody else. All they'll do is drag you into it, charge you with something, conspiracy to commit a burglary, some fucking thing, and it'll stick." He flipped the cigarette to the tile floor, then held his hand out to her, pulling at the chain. Laura saw the bright red marks on his wrist where the cuffs had cut into the flesh. He held his hand open, once more waved for her to take it. Hesitantly, frightened, Laura reached out and clasped it. When Bing spoke now, it was in a soft voice that he had to fight to keep under control.

"Forget about what I said, that stuff about Tommy." Bing swallowed, hard. Tears were in his eyes. "That was bullshit, I was trying to scare you. To get you to pay attention." Bing squeezed Laura's hand, lightly. "You asked me last night if I thought I owed you anything, and I been thinking about that, Laura." He paused, and shook his head. "I know what I am. And I know what I should have been, what everyone thought I was gonna be. Look at me. I ain't no baseball star, I never even made double-A. I'm a loser." He paused again, and leaned down to swipe at his eyes with his free hand. Laura didn't dispute his statement. She wanted to, but she couldn't.

"And now here I am, locked up, and if I don't think fast, they're gonna charge me with murder. I think I got a way out, you gave me an idea, but you have to stay out of it, you have to pretend you don't know anything about any of this. Please, let me do this for you, let me do one good thing for you. Even if they find out you worked for that dead guy, you can't say anything to the cops, you have to just shut up and let the lawyer handle it."

"Bing . . ." Bing squeezed her hand.

"Please. Trust me."

Laura softened her tone, not wanting to hurt him, but having to speak the words.

"Bing, no offense, but look where trusting you got me."

He looked at her, hurt again; tears leaped into his eyes. Bing lowered his head, shaking it slowly from side to side. She couldn't see his face, but she could see his shoulders; they were trembling as if he were crying.

"Bing, tell them the truth. Diana can take care of Tommy if they arrest me—"

"*Never!*" He looked back up fast now, his eyes hard and cold. Laura pulled her hand away and stood.

"Talk to them, Bing." She turned and walked toward the door. He called after her, but she didn't respond.

It was about five minutes after that when Lieutenant Nance approached Laura and told her that her husband had decided to make a formal statement, just as soon as his lawyer arrived.

Laura looked up when she heard her name mentioned, with venom. She saw Big Bing, rail-thin, stooped and ancient, his face a road map of red veins and burst capillaries, standing on the other side of the lobby, preparing to walk through the metal detector. A middle-aged man with a paunch stood on the other side, waiting for him. The second man was carrying a briefcase in his left hand. He'd breezed into the place without going through the metal detector, Laura had somehow noticed that, which meant he had to be Bing's lawyer. The lawyer Bing had talked about. Big Bing was arguing with the policeman guarding the machine, asking him if he thought he was a fucking criminal. Why did he have to walk through that thing? He'd heard they give you cancer. He was only being Big Bing. But he lost his audience, as the lawyer, shaking his head, turned away and began to walk toward Laura.

"Mrs. Bingham?" Laura stood up and shook his hand. "I'm Howard Metzle." Laura said hello. The lawyer put his briefcase into his right hand, and lifted his left to his head. He massaged his temples as if he had a headache. Laura decided he'd only done it so she could get a glimpse of the gold Rolex, and see the light from the overhead fluorescents bounce off his diamond pinky ring.

Laura said, "You keep that little drunk away from me, Mr. Metzle." Metzle looked over to where Big Bing was finally emptying his pockets into a shallow, round plastic dish. The guard looked on, bored.

"He's something, isn't he?" He looked back at Laura. "I agree with your opinion of him, but we can't let family disunity prevent us from reaching our goal. I know the two of you, you and Bing, are separated, I've heard all about it. But we have to work together if we're going to get your husband out of here. Now, how far are you willing to go?" Laura raised her eyebrows. "Would you make a statement that your husband was with you at the time of the murders?" Metzle paused, as if trying to think of a delicate way to tell her what he'd already decided. "Would you say you were—uh—*reconciling* last night? In the—er—*physical* sense?"

Laura thought about what Bing had said to her. He'd told her to forget about Tommy, but she couldn't. She stood as tall as she could, tried to appear confident as Big Bing swaggered over toward them. The smell of alcohol preceded him by several feet. He was wearing a bowling shirt. His meatless arms stuck out of the sleeves like bent twigs.

"So, look who's here. Look who's so all of a sudden concerned. The grieving wife." He looked around, Big Bing feigning surprise. "You see any reporters around anywhere, Howie? Anyone this bitch can pose for, play the victim?" Laura looked at Metzle.

She said, "Let this drunken little asshole say *he* was fucking Bing last night. He's been fucking him for almost forty years now; let him give his son an alibi. I won't lie to the police for Bing, and I won't lie to them to make your job easier for you."

"Now hold on one minute, little lady—"

"I'm not your little lady, and don't you cut me off until I'm through." She turned to Big Bing. "Your son has only a slim chance of getting out of this thing alive, Mr. Bingham. If you want him to make it, you better get out of here right now this minute, and let your lawyer handle it, because *you* sure won't be any help to him."

"Fuck this whore." Big Bing said it with disgust, dismissing Laura as he turned to the lawyer. He'd spoken loudly enough for people in the lobby to turn and look their way. Metzle stood there, shocked, trying to maintain his dignity with an appearance of aloof disinterest. "Let's go see my kid." Big Bing turned to Laura, shoved a bony finger into her chest. "As for you—"

"Take your hand off her, right now." It was a man's voice, and Laura, who was about to attempt to rip Big Bing's finger free from his hand, stopped and looked to see who it was. Then was glad she did.

It was the cop from last night, the one who looked too young to be a policeman. The college student. He was standing right there next to them, glaring at Big Bing. Big Bing took his hand away, put his hands on his hips, opened his mouth to crack wise, but must have thought better of it. The cop was glaring at him, looking for a reason to place him in custody. Laura looked away from him—what was his name? Jake, Diana had called him. She looked over at his partner, who was standing there next to him, looking back at her with a puzzled expression on his face. She smiled at him again, as she had last night, at the cop who'd gotten shot in the ear over at the Chicago Hilton and Towers, Laura smiling at the detective she'd been trying to reach: Alex Mondello.

WAS THIS GUY for real? Diana had to find out. After she let Mrs. LaRitcha into Laura's loft to wait for Tommy to get home from summer camp, Diana walked out the front door and headed north on Michigan Avenue. Across the street, the office workers were just starting to swarm out of the South Loop buildings; their side of the street was crowded. Diana, dressed in hot pants and a matching white halter top, would attract the usual amount of attention over there, so she stayed where she was, away from them all. She didn't strut or smile at the few whistles or comments that came her way. Today, she stayed on the Grant Park side of the street. Today, her mind was elsewhere.

Her mind was on Mr. X.

There had been something about that voice, something so familiar . . . She couldn't envision a face for him yet, couldn't match the voice with an image, but she was close to doing so, she knew it, his face was right there, floating just on the edge of her memory.

He wasn't someone she knew, not someone she'd formally met. And it wasn't a voice from the past, from Al's sex line, either. It was, rather, a voice she'd only heard one time, maybe two. Perhaps even on the radio, or on television, but she'd heard it. She didn't doubt that for a second; she knew the man's voice, she'd heard it somewhere in her recent past.

She'd heard the voice cursing, too!

Diana nearly stopped dead on the sidewalk when she had that revelation. As she came to the Hilton and Towers, she finally walked rapidly across the street, moved through the heavy sidewalk traffic, heading west, past Wabash then State Street, and down to the Dearborn Station, Diana walking a little more quickly now, sweating in the almost unbearable heat, her mind racing a mile a minute because she knew she was on to him, knew that she was close.

What stranger had she heard cursing at her, lately? Or, if not at her, at somebody close to her, in the vicinity? The way he'd said "fuck," there was a ring to it, she'd heard him say it before. Think, goddamnit! Where had she heard that voice?

Otis was smiling at Diana when she walked into Mail Boxes, Etc. "Back already? You can't be expecting mail today, you just rented your box."

"A messenger's bringing something over for me, did it arrive yet?"

"Not yet, but you're welcome to wait inside for it, with the air-conditioning."

There were a number of people in the office with her, collecting their mail, making copies, faxing things off. Diana walked over to the far end of the counter, and beckoned for Otis to come closer. Still smiling, without a trace of erotic interest, Otis came over, stood behind the counter, and smiled at Diana. He asked her how he could help her.

"Honey, there's a man coming here to bring me something. Would you do me a little favor? I'm going out into the Station; I'll stand right over by those stairs. When he comes in, just look over at me, but don't let him know who I am. Will you do that?"

Otis wasn't smiling anymore, he was looking at her calmly, with a steady but suspicious gaze. "I'm not sure I want to get involved with whatever this is, uh—" he had to think to remember her name, then got it "—Diana."

Diana leaned over the counter, and whispered close to Otis's ear.

"It's nothing illegal, Otis, I wouldn't do that to you. I just want to see who he is without him seeing me. Just this one time. Please?"

"All right, but don't make a habit out of this, I won't do it but this one time."

"You're a doll."

"Yeah. That's me, Otis the doll," Otis said sourly, then walked away to help another customer.

They would bring Bing into the large interrogation room for his statement, the one they used for lineups because the observation room was so large. There were plenty of cops who wanted to view this, to watch the investigator's technique, to see if he conducted the questioning in what they themselves would judge to be the proper manner. The interviewer would catch hell if he didn't. There were too many cops watching for him to get away with making mistakes.

Lieutenant Nance himself had decided to take the statement. He was already waiting in the room, patiently, while Bing consulted with his lawyer in one of the building's conference rooms. There was a stenographer in the room; a tape recorder was on the table. To triple-ensure that they got it all down properly, a video camera had been set up on a small table over in the corner. Nance was wearing his suit jacket, with his tie up, which Mondo personally thought to be a mistake. He himself would have preferred informality with a big dumb lug like Bingham. But it wasn't his show, and everyone did what felt best for them. Mondo's hangover was killing him. His ear was on fire. He didn't want to take any more pain pills, though; they'd dull his mind. He'd taped his ear, had finally stopped the seeping blood. The top part of it was gone, but he could hear: he'd adjust, he'd been shot before. The bright lights in the interrogation room were making his temples pound. He reserved his place in the front row by putting his large wax plastic cup of White Castle Coke down on the seat of the metal folding chair. He went to join his partner, Jake, who was out in the detective roll call room.

Which was now dark, with the window shades pulled down; Mondo appreciated the darkness. The flickering images of a television set was the only light in the room. A disembodied young black voice was narrating the videotape he'd shoved into the VCR.

"Here it is, here it comes," the man's voice held excitement. "Sixteen months we been on this motherfucker, the shooter does our job for us in sixteen seconds." On the screen, Mondo could see a short, muscular, swarthy young man with thick black wavy hair crouched down behind a four-door vehicle. He was wearing a T-shirt and cut-off jeans; there were sandals on his feet.

He was holding a pistol in one hand.

It was a parking garage surveillance tape, the images flickering and grainy, but clear enough to make out what was happening; more than clear enough to make out the young man's face.

He would stick his head up from time to time, watching a car parked two spaces away from him.

"I been on this guinea motherfucker—Mondo, that you come in? No offense, man, but this guy's a true greaseball." His apology over, he continued his narration. "Almost a year and a half. I had him cold for two murders, but didn't have enough proof to convince the ASA."

"The young guy?" Mondo recognized Jake's voice. His eyes were beginning to adjust to the darkness; he could see several forms standing around, watching, listening.

"Naw, not him, he's just some zip from the Old Country, sent down from where they had his ass stashed in Jersey City. *Him*, there he is! I been watching him forever."

"Is that Fiore?"

"None other. The godfather himself. Of what little there is left in this town to be the godfather of."

There was no sound track on the tape, just the sight of what was going on. Mondo watched Fiore walk around the side of the second car, watched him press the button to disarm his vehicle alarm. Watched him put his hand on the door, then watched the younger man stand up, carefully aim the weapon with both hands, and fire shot after shot into Marco Fiore's broad, fat body, from behind. Mondo, not expecting it, was glad that the room was dark; he jumped.

"Now here, here, here comes the best part." The young detective narrator was more excited than ever now. "Watch this shit happens now!"

The young killer walked around the car, bent over and fired one more shot into the back of Fiore's head. He dropped the gun on Fiore's corpse, then stood up. He calmly stepped away from the body. He ran his hand appreciatively over the top of Fiore's brand-new Cadillac Coupe de Ville, his lips turned down in grudging approval, nodding his head as he walked around the vehicle, the man impressed with the car as he inspected it. "See that shit? I can hear him thinking: 'Best of all, it's a Cadillac.' Just like he seen on the commercials on Jersey City TV." The killer walked over to Fiore, flipped him over, then grabbed his keys away from where they'd fallen under the body. He stood again, got into the car, started it up and drove away. Whoever had the VCR remote hit the Rewind button, and somebody else went over and flipped on the overhead lights.

"Perfect hit." The black detective was saying. Mondo couldn't remember his name. "Except he didn't understand the concept of having video surveillance cameras in indoor parking garages. They probably never heard of cameras in his thatch hut in Sicily." The narrator looked at Mondo, then spoke to him, trying to see if he was in any trouble over making a disparaging remark about Italians. "What do you think, Mondo, do I have his ass cold, or don't I?"

"The ass of the guy who killed a swamp guinea like Fiore? If you charge him with more than Grand Theft Auto, you ought to turn in your badge." There was general laughter in the room, and Mondo caught Jake's eye, motioned for him to join him in the interrogation room, then walked out before the laughter fully died.

Diana said, "That was him?"

Otis said, "That was the usual Ace delivery man."

"All right, Otis, how do I run down who sent me the envelope?" Otis looked at her for a moment, then down at the envelope on the counter. There was no return address on it. He shook his head.

"You can't."

"You could."

Otis looked at her, then shook his head. When he spoke his tone was stiff, cold and formal. Otis was no longer being the friendly store proprietor.

"Ma'am, you have to understand something, I'm running a legitimate business here, not a private detective office. What you do with your box, your time, and your life is none of my business. Don't try to make it mine. You want to find out who sent this over? You have to go over to the delivery company, give them the package and ask them."

Diana turned on all her charm. "Come on, just this one time? Please?"

Otis was firm. "You want to pick up your mail late? You want to get a front door key for twenty-four-hour access to your box? You want to fax something or overnight it, anywhere in the world, Diana, then I'm your man. Anything else, you have to find out on your own. Now excuse me." Otis turned to a woman who was impatiently waiting at the other end of the counter, the woman dressed in light summer clothing, holding a small box in her hands. She was middle-aged, with ratted hair. She was wearing too much makeup. Diana glared at her.

"Am I interrupting anything?" The woman asked it in a way that expressed her indignation over having to wait. Otis shot an angry look at Diana.

Otis chose to take the woman literally, at her words. He said, "No, ma'am, I'm all through over here." He turned his back on Diana, told her, "Have a nice day," over his shoulder, as he walked away toward his customer.

• • •

She walked out of the air-conditioned building into the still broiling late afternoon sun, Diana impatiently pulling at the tape that secured the small, flat envelope.

There were two twenties and a ten inside.

No note, nothing else, nothing to identify the sender. Diana absently stuffed the money into her purse, then dropped the wrappings into the garbage can attached to the wall. She looked over at the people who were having an early dinner or an after-work drink at the Mexican restaurant next door; the restaurant was part of the Dearborn Station complex. They were sitting in their heavy black wrought-iron chairs, at metal tables, drinking their Margaritas or imported beers, seeming cool under their wide blue-and-white table umbrellas, seeming not to have a care in the world. Directly across the street was another restaurant with outdoor tables. The umbrellas over there were green. That restaurant, too, was filled at this hour. Mostly couples, or four to a table that were set right up to the curb, the patrons seeming not to notice the buses that passed just a foot or two away from them.

Everyone seemed so happy, so at peace with their world and their places in it. They seemed to believe they were safe.

Yesterday, even earlier this afternoon, Diana would have loved to join them. She and Laura, at a table for two, sipping something cool through straws while they put their heads together and discussed Laura's Love Line. And the lonely, horny, frustrated poets who called it. Now, her entire world had changed. Diana was afraid. Fifty dollars a minute couldn't keep her talking to a man like this Mr. X. Not for long, anyway. Maybe one more call, maybe two, and then she'd have to cut him off, tell him not to call anymore. She cursed herself for not having Caller ID installed on the lines.

Diana suddenly felt paranoid, felt someone watching her. She looked around quickly, and in spite of the heat, she shivered.

"Shit."

Diana spoke the word aloud, wondering how ugly words spoken over a telephone line could have upset her as badly as these had. She was terrified now, thinking of what the man had said he'd do to her. Walking over here she'd had a plan. She'd thought she'd catch a glimpse of him, and she'd take it from there according to how big he was, how mean he looked. She'd pictured herself approaching him and shouting in his face, cursing him, threatening him, warning him of dire occurrences if he ever dared call her again, or her best friend, Laura. She'd pictured herself taking his wallet away from him, taking all his cash as payment for the terrible things he'd said to her.

Now she imagined him as being much larger than life, huge; a sub-human, predatory beast who would come for her in the night and fulfill the ugliness he'd promised to deliver such a short time ago.

Diana stepped off the small concrete stair that led into Dearborn Station, turned right on Polk, and headed for Michigan Avenue, deep in thought.

She never noticed the tall man in the broad-brimmed summer hat who'd been sitting at a table for one at the Mexican restaurant, and she did not look behind her as she made her way back to the loft, to see that he was, at a distance, following her home.

MONDO TRIED TO forget about the piece of paper in his shirt pocket. He tried to, but he couldn't. It was as if the paper were smoldering, about to burst into flames, Mondo at all times conscious of it, feeling its weight against his nipple. The paper had Laura's name and phone number written on it. She'd gotten him to the side before she'd stormed out of the place, and nearly begged him to give her a call the second he got out of the station.

He would, too, he was sure of it. Just looking at her made him feel warm, made him feel, for the first time in a while, profound sexual longing. He'd gotten by for so long on fantasy, on his imagination— even when he was still sleeping with Sheila, he'd have to pretend he was with somebody else in order to enjoy it. Mondo was grateful that Elaine Hoffman was working midnights. They'd had close but

guarded conversations, skirting around their sexuality, and she'd
kissed him once, the two of them standing right around the corner,
as they'd stood in the summer night air. Elaine had grabbed him,
pulled him close, shoved her lips onto his, but it hadn't done much
for him. She'd made Mondo highly aware that he could have her if
he chose. He hadn't yet decided if that would be a mistake, sleeping
with someone he worked with. Now that his marriage was over, no
longer just on the rocks, he'd have to think about Elaine a little more
seriously, think about how it might work out.

But he wouldn't think about her now. Because now, the suspect,
Norman Bingham, Jr., was being escorted into the interrogation
room.

The mood in the dark, packed surveillance room changed in a
second, went dead silent. There was no more kidding about the
darkness, no more fag jokes, no more overly loud, comical orders
for a medium popcorn and a large Coke. The cops were leaning forward, looking at the suspect, looking at Nance, too, to see how he
would play it. Bingham's attorney was with him, impatiently standing next to his client, waiting for the officer who'd escorted them in
to remove Bingham's handcuffs. Bingham sat down in the chair opposite Nance, rubbing his wrists, grabbing hungrily at the pack of
Marlboro Lights that Nance had placed facing him on the table sep-
arating them. Bingham sat stone-faced, smoking, while Nance and
the assistant state's attorney ran through the identification process,
went down the list, by the book: stating their names, those of themselves and of the other two police officers in the room; reciting the
time and date, then asking the suspect his name, his address; ascer-
taining Bingham's full understanding of the charges he was facing,
checking to see that he understood he could stop the questioning at
any time he chose.

At last, it was time to get down to business. Nance played it cool,
didn't look over at the two-way glass at all, just leaned forward in
his chair and spoke in a deep, professional tone of voice.

"Mr. Bingham, would you tell me your whereabouts at approxi-
mately two o'clock this morning?"

"Sure." Bingham paused, closed his eyes for a second. Mondo
touched Jake's arm and leaned toward his partner, and Jake, sitting
next to him, inclined his head toward Mondo's lips.

Mondo whispered, "He's making sure he remembers the lie he's
about to tell."

In the interrogation room, Bingham said, "I was over at Twenty-first and Wabash, seeing my boss, Mr. Allan Beck." There was a gasp somewhere behind Mondo; a couple of grunts of surprise, several muttered curses.

Bingham said, "I went over there to collect five grand he owed me for security work I'd done for him over the last few months. He paid me, and then he gave me a bunch of files." Bingham sat back in his chair, dragged on his cigarette, and closed his eyes again. The ASA was glaring at Bingham's lawyer, a small-time scumbag Mondo had seen around; he couldn't remember the guy's name. The lawyer was smirking openly. He thought he had them over a barrel, and he was too dumb to keep it to himself, to hide his glee, even with a camera rolling.

Bingham said, "He took the files out of his Rolodex. They were a bunch of guys he said were deadbeats, didn't pay what they owed. My job was to call them and talk to them, find a way to collect their debt. You can imagine, it's kind of tough, when they don't leave a Visa or MasterCard number, or the other one, that American Express." Nance was looking at him, deadpan, not interrupting, although at this point, Mondo thought he should have. He was letting Bingham play to the tape; the kid was already speaking to the jury, even embellishing, improvising as he went along, perfecting what he thought to be his airtight alibi.

"Mr. Beck had somebody with him, another member of his security detail, a big—uh—colored guy, I don't know his name. They'd both been drinking pretty heavy—I could smell booze all over them—and I think they'd been arguing. When I came in, there was a lot of tension in the air. Anyway, I collected my money, took the files, then left and went back to where I'd parked and found out that some asshole had kicked in the driver's-side window on my car. I drove home, parked in front of my place, and the next thing I know these two cops come in and started beating me up." Bingham leaned into the camera and turned his face from side to side, so that the welts on his face were clearly visible. He lifted up the sleeves of his shirt, then turned his arms toward the camera, one at a time. "The two coppers," he said in wonder, "man, they beat the living *shit* out of me."

"I think my client has said enough." The lawyer had finally realized that he had better straighten up. He was looking soberly at Nance. He put a protective hand on Bingham's arm. Nance's facade had at last cracked. He was staring at the lawyer in surprise, his mouth partially open. Bingham pushed his hand away, leaned forward in his chair.

"No, there's something else I want to say." The lawyer tried to speak, but Bingham waved him off. Mondo knew that it was part of the act, that they'd set the little game up in advance when they'd been alone. When Bingham spoke, his voice was intense, pleading. He leaned forward in his chair and said sincerely, "They were both alive when I left, man. Whoever killed them's still out there somewhere, running around the city, and all you guys can do is accuse me of something I didn't do and beat me up when I say I didn't do it. The truth is, you could have knocked me over with a feather when the Homicide guy, Phillips, told me that Beck and the cop were dead. I didn't even know the big black guy was a cop! I got scared then, what else could I do but shut my mouth? I was getting paid under the table, shit, I was collecting debts strong-arm. If I told you guys the truth, the IRS would be on my ass, too, and you wouldn't have believed me, anyway." Bingham placed both forearms on the table, stared soulfully into the camera, and said, "But I didn't kill them. I swear to God, I didn't kill anybody."

"That's enough, Norm, I don't want you saying one more word," the lawyer said, and Norman Bingham, Jr., collapsed back into his chair, covered his face with his hands, and began to cry.

"Gentlemen, the clock is ticking. I prohibit you from any further discussions with my client. He's made his statement, the general text of which I will be presenting to the media just as soon as I leave this room. You've had my client for over eighteen hours. The maximum you can hold him on suspicion is seventy-two. I suggest you don't use the rest of the time the law allows you." He motioned for the suspect to rise, and Bingham did, wiping at his eyes with the back of his hands, sniffling . . .

"Take my client back to his cell, please." The lawyer turned to the room in general. "Good day," he said solemnly, and walked out of the interrogation room.

"Jesus Christ." It was Jake, the words spoken in near awe. Someone turned the lights on, and the cops in the surveillance room rose to their feet, stretching, yawning, cursing, already tearing into Nance, talking about how badly the lieutenant had fucked up, how he should have cut the guy off the second he opened his mouth and Nance saw the lies start flying out. The door to the room opened suddenly, and Mondo turned around, sucking up the last of his Coke, saw Captain Merlin Royal standing in the doorway with his hands on his hips. Royal did not look pleased.

"Mondello, Phillips, I'd like to see you in my office." He stood there for a second, purposely, knowing they would look at each other before responding. He nodded his head when they did, then bellowed, "Right fucking *now!*"

"What do you think?" Jake was apprehensive as he followed Mondo up the staircase. He tried to cover it up, but there was no way around it; he was frightened.

"It's got nothing to do with you. You're my partner and you were in the room with me, that's all."

"You don't think it's about Bingham?"

"*Bingham?*" Mondo nearly stopped on the stairway. He proceeded on up the stairs, using the bannister to pull himself along, Mondo shaking his head. "What would Bingham have to do with any of this?"

"I set him up."

"I didn't."

"What is it, then?"

"That son of a bitch, that ass-kisser Reed. That's what it's about." Jake had completely forgotten about Jimmy Reed.

"I'll bet he already filed suit against the department in general, and against me in particular. I destroyed his political career before it started, with one punch." Mondo was gasping for breath as he climbed; Jake could hear him wheezing. He spoke between breaths. "Who'd vote for a guy so dumb he'd openly cheat on his wife like that?"

"Yeah, but what about Bingham?" They were at the top of the landing now, and Mondo stopped, leaned forward, put his hands on his knees and sucked in deep breaths of fetid air. He looked up at Jake, ignoring the looks he was getting from the Homicide squad afternoon-shift coppers.

"Bingham? What are you, nuts? Bingham didn't kill anyone." Mondo stood, blinked his eyes several times, rapidly, and looked around the room. He was holding it together pretty well, but it was obvious to Jake that the hangover was bothering him far more than he had been letting on. Mondo said, "He was lying through his teeth about the reason he was there, but he didn't kill Roosevelt or Beck."

"What?"

Mondo looked at Jake. He said, "Trust me. He didn't kill them."

They heard the door to the captain's office open, and Mondo turned quickly and began to walk toward it. Jake followed. Royal appeared in the doorway, hands on his hips, glaring, then he disappeared inside. The door stayed open.

How could Mondo know? How could he be so sure? Forget the Vision, forget seniority, all the years on the job watching punks like Bingham try to squirm out of indictments. How could Mondo stand there and state without doubt that Bingham hadn't killed Roosevelt and Beck?

Unless he'd done it himself, and was now trying to cast suspicion elsewhere, thinking that Norman Bingham was too obvious a mark to lay the murders on.

"Are you sure?" Jake whispered it at Mondo's back.

"As sure as I could be, without being there," Mondo said, a little too patly for Jake's taste. Then he added, "But I'd bet my pension he knows who did it. Your man isn't a killer, Jake; he's a material witness."

"Mondo!" Jake reached for his arm, wanting him to explain his statements, but Mondo pulled away and walked into the captain's office. Jake followed, and closed the door behind them.

DIANA HADN'T TURNED on her voice mail before leaving the loft; she'd let the answering machine pick up her half of the calls. Now the machine had played itself out, all the way to the end of the tape. Diana rewound the tape and sat on her couch with a pencil held over a legal pad, taking down the names and numbers of the men who wanted callbacks. She knew that whoever had put their number on the computer bulletin board had done them a huge favor, had ensured the early success of Laura's Love Line.

She also knew that it wouldn't last.

They were the new thing to try, the hot new number for horny studs to check out, until someone else started up a brand-new line, and then, Diana knew, they would lose at least half of their customers. The trick would be in keeping the other half, regulars who would call them once or twice each week. The trick would be to cull the generous tippers from the guys who only paid the flat rate; *those* would be the ones who would put Laura through college and pay for Diana's final operation.

She knew they wouldn't hang onto such men for long if they weren't here to take the calls.

Laura was off trying to visit Bing. Diana hadn't checked upstairs yet, but she had enough experience with police stations to know that Laura wouldn't be back yet; if Bing hadn't yet been charged with a crime, she probably hadn't even been allowed a visit. But knowing her, Laura would stay there, out of some misguided sense of loyalty to a man who didn't care about her, or about her son, one way or another.

So it would be up to Diana to grab and keep the best customers. To make them keep coming back for more. Lusting for her. The thought made her stiff. And she wouldn't be able to do it if she spent the rest of her life dwelling on some freak who had called and made a bunch of ugly threats, then paid five times the going rate as his penance.

In the safety of her apartment, with the lights on, she felt safe. To hell with Mr. X. To hell with his fifty dollars. Diana would warn Laura about him just as soon as the girl got home, tell her not take his calls, and when he called Diana, she'd deal with him. She forced the freak from her mind, picked up the headset, and carefully adjusted it atop her hair. She looked down at the pad and began to dial a number, then stopped in mid-dial, stricken.

She'd remembered where she'd heard the voice. The voice of Mr. X.

Diana hit the cut-off button, took the headset off, and sat back. A slow, sly smile began to spread across her face. She slapped at her knee in joy, but she had to fight her fear to do it. The son of a bitch, he'd be a tough nut to crack, and it might even be dangerous—he was a big, mean bastard. But she'd bet his career and his marriage meant a lot to him. A whole, big lot. Diana had to find out exactly how much. She'd call him and find out, run it past him and see what he said.

She assured herself that there wouldn't be much the man could do; after all, he had a phone number, but he didn't know where she lived, now, did he?

Diana looked the direct number up in the book, dialed the number, and some man who answered the phone told her that her party was in "conference" and couldn't be disturbed: Would she like to leave a message? Diana was about to say no, then thought better of it, and gave the man her beeper number. Told him she'd be available to return the man's call in twenty minutes. If the conference was over by then, would he please ask the man to beep her? He'd want to hear what she had to say, in fact, the matter was urgent.

MONDO **CAME OUT** of the captain's office fast and slammed the door behind him hard enough to startle everyone in the squad room. He stood there and waited, in case the captain wanted to make a federal case out of it, but the man was behind his desk, smoking a Pall Mall, ignoring Mondo while he tore Jake a new asshole. Mondo looked up, and everyone in the squad room hurriedly looked away, except for Lieutenant Millkiss, the afternoon Homicide shift commander, who was waving something at him, a thick handful of small, yellow while-you-were-out message slips. Millkiss didn't seem at all concerned about Mondo's negative state of mind.

"Hey, Mondo, what the fuck are the rest of us around here, your personal secretaries? Brian and his crew took calls for you all day, and they're still coming in. This one on top? It's from some broad,

says you'd want to talk to her." He squinted at the paper. "Says here
it's urgent." Mondo wandered over to him, took the papers from his
hand, and grunted his thanks. He looked at the top message and
started, then put it on the bottom, then thought better of it and
transferred it to his shirt pocket, next to the other piece of paper.

"I need to see the union rep."

"What happened?"

"I'm on medical leave, I got shot, and that bastard threw me out of
the building, says I got no business even viewing interrogations. I'm
gonna file a grievance."

"You on full pay?"

"Yeah."

"Then what's your beef? You don't want to see the rep, Mondo,
save him for something important." Millkiss's face was unreadable.
Mondo wondered how many of the people in the room knew about
what had happened last night, knew of his public cuckolding.

"I ever run into that bastard Reed again, I swear to God—next
time I'll kill him."

"Christ, Mondo, keep your voice down, you know better than to
talk like that. What's the matter with you?"

"Do me a favor, Millkiss. When Phillips comes out, tell him I'm
taking a cab back to my motel, okay?"

"No problem."

"Thanks." Mondo stuffed the remaining message slips into his
pocket without even bothering to look at them, then left the Homicide squad room, walking rapidly through the swinging gate, going
down the stairs a lot easier than he'd come up them.

Jake sat across the desk from the captain, accepting it all without
comment, waiting for a chance to say something. The captain would
have to give him the opportunity to speak. Wouldn't he? Maybe he
wouldn't at that; the guy was pretty wound up right now. Accusing
Jake of improper investigation techniques, threatening to throw his
ass out of the squad this minute. Telling Jake that he had no business running personal, private investigations on his goddamn day
off. Jake tried to tell him that the captain himself had ordered Jake
to find Mondo, but the captain wasn't hearing it. Jake had never
seen him like this, so upset.

At last the captain stopped, lit a fresh cigarette from the butt in his hand, then swiveled in his chair and faced the filthy window. Jake wondered what he was looking at. The window was so heavily nicotine-stained that it seemed to have been painted brown. Jake didn't know if he'd been dismissed yet, so he didn't move. He waited, hoping that when the captain turned around again he'd be calm, back in control. Because Jake wasn't through; he still had to ask the man for his help in one more important matter.

"Mayor's berserk over all this that happened. His fund-raiser was a bust, and how many of those rich, white assholes you think will show up at the next one? They've been talking to their lawyers all day, gonna sue the mayor for not warning them he was being stalked; sue the department for not issuing a warning. On top of that, the mayor lost the man he thought would be his new pet in the Tenth Ward, the next alderman. Little lapdog ass-kisser that Reed is, he'd have been good in the City Council." The captain didn't swivel back around; it was as if he were speaking to the wall, or to the filthy window. "Mayor gets a bug up his ass, it trickles down, like Reagan used to say. What Mondo did got the superintendent crazed—and all the political appointees are shitting in their pants, too." The captain swiveled back now, and Jake found himself wishing that he hadn't. The look on the captain's face wasn't one of conciliation.

"They all want Mondo, handed to them on a silver platter. The best man I've got, the most experienced, most intuitive, and for damn sure the brightest. He's Tulio without the ego." The captain shook his head. "The man leaps onto a table and attacks an assassin, saves the mayor's *life,* and what does he get? You think he'd get a medal. Instead, they want his badge. For what? For punching a fucking wife-stealer in the head."

"It doesn't make sense." Jake threw it out there as a lure, to see if the captain would chew his head off for daring to speak. The man didn't get angry, but rather nodded his head in agreement.

"It doesn't, at that. You want to know what really frosts me, Phillips? The worst part of this entire thing? I've been in three meetings this month with superiors who want to restart the Special Victims squad. How do you like that? There I was, with Mondo in mind to run it, you as his second in command, then all this has to happen. I get the calls from Mondo's wife, he goes and attacks a multimillionaire socialite friend of the mayor. *You* decide to go out on your day off and crack cases that don't stay cracked, and now you're sitting there, waiting for me to shut up, so you can ask me a question you already know is gonna do nothing but piss me off."

Jake fought to keep his face straight.

"I'm going to wind up not being able to use my two best men on Special Victims over this bullshit. That's what really gets to me, Phillips. So what is it, what do you want? How badly are you gonna cut your own throat this time."

Jake cleared his throat before speaking, had to fight the urge to say nothing. But he couldn't do that. He had to make sure, had to find out—at least to his own satisfaction—who had actually killed Roosevelt and Beck.

Jake kept his face straight when he said, "Captain, sir, I was wondering, seeing as how my career's already destroyed and all, could I possibly get your help seeking a warrant, before you go home?"

"You heard me, you perverted motherfucker, I want fifty grand in hundreds, a one-time payment. I got your motherfucking voice on tape, there's no disguising it. How'd you like your wife to get a copy of it, how'd you like the media to get copies? You want to hear your voice on *Good Morning Chicago* everyday, all that shit you were saying to the lady?"

Mr. X fought hard to keep his voice calm, to not allow the terror he was feeling to enter his tone. He said, "I have no idea what you're talking about." He was sure of only two things: the voice was black, and male. That was all Mr. X could tell from the voice, and that wasn't telling him much. Whoever had taped him and figured out who he really was could have hired this jig to call and make the extortion attempt. He had to keep him talking, had to get proof of who this man was representing. Although in his heart he thought he knew. The man had to be representing that new bitch, Diana. He hoped that was the case. There'd been so many of them, it would be very difficult to track any of the others down. But it had to be Diana. If it was anyone else, why would the man have waited this long to make his move?

He said, "As a matter of fact, I'd like very much to hear the tape."

"*Fucks* you!" the nigger shouted. "Fucks you, fucks your wife, your kids, and your goddamn career! I'm gonna de*stroy* you, white boy, I'm gonna see you twist on the spit."

Mr. X took a shot. "Tell Diana I said hello," he said, and there was the slightest intake of breath on the other end before the man asked, Diana who? It was all Mr. X needed to hear. He softly hung up the telephone, and thought for a minute. Then he picked up the telephone.

Diana hadn't used her male voice in a long time. It bothered her to do so, but she didn't dwell on that now. Not after what the man had said; she'd moved too fast, and he'd figured out her game. Dear God, why hadn't she waited a week, or a month? What was *wrong* with her? Greed had gotten the best of her, had made her act like a fool.

The phone rang, and she looked at it. She felt a burst of rage.

"Hello?"

"Is this Diana?" It was him. Diana fought to keep her voice calm, to work her way through this.

"Yes it is. Who's calling?"

"Oh, I think you know."

"It's X, isn't it?"

"Yes, and I agree to your terms."

"Terms?"

"Don't play games with me, you dense cunt!" His voice was a malignant whisper, ugly, as it had been earlier. He paused, and Diana didn't say anything. The ball was in his court. When he spoke again, he had himself under control.

"I said I agree to your terms. All you have to do is verify that it's you who had the call made to me."

"How would I do that?"

"What was the amount you asked for?"

Diana paused, then said, "Fifty thousand dollars, a one-time payment."

"I agree to your terms. It will take me some time to get that much cash together. But I need the tapes—*all* of them, Diana."

"You'll get them."

"We'll have to meet to make a trade."

"Not on your life."

"Send your man, the pimp who called. We'll meet at Dearborn Station, where I sent your money this afternoon, in broad daylight so nobody has to worry. I'll call with the details when I get the cash together. And Diana?"

"Yes?"

"I trust that you or none of your agents will ever try to reach me again."

"You've got three days, Mr. X. Then I'll call your *wife.*" This time Diana hung up first. She sat there looking at the phone, waiting for it to ring again. When it didn't, she made a fist, pumped it in the air, and shouted for joy. "*YES!*"

Diana stood, stretched, smiling broadly, having climbed into the ring and won with a first-round knockout with a heavyweight. She looked at the legal pad on the table, then bent over and tore off the page she'd been writing on, held it in both hands and made a ceremony out of ripping it in half, then tearing the two halves into tiny little pieces. She kicked the phone off the table. Went over to the answering machine and shut it down. She wouldn't be taking any more calls. In the morning she'd arrange for her number to be disconnected.

It would be Laura's now, the love line, all of it. It would be Diana's going-away present to Laura and little Tommy.

Jake came out of police headquarters, looked left, then right, and finally spotted Mondo a block away, on the corner by the parking lot, using the pay phone. What was the man doing? There were a couple of dozen lines right there in the Homicide squad room. Jake bet that he was calling his daughters, that's why he'd felt he had to use the pay phone. Jake hoped to God that was what he was doing. Or maybe he was calling Elaine; Jake had forgotten about her. Elaine would be good for Mondo. He walked toward Mondo slowly, saw him hang up, saw him put his head down on the top of the telephone, saw him rest it there for a while.

Mondo jumped when he saw Jake standing beside him. "How long you been there!" he demanded, and Jake held up both his hands, placatingly.

"Take it easy, Mondo! Jesus, I'm your partner."

"Not anymore, kid. You heard the captain, I'm not part of the squad anymore. I don't have any partners. It's me and the doctors now."

"Listen, Mondo, the captain was just blowing off steam. And Reed isn't even filing a lawsuit; he couldn't afford the negative exposure. It would kill his business." Jake smiled. "He'd have to reshoot all his commercials, the ones with his wife and kids, talking about how the houses they sell will last into the next century."

"Fuck Reed. And fuck the captain." Jake waited for Mondo to say, and fuck you, too, but he didn't. Instead, he closed his eyes, then rubbed his temples lightly with trembling fingers. "Jesus Christ, Jake, what with this heat, I swear, this hangover's gonna kill me." It didn't look like much of an exaggeration; Mondo was sweating rivers, his new shirt was already soaked through.

"Mondo, the investigation's still open. They think they've struck out with Bingham, and they're probably gonna forget about trying to get him to cop to the murders, they'll charge him with the arson. I've got conditional approval for a warrant on a place on the South Side. I begged the captain to let us work it, you and me, together, just the two of us. All we need to do is ride down to Twenty-sixth and Cal, get it signed by the Night Court judge. He's waiting for us, the captain told him we're coming."

"Us? After the way he just chewed my ass out?"

"He chewed you out, he talked about your medical leave, but Mondo, he didn't suspend you. He didn't take your badge, he didn't take your gun, come on. You know how the guy is, he was pissed off, that's all." Jake didn't think it would be prudent to tell Mondo what the captain had said about the Special Victims Bureau. It was an even trade. He hadn't told the captain about his suspicions toward Mondo, either.

"I guess he didn't," Mondo said. "The hangover got me thinking funny; I swear to God, my head's gonna explode."

"We'll stop and grab some aspirin or something. Come on, we've got work to do."

"Jake, I can't. I've got something to take care of right away, right this minute." Jake waited until some uniformed officers passed them before he spoke. He watched Mondo nod to them, saw him wince, as if doing it caused him pain. He took his time, calming himself down inside. He was angry, confused, and he couldn't let either emotion show.

He said, "Mondo, listen to me. This is important. You're the senior man, and you've been good to me; I respect you, and I'm grateful to you. I think the man that killed Roosevelt and Beck rents an office on the South Side. I believe that." Jake took a deep breath, stepped back a foot or two in case Mondo took his next words badly. "I know it's either him or you that did them, Mondo. I want to eliminate you, and the only way to do that is to grab this guy, this," Jake

fished a piece of paper out of his jacket pocket, said "Luis Rodriguez."

"Rodriguez? That's a scam."

"I believe you."

"But you don't believe I didn't kill Roosevelt."

"Mondo, I'm not sure."

"And you're young enough and dumb enough to stand there and
tell me you still suspect me. When nobody else in the department
does. And you want me to serve a warrant with you, in a place just
the two of us know about." Mondo shook his head in disgust. "Jesus
Christ, Jake, haven't you learned anything in all this time?"

"Are you coming, Mondo, or not?" Jake didn't bother to tell him
that the captain knew where they were going. The captain, and the
judge who would be signing the warrant. He'd said it once, it wasn't
his fault if Mondo had too much of a hangover to pay attention. Nor
would he tell him that finding the real killer would get Mondo off
the hook, not only for the killings, but for punching Reed last night.
He was so damn smart, let him figure it out for himself.

Mondo sighed. "I'll tell you what I'm doing. I'm going back to the
motel. You go get the warrant signed. Do what you got to do."
Mondo wiped at his sweating brow, looked at his fingers, then
wiped them on his pants. "Jesus Christ, I'm sweating scotch."

"You're not coming with me?" Jake eyed Mondo the way he'd
looked at hundreds of suspects; coldly, cruelly, as if whatever
Mondo now said would automatically be proof of his guilt.

"Hey, kid," Mondo said. "I was a cop since you were in—what—
the fourth grade? I personally put more bad guys in the joint than
you'll ever even look at in your entire career. I took you under my
wing when nobody else wanted you. I gave you credibility, and
don't you think for a minute I didn't have to stand up for you more
than once with guys who were loyal to Jerry. Now you want to play
games with me, and you want me to run around like a fucking
rookie patrolman, trying to ease your suspicions?" Mondo grabbed
his crotch and lifted it toward Jake in a quick, violent gesture.

Mondo said, "Hey, Phillips, suspect *this,* all right?"

IT TOOK **MONDO** a little while to calm the guy down at the motel's front desk. The man kept waving his hands in the air and lapsing into Farsi while he begged Mondo not to stay another night. Mondo waved his packages around, trying to get a word in edgewise, trying to tell the man that all he wanted was to take a fucking shower. At last Mondo convinced him that he would be no threat to his business, and the man grudgingly told him he could keep the room another night. But he'd have to pay. Mondo put his packages down and slowly took out his wallet, handed over his credit card and told the man that he'd be moving the police car out of the parking lot the second he got his receipt—oh, and not to bother calling his room if somebody went crazy with an automatic pistol in the middle of the night. The man hesitated, biting his lower lip, turning the card over and over in his hands, then he finally handed it back, and grandly announced to Mondo that he could stay one more night, free of charge. "Ahn de hoose," he said. Mondo thanked him.

As soon as he was in the room, Mondo stripped off the clothes he was wearing and headed into the shower. He stayed in there a long time, until the hot water ran out. He dried off and dressed, then pulled a chair over to the window and sat in front of the air conditioner, ignoring its creaking while he used the remote to turn on the late afternoon news. There was big news today, lots of shit happening. An assassination attempt against the mayor; the killing of an off-duty cop; then a lawyer Mondo had seen just a few hours ago was shown standing on the sidewalk in front of police headquarters, shouting self-righteously about police brutality against his client. Mondo smiled, and shook his head. When the news was over he flipped off the television and waited for darkness to fall.

Jake was stepping all over the rules and he knew it. If Royal ever found out about this . . . but hell, he'd have to, one way or another. How could Jake keep it from him? If things worked out, if this was the right place, then he'd have a major, high-profile arrest, and Royal would be right in the middle of it. He'd say and do all the right things in public, but he wouldn't forget—or let Jake forget—that Jake had acted contrary to orders.

And if things didn't work out, if Jake's suspicions were way off base, then the man who rented this office would wind up suing the department, and Royal, as Jake's superior, would be included in the documents.

Either way, Jake was in trouble.

So what should he do? Call in for a backup? If he did, he'd have to wait around for someone to show up. On a blistering August night, at a time when crime wasn't exactly on an extended summer vacation. Not to mention that he'd have to share his suspicions about Mondo with a stranger, some detective unknown to him.

Jake was having his doubts now; it was clear to him that what he was doing was pretty much as Royal said—it had become Jake's personal crusade. He didn't think he had any time to waste waiting around for a detective who might or might not bother to show up. He was supposed to be doing this with Mondo, only Mondo wasn't around. And if Jake's suspicions were correct, then he had to move fast. Because he wasn't altogether certain that Mondo had ducked out of this due to a hangover. He might well have ducked out of it because Mondo himself was the killer.

Jake sat in his running car with the air-conditioning on high, the cold air blasting onto him as he tried to make up his mind. He was parked right in front of the office building. There weren't many people using the main entrance; in fact, he hadn't seen anyone come in or out. Jake believed it was a building used more for maildrops than for business, the sort of place where you could have packages delivered to a legitimate street address and not have to worry about someone figuring out your scam, as they might well do if you used a P.O. box. And, too, using a place like this, a con man could somewhat avoid attracting the suspicions of the federal postal service. They might be slow, but once they got into something, they were like any other federal agency; they came down on you like a ton of concrete, and they were usually just as smart.

Jake looked at his watch, then angrily shook his head. He hadn't called home since dawn, when he'd let Marsha know that he wasn't a suspect in Roosevelt's murder. He hadn't told her that Mondo was. She'd have noticed the wet towel, would have known that Jake had stopped home, but he hadn't left a note, or a voice message on their answering machine. Marsha would be angry by now. Probably worried, too. He had to get home soon, or at least call and check in.

Jake shut the car off and got out of it, locked the door behind him, then wandered over and casually checked the front door, which was nothing more than a sheet of plain, thin glass with a cheap lock and a steel handle. Jake gently pulled it toward him, felt the lock ready to give just from that subtle pressure. He looked around. There was no one on the street. He pulled hard, and the lock popped. Jake kicked the tongue of the lock into the gutter, stepped inside and pulled the door closed behind him. He headed for the stairway.

STE 4E. That's what the mailing address was, where the telephone bill was sent to someone who claimed to be Luis Rodriguez. Like hell. Jake stopped halfway up the stairs, between the third and fourth floors. He transferred the warrant from his inner sport coat pocket to his left hip pocket. He took out his pistol. He wished he weren't alone. He wished he were wearing a vest. His heart was pounding, loud in his ears. Wishing would get him nowhere; he was alone, without a vest, and wasn't about to take any chances.

Jake held the pistol in both hands, up high, next to his head. He took the remaining stairs two at a time, turned left, and ran down the dark hallway toward suite 4E. He didn't bother knocking, didn't announce himself as a police officer. He just kept moving, fast, Jake lowering a shoulder at the last second and hit the cheap wooden door at the lock, it flew open, and he nearly fell inside. When he got his balance he lowered his gun and swept it around the room, his face grim, his finger on the trigger.

The room was empty, and dark.

Jake cursed, put his weapon away, then kicked the door shut behind him and looked around. There was enough illumination from the tall vapor lights on the street outside for him to see around the place; he didn't want to touch the light switch.

The room had hardwood floors, and unfinished walls. Jake stood just inside the door, his hands in his pockets so he wouldn't inadvertently touch anything, looking at the place where desk and chair legs had scratched the wood and made circles in the dust. A small rectangular space was next to where the desk had been; a wastepaper can had probably been set there. They were the only signs that the room had ever been occupied—it looked like an office in progress rather than a place that anyone worked in. Or made phone calls from.

Jake left the room with a heavy heart, walked halfway down the hallway, then had a thought that lifted him. He stopped. He walked back to the room, pulled the door shut, and slapped one of the Crime Scene stickers onto the angle where the door met the frame. The sticker wouldn't hold the door closed; a good breeze would break the seal, but anyone noticing it would leave it alone, the honest ones thinking that they could get in trouble for merely touching the door. Anyone with a larcenous mind could break the seal and look inside, and would immediately see that there was nothing in there for them to steal. Jake hoped the seal would keep out any of the building's occupants who might for any reason be curious, at least until he could get a crime scene tech in here, and get the electric sockets and the light switch and the windowsills dusted for fingerprints.

The fact that the room was empty no longer made him feel depressed. In fact, the opposite was true; Jake now felt elation. Because whoever had emptied the place out had had a good reason for doing it, and Jake thought that that reason might be murder.

He made the call from the car radio, and had to explain what he wanted to the evidence tech when the woman finally arrived, an hour after he'd called. The woman seemed to recognize him, and she took him at his word without a lot of questions, for which Jake was grateful. Even with his newfound status, it wasn't easy for him to talk calmly to the woman; Jake had to hide his excitement. Because while he'd been waiting he'd found something much more interesting than the empty room.

He'd found a desk around back in the alley, three buildings down, but the building it was behind was a vacant, burned out hulk. He knew without doubt that this was the desk out of 4E. Next to the desk, lying on its side in the alley, was a filthy, plastic, office-sized trash can. The can had been half-filled with wadded-up paper towels and toilet paper, and Jake had been very careful looking through it, imagining what they'd been used for. He'd used a stick he found in the alley to poke around inside the can, Jake wearing thin latex gloves on his hands. He'd spotted the hands-free phone setup in the middle of the can, found it maybe a minute or so before he decided to save himself a lot of paperwork and trouble, decided to carry all the stuff back upstairs where it belonged, to suite 4E.

Where it now was, back in its place, Jake knowing where to put everything from the displaced dust on the floor. The tech was carefully dusting everything, working by the numbers. Having been told that it was the office of a possible murder suspect, the woman was being very careful, she knew that the Homicide dick was watching her every move.

Jake had to hide his joy when she lifted clear prints, first off the telephone headset, then from under the top drawer of the desk, then from the side of the wastepaper basket. The bastard wasn't nearly as slick as he thought he was. Luis Rodriguez. Jake would bet his wife's inheritance that the killer was more of a WASP than Donald Trump.

While the tech was still working, Jake went down and called for one of the locksmiths the department used to come and change the locks on the office door. He had to wait for the guy, then wait for him to install the new lock, then wait while the locksmith filled out the voucher. Jake impatiently signed it. Before he locked the door and left, Jake dropped the warrant on top of the desk. He didn't think that Luis Rodriguez would ever be coming back to get it, but still, it had been served. And if everything turned out all right, nobody would ever know that Mondo hadn't served it with him.

Jake knew that he was required to go back to the station to fill out his report and inventory the new keys, but he was too tired to do that right now. He had been on the go for nearly twenty hours, working on three or four hours of sleep. It was time to go home, try to smooth things out with Marsha, and, if he was lucky, get some rest before the evidence tech called him with the FBI run on the prints she'd lifted. Jake had given her his home phone number, and told her he'd be in her debt if she called him right away. She'd promised him that she would. Jake pushed the broken entrance door closed, got into his car, and headed for home, wondering where Mondo was, hoping that, before the night was over, he wouldn't have to get a warrant sworn out, mandating his partner's arrest.

THE BLINDS SURROUNDING Jimmy Reed's glassed-in corner office were all closed, a sign that Mr. Reed wasn't to be disturbed under any circumstances. He usually only twisted them closed when he had someone in there with him who was about to get fired, but he was alone today, Sheila and Angelina—the only other saleswoman still in the office—both knew it. In fact, they were painfully aware of his presence; an uncomfortable silence had grown between them since Jimmy'd come in. They couldn't hear him talking on the phone, couldn't hear anything through the thick, black plastic. Sheila pictured him in there, all by himself, staring sadly at the wall, and her heart nearly broke. She almost jumped with joy when Angelina informed her that she had to go out on a late showing.

Should she go in there and try to talk to him? Did she have the nerve? They already had what you might call a relationship, even more so after last night. But the relationship had never been consummated, it was made up mostly of brief, stolen kisses, grabbed in doorways or in cars, Jimmy pushing Sheila's hand away when she reached for his crotch, or when she tried to unbutton his shirt and get her hand inside. He was far more of a gentleman than her husband could ever be; he was absolutely nothing like Alex suspected him of being. Jimmy was not a lecher, not a home wrecker, not an adulterer. Jimmy Reed was a man of honor. A war hero, too, a man who'd served his country honorably and well. He'd often tell her about those days, in a low, far-off voice, whereas Alex never would, no matter how many times she asked him.

It had taken her a long time to figure it out, but now Sheila knew that Alex just wanted a woman to take care of him, to be there when he needed her, like a servant, on twenty-four hour call. Alex didn't understand that women were sensitive, that they had feelings, or that women were equal to men, too, not just people he could use to cook, clean, sew, and screw for him. It was what his mother had been for his father, an indentured servant, and Alex had expected the same out of his marriage. He was also more than likely overcome with jealousy when he thought of Jimmy Reed. Alex was a Neanderthal, middle-aged and stuck in his dead-end job, while Jimmy was a multimillionaire, self-made, with more class in his little finger than Alex had in his entire body. And he was sensitive, caring, loving and thoughtful, things Alex couldn't imagine being.

But that didn't mean that Sheila had the right to barge into the boss's office. He was adamant about that; nobody was to interfere when Jimmy had the blinds closed, not even his wife. He might even fire her if she went in there, if she broke his rules.

Would he do that? Sheila wasn't sure.

A look had passed between them when he'd finally come in, just about a half an hour ago. His poor nose had a large bandage taped across the bridge. The tape stretched all the way to the middle of both his cheeks. The side of his face had a large lump on it, discolored and ugly. His ear was so dark red that in the overhead lights it looked black. As she thought about it, Sheila decided that she couldn't take it any longer; she had to know how he was.

She rose, pushed her chair back into its space under her desk. She'd take her purse in with her, she could tell him she was leaving for the night, just wanted to see how he was before she went home to her daughters. If he got mad, she'd give him that excuse, and leave the building quickly. If he didn't get angry, well, she'd just have to play it by ear.

Sheila felt a tingling of excitement in her spine as she walked toward Jimmy's private office. He'd held her in his arms last night, had kissed her over and over again, had told her she'd be all right. Jimmy had done that in front of his own wife, and where had her husband been? Risking his silly life for a stranger, for a mayor he hadn't bothered to vote for, a man he didn't even like.

No, she'd be better off without him. She'd be *far* better off with Jimmy. If he wasn't mad at her, if he didn't blame her for last night.

Sheila had that thought and stopped. My God, could he blame her for what had happened to him? She stood there thinking about it, then came to a decision. If he did blame her, she had to know. She walked resolutely to the door, knocked on the glass, then waited. She heard rustling from inside, heard Jimmy ask who it was. Sheila turned the knob, and discovered that the door was locked from the inside.

"Jimmy? It's me, Sheila. Angelina's gone for the night." She heard soft rustling sounds coming from inside the office. Were they angry noises? Was he pushing things around? Between the thick glass and the heavy blinds, Sheila couldn't be sure. She waited. She heard the lock snap open, then the door was opened wide, and her fears deserted her as Jimmy, smiling, looked around the office anxiously, then, when he was certain it was empty and they were alone, he took her in his arms and kissed her hard, on the mouth.

"I'm sorry, I don't know what came over me," Jimmy said. He was behind his desk now, looking at Sheila sheepishly. He lifted his hands in a gesture of futility, let them drop on a large stack of messages, contracts and other paperwork that had piled up in his absence. Sheila still felt tingling in the spots where his arms had touched her, on her back, and around in front, where their bodies had briefly joined. Her lips felt as if they were on fire. She was breathing heavily; she hadn't expected that sort of reception, hadn't been prepared for it. She felt like a homely school girl who'd just been asked to the prom by the homecoming king. She hoped she was at least partially together when she responded.

"That's all right . . ." Damn. It came out sounding so lame. "I mean, it was bound to happen sooner or later, wasn't it? After last night?" There. That was a little better. Jimmy grabbed a bunch of messages and threw them into the air. They drifted down to the floor and the desk like pink snow.

"Last night." His gaze was direct now, there was no fooling around anymore. "That husband of yours. He cost me my political future."

"I'm sorry."

"What are *you* sorry about? It's not your fault he's a violent son of a bitch." Jimmy's voice was filled with concern. He got out of his chair, walked around the desk, then knelt down on one knee in front of Sheila, taking both her hands in his own. He kissed one of them.

"I didn't mean you were at fault. We can't—after what happened, Sheila, we have to stay together through this all, it's more important than ever." Sheila was having trouble fighting back the tears. Jimmy squeezed her hands, gently.

"I'd abdicate the throne for a woman like you, Sheila." He spoke now in a Southern accent. "A seat on the damn City Council ain't shit." Sheila smiled and returned the squeeze, pulled one hand free, draped it atop Jimmy's shoulder. She softly stroked his neck, using only the tips of her fingers. Jimmy closed his eyes. For a moment, she thought he was going to lower his head into her lap, and she wished he would, but he tilted his head backward instead, and kept his eyes closed, enjoying Sheila's touch. Sheila stroked him a little harder.

"It's just that I've been under so much pressure today. More than ever, after what happened last night. The mayor's incensed, he was embarrassed in front of the governor and all of his regular deep-pocket contributors. He wants your husband's badge. I do, too, I think you should know that. I want him off the force. Not just for my own sake, because of what he did to me, but for the public safety as well. He has to be stopped before he does this to anyone else." He leaned his head into the back of her hand, tried to trap her fingers between his head and his shoulder. Sheila pulled her other hand free. Jimmy let his hands fall onto her thighs. She rubbed both sides of his neck now, gently, softly stroking him. He softly rubbed her upper thighs, an absent gesture, and gentle.

"God knows how many other people he's already hurt." His voice was a croak.

"Do we have to talk about him, Jimmy?"

"I just want you to know, before we go any further, I'm gonna go after the son of a bitch, Sheila, I want him in prison if I can swing it." He hadn't opened his eyes, his voice never lost its softness, he was simply giving her a statement of fact. "I don't want you to get into something with me if you have a problem with that."

"He should have been locked up a long time ago." Jimmy smiled, turned his head, reached up and took one of her hands, then he kissed the palm, softly licked the underside of her wrist.

"Let's get out of here." Jimmy's voice was husky. "I'm staying at the Four Seasons, and I've been gone all day, running around trying to take care of all this garbage. I need a shower, I've got to clean up." He opened his eyes now, took her hands again in his, stood up and pulled her to him, held her tight, close. Jimmy kissed the side of Sheila's neck. "This is such a relief, Sheila, my dear God, I can't tell you how much this relaxes me."

Sheila almost laughed. He hadn't seen *anything* yet. But he would, soon.

She whispered, "Let me go home and change."

"I have to go get some clothes, I have to see my kids, talk to them myself, too, explain things to them, what happened last night, why Daddy didn't come home. God knows what their mother's told them. I'll need someone to talk to after *that*. I'll make a dinner reservation before I leave the house. Where would you like to eat?"

"I thought room service would be appropriate, at the Four Seasons." Sheila paused. "A midnight snack, perhaps, afterward . . ." Jimmy started then pushed back, holding Sheila by the forearms.

"Are you sure we're ready for this? My God, we both only separated from our spouses last night."

What a sweetheart he was. Sheila hurriedly responded, trying to erase his fears.

"It's the right thing, Jimmy. There's no other way for us to go." Jimmy smiled.

"I'll meet you at the hotel, say, nine-thirty, ten?" He reached into his pocket, took out one of those magnetic cards they give out at hotels now, instead of keys. "Take this, so you won't feel out of place waiting in the lobby or the bar. I'm in forty-one-fifteen. It's a corner suite."

"I'll be waiting, Jimmy."

His face was somber now as he pushed away, then hurried over to his desk, grabbed a bunch of papers and shoved them into a leather briefcase.

"I'll get there just as soon as I can." There was no hiding the excitement, the pure *desire* in Jimmy's voice.

Sheila smiled and left the office, already knowing that she would spend the entire night with Jimmy Reed at the Four Seasons Hotel. She formulated a lie as she walked to her car, aware that the girls were too young to understand. She had to think of something that the girls would believe, so that they wouldn't think less of their mother for what she was about to do.

IT WAS HARD for Jake to believe that Lynne was almost two. Three months, and she'd be there, another milestone in her life gone by, another year passed. She was struggling to get out of his arms now, Lynne wanting, as usual, to run and play at bedtime. Jake held her to him, gently but firmly, and cuddled her, shushed her as she threw out a short, trial scream to see if he'd give in. He wouldn't. He couldn't put her in her crib and let her scream, either, although Marsha got mad at him when he refused to do that. She would tell him that it was a power thing, the baby was trying to find out who held control in the household. Jake believed it, but he didn't care. She'd have enough problems in her life when she got older; Jake wanted his daughter's first years to be ideal. When Jake was home at night he would rock Lynne at her bedtime, feed her her bottle—again over his wife's objections, she thought that Lynne was far too old to still have a bottle—and talk her to sleep. He would sing lullabies that he made up as he went along, looking down at that angelic face, and watch her little eyes close by centimeters, almost against Lynne's will.

Tonight he had the strong urge to change his voice patterns, make it a little louder, as his daughter drifted off to sleep, so it would wake her; Marsha was sitting at the kitchen table waiting to have a discussion Jake wasn't at all certain he wanted to have right now. He'd told her what had happened, had given in to her demand that he explain where he'd been all day, what he'd been doing on his day off. When he got to the part about the cuff link, she'd blanched, and when he told her about the desk and the wastebasket in the alley, she'd turned to ice and *glared* at him. He should have kept his mouth shut. Jake knew that now. But he was tired and feeling guilty, and he'd blurted it all out without giving any thought to Marcia's possible negative reaction.

Lynne was finally sleeping now, so there was no way to put off the discussion. Jake stopped singing and stared out at the city for a second, then rocked a little harder, then a little harder still, working it a little bit at a time, until he could stand without disturbing the child's sense of his rhythm. He carried her to her crib. When he put her down she started, made a frightened sound, and lifted her baby arms out to him, fingers stretching. Jake patted Lynne's belly, then rubbed it, talking to his daughter softly, telling her he was there, that there was nothing to be afraid of. He didn't add that he was the one with something to worry about. He backed out of the room, watching Lynne, thinking about her and her future, about the wonderful life she had ahead of her. If he could keep her safe, if he could protect her from the city. From the city and all the ugliness that was endured within its borders.

• • •

"Mrs. Rafael was at the gas station, Jake, this morning, getting ciga-rettes when you left." Marsha was trying for a neutral tone, Jake knew, but it was coming off cold; she was lecturing. The sentence drove him off stride, too: What the hell did their neighbor have to do with anything that had happened today?

Rather than ask Marsha, Jake said, "Is that right?" He wondered if he'd somehow snubbed the poor, old fat woman who lived on their floor, across the hall, if he had in some way hurt her feelings. If he hadn't, then what the hell was all *this* about?

"She told me what you did to that man in the deli doorway, Jake."

"In the doorway . . . ?" It took Jake a moment to remember it, and when he did, there was no keeping the look of guilt off his face.

"How could you do that, Jake? How could you brutalize a man like that?"

"Marsha . . ." He used his warning tone, telling her that she was getting into territory she had no business exploring.

"Marsha, hell. You brutalized that man, Jake, you slammed his head against the wall. If somebody had been at the gas station with a video camera you'd be on suspension right now, if not under arrest."

"The guy was a mugger, Marsha, for Christ's sake, he was work-ing a scam with a woman and a little kid."

"Oh, you deduced that, did you?"

"I didn't have to. The woman asked me for a bus token or some damn thing, and I turned her down, and before I even got to my car that punk was out of the deli doorway, about to kick the shit out of her for disobeying his instructions, for not getting me to turn my back toward him so he could leap out of the doorway and smash in my skull."

"Is that right?" Jake recognized her tone. It was the way she talked before she dropped a bomb. "You got a confession from him awfully fast. I wonder." Marsha paused. "If he was a crack-addled mugger, why didn't he attack Mrs. Rafael?"

"Are you serious? Mrs. Rafael wears muu-muus, for Christ's sake. She's a drunk who can't sleep at night, and she looks it. She's sev-enty years old and she keeps her money in a change purse stuck down her bra. She looks like a cleaning lady, Marsha. Why would he wreck his scam, and risk arrest, go to jail over someone like her?"

"Oh, I see, now. He was waiting for someone who was obviously rolling in dough to come out of the building. Like you."

Jake ignored her sarcasm. "I was wearing a sport coat, a tie. Yeah, you'd think I was holding some money."

"Did you ever stop to think that maybe those people were desperate?"

"Marsha, please, let's not get into that."

"No, *let's.*" She was leaning forward in the chair now, her arms crossed under her breasts.

Jake said, "You're mad because I didn't call all day. I'm sorry. I came home, but you weren't back yet, you were still at your mother's. There's no reason to get into all this other shit just because I didn't call."

"I wasn't at my mother's. Please don't tell me where I was."

"Well, wherever the hell you were, you weren't home, all right?"

"Jake, don't raise your voice. I waited until Lynne was asleep before saying a word to you about any of this, you owe me the courtesy of responding without anger."

But how was he supposed to do that when he was angry? And her crack about waiting until Lynne was asleep was bullshit, as far as Jake was concerned. All waiting had done was give her more time to think up more garbage she could lay on him. He should have kept his mouth shut, he knew now. He shouldn't have said a word to her.

"When you joined the police department you told me you were doing it to make a difference. You didn't say you were doing it so you could exploit the power of the badge, so you could brutalize *suspected* muggers, Jake, and terrify their wives and children."

"That wasn't his wife."

"Oh, you know that, do you? How do you know, 'cause they were black?"

"Now I'm a bigot."

"Now you're getting defensive. Looking for an argument, rather than reasoning things out between us, discussing them, the way we always have. Jake, I'm trying to understand. And I'm sure your reaction probably makes perfect sense to you, in some way, because if you get angry, then you can storm into the bedroom and slam the door, or better yet, storm out of the apartment. Then you won't have to face up to what you did, right?"

"What'd I do?" Jake fought to keep from shouting. He whispered harshly, conveying the same message that he would have if he'd been screaming. "I told some psychopath who would happily bust your head wide open for the change in your pocket to keep his ass off my street, to stay off Dearborn! I was protecting my family, my neighborhood!"

"And how many times have you heard that same remark from

people who've killed kids who were stealing hubcaps? Or from mob guys who use that as their rationale for violence? Your being a cop doesn't give you a divine right, Jake. In fact, it holds you up to a higher standard, in a harsher light."

"I know all about being in harsher lights, Marsha, and you don't."

"Jake, you know better. That man has as much right on this street as you or I have." The calmness in Marsha's voice infuriated Jake. He began to breathe harshly, looking around him angrily, as if seeking something in his personal environment on which he could vent his anger.

"And tonight, you disturbed a possible major crime scene, Jake, you might have even manufactured evidence against an innocent man. You en*trapped* whoever rents that office! I'm not a cop or a lawyer, but my God, Jake, you don't have to be a Supreme Court justice to see that you're stomping all over the Constitution! Don't look at me like that, I'm your wife, I'm not one of your fellow officers. I'm certain that late at night, in the cop bars, what you did tonight would be seen as some great, inspired move. But the fact is it's a *crime,* Jake! Cops aren't supposed to commit them, they're supposed to stop them. Or at least solve them after they occur." Marsha put her hands down on the table, half stood in front of him. Jake stared at her, hard, but she didn't seem to be getting the message.

"You weren't a criminal when you joined the department, Jake, you didn't act like that."

"Marsha, you don't understand."

"Oh, of course not, how could I? I'm not a cop."

Jake took a deep breath before he responded. He would not react in anger, he would not play into her hands. She was a psych major; he would never win with Marsha if he used his temper instead of his intellect.

Jake said, "I didn't mean it that way. Look, you don't see, every day of your goddamn life, how easy it is for killers to weasel their way out of convictions. You've never had an airtight case blown out of the water because one of the jurors was impatient to get home because he had yachting plans for the weekend, or one of the other juror's husband's couldn't change a diaper properly, or get the kids off to school. The system's fucked, Marsha, it's falling apart. If you saw, one time, what I see day in and day out, believe me, you'd not only congratulate me for what I did this morning—and tonight—but you'd want to move to the country and put a moat up around the property."

"Jake, listen to you." Marsha had slumped back in her chair now and was watching him closely, almost sadly. "Listen to what you're *saying*." Now her voice was plaintive. "This is not the way you used to talk to me, Jake, not the way you used to act, either."

"I've changed. So have you. We all change as we get older."

"Lose some of that old idealism, is that what you mean, Jake?"

"Marsha, please."

Marsha nodded her head as she watched him, moving it almost involuntarily, up and down, slowly. They were having a Moment, nothing more. Jake told himself that because he was terrified it was something more, that something ugly was about to happen between them.

"I wasn't at my mother's this afternoon, Jake," Marsha said, and Jake raised his eyebrows in inquiry, letting her know that he'd listen if she wanted to tell him where she'd been, but he wouldn't press it if she didn't. "I've—" Marsha paused, took a breath, then hurriedly said, "I've been seeing somebody, Jake, for a couple of months, now."

"What?" Jake glared at her, and now Marsha nodded again, just once, decisively.

"A psychiatrist, Jake. A shrink, I've been seeing him for a few months now." Marsha's eyes narrowed. She had him, and he knew it. "But you right away had to jump to the worst conclusion, didn't you, Jake? You immediately had to think that I was cheating on you."

That was it. To hell with being reasonable.

Jake shouted, "Well Jesus Christ almighty, Marsha, you want to talk about entrapment! What the *hell* did you say it like that for? 'I'm seeing somebody, Jake.' What the *fuck* was I supposed to think?" Jake rose now, and shoved his hands in his pockets, because if he didn't, he knew, he'd punch a hole in the wall. "You want to play games? You want to play with somebody's head? Go play with your mother's, with your sister's. They're experts at it, you'll all have a good time." Jake walked over to the closet, to grab his gun off the shelf, his sport coat off the hanger.

"Jake, if you leave now, don't come back for a few days. That'll give me time to pack up and move out." Marsha's tone was soft, not angry. Jake held the closet door open, looked at her over his shoulder.

"That's the way to do it, Marsha. I don't sit here and pander to your manipulations, then you're taking your ball and going home, is that it?"

"In this case, the ball's my daughter. And I won't have her raised the way you were raised, Jake."

"What did you say? What the hell did you just say to me?" Jake slammed the closet door closed, stalked back to the table and stopped.

Marsha was looking at him, fearfully. Leaning back in her chair, her hands coming up in a defensive gesture. He stepped back and she relaxed a little, with a hurt look in her eyes, on her face.

"Jake, you were going to hit me."

"No I wasn't. Don't tell me what I was going to do."

"You've never come at me with your fists at your side, Jake. Not in four years of marriage. What were you planning to do?" Jake fell into the chair, lifted his legs then let the heels of his feet flop to the carpet. He closed his eyes and shook his head, blew out a hard breath.

"I'm as tired as I've ever been, and I'm scared to death about Mondo." He shook his head again, then reached up and gently rubbed his forehead, wearily. "I shouldn't have said anything, I shouldn't have said a word."

"The same way your father never said a word to your mother, Jake. Is that the relationship you—"

Jake smashed his fist down onto the table. "Will you stop comparing me to that son of a *bitch!*" In the other room, he could hear Lynne cry out. Not loudly, the child wasn't even sure she was awake yet. She was just clearing her lungs, getting ready for the real scream, the one she'd let loose if she decided to wake up.

"Are you happy now, Jake?" Marsha said, then got up from the table and walked away from him, resolutely, heading into the baby's bedroom, and all Jake could think of to do was look after her with a stricken expression. Marsha stopped at the doorway, turned and looked at him with an expression he had never seen before; she was curious, but at the same time frightened, and disgusted.

"Was it a mistake, your becoming a cop, Jake?"

"My mistake was in marrying a fucking debutante," Jake said, and was immediately sorry when he saw the look of pain that crossed over her face before Marsha caught herself. Then her face went blank and she turned and walked into the baby's bedroom.

Leaving Jake to sit at the table, staring off into space, until the phone in the kitchen rang and finally startled him out of his numbness.

LAURA SAID, "**I** wasn't sure you were coming," as she opened the door of the loft for Detective Sergeant Alex Mondello. She stood back and he walked in, breathing heavily. She said, "I'm sorry about all those stairs, but the elevator's been out since July." She was staring at his pistol, the hogleg hanging off his right side, next to his belt badge. Mondo wasn't wearing a sport coat.

"That's all right," Mondo said. He came inside and looked around, noticed that the place was a lot bigger than he'd expected, but far more cheaply furnished than he'd imagined. It looked as if Laura had gotten the furniture out of the alley. On the other side of the huge room, a gigantic older woman was sprawled out on an old, dirty couch, watching a Monday Night Football preseason game on the portable black-and-white television set. The old woman looked over at him, then past him, at Laura.

"You want'a I should go now?"

"Please stay, Mrs. LaRitcha," Laura said, then waved her hand at Mondo. "Come in, let's go sit down."

Mondo heard noises in the bathroom, sounds he was used to; running water, teeth being brushed too quickly; the sounds impatient children make when told to do something that didn't appeal to them. Mondo was puzzled, this wasn't what he had expected. A kid in the toilet, a diesel truck of an old woman watching a football game, and all the noise. He could barely hear the television above the sound of the old floor fan.

"It's hot, isn't it?" Laura said to him, and he half-smiled. Not a good opening gambit, if her goal was to get Mondo into the sack. Which he was doubting more and more with every passing second. So, why the hell had she insisted that he come? To get her husband off the hook? She would never know how badly Mondo wanted the man to take that fall. But that didn't mean that he couldn't feel her out, find out what she knew. You never could tell . . .

He said, "In a month we'll be complaining about how cold it is." Mondo nodded toward the TV. "Football weather, winter. It's on the way."

"I can go on my roof with a pair of binoculars and watch the Bears home games at Soldier Field." Laura sat down at the cheap Formica kitchen table. Mondo lowered his voice and leaned forward, so the woman on the couch couldn't hear what he was saying. He kept his face and tone professional; he was questioning her and he wanted her to know it.

"You said it was urgent, when we talked at headquarters, and in the message you left for me earlier today. What's going on, Laura? What do you want from me?" Mondo noticed her quick look of discomfort, and he forgot about his hangover, and about his disappointment at the fact that they weren't alone. He knew he was onto something. He tried another tack; he reached out and touched Laura's forearm. "Come on, you can tell me, Laura. I owe you."

"*You* owe *me?*"

Mondo shrugged. "Seeing you last night, outside the hotel, took away the pain of getting shot in the head."

"Oh my God, I'm so sorry, I've been so wrapped up in my own problems . . . How *is* your ear?" Mondo turned his head so she could see it.

"Just a bandage now is all I need. I got lucky."

"But you got shot."

"I've been shot before, Laura. More than once."

The door to the bathroom opened before Laura could respond, and a short, squat, lumpish kid wearing white pajamas came hulking out. The kid was all bent over; his back was turned to them. Mondo turned in his chair to look at him, at his dwarfish size, his form. He kept his face impassive.

"That's my son, Tommy," Laura said, then raised her voice and said to the kid, "Tommy? Honey? Come over and say hello to Mr. Mondello." Mondo watched Tommy walk shyly across the room, heading on an angle away from him, toward Mrs. LaRitcha, who opened her arms to accept him without ever taking her eyes off the football game. The boy's tongue was protruding from his mouth, it lolled over to the left side of his chin. Tommy didn't look directly at Mondo, but rather behind him, looking from the wall, then to his mother, as if frightened to focus on Mondo himself.

"Mr. Mondello, this is Tommy." Laura seemed puzzled. "Tommy? Where are your manners? Come over and shake Mr. Mondello's hand."

"Don't want to." The voice was far too deep for a child, a mannish voice, the words heavily mumbled.

"Tommy!"

"That's all right, Laura," Mondo said, embarrassed. The kid was a mongoloid, a Down's syndrome child. You couldn't expect him to come over and shake hands with a total stranger. Mondo thought he understood why the woman had stayed with her loser of a husband as long as she had.

Laura said, "No, it's not all right. Tommy's not usually rude."

"You leave'a him alone," Mrs. LaRitcha said. "He know in his head wha' he a'like and no a'like. He no a'like the gentlemens, he's'a got the right." Mondo couldn't help himself, he smiled.

"Look, it's all *right.*"

"Tommy's got a big day at camp tomorrow," Laura said, changing the subject, then she raised her voice again. "Don't you, Tommy?"

The kid shoved his face into the fat woman's shoulder, burying it there. When he spoke, Mondo could hardly understand him.

"I'm going *swimming!*"

"Good for you, Tommy, be careful." Mondo spoke and the kid looked up, stood as straight as he could and put his hands on his hips.

"I'm a very good swimmer, you know." Challenging Mondo. Was he jealous because Mondo was sitting there with his mother? Mondo looked at him, and smiled.

"I'll bet you are."

"I can swim better than you!"

"I'll bet. I swim like a rock."

"You can't fool *me,* Mr. Mondello. Rocks don't know how to swim."

"He remembered my name?" Laura didn't respond. But the woman on the couch did.

" 'Ey, he's'a no stupeedo, meester. Don't mistake'a that he ees."

"He only heard my name . . ." Mondo let the words fade away, then shut up. He knew he couldn't win; whatever he said now would only make his embarrassment worse. He felt resentment beginning to bubble, just under the surface. What was he doing here, with all these people? Mondo took a deep breath, let it out slowly. He did it again, but it didn't help much. The large, open space of the loft suddenly felt too small for him; too enclosed. He suddenly noticed the heat, as if the sun was still up, beating down on the back of his head. Laura rose from her chair, walked over and Mondo watched her, trying to enjoy the sight, trying not to notice that the kid was still watching him. He hoped she wasn't going to drag the kid over here, make him shake hands or something, recite a goddamn simpleton poem he learned at his retard school. He wished he was in a bar, or in his motel room. He wished he were anywhere but in this loft.

Laura took the boy by the hand, and then, to Mondo's great relief, she walked him to his room. She kissed him at the doorway, told him to say his prayers. She lowered her voice and said something else to the kid, and Tommy responded in a slurred whine that Mondo couldn't make out. The kid sulked into the room, and Laura walked back toward Mondo, forcing a smile, looking as uncomfortable as Mondo felt.

Mondo didn't waste any more time. "What was it you wanted, Laura?" He was no longer feeling very seductive. Or even polite. This wasn't his problem, and he wasn't about to get involved. This family had enough problems already without his getting involved with Laura, no matter how pretty she was. And he was sure she didn't know anything. So his plans were out the window, at least for tonight.

"You don't have to be afraid, it's not contagious." She couldn't seem to help the hint of anger in her voice. "All he's got to offer is love, Mondo. He's profoundly affected by his disease, his IQ is very low, but he's not moronic, and he *feels,* the exact same way we do, and he's very sensitive."

"Did I do something?"

"You didn't have to." Laura wiped angrily at her eyes. Mrs. LaRitcha was still absorbed in the football game, not seeming to be paying them any attention. Mondo got to his feet. Laura said, "No, please, don't go." Against his better judgment, Mondo sat back down. "I didn't mean to be rude," Laura said, then looked away. "I just, I don't know, I thought you'd be different."

"From whom?"

Laura looked straight at him now, dead on, her eyes alive. "From every other fucking human being on the planet, that's from whom. Everyone either patronizes him or pretends he isn't there, or stares at him, like he's a freak." Laura waved a hand in the air. "It's not your problem, I'm sorry. I need your help, and I'm pushing you away."

"I don't know how I can help you, unless you have some control over your husband, if you can somehow get him to tell us the truth." Mondo heard the couch creak, and looked up, saw Mrs. LaRitcha struggling to her feet, watched her walk over to the TV set and shut it off. She waddled to the door. There seemed to be something wrong with her feet.

"Is'a half'a'time. I go watch'a the rest of eet een my own compartment."

"You're sure?"

"I'm'a sure." She leveled a deadly glare at Mondo. "Call'a me up on the telephone, if'a you need me, honey."

Laura said, "I think I'll be home the rest of the night." The woman grunted, looked at Mondo, hard. "The boy, he's afraid of your gun," she said, and walked out without another word. Mondo could hear her on the stairway, wheezing, cursing to herself, pulling her bulk up the stairs. He could relate to that.

At last, they were alone. Maybe he could still discover things here, maybe the night wouldn't be a total loss.

"She loves Tommy, she really does."

"He seems attached to her."

"With a father like Bing, and the sort of grandparents that he has, Tommy would have gotten attached to an attack dog that licked his hand."

"I can imagine."

"Can you?" Laura got up, went into the kitchen, then came back with a telephone in her hand. She sat down in the chair, punched a number into the keypad that was built into the belly of the handset. She spoke as she dialed.

"Bing wanted an athlete. His father wanted another Bing. *My* parents think Tommy's God's punishment for my getting pregnant out of wedlock." She held the phone to her ear, looked over at Mondo, cynically. "And you say you can im*a*gine?" Laura took the phone away from her ear, pressed a button, then listened again. "Voice mail," she said, as she took the phone away yet again, squinted at it, then pressed another button. "I just got it today, I'm not used to the commands. Can you be patient for just another minute? There's a point to all this, believe me." Laura's face was determined. Mondo watched her, marveling at her beauty. How could someone so beautiful have had a kid with such screwed-up chromosomes? He felt a stirring of hope. With the kid in bed, the old lady gone, who knew? Something might still work out between them.

"*There* it is. Wait, let me rewind and pause it," Laura said, and took the phone away from her ear for the last time, pressed a button, then handed the phone to Mondo. "Press five, then the star button. Then listen to this son of a bitch." Mondo looked at Laura quizzically, and she nodded at him encouragingly. He shrugged, pressed five, then the star key, then put the phone to his ear, and was right away glad that he had done what she'd instructed because he could smell her perfume on the telephone. Something flowery and understated. The smell made him feel almost happy.

Until he heard the guttural, snarling voice on the phone, some outfit slob, no doubt about that, warning Laura one last time about what would happen to her if she didn't follow orders, right away.

After the message was over, Mondo held the phone away from his ear for a second. "How do you rewind it?"

"Three, then star." Mondo hit the buttons, listened to the message again.

Things began to fall into place for him, other things, but still, things that were related to this phone call. Things that had been dancing around on the edges of Mondo's mind all afternoon.

"Here." Mondo handed the phone back to Laura. He'd heard enough. "Don't erase it."

"I won't." She seemed embarrassed now, ashamed of herself. What could she be, twenty-four, twenty-five years old, tops? He shook his head, not bothering to hide his disgust. Laura seemed to sense what he was feeling. She looked at him with the same determination he'd seen earlier, when she'd so vehemently defended her child.

"Before you make any judgments, let me tell you something, all right? Let me say it, then you can walk away if that's what you want, and no hard feelings. I left my husband at the end of May. I had my son in the middle of my senior year of high school, and back then there weren't any day care centers, not even in the public schools. I went to a Catholic school, so I had to either drop out, or get expelled. I never got my diploma. After I left Bing, I waited tables at four different restaurants in this city. I had to work the late shift, because the senior girls got their pick of when they worked. I slapped more hands of more drunks off my ass in the past three goddamn months then I ever did when I was tending bar and hopping tables at Bing's father's tavern, and back then I was working with drunks all day and night. I got my GED this summer, and those papers at your elbow are my financial assistance forms for college. I'll be starting at Circle in January, *and* I've been accepted in the Honor's course." Laura paused.

"I made up my mind about something this summer, Mondo, and I still believe it today, even with all that's happening: If men are going to treat me like a whore, I'm going to get paid for the insult."

"So you make dirty phone calls."

"I fill a need. I get paid for that."

"How long you been at it?" Mondo asked, and Laura hesitated, as if embarrassed to tell him the truth.

"What's today, Monday? I started Friday night."

"What?"

Laura gave him a level look. "I worked for Al over the weekend, Mondo, for the late Al Beck."

"I know," Mondo said. He had made that connection some time back. "I know you did, Lori," and he saw her face crumple with fear as he leaned back in the chair, crossed his legs, and stared at her, hard. "Now I think it's time we stopped playing around, Lori, and you tell me everything you know. I won't be asking you twice."

JAKE WAS GASPING for air as he left the cramped and busy Crime Scene offices. He was shaking his head back and forth, in disbelief. He had to get it together before he went back upstairs, before he confronted anyone, Jesus, before he ran into Mondo. He might show up here, fishing for information, wanting to see what had happened when Jake had tried to serve the warrant. Jake went into the bathroom, locked the door, went over to the sink and turned on the tap and threw cold water on his face, cupping his hands and dashing his face with the icy water over and over, until he felt a little better. Then he stood there, holding onto the sink with the palms of his hands, gazing into the mirror, making connections, forming links, figuring things out and putting it all together until it made some kind of sense to him.

There was a rattle on the door handle. Jake stood and grabbed some paper towels off the roll hanging on the wall, wiped his face as he walked over to the door and unlocked it with his free hand.

Captain Merlin Royal walked in, slowly, glaring at Jake. He shoved the door closed with his foot, locked it behind him without taking his eyes off Jake. He held out his hand. "You got the fucking sheet, Phillips?" Jake nodded to where he'd left it, on top of the garbage can. The captain looked over at it, but did not move to touch the sheet. He just looked up at Jake, unsurprised and angry.

"My ass has been in a sling over this since Roosevelt got killed. I went to bat for Mondo," the captain shook his head. "Jesus Christ almighty forgive me, I suppressed *evidence,* trying to do him a favor. It was all right there in front of us the whole time though, wasn't it, Phillips?"

"I was going to call you."

"Yeah? When was that, Phillips? *After* you broke the case? What, call me from the Channel Five newsroom, when you're doing an interview about how you broke the case, no problem, on your fucking day off?"

Jake looked up, hurt, but the captain ignored him, Royal shaking his head and glancing one more time at the sheet atop the trash can.

"Call Mondello right now, beep him. Get him to meet you somewhere. He trusts you, he'll do it. The second he sits down, you draw down on him, and if he moves, you whack him over the head with your pistol. I'll have backup there, we'll take him into custody. It's for his own good. We *have* to do this, Phillips!"

"Captain—"

Royal slammed his fist down on the trash can. The top of it buckled downward, the swinging doors caved in. The paper on top of it was torn by the blow; it fluttered to the ground. The captain looked at his hand, opened his mouth, then shut it, as if he didn't believe what he'd just done. When he spoke his voice was sharp and commanding, but he had control of it, he wasn't shouting.

"Shut up! Don't you say one more word to me, Phillips, I'm warning you. I'm tired of listening to you. More people could die here, this thing isn't over. The guy went over the edge last night at the hotel, and none of us wants to believe it. Don't feel bad, the mayor won't believe it, either. But after last night, *anybody's* at risk. Anybody who saw what happened. He'll blame you all. The guy's a psycho." The captain looked away, thinking. "Crime Scene tech called me at home, to break the news. She's looking for a spot in Homicide, I can trust her to keep her mouth—" The captain shouted "*Shit!*" He grabbed Jake's arm. "Come on, let's go."

"Mondo—"

"Mondo can wait, shit, I forgot about the wife. The wife'll be most at risk. You know her, right?"

"I met her."

"Phillips, listen to me. We've got to keep this in-house until the bastard's in custody, we can't take any chances that he'll get away or go on a killing spree."

The captain turned and reached out to unlock the door, and Jake fought his fear, reached out and stopped him. The captain turned slowly, giving Jake the sort of look he would give to a madman. Jake spoke quickly; there was a chance that the captain might hit him.

"Captain, look, we've got nothing solid at this point but finger-print ID. We're acting on our anger, on emotions. We've waited this long, let's wait five more minutes, please. Just give me five minutes with the suspect, with Bingham, five minutes, that's all I ask. I've got an idea—Mondo gave it to me himself. If it works out, we might have him cold, dead to rights. If not, he could walk with a slick lawyer, the same way Bingham will." The captain looked at Jake, and Jake knew the second he had him, without the captain having to speak a word.

"Come on." The captain threw open the door and ran out, and Jake followed him. The two of them raced down the hall, to the Criminal Investigation detective's squad room.

Laura sat, nervously waiting, wondering how a man could change from hot to cold so quickly. Mondo had gone from a genial guest to a tyrant, all cop, questioning her coldly, his voice devoid of emo-tion. He wanted to know what she knew, how much she knew, and when she'd learned it, and he told her, right up front, that she was in no position to bargain. No deals. Tell it all, tell it straight, if she lied once, she went down, he'd see to it that she was indicted along with her husband as a co-conspirator. After she'd told him all she knew, he'd made her hook up her telephone line, the sex line, both phones, but not the answering machine. Then he'd warmed up just a little bit, not much. He'd told her he would get the outfit punk off her back, and they'd be square. All they had to do was to wait for the guy to call back. Laura had asked, What if he didn't? Mondo did-n't want to even entertain that notion. He'd told her that he'd think about his next move while she waited, that she was to get a number and call back anyone else who called.

Her goal was to get Bing out of jail, and it looked as if Mondo could pull that off. In return, she had to find out for him exactly what Bing had seen. What he remembered, descriptions of everything. Mondo didn't care how she got the information, either, he'd made that clear. The son of a bitch. Now he was downstairs, getting something out of his car. His own recording device, one that was far more advanced than the cheap machine Diana had bought her.

Diana!

Laura hadn't thought of her all night, since coming home. She looked at the door, knew that she'd be able to hear Mondo's feet on the stairway when he came back up. Laura put on the headset, punched in Diana's number, then waited while it rang. She hung up on the voice mail. Diana must be on the line. At least one of them was making money. Laura thought about going over and locking the door, then dialing nine-one-one. If she did that, she'd get arrested. At least. The way Mondo had been looking at her, God knew how he'd react if she locked him out. Laura bit at a knuckle. She'd left her husband because she was tired of being helpless, at the mercy of some man. And now where was she? A lot worse off than where she'd been, so much for independence. She should have taken Bing's advice, she should have never said a word to any cop. God-damn Diana, goddamn her to hell, for telling Laura to call Mondo if she was ever in trouble and needed an honest cop. He was like all the rest. All these fucking men were the same . . .

The phone rang.

Laura looked at it.

She should wait, she should wait for Mondo. She didn't hear his footsteps on the stairs. If it was the extortionist on the phone, she'd have to talk to him alone.

But even if it was, she knew how to drive him crazy. She'd simply curse him, then hang up on him. He'd call right back, his ego would make him, then Mondo could capture his voice on tape, or else scare him off with threats.

How had she ever gotten herself into a mess like this? Laura was quitting, this was it. She'd sling hash all day, sixteen hours a day, but she wouldn't do this for one more night. Laura's Love Line was going out of business, first thing tomorrow morning.

She hit the button on the headset that turned on the line, and she said hello as softly as she could, but there was a catch in her voice, and she knew it.

"*LLLLLAAAAUUURRRRRAAAAA!!!!!*" The sound of the voice made Laura jump. She got to her feet, listening, one hand to her ear. It was a male voice, but not the mobster's. The sound was that of an animal, one in incredible pain.

An animal that knew her name, who she was.

"IS THIS LAURA!" the voice demanded, in a reptilian whisper.

"Yes, yes it is." She couldn't keep the fear out of her tone of voice. In spite of the heat, Laura shivered. "Who's this?"

"THIS IS *XXXXXXXXX.*"

"Who?"

"This is X you bitch and don't pretend you don't know who I am!" The words were spoken all in a rush. It took Laura a second to understand what he had said. X? Was that supposed to mean something to her? It had to be just some freak who'd gotten her name and number from the computer bulletin board, who got his jollies off on women's terror. Getting off without paying, either. She'd hang up on him, that's all.

But as she was reaching to disconnect the call, his voice came back to her, filling her head; the man was no longer screaming.

"And how's that retardate fucking son of yours, you dense bitch?"

He seemed amused now, this freak. There was a laugh in his tone, then a loud giggle came over the line.

At the insult to Tommy, however, Laura Bingham lost her fear.

"Fuck off, you asshole!" Laura said, and made a face at the sound of the high-pitched scream that came over the line; she cut it off in mid-howl.

The phone rang again immediately. Laura clicked the headset on.

"I'm taping the call, you son of a bitch, and I'm turning it over to the FBI."

"Oh, you do that, Laura honey. Or shall I call you Lori?" Lori? Mondo had called her Lori. It was the name she'd used over the weekend, working for Al. She assumed Mondo had gotten the information from the card Bing had said he'd thrown away, the lying bastard.

But now Laura wasn't so sure.

This man had called her Lori, as Mondo had. And now he'd called her dense. But it didn't sound like Mondo. It didn't sound like him at all.

Laura said, "I know you, don't I?"

"We've spoken before." He was playing with her again, Jesus, this guy was a sicko. First he was screaming, keening, wailing, howling in agony, and now he was all lilting-voiced and joking around, playful. But Christ, was he breathing hard, as if he'd just finished a race.

Laura got it then, and blurted out her memories.

"You're the man from last night, the one who tried to get me to give out my home phone number."

"Oooooh!" The freak was playing again, singing the syllables out, sketching them as a child would. "Laura gets to die-ie, Laura gets to die-ie!"

"Come on up and see me, you faggot, as soon as you grow the balls." She'd said it for the reaction, to see what he'd say. He'd somehow known about Tommy's disease; that couldn't have been a shot in the dark.

"YOU DARE CALL ME QUEER? I'LL *SHOW* YOU HOW QUEER I AM!" His voice was commanding now, deep, sounding entirely different from any voice he'd used earlier. Laura began to shiver again. So hard she couldn't stop.

"YOUR TEETH SHOULD BE CHATTERING!" the man shouted, then he was joking again, the freak was completely out of control and didn't even know it. "Because you're going to die, Lori! And it's so cold there, so very, very cold . . ." He hissed now, like a snake, his words coming over the line in a harsh whisper. "Let me share a secret with you. I wasn't going to tell you, but I don't like surprises, do you? I'm down at Diana's, at her loft, Lori, right downstairs from yours. I'm with what's left of Diana. You see, I ate most of her." He giggled again. "I always like dark meat best."

"*NO!*" Laura shouted the word into the phone, then tore off the headset and threw it angrily to the floor. She raced to the door, tore it open, then stopped. She was shaking, crying, sobbing with each breath.

Tommy. She had to think of Tommy. She had to get herself under control and think about her son.

Laura stepped back, closed and locked the door. She walked quickly to the kitchen and grabbed her longest, sharpest knife out of the cutlery drawer. She held it in front of her as she walked to her son's bedroom.

Tommy was awake, looking up at her, no longer in his bed but rather cuddled into a ball in the corner, sucking his thumb and crying. Laura ran to him, knelt down beside him, dropped the knife to the floor and pulled him into her arms.

"Did Mr. Mondello make you say all those mean things, Mommy?"

"No, no, honey, it's all right, sweetheart, it's okay. It was just a mean phone call, you know about those, we've talked them over, remember?" Laura was fighting to remain calm, for Tommy's sake. She looked down at his round face and nearly burst into tears herself at the pain she saw, the suffering and confusion etched onto his heavy little features. She kissed his cheek, kissed away his tears. Tommy didn't know what self-pity was; he wasn't crying for himself, he was crying for his mother, because she was upset. "I love you baby. Now come on, we're going out for a little while."

"Where are we going?" Tommy seemed surprised. "You want me to go out in my pajamas?"

"Just for tonight."

"Where are we going, Mommy?"

Laura thought about that, briefly. There was nowhere they could go. The police were out of the question. She'd tried that already, and look what had happened.

There was a heavy pounding at the outside door, and Laura and Tommy both jumped at the sound. Laura picked up her knife, and stood.

"You stay right here, Tommy." She liked the way her voice sounded. Strong, confident, steely. She sounded in control—a lot better than she felt. Inside, she was shaking, fighting the urge to vomit.

"Mommy, don't go, please don't hurt anybody. Whatever he said, Mr. Mondello didn't mean it!"

Mr. Mondello? Mr. *Mondello?!* Laura looked down at her crying son. "Why didn't you want to shake his hand, Tommy?" She had to fight not to comfort him, not to fall to her knees and try to stop his tears.

Through those tears, through his sobs, Tommy said. "He's a mean man, Mommy. I can tell, I can always tell. He's not mean like Grandpa Bing is, he's worse, he's a *whole* lot worse."

Oh God, Laura thought, putting it all together, Mondo's being gone when that crazy bastard called, calling her Lori, knowing about Tommy, his accidentally running into her at the police station . . .

Perhaps Mr. Mondello truly is mean. Mean, and very sick.

Maybe he even calls himself X when he calls women on the phone to terrorize them.

NOBODY CAME TO the door at first, so Jake leaned into the bell. He took his finger away and put his ear right next to the door, listening for the sounds of voices, a television or radio, something. There *was* something, something that sounded like a cat crying, far off, maybe in the basement, or locked in an upstairs room.

"Try it again," the captain said. Jake held his hand up for silence.

"I think I hear something."

"I'm going around back."

Jake stood sweating in the midnight heat, in front of the well-kept house on the East Side, listening and afraid, trying to fight his fear. He was holding the screen door open with his shoulder. The night darkness was broken by the light cast from the streetlamps, long shadows falling from the trees, the cars, the fences. A good, quiet neighborhood, working people asleep in their bungalows.

The sound of shattering glass broke the silence, and Jake jumped. He pulled his pistol and ran around to the gangway, through the driveway, racing to the back door, where the captain was. Jake turned the corner in a skid, doing it all wrong but he didn't give a shit, he was pumped up, they were *there.* He skidded to a halt, nearly fell, got his balance, then raced up the paved back steps, then on into the house through the shattered back door.

The captain was in the kitchen, giving CPR to the beaten, shattered body of the bleeding naked woman who was lying on the kitchen floor.

"It's Mondo, Laura, open up for Christ's sake."

"Go away!"

"What?"

"Get the fuck away from my door, I swear to God, I've already dialed nine-one-one!"

"Good. They can send a wagon for you, a matron to body-search you before they lock you up with the dykes at the County. Go ahead, call the cops."

"Go *away!*"

"What's gonna happen to the kid if they take you away, Laura? I agreed to help you, even after I didn't have to. What's your problem all of a sudden?"

"Mondo?"

"What?"

Laura threw the door open wide, held the knife in both hands, up high, blade pointed toward Mondo, ready to strike if she had to. Mondo saw it and raised both hands to shoulder level. He was holding a small black leather satchel in his hand. It could be the tape recorder he claimed he'd gone to get. He took a step back. "Calm down now, Laura, just calm down. What got into you in the past ten minutes?"

"What took you so long, Mondo!"

"What?" He shook his head, exasperated. "You ever notice the bar downstairs, how crowded it is? You can't park anywhere on this street before three in the morning."

"What did you do to Diana?!"

"To *who?*" Mondo looked puzzled.

Laura raised the knife. "To Diana, you son of a bitch!"

"All right. Listen to me, Laura. I don't know any Diana, I don't know what the hell you're talking about . . . Now why don't you just calm down and give me the knife? What do you say?"

Laura almost did, his voice was nearly hypnotic. It would be so easy to give him the knife, to give him everything, to let him take it all over and deal with it. Big, strong Mondo could solve all the problems.

NO!

She couldn't give in. If Mondo was the man who called himself X, she and her son were in grave danger, even if he hadn't touched Diana. The man on the phone had been disturbed. He needed to be in a nuthouse. She raised the knife again, and was pleased to notice that when she now spoke, the hysteria that had been in her voice was gone.

"Diana's downstairs, Mondo, in her loft, two flights down. You want the knife? Go down there and see if she's okay. If she is, you come back up with her. You do that, and I'll hand over the knife, no problem. If she doesn't come upstairs with you, don't you bother to come back alone—I'll cut your throat if you do."

"All right, I'm going," Mondo said. He'd taken a step down while

Laura had been speaking, and he'd lowered his hands. He was giving her a strange look. Laura hoped that she'd be apologizing to him in a minute, that her suspicions had been wrong. "Laura?" Mondo said. "What happened while I was gone?" He seemed to really want to know.

"Let's just say I got a phone call." Laura watched for Mondo's reaction; there wasn't one. "From some bastard who calls himself X."

"X? Like in Malcolm? Was it a black guy?"

"It might have been you."

"Me." Mondo shook his head and turned his back on her. Laura watched him closely. If he made one move for that gigantic gun at his side, she'd let him have it, jump down the stairs and stick the knife right into his back. She could do it before he cleared the weapon, she knew it. Laura stepped out onto the landing, so she could get a jump on him if she had to. She stood by the railing, but Mondo didn't look back at her, and didn't put his hand anywhere near his gun. He seemed to be humoring her.

"Two floors down. She got a number?"

"Diana's got the whole floor."

And then he was around the bend, out of Laura's sight. She could hear him knocking, could hear him call Diana's name. He hadn't seemed to recognize the name; maybe he'd recognize Diana when he saw her, if he hadn't already seen her. If he hadn't already killed her. Laura didn't hear anything for a minute, not a sound.

Then in quick succession, she heard four things:

Mondo screaming in surprise;

then his shout for her to get into her apartment, *now;*

then there was the sound of a tremendously loud gunshot, blasting in the hallway;

and lastly, over the ringing in her ears, Laura heard the sound of footsteps pounding up the stairs toward her.

"Where's he at? God in Heaven, we have to stop him . . ." The captain was talking to himself, sitting at the kitchen table, absently watching the paramedics carry out the children on stretchers. They'd been found upstairs, in shock, locked in their bedroom closets. They'd seen what their father had done to their mother. The bastard had made them watch.

"She's gonna make it, Captain," Jake said. The woman had been sodomized, for Christ's sake, in front of her teenage kids, dragged out of her bathroom in the middle of her shower. She'd need reconstructive surgery on her face, and therapy, but she'd make it. She'd probably never trust men again, though. Jake couldn't blame her. If you couldn't trust a man you'd been married to for most of your entire adult life, who could you trust?

Right now, Jake trusted the captain, was holding a lot of faith in his sudden lack of good judgment. He had to; he needed things from him, authority to act, for one. If not approval, then he had to get the man to at least turn his head and look away. It had been some time since the captain had been out on the street, had seen anything like this. He wasn't used to it; the sight had taken its toll. Jake used it to his advantage. He sat down next to the man, with uniformed squad car officers and Crime Scene coppers working or loafing all around them, wanting to catch a boss's attention, show how hard they were working.

When Jake spoke, it was a whisper. "Captain, cut me loose. I can find this bastard, tonight."

"We got to find him, he's got a gun." The captain's voice was distant.

"I went outside my authority, I put out the warning. I'm sorry. There'll be uniformed people checking every hotel and motel in the city, and looking for his car. They know he's armed, and dangerous. And if we don't get him that way, someone'll recognize him from the TV or papers. The press's outside right now, Captain. They smelled blood when I called nine-one-one. It's a madhouse."

The captain looked up. "What'd you say? You want me to cut you loose?"

Jake nodded just one time, his eyes giving away nothing. The captain looked at him for a long moment, then slowly began to nod his head.

"You know something, don't you?" There was awe in the captain's voice. He waited until he was sure that Jake wasn't going to respond, then he said, "Maybe I don't want to know." Jake still didn't say anything. The captain said, "Let me tell you something, Phillips. This is your day off. I don't have twenty-four-hour cops working for me." He waved his hand. "Go on, get out of here. Go home to your wife." Jake thanked him, and left.

He ran out the front door, into a daylight-at-midnight scene, bright lights, TV crews in place, their Minicams set up and ready to go, the reporters calling out to any cop they saw, trying to find out

what had gone on inside. There were squad cars everywhere, blocking entrance and exit. Jake screamed on the run to a bunch of uniformed officers, told them to clear a path for his car, right fucking
now, and he jumped into his Caprice, put the flasher on the roof
with one hand as he started the car with the other. He powered
down his window.

"You, hey you!" Jake hollered at a young female officer, who
looked surprised that he had taken notice of her. "Make sure *none*
of those reporters follow this car, you hear me?" The woman nodded. She wasn't surprised anymore, her facial expression was determined as she jumped into an idling squad and threw it in
reverse. The second Jake pulled out, the woman backed the squad
car into the middle of the road. There was a loud honking, as one
savvy reporter who'd seen what Jake was doing nearly broadsided
the squad car as he tried to follow Jake. Jake saw it in a brief glance
into his rearview mirror, nodding his approval at the woman's
smart move. He couldn't have anyone following him, not now. He
needed to be alone when he found Sergeant Mondello.

Laura grabbed the sex-line phone with trembling fingers, hit nine-
one-one, then put the phone to her ear. There was a loud screech-
ing, a wild beeping sound, wild noises coming out of the earpiece.
There was a heavy kick at the loft door. It shook nearly off its
hinges. Goddamnit, god*damnit!* She'd left the headset turned on
when she'd torn it off her head—she didn't have a line. "Tommy!
Get back in your bedroom!" The boy had come into the room, was
now cowering, close to the door. "RIGHT NOW, TOMMY!"

There was another kick at the door, then another, and at last the
lock gave out. Laura ran to the kitchen phone, was reaching for it
when a hand grabbed at her throat from behind. She could smell
the acrid cordite smell coming out of the barrel of the gun that was
pointed at her temple.

Jake raced downtown, running stoplights, ignoring the curses of
other vehicles and the shouts from the punks on the street corners,
Jake driving sixty and seventy on stretches of Lake Shore Drive in
areas where the posted speed was twenty-five to thirty. He had to
get from 103rd Street to Thirteen and Michigan, quick. To the
woman's house, where Mondo would be. Jake had watched as she'd

written her phone number and address down in Mondo's notebook. He'd heard the woman, Laura, nearly beg Mondo to call her just as soon as he was done at Headquarters. She'd said that it was urgent, she'd made Mondo promise he'd call. Jake had already called Mondo's hotel; he knew he wasn't there. He had to get there, to the woman's place. He had to, before the next victim died.

Laura heard Tommy scream, the child fighting his paralyzing terror as he tried to defend his mother. "Leave my mother alone—" She felt the gun leave her head for a moment, heard Tommy grunt as the man slapped at him. She heard her son fall to the floor. Laura stabbed behind her with the knife, felt it hit something, something that gave, Laura lashing out blindly as she turned. Everything was suddenly brighter, all the colors; sounds were now coming into her ears as if through a long tin tunnel. She saw blood, saw a *lot* of it, bright red, shooting out, coming out of the wrist of the man, the son of a bitch, X.

She'd stabbed his gun arm. He'd dropped the weapon; it fell almost on top of Tommy. Laura didn't take time to look down at her son; she couldn't afford the luxury of trying to see if he was all right. The bastard was advancing, snarling, the big gun gone, but he didn't seem to care. He didn't seem to care about the knife in Laura's hand, either. She backed to the kitchen counter, made a high-pitched sound when her hips touched it. She slashed at him, and he backed off. Laura advanced, swinging the knife at his belly. He backed off, danced into the living room. There was a ribbon of blood beginning to stain the front of his shirt. She'd cut him.

"Come on, you sick fucker," Laura hissed at him, waving the knife from side to side, crouched down, the weapon held tightly in both hands. "I'll cut your *heart* out, you motherfucker." The man was afraid now. Blood was coming out of his right wrist, was soaking the front of his shirt. She hoped she'd cut an organ, that he'd drop over, that he'd die. She was feeling sick, her vision was blurred. She waved the knife and took a step toward him. "Come *on,*" she snarled, again.

Instead of backing away from the knife, this time the man moved in. It startled Laura, she hesitated, then he grabbed the knife, held the blade in both hands, the man ripping it from her hands and throwing it away from him. His palm was torn open, God, Laura could see the bones in his hand. He was snarling back at her, his lips curled back, the man cursing her as he moved in on her.

"Cunt, you dense *cunt!* You'll watch me butcher your child!"

Laura was against the wall now, watching him, waiting for his move. She wanted to time her kick to his balls—she couldn't afford to miss.

But she did.

He was on her fast, had her by the hair, his blood was getting into her eyes as he slapped her now, as he slammed her head into the wall. She could feel the plaster caving in around her head, felt the hole in the wall that her head was making in it. Laura tried to knee him, but she was losing strength fast, Laura scratching at him, clawing at him with her fingernails, then feeling something soft and squishy, feeling her finger go in deep.

The man backed off, howling in pain, grabbing at his eye. He was bent over forward when the night was torn apart by an explosion, then he was thrown back, his arms flailing, an expression of surprised agony on his face as he fell in a heap to the floor. Laura watched the body, fascinated, repelled, too shocked to look away. There was another loud explosion, and the body on the floor jumped. Then another, then another. At last the body lay still.

"*Tommy!*" Laura dropped to her knees next to her son, lifted his head and cradled it in her arms, gently touching his forehead, saying his name over and over, frantically.

"Laura." The voice was soft, the word spoken in a monotone. "Laura." Laura looked over at the doorway.

Mondo was leaning heavily against the shattered door frame. His shirt was soaked red from the blood he'd lost. He was holding his left side with one hand, the other held his huge gun, loosely. As Laura watched, he lost his grip, and the gun slipped from his fingers to the floor.

"Get the gun, Laura, go over and shoot him, in the head, make sure he's dead." Mondo fell heavily to the floor, in a sitting position.

"He's dead, he's already dead, he has to be."

God, she had to get herself under control. X was dead and Mondo might be dying, and Tommy was hurt. Laura somehow got to her feet and ran to the kitchen, grabbed the phone and dialed nine-one-one. She was screaming into it, trying to explain things to the dumb, calm son of a bitch on the other end. She shouted at him until he understood, and she left the line open as she ran back to her son.

Mondo had somehow grabbed his gun, was now crawling toward

the dead man on the floor, dragging the heavy pistol along with him. Laura walked over to him, crouched down, and took the gun out of his hand.

"The ambulance is on the way, the cops are coming."

"Shoot him in the head, Laura, you have to make sure."

"He's dead."

"*Shoot* him, goddamnit, or give me back my gun." Mondo paused. Speaking seemed to hurt him. Through clenched teeth, he said, "You don't know what he did downstairs, what he was going to do to you. To your kid."

Laura looked at him, at his pleading eyes. She imagined Diana downstairs, her best friend dead. She remembered what the man, X, had said to her on the phone. That he'd eaten her. He had been planning to kill her son; butcher him in front of her eyes, he'd said. Tommy was unconscious. He would never know.

And Laura knew how often even the worst criminals beat the system.

She walked over to X, where he was lying, pointed the pistol at his head, and pulled back the hammer. The gun was a lot heavier than she thought it would be. She heard the sound of feet pounding on the stairway. She turned toward the sound, the gun still in her hand.

Then the young cop, the handsome one, was pointing his gun at her, shouting from the doorway for Laura to drop the weapon.

THE FIRST THING Mondo saw when he woke up was Jake Phillips, standing by the side of his bed. Jake hadn't shaved in a while, which meant that Mondo had been here for more than a day. Mondo tried to speak, but it only caused him to cough. He felt wires, tubes sticking in him. He felt like a robot.